W9-BYX-579

From the Pages of
the Inferno

Midway upon the journey of our life
I found myself within a forest dark,
For the straightforward pathway had been lost.
(Canto I, lines 1-3, page 3)

"And a fair, saintly Lady called to me
In such wise, I besought her to command me.
Her eyes were shining brighter than the Star."
(Canto II, lines 53-55, page 9)

"Bestir thee now, and with thy speech ornate,
And with what needful is for this release,
Assist him so, that I may be consoled.
Beatrice am I, who do bid thee go."
(Canto II, lines 67-70, page 10)

"All hope abandon, ye who enter in!"
(Canto III, line 9, page 14)

"Lost are we, and are only so far punished,
That without hope we live on in desire."
(Canto IV, lines 41-42, page 20)

They go by turns each one unto the judgment;
They speak, and hear, and then are downward hurled.
(Canto V, lines 14-15, page 25)

"Envy and Arrogance and Avarice
Are the three sparks that have all hearts enkindled."
(Canto VI, lines 74-75, page 33)

"But fix thine eyes below; for draweth near
The river of blood, within which boiling is
Whoe'er by violence doth injure others."
(Canto XII, lines 46-48, page 61)

"Therefore let Fortune turn her wheel around
As it may please her, and the churl his mattock."
(Canto XV, lines 95-96, page 80)

"Behold the monster with the pointed tail,
Who cleaves the hills, and breaketh walls and weapons,
Behold him who infecteth all the world."
(Canto XVII, lines 1-3, page 86)

Justice of God! O how severe it is,
That blows like these in vengeance poureth down!
(Canto XXIV, lines 119-120, page 125)

Rejoice, O Florence, since thou art so great,
That over sea and land thou beatest thy wings,
And throughout Hell thy name is spread abroad!
(Canto XXVI, lines 1-3, page 132)

"And all the others whom thou here beholdest,
Sowers of scandal and of schism have been
While living, and therefore are thus cleft asunder."
(Canto XXVIII, lines 34-36, page 144)

And by the hair it held the head dissevered,
Hung from the hand in fashion of a lantern,
And that upon us gazed and said: "O me!"
It of itself made to itself a lamp.
(Canto XXVIII, lines 121-124, page 147)

Then I beheld a thousand faces, made
Purple with cold; whence o'er me comes a shudder,
And evermore will come, at frozen ponds.
(Canto XXXII, lines 70-72, page 167)

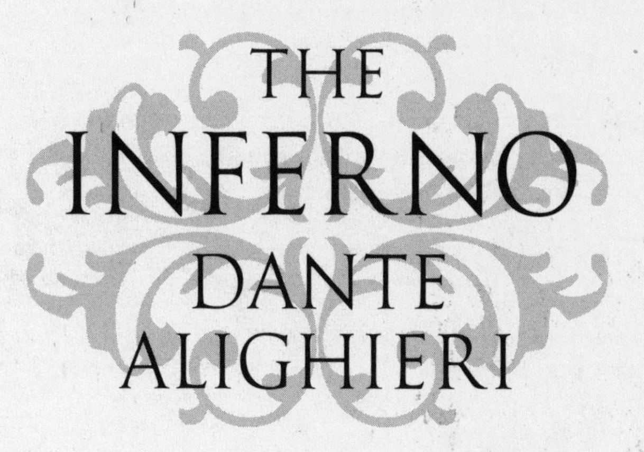

THE INFERNO

DANTE ALIGHIERI

TRANSLATED BY

HENRY WADSWORTH LONGFELLOW

With an Introduction
and Notes by Peter Bondanella

Illustrations by
Gustave Doré

George Stade
Consulting Editorial Director

BARNES & NOBLE CLASSICS
NEW YORK

BARNES & NOBLE CLASSICS
NEW YORK

Published by Barnes & Noble Books
122 Fifth Avenue
New York, NY 10011

www.barnesandnoble.com/classics

Dante is believed to have composed *The Divine Comedy* between 1308 and 1321, just before his death. Longfellow's translation of *The Inferno* first appeared in 1867; the present text derives from the Bigelow, Smith & Co. edition published in 1909.

Published in trade paperback format in 2003 by Barnes & Noble Classics with new Introduction, Notes, Biography, Chronology, Map, Inspired By, Comments & Questions, and For Further Reading.
This hardcover edition published in 2005.

The Inferno
ISBN-13: 978-1-59308-331-1
ISBN-10: 1-59308-331-9
LC Control Number 2004110472

Produced and published in conjunction with:
Fine Creative Media, Inc.
322 Eighth Avenue
New York, NY 10001

Michael J. Fine, President and Publisher

Printed in the United States of America

WCM

9 11 13 15 17 19 20 18 16 14 12 10 8

Dante Alighieri

Dante Alighieri was born in Florence in 1265 to Alighiero Alighieri, who appears to have been a moneylender and property holder, and his wife, Bella. Alighieri's was a family of good standing. Much of what we know of Dante's earliest years comes to us from *La Vita Nuova* (*The New Life,* completed around 1293), in which he tells the story of his idealized love for Beatrice Portinari, whom he encountered just before his ninth birthday. Beatrice died in 1290 but remained Dante's idealized love and muse throughout his life. Sometime around 1285 Dante married Gemma Donati, with whom he had three sons and a daughter.

Dante's public life is better documented than his private life. It is known that he counted among his closest friends the poet Guido Cavalcanti and the philosopher and writer Brunetto Latini, who is generally credited with bringing classical literature to thirteenth-century Florence. Dante began an intense study of theology at the churches of Santa Maria Novella and Santa Croce in 1292, and was well-versed in classical literature and philosophy as well as religious thought. Membership in a guild was a requirement to participate in the government of Florence, and Dante partook of this privilege after enrolling in the Arte dei Medici e Speziali (Guild of Physicians and Apothecaries) in 1295. He was elected to serve as a prior, the city's highest office, in 1300.

By early 1302, however, Dante had fallen out of favor in Florence. The Guelphs, the ruling body with whom Dante's family had long been associated, had split into two factions, the White and the Black Guelphs. Dante aligned himself with the Whites, who were opposed to the intervention of Pope Boniface VIII and his representative, Charles of Valois, in Florentine politics. While Dante was in Rome with a delegation protesting papal policy, Charles of Valois entered the city and a proclamation was issued banishing Dante and others, ordering them to be burned alive should they fall into the hands of the Florentine government.

Dante never returned to Florence, even after the exiles were granted a pardon. He probably began *La Divina Commedia* (*The Divine Comedy*) around 1308, during his extensive travels throughout Italy. The work brought him fame as soon as it began to circulate (in hand-copied form, at a time when the printing press had not yet been invented). Dante's travels took him to Verona, where he resided on and off for some six years, and finally to Ravenna, where he died on September 14, 1321, after falling ill in Venice.

Dante Alighieri is considered to be one of the world's greatest poets. In the words of the twentieth-century poet T. S. Eliot, "Dante and Shakespeare divide the world between them. There is no third."

Table of Contents

The World of Dante and the *Inferno*

1265 In May or June (exact date unknown), Dante Alighieri is born to Alighiero Alighieri, a Florentine moneylender and renter of properties, and his wife, Bella, daughter of a family of good standing. (Dante discusses his ancestry in *Paradiso* [*Paradise*], cantos XV and XVI.)

1272 Bella dies.

1274 According to his later collection of poetry and prose *La Vita Nuova* (*The New Life*), Dante lays eyes on Beatrice Portinari for the first time during festivities on May 1. Throughout his life and career Dante cites Beatrice as his muse and as the benevolent force in his life, maintaining that she inspired the best part of his work.

1281 Dante, some scholars contend, studies at the universities of Bologna and Padua.

1282 Dante's father dies, leaving a modest inheritance of property.

1283 Dante passes Beatrice in the street and she greets him. The encounter inspires a visionlike dream, which Dante recounts in a sonnet that he circulates around Florence. One of the readers, the poet Guido Cavalcanti, becomes Dante's friend and mentor. About the same time Dante finds a role model and teacher in Brunetto Latini, a writer and influential Florentine politician and man of letters.

c.1285 Dante is married to Gemma Donati, to whom he was bethrothed when he was twelve and Gemma was ten.

1287 Beatrice marries Simone de' Bardi, member of a wealthy clan.

1288 Dante's son, Giovanni, is born. Dante and Gemma will have three more children, Pietro, Iacopo, and Antonia.

1289 It is believed that Dante, having been trained in knightly warfare, fights in the battle of Campaldino on June 11, when the Guelphs, with whom Dante sympathizes, defeat the Ghibellines. On August 16 Dante goes into battle again, this time against the Pisans to restore the fortress at the village of Caprona to the Guelphs, from whom the Ghibellines have captured it.

1290 Beatrice dies in June.

1292 Dante begins to study theology, first at the Dominican church of Santa Maria Novella, then at the Franciscan church of Santa Croce. His theological readings will have a profound influence on his works.

c.1293 Dante completes *La Vita Nuova,* which he had begun around 1283 to celebrate his beloved Beatrice.

1295 Dante enrolls in the Arte dei Medici e Speziali (Guild of Physicians and Apothecaries), which includes philosophers as well. Membership in a guild gives him a say in the Florentine government. Dante's friend and mentor Brunetto Latini dies.

1300 Dante, a persuasive and eloquent speaker, is appointed to Florence's highest office as one of the city priors. He holds this office from June 15 to August 15. Florence is once again divided into warring factions, the White and the Black Guelphs. Dante's sympathies lie with the Whites, who favor independence from papal authority; in what he considers to be the best interests of Florence, he must concur with the priors when they send Guido Cavalcanti, a Black and his longtime friend, into exile on the Tuscan coast, where he dies of malaria. Dante travels as part of a mission to the city of San Gimignano to rally Tuscan cities against the territorial ambitions of Pope Boniface VIII.

1301 Dante goes to Rome to ask Pope Boniface VIII to help prevent the French Charles of Valois, a papist sympathizer, from entering Florence. Charles takes the city in November, and the Blacks harshly regain power.

1302 On January 27 Dante is accused of corruption and bribery, fined, and sentenced to two years in exile. When he does not reply to the charges, his home and possessions are confiscated, and on March 10 his sentence is increased; he is now banished for life and condemned to be burned alive if he ever returns to the city.

1303–1304 Dante travels throughout central and northern Italy and affiliates himself with other Florentine exiles. He appears to have been much dissatisfied with his colleagues. Dante arrives for a stay in Verona, as a guest of Bartolomeo della Scala, son of a local ruling family.

1306–1308 Dante works on *Il Convivio* (*The Banquet*), a philosophical treatise on poetry influenced, in part, by the writings of Aristotle. Throughout these years he travels to Lucca (where some think he encounters his eldest son, Giovanni), Arezzo, Padua, Venice, and other cities. It is believed that Dante probably begins work on *La Divina Commedia* (*The Divine Comedy*), turning first to the *Inferno*, in 1308; he will complete the larger work shortly before his death in 1321.

1309–1311 In January Dante attends the coronation, in Milan, of Henry VII of Luxemburg as King of Lombardy. Dante views Henry as the rightful ruler of Italy and writes two impassioned letters to the Florentines, imploring them to open their gates to Henry.

1312 Dante begins a six-year stay in Verona, interrupted by frequent travels, as a guest of Cangrande della Scala, a powerful political leader. While in Verona, Dante revises the *Inferno*, writes and revises *Purgatorio* (*Purgatory*), and begins *Paradiso* (*Paradise*). His second son, Pietro, joins him in Verona.

1313 Henry VII dies, putting an end to Dante's hopes of returning to Florence.

1315 Dante refuses an offer from Florence allowing him to return if he pays a reduced portion of a fine imposed upon him at the time of his exile; he calls the pardon "ridiculous and ill-advised." Another decree is issued against Dante, as well as his sons, condemning them to beheading if they are captured. The *Inferno* gains recognition throughout Italy.

1319–1321 Dante stays in Ravenna as a guest of Guido Novello da Polenta. Two of Dante's sons, Pietro and Iacopo, his daughter, Antonia, and his wife, Gemma, join him. Antonia enters the convent of Santo Stefano degli Olivi in Ravenna, taking the name "Sister Beatrice."

1321 Dante travels to Venice to help negotiate a peaceful resolution to a disagreement that has arisen between Ravenna and Venice. During his return to Ravenna across marshy lands, he contracts malarial fever; he dies on the night of September 13–14. He is buried "with all the honors deemed worthy of such an illustrious deceased man," writes Giovanni Boccaccio, the author of another great fourteenth-century Italian masterpiece, the *Decameron.* Dante's remains are in Ravenna's church of San Francesco, though Florence has tried repeatedly to have them moved to the poet's place of birth.

1337 Florence establishes the Chair of Dante, an academic position for the preservation and study of Dante's works. This position was first held by Giovanni Boccaccio, who was not only a friend of Dante's, but whose own literary perspective was influenced by the poet's writings and who was one of Dante's first biographers.

The Story of the *Inferno* in Brief

BY HENRY FRANCES CAREY

CANTO I. The writer, having lost his way in a gloomy forest, and being hindered by certain wild beasts from ascending a mountain, is met by Virgil, who promises to show him the punishments of Hell, and afterward of Purgatory; and that he shall then be conducted by Beatrice into Paradise. He follows the Roman poet.

CANTO II. After the invocation, which poets are used to prefix to their works, he shows that, on a consideration of his own strength, he doubted whether it sufficed for the journey proposed to him, but that, being comforted by Virgil, he at last took courage, and followed him as his guide and master.

CANTO III. Dante, following Virgil, comes to the gate of Hell; where, after having read the dreadful words that are written thereon, they both enter. Here, as he understands from Virgil, those were punished who had passed their time (for living it could not be called) in a state of apathy and indifference both to good and evil. Then pursuing their way, they arrive at the river Acheron; and there find the old ferryman Charon, who takes the spirits over to the opposite shore; which as soon as Dante reaches, he is seized with terror, and falls into a trance.

CANTO IV. The Poet, being roused by a clap of thunder, and following his guide onward, descends into Limbo, which is the first circle of Hell, where he finds the souls of those, who, although they have lived virtuously and have not to suffer for great sins, nevertheless, through lack of baptism, merit not the bliss of Paradise. Hence he is led on by Virgil to descend into the second circle.

CANTO V. Coming into the second circle of Hell, Dante at

the entrance beholds Minos the Infernal Judge, by whom he is admonished to beware how he enters those regions. Here he witnesses the punishment of carnal sinners, who are tossed about ceaselessly in the dark air by the most furious winds. Among these, he meets with Francesca of Rimini, through pity at whose sad tale he falls fainting to the ground.

CANTO VI. On his recovery, the Poet finds himself in the third circle, where the gluttonous are punished. Their torment is, to lie in the mire, under a continual and heavy storm of hail, snow, and discolored water; Cerberus meanwhile barking over them with his threefold throat, and rending them piecemeal. One of these, who on earth was named Ciacco, foretells the divisions with which Florence is about to be distracted. Dante proposes a question to his guide, who solves it; and they proceed toward the fourth circle.

CANTO VII. In the present Canto, Dante describes his descent into the fourth circle, at the beginning of which he sees Plutus stationed. Here one like doom awaits the prodigal and the avaricious; which is, to meet in direful conflict, rolling great weights against each other with mutual upbraidings. From hence Virgil takes occasion to show how vain the goods that are committed into the charge of Fortune; and this moves our author to inquire what being that Fortune is, of whom he speaks: which question being resolved, they go down into the fifth circle, where they find the wrathful and gloomy tormented in the Stygian Lake. Having made a compass round a great part of this lake, they come at last to the base of a lofty tower.

CANTO VIII. A signal having been made from the tower, Phlegyas, the ferryman of the lake, speedily crosses it, and conveys Virgil and Dante to the other side. On their passage, they meet with Filippo Argenti, whose fury and torment are described. Then they arrive at the city of Dis, the entrance to which is denied, and the portals closed against them by many Demons.

CANTO IX. After some hindrances, and having seen the hellish furies and other monsters, the Poet, by the help of an angel, enters the city of Dis, wherein he discovers that heretics are punished in tombs burning with intense fire; and he, together with Virgil, passes onward between the sepulchres and the walls of the city.

CANTO X. Dante, having obtained permission from his guide, holds discourse with Farinata degli Uberti and Cavalcante Cavalcanti, who lie in their fiery tombs that are yet open, and not to be closed up till after the last judgment. Farinata predicts the Poet's exile from Florence; and shows him that the condemned have knowledge of future things, but are ignorant of what is at present passing, unless it be revealed by some new-comer from earth.

CANTO XI. Dante arrives at the verge of a rocky precipice which incloses the seventh circle, where he sees the sepulcher of Anastasius the Heretic; behind the lid of which, pausing a little to make himself capable by degrees of enduring the fetid smell that steamed upward from the abyss, he is instructed by Virgil concerning the manner in which the three following circles are disposed, and what description of sinners is punished in each. He then inquires the reason why the carnal, the gluttonous, the avaricious and prodigal, the wrathful and gloomy, do not suffer their punishments within the city of Dis. He next asks how the crime of usury is an offence against God; and at length the two Poets go toward the place from whence a passage leads down to the seventh circle.

CANTO XII. Descending by a very rugged way into the seventh circle, where the violent are punished, Dante and his leader find it guarded by the Minotaur; whose fury being pacified by Virgil, they step downward from crag to crag; till, drawing near the bottom, they catch sight of a river of blood, wherein are tormented such as have committed violence against their neighbor. At these, when they strive to emerge from the blood, a troop of Centaurs, running along the side of the river, aim their arrows; and three of their band opposing our travelers at the foot of the steep, Virgil prevails so far, that one consents to carry them both across the stream; and on their passage Dante is informed by him of the course of the river, and of those that are punished therein.

CANTO XIII. Still in the seventh circle, Dante enters its second compartment, which contains both those who have done violence on their own persons and those who have violently consumed their goods; the first changed into rough and knotted trees whereon the harpies build their nests, the latter chased and torn by black female mastiffs. Among the former; Pier della Vigne is one who tells him the cause of his having committed suicide, and moreover in what manner the souls are transformed into those trunks. Of the latter crew, he recognizes Lano, a Siennese, and Giacomo, a Paduan: and lastly, a Florentine, who had hung himself from his own roof, speaks to him of the calamities of his countrymen.

CANTO XIV. They arrive at the beginning of the third of those compartments into which this seventh circle is divided. It is a plain of dry and hot sand, where three kinds of violence are punished: namely, against God, against Nature, and against Art; and those who have thus sinned are tormented by flakes of fire, which are eternally showering down upon them. Among the violent against God is found Capaneus, whose blasphemies they hear. Next, turning to the left along the forest of self-slayers, and having journeyed a little onward, they meet with a streamlet of blood that issues from the forest and traverses the sandy plain. Here Virgil speaks to our Poet of a huge ancient statue that stands within Mount Ida in Crete, from a fissure in which statue there is a dripping of tears, from which the said streamlet, together with the three other infernal rivers are formed.

CANTO XV. Taking their way upon one of the mounds by which the streamlet, spoken of in the last Canto, was embanked, and having gone so far that they could no longer have discerned the forest if they had turned round to look for it, they meet a troop of spirits that come along the sand by the side of the pier. These are they who have done violence to Nature; and among them Dante distinguishes Brunetto Latini, who had been formerly his master; with whom, turning a little backward, he holds a discourse which occupies the remainder of this Canto.

CANTO XVI. Journeying along the pier, which crosses the sand, they are now so near the end of it as to hear the noise of the stream falling into the eighth circle, when they meet the spirits of three military men; who judging Dante, from his dress, to be a countryman of theirs, entreat him to stop. He complies, and speaks with them. The two Poets then reach the place where the water descends, being the termination of this third compartment in the seventh circle; and here Virgil having thrown down into the hollow a cord, wherewith Dante was girt, they behold at that signal a monstrous and horrible figure come swimming up to them.

CANTO XVII. The monster Geryon is described; to whom while Virgil is speaking in order that he may carry them both down to the next circle, Dante, by permission, goes a little further along the edge of the void, to catch sight of the third species of sinners contained in this compartment, namely, those who have done violence to Art; and then returning to his master they both descend, seated on the back of Geryon.

CANTO XVIII. The Poet describes the situation and form of the eighth circle, divided into ten gulfs, which contain as many different descriptions of fraudulent sinners; but in the present Canto he treats only of two sorts: the first is of those who, either for their own pleasure or for that of another, have seduced any woman from her duty; and these are scourged of demons in the first gulf: the other sort is of flatterers, who in the second gulf are condemned to remain immersed in filth.

CANTO XIX. They come to the third gulf, wherein are punished those who have been guilty of simony. These are fixed with the head downward in certain apertures, so that no more of them than the legs appears without, and on the soles of their feet are seen burning flames. Dante is taken down by his guide into the bottom of the gulf; and there finds Pope Nicholas the Fifth, whose evil deeds, together with those of other pontiffs, are bitterly reprehended. Virgil then carries him up again to the arch, which affords them a passage over the following gulf.

CANTO XX. The Poet relates the punishment of such as presumed, while living, to predict future events. It is to have their faces reversed and set the contrary way on their limbs, so that, being deprived of the power to see before them, they are constrained ever to walk backward. Among these Virgil points out to him Amphiaraüs, Tiresias, Aruns, and Manto (from the mention of whom he takes occasion to speak of the origin of Mantua), together with several others, who had practised the arts of divination and astrology.

CANTO XXI. Still in the eighth circle, which bears the name of Malebolge, they look down from the bridge that passes over its fifth gulf, upon the barrators or public peculators. These are plunged in a lake of boiling pitch, and guarded by Demons, to whom Virgil, leaving Dante apart, presents himself; and license being obtained to pass onward, both pursue their way.

CANTO XXII. Virgil and Dante proceed, accompanied by the Demons, to see other sinners of the same description in the same gulf. The scheme of Ciampolo, one of these, to escape from the Demons, who had laid hold on him.

CANTO XXIII. The enraged Demons pursue Dante, but he is preserved from them by Virgil. On reaching the sixth gulf, he beholds the punishment of the hypocrites; which is, to pace continually round the gulf under the pressure of caps and hoods, that are gilt on the outside, but leaden within. He is addressed by two of these, Catalano and Loderingo, knights of Saint Mary, otherwise called Joyous Friars of Bologna. Caïaphas is seen fixed to a cross on the ground and lies so stretched along the way, that all tread on him in passing.

CANTO XXIV. Under the escort of his faithful master, Dante not without difficulty makes his way out of the sixth gulf; and in the seventh, sees the robbers tormented by venomous and pestilent serpents. The soul of Vanni Fucci, who had pillaged the sacristy of Saint James in Pistoia, predicts some calamities that impended over that city, and over the Florentines.

CANTO XXV. The sacrilegious Fucci vents his fury in blasphemy, is seized by serpents, and flying is pursued by Cacus in the form of a Centaur, who is described with a swarm of serpents on his haunch, and a dragon on his shoulders breathing forth fire. Our Poet then meets with the spirits of three of his countrymen, two of whom undergo a marvelous transformation in his presence.

CANTO XXVI. Remounting by the steps, down which they had descended to the seventh gulf, they go forward to the arch that stretches over the eighth, and from thence behold numberless flames wherein are punished evil counsellors, each flame containing a sinner, save one, in which were Diomede and Ulysses, the latter of whom relates the manner of his death.

CANTO XXVII. The Poet, treating of the same punishment as in the last Canto, relates that he turned toward a flame in which was the Count Guido da Montefeltro, whose inquiries respecting the state of Romagna he answers, and Guido is thereby induced to declare who he is, and why condemned to that torment.

CANTO XXVIII. They arrive in the ninth gulf, where the sowers of scandal, schismatics, and heretics, are seen with their limbs miserably maimed or divided in different ways. Among these the Poet finds Mohammed, Piero da Medicina, Curio, Mosca, and Bertrand de Born.

CANTO XXIX. Dante, at the desire of Virgil, proceeds onward to the bridge that crosses the tenth gulf, from whence he hears the cries of the alchemists and forgers, who are tormented therein; but not being able to discern anything on account of the darkness, they descend the rock, that bounds this the last of the compartments in which the eighth circle is divided, and then behold the spirits who are afflicted by divers plagues and diseases. Two of them, namely, Grifolino of Arezzo and Capocchio of Siena, are introduced speaking.

CANTO XXX. In the same gulf, other kinds of imposters, as those who have counterfeited the persons of others, or debased the current coin, or deceived by speech under false pretences, are described as suffering various diseases. Sinon of Troy, and Adamo of Brescia, mutually reproach each other with their various impostures.

CANTO XXXI. The poets, following the sound of a loud horn, are led by it to the ninth circle, in which there are four rounds, one inclosed within the other, and containing as many sorts of Traitors; but the present Canto shows only that the circle is encompassed with Giants, one of whom, Antæus, takes them both in his arms and places them at the bottom of the circle.

CANTO XXXII. This Canto treats of the first, and, in part, of the second of those rounds, into which the ninth and last, or frozen circle, is divided. In the former, called Caïna, Dante finds Camiccione de' Pazzi, who gives him an account of other sinners who are there punished; and in the next, named Antenora, he hears in like manner from Bocca degli Abbati who his fellow-sufferers are.

CANTO XXXIII. The Poet is told by Count Ugolino de' Gherardeschi of the cruel manner in which he and his children were famished in the tower at Pisa, by command of the Archbishop Ruggieri. He next discourses of the third round, called Ptolomea, wherein those are punished who have betrayed others under the semblance of kindness; and among these he finds the Friar Alberigo de' Manfredi, who tells him of one whose soul was already tormented in that place, though his body appeared still to be alive upon the earth, being yielded up to the governance of a fiend.

CANTO XXXIV. In the fourth and last round of the ninth circle, those who have betrayed their benefactors are wholly covered with ice. And in the midst is Lucifer, at whose back Dante and Virgil ascend, till by a secret path they reach the surface of the other hemisphere of the earth, and once more obtain sight of the stars.

Introduction

Dante's Life and Times

We know little about the private lives of Homer and Shakespeare, the only two poets who may be said to rival Dante's influence in the Western tradition or, indeed, his genius. Some critics have raised doubts about the authorship of the *Iliad* and the *Odyssey*, and about the rich poetry and drama of Shakespeare. But Dante Alighieri, the man whom the nineteenth-century British writer and critic John Ruskin called "the central man of all the world," is unquestionably the author of the great epic poem we call *The Divine Comedy*, of which the *Inferno* is just one of three parts. Dante the man remains inextricably tied to the content and action of *The Divine Comedy* both as its narrator and as its central protagonist. Many of the important events in his life figure prominently in the work, and the reader, to whom a good many of these biographical details are not immediately transparent, must seek out information in annotations that centuries of scholars and commentators have compiled.

The problematic quality of autobiographical details in Dante's works is that they may allude to real, historical events that actually occurred, or to fictional events from Dante's fertile imagination. It is not always easy to separate the fact from the fiction. Dante the Poet is also the epic's protagonist, Dante the Pilgrim. It required a breathtaking act of poetic license for Dante to make himself the hero of an epic, a genre usually populated by warriors and heroes. The results, however, have silenced any critical objections to his presumption. Scholarly debate over Dante's poem has continued since its first appearance in manuscript in the early fourteenth century. The unbroken tradition of writing about Dante from that time to the present remains unparalleled in its complexity and breadth by that on any other major Western author, including Shakespeare. And yet problems arise from the fact that in spite of the great deal we know about Dante (much of this gained from the poem itself), there is not a single extant autograph manuscript of his many works, including his poetic masterpiece. Every one of his many works has come down to us in such a complicated manuscript tradition that his contemporary editors can still carry on heated debates about which text should be accepted as the best one or whether, indeed, some of his minor works are actually to be attributed to his own hand.

Born on some day between May 14 and June 13, 1265, in the Tuscan city of Florence, Italy, a child was christened in the Baptistery of San Giovanni on March 26, 1266, with the name Durante Alighieri, later contracted to Dante Alighieri. Dante's family—the father Alighiero and the mother Bella—was not particularly wealthy or distinguished but was sufficiently well off that Dante could later participate in the republican government of Florence, eligibility for which rested primarily upon economic status. According to Dante's testimony in *La Vita Nuova* (*The New Life*), he first encountered a girl named Beatrice Portinari when they were both eight years of age; he saw her again nine years later in 1283. A decisive encounter in his poetic and intellectual development, this meeting inspired Dante's unrequited love for Beatrice (who died in 1290) and led him to begin writing poetry. Dante married a woman named Gemma Donati (the marriage contract is dated 1277), and he apparently had four children.

Dante must have enjoyed a very good education, probably from the schools that had grown up around the ecclesiastical centers in Florence—the Dominican church of Santa Maria Novella; the Augustinian church of Santo Spirito; and the Franciscan church of Santa Croce. He certainly received stellar training in Latin grammar (he would later compose a number of works in Latin) and must have read extensively in the Latin classics and rhetoric books typically employed in medieval education. The poet also came under the influence of Brunetto Latini (1220–1295), under whose tutelage he probably encountered not only the works of Aristotle and Cicero but also important works written in Old French, such as *The Romance of the Rose,* and the troubadour lyrics written in Old Provençal. One work attributed to Dante but still contested by some scholars, and probably written between 1285 and 1295, is *Il Fiore* (*The Flower*), a series of 232 sonnets summarizing *The Romance of the Rose.*

The lyric poetry Dante produced between the early 1280s and the mid 1290s holds much greater importance in his poetic development. These ninety or so poems of undoubted attribution represent a kind of artistic workshop for the young aspiring lyric poet. The poems display a variety of metrical forms: sonnets, sestinas, *ballate* (dance songs with repeating refrains), and *canzoni,* odelike "songs," as the name implies, consisting of a number of stanzas and a shorter envoy. Dante considered the *canzone* to be the noblest form of poetry. This kind of poetry was popular among the major groups of lyric poets Dante admired, imitated, and sometimes criticized: the Provençal troubadours, such as Arnaut Daniel and Bertran de Born; the Sicilian School of poetry that flourished from around 1230 to 1250, the members of which included Pier della Vigna and Giacomo da Lentini, the probable inventor of the sonnet; the Tuscan school led by Guittone d'Arezzo; the Bolognese group of poets led by Guido Guinizzelli; and what came to be known as the *dolce stil novo* poets (the "sweet new style"), a group of Tuscans including not only Bonagiunta da Lucca, Cino da Pistoia, and Guido Calvacanti, but also Dante himself. Dante places a number of these individuals in *The Divine Comedy* as testimony to his own literary development and to his argument that poetry represents one of humanity's most noble callings.

Had Dante stopped writing poetry with his lyric production and never composed *The Divine Comedy,* he would be remembered only by medievalists as the author of a moderately interesting Latin treatise on political theory, *De Monarchia* (*On Monarchy*), completed during the last decade of his life, and an unfinished Latin treatise on vernacular language and its use in poetry, *De vulgari eloquentia* (*On Eloquence in the Vernacular Tongue*), probably written between 1302 and 1305. Without *The Divine Comedy,* there would have been little reason for Dante to have composed his unfinished Italian *Il Convivio* (*The Banquet*), a philosophical consideration of poetry that is also inspired by religion. In fact, rather than being admired for the often abstract and ethereal love lyrics typical of the "sweet new style" (another historical label that would not have existed without *The Divine Comedy,* since the term itself comes from a line in his epic poem), Dante would be recognized primarily for *La Vita Nuova* and four explicitly sensual lyrics called the *rime petrose* (literally the "rocky rhymes") that reveal his interest in metrical experimentation and a highly sophisticated understanding that the courtly love celebrated by the Provençal poets—often Dante's models—was firmly based on requited lust rather than unrequited love. Such a poetic reputation would not have attracted much critical attention during the past six centuries from anyone but highly specialized scholars.

Dante's love poetry, however, led to the stroke of genius that ultimately saved him from so unremarkable a future. Dante had the immensely clever idea of taking thirty-one of the lyric poems he had composed treating an unrequited love for a girl named Beatrice and of setting them within a prose frame. Although not widely read and immediately eclipsed by the appearance of his great epic, *La Vita Nuova* (probably completed around 1293) represents a fundamental step forward in Dante's poetic and intellectual development. The Italian prose framework of the work allowed Dante to comment on his own work. The idea of a poet who presents a series of poems on love and then includes his own readings of the works was a unique invention that flirts with a postmodern conception of literature as an ironic revisitation of what has been written in the past. *La Vita Nuova* represents a precocious first step toward Dante's decision to become the protagonist hero of an epic poem filled with self-critical images of its author. This little work already contains the key distinction in *The Divine Comedy* between protagonist and narrator, who are the same person but are viewed from different perspectives. But even more important was the revolutionary role of Beatrice in *La Vita Nuova*. By the addition of the prose commentary, Dante projects Beatrice as one whose name, life, and effects upon the narrator are associated with blessing and salvation and especially with the number nine (the square of three, the number of the Trinity). Her death nearly destroys the narrator of *La Vita Nuova,* but in the process of mourning, Dante envisions a Beatrice who has become a figuration of Christ and a guide to his salvation even before her dramatic appearance in *The Divine Comedy*.

Did Beatrice really exist? We know that there was a real person named Beatrice Portinari who died around the time Dante says his Beatrice did. Did she really have such an influence upon the young Dante, or does Dante simply invent this conceit in order to embark on a revolutionary treatment of a woman's role in a poet's life? It is impossible to prove or disprove this influence, for we only have Dante's word. Whether or not the young Dante was so struck by Beatrice at the age of eight that she led him to poetic glory, Dante states that this early *innamoramento* transformed his life and mind. In the process, Dante raised the poetry of praise, the most traditional role of medieval love poetry, to the highest possible level, surpassing the traditional claims of courtly poetry that a woman's love (sexual or chaste) refined a man. Dante affirmed that a woman's love could lead a man or a poet to God, and this bordered on blasphemy. It was, at the same time, a step back from the avowed sensuality of troubadour lyrics and the creation of a literary relationship between the lover and his beloved that would later come to be labeled "platonic."

For approximately a decade between the time *La Vita Nuova* was completed and his exile from Florence in 1302, Dante divided his activities between writing and active participation in the communal government. In 1289 Dante took part as a cavalryman in the battle of Campaldino, in which the Florentine Guelphs were victorious against the Ghibellines of the nearby Tuscan city of Arezzo. Guelph and Ghibelline traditionally refer to Italian political factions allied, respectively, to the papacy and to the Holy Roman Empire. But the intense and bitter rivalries within the city-state governments of Italy made things more complicated than that. If your enemy was a Guelph, you became a Ghibelline, and vice versa. Conflicts between families and clans were often more important than the more weighty issues of empire versus papacy. Florence was traditionally Guelph, as were most of the city-state republics intent upon removing themselves from the restrictions of either church or state, but even the Guelphs divided into warring factions. The Black Guelphs were most extreme and had the closest ties to the papacy. The White Guelphs (Dante's party) were generally more moderate in their politics.

In 1300 Florence boasted a population of around 100,000; it may have risen to 120,000 before the Black Plague of 1348 devastated the city as it did most of Western Europe. This Italian city-state was a crucial player in the politics of the period because of its central location, its vibrant republican government, and particularly its enormous wealth. Its flourishing textile industry (specializing in luxury goods of wool and silk but also more humble fabrics made from cotton and linen) and its international banking business dominated world trade and commerce—even rivaling that of Venice, a commercial city and seafaring republic. Florentine politics reflected not only the struggle between Ghibellines and the two factions of Guelphs but also class conflict between the impoverished mass of humble workers, on the one hand, and the two groups of economically well-off people who governed and who were themselves often in conflict: the elite, upper-class patricians who represented a small number of powerful families and were not really noble in the medieval or feudal sense and the more numerous but less prestigious middle-class merchants, artisans, notaries, lawyers, manufacturers, and shopkeepers who were members of the various guilds and corporations in the city-state. The politics of the city remained turbulent because of friction between various groups. Although members of the groups were often connected to each other by ties of family, religion, and friendship, conflicts often turned into violence, riot, and warfare, with financial ruin and exile being the favorite punishment for those who lost the struggle. Constant internal conflict led quite naturally to a search for outside allies, further complicating the situation within Florence.

In the fourteenth century, the Florentine florin served as the standard currency for the entire European economy. Its value was carefully maintained: 24 carats of purely refined gold accepted almost everywhere in the known world as legal tender. Rapid commercial communications operated by the Florentine banks, the invention of double-entry bookkeeping, and shrewd dealings abroad made Florence the capital of the major service industry of the Middle Ages. When Tuscan banks began to collect papal revenues all over Europe, the profits were enormous. Based upon high banking charges and incredible profits from the luxury goods produced by the textile industry, the Florentine economy supported a huge building program between 1250 and 1320. The popular monuments now visited by busloads of foreign tourists each year—the Bargello, the churches of Santa Croce and Santa Maria Novella, the duomo of Santa Maria del Fiore, the Palazzo Vecchio, numerous family palaces—were all begun during Dante's lifetime. Florentines were so omnipresent in the economic life of Western Europe that they were called the "fifth element" by a pope—the other four elements, of course, were earth, fire, air, and water. Florentine bankers collected taxes for various foreign monarchs and loaned money to both sides in European wars, gaining the reputation as usurers for their trouble. Florentines ran at least one European navy, and like their counterparts in Venice, they journeyed as far as China and India in search of profit. In the process, they began to patronize architects, painters, and sculptors in such an enthusiastic and sophisticated manner that the city soon became the artistic capital of the known world. By the time Dante, Petrarch, and Boccaccio died, they had virtually created Italian literature and fixed the Italian language in the form that we know it today. Unlike Old French or Old English, Old Italian is just Italian thanks to the example of Dante and his two brilliant successors, together known as the "three crowns of Florence."

Religious life in Florence was vibrant, and the cloister and pulpit concerned Florentine citizens as much as the bank and the factory did. In fact, a significant part of the city's remarkable artistic production was directly linked to religious patronage. Religious organizations also contributed a great deal to the daily life of the city. The life of a medieval Florentine was marked from the cradle to the grave by religious ritual; time was told by canonical hours, and the passing of the seasons was marked by religious holidays, saints' days, and church processions. Moreover, the city's clerics provided much of the education and religious confraternities supplied much of the social assistance before the advent of a welfare state. One of Tuscany's wealthiest citizens in the next century, Francesco Datini, began his ledger book with the telling phrase: "In the name of God and profit." The relationship between economic wealth and moral corruption, the latter caused by a society that avidly pursued profit and tried to retain its religious devotion, would provide Dante with one of the key themes in the *Inferno*—the moral and ethical corruption of both Church and society brought about by the wealth produced by the "new people" that Dante's essentially conservative social views could not abide. Florence also boasted some of the greatest reformist, fire-and-brimstone preachers of the time, figures who reflected the great popular piety of both the masses and members of the ruling classes and the intelligentsia. Echoing the concerns of these preachers, Dante sometimes seems like an outraged Jeremiah, but his moral indignation over corruption and evildoing was shared by many of his fellow citizens. In spite of Dante's reservations about the "new people" who were busily making Florence into the most exciting place in the Western world, Florence soon became a cultural and commercial center that would rival Athens and Rome in its brilliance during the period between the thirteenth and the sixteenth centuries.

Once the merchant class determined that internal conflict was bad for business, the city government found a novel way to limit the strife. In 1293 a fundamental constitutional change, the *Ordinamenti di Giustizia* (Ordinances of Justice), took place in Florence, supported by the Guelph faction. Essentially, it limited political participation in the republican government of the city to members of the major guilds or corporations—basically merchants, bankers, magistrates, notaries, and the moneyed classes. It is important to remember that medieval guilds were not modern labor unions: Membership usually excluded common workers and included only people with property or money. In 1295 Dante joined the Arte dei Medici e Speziali (Guild of Physicians and Apothecaries)—the same guild to which most artists in Renaissance Florence subsequently belonged, because apothecaries provided the materials for paintings. He was elected to serve a two-month term as one of the seven city priors, but fulfilling his civic duty proved to be disastrous for Dante. The elevation to this office identified him as an important White Guelph and made him a target when the more radical Black Guelphs seized power from the White Guelphs. While serving as one of three Florentine ambassadors to Pope Boniface VIII in Rome in 1302, Dante was sentenced first to exile and then to death if he should ever again set foot in his beloved native city of Florence.

Dante's exile lasted until his death, in 1321, from malaria at Ravenna, where he enjoyed the protection and patronage of Guido

Novello of Polenta, after receiving the same type of hospitality from Cangrande della Scala in Verona. He wrote *The Divine Comedy* during his long years in exile, and his body was laid to rest in Ravenna, not in Florence, where it remains to this day. In spite of Dante's life in exile and the composition of the poem outside his native city, *The Divine Comedy* has a distinctive Florentine and Tuscan character. The poem often reflects the partisan struggles that swept over Italy during Dante's day, and in so doing allowed the poet ample opportunity to pay back his political foes. Many of the most memorable figures in the *Inferno* are essentially minor historical characters who played a role in the internecine factional struggles of fourteenth-century Florence and who had a personal effect on Dante's life. Many minor historical figures—although condemned to a Hell of Dante's invention, their depictions inspired by Dante's rancor and righteous indignation or, occasionally, by his admiration—have been transformed by Dante's poetry into major literary characters.

An Overview of The Divine Comedy

Several times in the poem, Dante refers simply to his creation as *The Comedy.* A subsequent sixteenth-century edition of a manuscript published in Venice during the Renaissance added the adjective "divine" to the title, where it has remained ever since. The poem is an epic, owing a good deal of its structure and content to the epic tradition that began in Western literature with Homer's *Iliad* and *Odyssey*—works Dante could not have read, since he knew no Greek. Few readers of Virgil's *Aeneid,* however, would ever know the Latin epic better than Dante, who absorbed many of the lessons he might have learned from a direct reading of Homer through an indirect encounter with Homer in Virgil's poem. In celebrating the birth of the city of Rome, destined to rule the classical world by Virgil's lifetime, the Latin poet could not have predicted that his imperial capital would eventually become the capital of Christianity, or that the Latin race would be fully Christianized. The link of Rome to both the Roman Republic and Empire, on the one hand, and to the rise of Christianity, on the other, was never far from Dante's mind when he considered what Rome meant to his own times. Virgil's Latin epic became the single most important work in the formation of the ideas that would eventually produce *The Divine Comedy*. Dante also read carefully other Latin epics that are less popular today. One such book was Lucan's *Pharsalia*, a Latin work that described the Roman civil wars and was also full of horrible monsters and marvelous sights. He admired two Latin epics by Statius: the unfinished *Achilleid*, a treatment of Achilles in the Trojan War, and the more important *Thebeid*, a poem treating the fratricidal struggles of the sons of Oedipus in the city of Thebes. Ovid's *Metamorphoses* provided Dante with the most influential repository of poetry about classical mythology.

However, there is really no classical precedent for the overall structure of *The Divine Comedy*, in which the author is also the epic protagonist, an Everyman who is not a warrior or a city founder. Homer or Virgil would never have dreamed of making themselves the heroes of their epic works. Dante the Pilgrim in Dante the Poet's epic takes a journey that the poet believes must be taken by every human being. No matter how many trappings of the classical epic *The Divine Comedy* may contain—invocations to the muses, masterful epic similes, divine messengers sent from the deities, lofty verse, and monsters and other figures cited from the literature or mythology of ancient Greece and Rome—the underpinning of the entire poem is fundamentally religious. It is a Christian epic and, more specifically, a Catholic epic. For the first time in Western literature, the values and ideals of an epic poem derive from the fundamental tenets of Christianity as they were understood during the Middle Ages. This means Catholicism as mediated by the dominant theology of the time—the Scholasticism of Saint Thomas Aquinas—as well as the writings, teachings, and examples of such figures as Saint Augustine, Saint Francis, Saint Benedict, Saint Dominic, Saint Bernard, and Saint Bonaventure. Ancient philosophy, in particular the works of Cicero, Boethius, and Aristotle, filtered through these Christian lenses, as did the traditional Ptolemaic picture of the universe as Earth-centered and the classical rhetoric and erudition often based on either Scholastic commentaries in Latin or Latin translations of Arabic commentaries on Greek texts.

The most important philosopher of the Middle Ages in Italy as in Europe was Aristotle, the sage Dante calls the Master of "those who know" (*Inferno* IV: 131). By the time Dante was born, more than fifty of Aristotle's works had been translated into Latin, although these works were often read alongside Scholastic or Arabic commentaries. Plato was virtually unknown during Dante's time, except for an incomplete Latin translation of the *Timaeus*. The emergence of Plato as a rival for Aristotle would not occur until the Medici family of fifteenth-century Florence sponsored the publication of Latin translations of the entire body of Plato's works.

In addition to his profound knowledge of Christian philosophy and theology, Dante had a familiarity with the Bible that was extensive for his time, an era when most Catholics may have only heard scripture cited in sermons, or read to them out loud during the celebration of the Mass, or even depicted in narrative fresco painting and tempera altar pieces in the churches. In the centuries before the Reformation declared that every man could be his own priest, few laymen actually read the Bible. Dante was certainly an exception to this general practice, and the Bible he would have read would have been some version of Saint Jerome's Latin Vulgate. In *The Divine Comedy*, Dante draws almost 600 references or citations from the Bible, compared to almost 400 from Aristotle and almost 200 from Virgil. Interestingly enough, the number of classical and biblical citations is almost identical, an eloquent testimony to Dante's conscious desire to synthesize the classical and Christian traditions in his poem.

The theme of Dante's epic work is the state of souls after death. Consequently, the entire work is subdivided into three parts, each corresponding to one of the three possibilities in the Christian afterlife. In *Inferno* XX: 1–3, Dante refers to the part of the poem devoted to Hell as "the first song" ("la prima canzon"). *Canzone* means both "song" in a generic sense but may also refer to a specific poetic genre, a relatively long composition, the rough equivalent of the ode, with a number of stanzas and an envoy. Dante valued the Italian *canzone* form for its rich poetic possibilities. At the end of *Purgatory*, in canto XXXIII: 140, he employs another, even more suggestive term for the three major parts of the work—canticle (*cantica*). If labeling his epic poem a *canzone* recalls Dante's origins in his secular lyrics, both the amorous and the moralizing variety, calling it a *cantica* reminds us of the religious nature of its content, since the term retains the biblical suggestion of Song of Songs (*Cantica canticorum* in the Vulgate Bible). The two terms Dante employs when referring to his poem also reflect Dante's intention to synthesize very different literary and philosophical traditions in his epic, blending the secular love lyrics of *La Vita Nuova* and the tradition of courtly love with the greatest lyric poetry of the Bible.

Besides the terms Dante uses to refer to the three parts of his epic poem (the number of parts suggesting the Holy Trinity), Dante employs the term *canto* (first mentioned in *Inferno* XX: 2) for the name he gives to the 100 subdivisions of the three canticles of his poem. *Canto* suggests both poetry and song and singing in Italian. The cantos in the poem are divided as follows: thirty-four in the *Inferno* and thirty-three in both *Purgatory* and *Paradise.* Dante obviously considers canto I of the *Inferno* to be a kind of general prologue to the work. Thus the poem may be said to reflect the following numerical structure: 1 + 33 (*Inferno*) + 33 (*Purgatory*) + 33 (*Paradise*) = 100. Given Dante's fascination with symbolic numbers, the suggestive quality of this arrangement is certainly intentional.

Dante's poem contains 14,233 lines of hendecasyllabic verse in *terza rima.* The length of each canto may vary from between 115 and 160 lines. Hendecasyllabic verse, following Dante's noble example, became the elevated poetic line of choice in Italian literature, just as the peerless example of Shakespeare's blank verse of iambic pentameter has privileged that poetic form in English. In general, the most successful English translations of Dante, such as Longfellow's, have always been in blank verse, not in rhymed verse. Italian poetry is not scanned by feet but by counting the number of syllables in a line. Since most Italian words are accented on the penultimate syllable, hendecasyllabic verse generally contains eleven syllables with the tenth accented. However, lines of ten syllables or even twelve syllables occur in the poem infrequently but still follow the general rule governing accents: In the first case, the tenth or last syllable is accented, while in the second case, the tenth syllable of a twelve-syllable line retains the accent.

Dante's great metric invention was *terza rima.* This incomparable narrative form has stanzas of three lines (tercets) in which the first and third lines rhyme with each other, and the second lines rhyme with the first and third lines of the next tercet. The formula for *terza rima* may be written as follows: *aba bcb cdc d... wxw xyx yzy z.* Note that each canto begins with a pair of alternating rhymes but ends on a single line. The rhyme scheme also makes run-on lines (*enjambement*) infrequent in the poem, since the focus is upon rhymes at the end of lines. English, compared to Italian, is relatively impoverished with rhymes, and this explains in large measure why most attempts to repeat Dante's *terza rima* have met with dismal failure in English translations. The Trinitarian association with a rhyme scheme that relentlessly repeats itself in series of threes seems obvious. What is less obvious but probably also intended by Dante is that *terza rima* helped to protect his manuscripts from changes by scribes (either accidental or intentional) and eventually by proofreaders after the advent of printing. We may not have an autograph manuscript of *The Divine Comedy,* but even after the passage of six centuries, the text of Dante's poem that has been established for us today represents an amazingly accurate version of what Dante must have written, thanks in part to the meter the poet invented.

Dante's Hell: Conception, Geography, and Its System of Punishments

Church doctrine in Dante's time (as today) holds that Hell's function is to punish for eternity human souls who died in mortal sin without a sincere confession of their faults that expresses repentance for their misdeeds. These miscreants do not qualify for the purifying punishments of Purgatory, where souls who do not die in mortal sin escape eternal damnation and suffer temporary expiation before receiving their blissful reward in Paradise. When Dante began his poem, he was certainly aware of biblical and classical views of the afterlife. In the Sheol of the Hebrew Old Testament and the Hades of classical antiquity, souls after death did not really receive retribution for their earthly sins or particularly attractive rewards for their earthly merits. But the Christian church, affirmed by the theology of such major writers as Augustine and Thomas Aquinas, conceived of Hell as a place where the good were separated from the evil, and deeds on earth were weighted and judged. Dante's famous notice over the gate of Hell underlines the eternity of Hell's punishment ("All hope abandon, ye who enter in!"), but it is also clear from a reading of the entire poem that Dante considers the greatest punishment possible to be not the incredibly original and grotesque physical punishments he invents for his work but, instead, the eternal loss of communion with God that is enjoyed by the blessed.

Dante's poetic genius partly resides in his many ingenious inventions for the shape and character of Hell. Dante's *Inferno* is a hollow cone shaped by the displaced territory after Lucifer's expulsion from Heaven and fall to Earth. It is situated under Jerusalem and consists of nine concentric circles that grow ever smaller and house more and more evil sinners. Ultimately, Hell ends at Earth's core, where Lucifer is imprisoned in ice. Contrary to popular opinion, fire and brimstone are not the typical infernal punishments, although they are present. The place is filled with a number of rivers, swamps, deserts, a burning plain, a huge waterfall, a frozen lake, the towers of the City of Dis, and the ditches and bridges of Malebolge (ten sections of a circle shaped like ditches, pouches, or purses). Because the science of Dante's day followed the Ptolemaic system of the universe in astronomy and Aristotle's teachings on physics and biology, Dante considered Hell to be in the center of Earth, which in turn was in the center of the universe, with the sun revolving around it. A great chain of being extended from gross matter, animals, and humanity to the nine orders of the angels, and then to God in the Empyrean Heaven. Dante's *Inferno* generally reflects traditional medieval thinking on astronomy and science, but the poet is also capable of enriching this tradition with his own ideas to enliven his picture of the Other World.

The most important rule in the *Inferno,* as well as in *Purgatory* and *Paradise,* is that Dante makes the rules. Laws can be broken or twisted to suit his poetic purposes, but they are always his alone. Such inventive details, often created by the author out of whole cloth, provide the reader with a rich, textured world of real individuals and a universe with its own specifically Dantesque regulations and customs. In many respects, Dante's *Inferno* is not an unfamiliar place. Its most interesting inhabitants are not classical monsters, mythological figures, or heroes but instead are contemporary Italians, figures from all over the peninsula. It is an all too human world that we all immediately recognize as the one in which we live. Jean-Paul Sartre once wrote that Hell is other people. Dante would have said: "We have met the damned, and they are we."

Apart from all of the entertaining and ingenious "house rules" in Hell that Dante invented, one of the great intellectual achievements of Dante's *Inferno* as a work of art is its original synthesis of the Christian and the classical worlds in Hell's organization. For example, the idea of a visit to the Underworld was suggested to Dante by the obvious example of Virgil's *Aeneid.* Since Virgil had been to Hell before, who else would be more qualified to guide an Italian poet who loved Virgil's epic work on another journey through the same territory? Numerous specific physical punishments in Hell require guardians or bureaucrats (not to mention torturers enjoying their work), just as a prison requires jailors and executioners. Thus Dante employs a wide variety of classical figures to serve in this capacity, including Charon, Minos, and the centaurs. The rivers of Hell are those of classical antiquity (such as Acheron, Styx, Phlegethon, and Lethe). Numerous classical figures, such as Alexander the Great, Brutus, Cassius, and Ulysses, appear in the various circles in which they suffer eternal damnation along with Dante's contemporaries. No more heuristic juxtaposition of ancient and modern, classical and contemporary, will occur in Western literature until the sixteenth-century appearance of *The Prince* and the *Discourses on Livy,* two books by Niccolò Machiavelli that effect a similar synthesis by founding a new realistic view of politics upon comparative analyses of ancient Romans and contemporary Italy or Europe.

The most counterintuitive aspect of Dante's *Inferno* is that the seven deadly sins of lust, gluttony, avarice/prodigality, sloth, wrath, envy, and pride—the obvious scheme for organizing the punishment for the sins of damnation—serve not to organize the physical layout of Hell but that of Purgatory, whose structure directly embodies these traditional seven deadly sins. The shape of the Mountain of Purgatory, however, resembles a reverse image of the shape of Hell. Instead of a hollow cone becoming narrower and narrower, the image of Purgatory is that of a mountain with seven terraces, each devoted to one of the traditional sins. In Paradise, Dante employs the nine angelic orders to organize the geography of Heaven into different regions leading up to the Empyrean. He also associates these different realms with planetary bodies as well as with the classical virtues (prudence, fortitude, justice, and temperance) and the three Christian virtues (faith, hope, and charity).

In the organization of Hell, Dante recognizes the seven deadly sins as well as the "golden rule" and punishes these infractions severely, but he structures the sins and punishments with an eye to classical notions of human failings, taking his ideas primarily from Aristotle with suggestions from Cicero. As a result, his system of punishment provides the greatest and most original synthesis of classical tradition and Christian thinking. Even though the system of punishments and the corresponding geographical structure of Hell are outlined at length by Virgil in canto XI of the *Inferno,* it has always confused readers of the poem and has been argued over by scholars for centuries. The problem is complicated by the fact that there are thirty-four cantos and three main divisions of sin, themselves subdivided into subcategories over nine circles.

In his *Nicomachean Ethics,* Aristotle spoke of Incontinence, Malice, and insane Bestiality. Dante follows these concepts to some extent, for in the first circles of Hell, he punishes sins of Incontinence that result from immoderate impulses. Here is the structure of the first part of Dante's Hell:

- The Beginning of the Journey (the Dark Wood, Virgil's Arrival, cantos I and II)
- Antechamber or Vestibule (neutral angels and the lukewarm, canto III)
- First circle, Limbo (the virtuous pagans, canto IV)

Sins of Incontinence:

- Second circle (lust, canto V)
- Third circle (gluttony, canto VI)
- Fourth circle (avarice and prodigality, canto VII)
- Fifth circle (anger and sloth, cantos VII and VIII)

The first circle (Limbo) and the sixth circle (heresy) are more difficult to associate with sins of Incontinence than are the other traditional deadly sins in circles two through five, because they have an intellectual and willful aspect. The sixth circle (rebel angels and heresy, cantos VIII, IX, X, and XI) lies within the walls of the City of Dis, and this break in the geography of Hell also marks the transition from the less grievous sins of weak impulses, such as lust, to the more dreadful sins dominated by willful malice to do harm to others, a deliberate misuse of reason, a gift from God to humans. Notice that Dante, in contrast to prudish religious thinkers, does not consider lust to be a very serious sin. Lust is important enough to send someone under its domination to Hell but is not a sin about which the poet is obsessed. Anything but a puritan or a religious fundamentalist, Dante realizes that betraying a friend is far more serious than giving in to one's sensual desires, because it breaks one of the essential bonds between men.

Sins of Malice, divided into two subcategories in the seventh circle and the eighth circle, involve either force or violence and fraud. In the seventh circle (violence), this category of sin is broken down into three subcategories, each of which breaks the admonition of Christ to love God, one's neighbor, and oneself:

- Violence against others, such as murderers or warmongers (canto XII)
- Violence against oneself, such as suicides (canto XIII)
- Violence against God, nature, and art, such as blasphemers, sodomites, and usurers (cantos XIV, XV, XVI, and XVII)

Simple and complex fraud or treachery are punished in the eighth and ninth circles. In the eighth circle of Malebolge, Dante presents ten subcategories of simple fraud, each punished in a different *bolgia* (which translates as "ditch," "purse," or "pouch").

- First Bolgia: panderers and seducers (canto XVIII)
- Second Bolgia: flatterers (canto XVIII)
- Third Bolgia: simonists (canto XIX)
- Fourth Bolgia: fortune-tellers and soothsayers (canto XX)

- Fifth Bolgia: grafters and barrators (canto XXI and XXII)
- Sixth Bolgia: hypocrites (canto XXIII)
- Seventh Bolgia: thieves (canto XXIV and XXV)
- Eighth Bolgia: evil counselors (canto XXVI and XXVII)
- Ninth Bolgia: sowers of discord (canto XXVIII)
- Tenth Bolgia: falsifiers and alchemists (canto XXIX); evil impersonators, counterfeiters, and false witnesses (canto XXX)

The ninth circle of complex fraud or treachery in a region called Cocytus (canto XXXI) contains four divisions and displays sins that break the most essential human ties—familial, political, and social:

- Caïna (treachery against relatives, canto XXXII)
- Antenora (treachery against party, city, or country, canto XXXIII)
- Ptolomea (treachery against guests, canto XXIII)
- Judecca (treachery against lords and benefactors, canto XXXIV)

The relationship between the sins Dante describes in Hell and two of Aristotle's moral categories—Incontinence and Malice—seems clear enough. Nonetheless, many of Dante's critics have raised questions over the third category of insane Bestiality. Most refer this third Aristotelian category to all sins of violence, but a few relate the category specifically to complex fraud in the ninth circle.

Dante expects his reader to keep in mind the location of each circle, the sin punished there, the specific description of the punishment, the sinners encountered in that area, and which canto contains this particular material. But sorting out this complicated material with its mass of detail may disorient a first reader of the *Inferno*. The inevitable question on a Dante examination—to discuss in detail the organization of sin and its punishment in the *Inferno*—has created hellish nightmares for generations of students. Perhaps Dante's ingenuity and graphic fantasy failed only to invent an appropriate place in Hell and a suitable punishment for two subcategories of his future readers: teachers who ask this devilish question and students who fail to answer it properly.

The general rule regulating the actual physical punishments in Hell, as opposed to their geographical location or their moral hierarchy from less to more serious, is called *contrapasso*. Finally defined relatively late in the *Inferno* (canto XXVIII: 142), *contrapasso* is a variation on the Old Testament's *lex talionis* (law of retaliation of retribution). Longfellow translates *contrapasso* quite neatly as "counterpoise." Dante's Italian term comes from the Latin translation of a Greek word found in Aristotle's *Nicomachean Ethics* and discussed extensively by Saint Thomas Aquinas in his commentary on the Aristotelian passage. The original Greek word meant "retaliation," clearly relating it to the *lex talionis* of the Old Testament, the proverbial "eye for an eye, a tooth for a tooth." Many readers of *The Divine Comedy* are puzzled by what they find to be a lack of compassion in this first canticle of the work, since nothing seems more foreign to the moral teachings of Christ than the righteous indignation of a progressively less compassionate Pilgrim as he meets sinners and comes to damn them as his understanding of the nature of sin matures. But the reader must never forget that the souls in Hell have died in mortal sin and have had ample opportunity to seek and obtain forgiveness and, in the worst-case scenario, to expiate their evil deeds in Purgatory.

What we may call the "house rules" of Hell are among Dante's most genial poetic inventions. The afterlife was never so minutely or so creatively described in the Bible or in classical writings as it is in Dante's *The Divine Comedy*. The *Inferno* contains any number of special laws that Dante devised for certain groups of sinners. For example, his invention of a vestibule to Hell for the neutral angels and lukewarm humans who never took sides or clear decisions in matters of ethical and political significance while alive has no real precedent. In like manner, his generous salvation of the virtuous pagans, especially classical poets he loved, would probably find few supporters among the theologians. The fanciful idea that certain particularly grievous sinners could have their souls condemned to Hell before their bodies died and that their bodies could be inhabited temporarily by a devil—in effect, being an empty shell on earth while the soul was being tortured in Hell—is a splendid invention hard to match. Medieval man told time by the stars, but in Hell there is no starlight. Yet Virgil manages to tell time in the dark. Damned souls in Dante's universe have the power to see the distant and near future but not the present. While they may be capable of giving Dante prophecies about his future, they have no idea what is happening in the present. On the Final Judgment Day, time will end and they will lose the consciousness of anything other than their sin and their eternal punishment. God's goodness prohibits the blessed in Heaven from feeling compassion or pity for the damned, since such a sentiment would diminish their bliss in Paradise. Hence the damned have only one hope in Hell—that Dante the Pilgrim will report favorable things of them in the world of the living. Earthly fame (as opposed to immortality in Paradise) is their one desire. Conversely, true accounts of their sinfulness reported back to the living by Dante the Pilgrim represent their worst fears. But at the Last Judgment, time will dissolve and this hope, too, will be lost. Many physical "laws" of Hell seem strange. Dante has physical weight and is not a shade like Virgil. Yet Virgil can pick him up bodily. Nor do Virgil and Dante feel the punishments as they pass through them, although the intensity of Dante's reaction to the sins he observes may also tell us something about the sins the poet feels are most typical of his own life and about the sins he most hates.

Hell is reserved for the real hard cases, and there is no reason to waste compassion on them—something Dante the Pilgrim must learn. Even though the principle is not enunciated until the canticle is about to come to a close, the punishments everywhere in Hell reflect the fact that they are either appropriate to the sin or, in some cases, are poetic reflections of the sin itself. The lustful (canto V) are driven by the winds of passion but held in an eternal (and therefore) hellish embrace. Hypocrites (canto XXIII) wear a heavy cloak of lead gilded by gold, just as their hypocrisy was covered by a golden tongue. Suicides who renounced their bodies (canto XIII) now have their bodily shapes torn apart. Flatterers (canto XVIII) who made their way figuratively by ample applications of their tongues to the objects of their flattery are now immersed in human excrement, produced by the same posteriors they so obsequiously kissed to further their nefarious causes. Dante's graphic depictions of the sins in Hell tell his readers a great deal about the nature of evil, but they also reveal much to us about natures of the characters we encounter in the afterlife. A person's sins may summarize his or her natures.

Reading the Inferno*: A Few Caveats*

An encounter with the *Inferno* (not to mention the rest of the epic) requires serious thought and work. This is a classic for which footnotes are essential, and the bibliography provides a number of works that will assist the reader in understanding this incomparable work. Few works of imaginative literature so richly reward the effort required to read them. In the first place, putting aside the erudition and information that gives the reader a better understanding of the poem, Dante's *Inferno* is first and foremost a poem, a work of the imagination of one of the world's most gifted poets, and not a treatise in theology. It is an adventure story, focusing upon a man named Dante. Thanks to his good connections in Heaven with his former love object, a woman named Beatrice who is now dead but residing in glory in Paradise, Dante receives assistance from above to visit the afterlife in order to escape the dangers to his soul. The character Dante (Dante the Pilgrim), who will eventually become the author of the poem (Dante the Poet), requires a guide. Beatrice sends him the classical poet Virgil, who resides in the Limbo of the virtuous pagans (one of Dante's most ingenious poetic inventions). These are privileged people who have not received Christian baptism. Normally, such individuals would not be saved, but since so many of the virtuous pagans are great poets Dante admired, Dante arranges things in Hell in such a way that they are saved in spite of the doctrines of the Catholic Church. They have been saved because of the human significance and ideals expressed in their literary works. Through the course of the journey that takes Dante and Virgil through Hell, an entire universe unfolds before our eyes. How best may we interpret this universe?

The first and fundamental thing to remember about the *Inferno* is that Dante the Pilgrim, the traveler, must not be confused with Dante the Poet. The Poet describes this journey from the vantage point of having completed it and having reached Paradise, while the Pilgrim lacks the knowledge the Poet has acquired. The reader of the poem is thus placed in the same position as the Pilgrim. As the journey progresses, the Pilgrim begins to learn, and it is the Poet's hope that the reader will learn along with the Pilgrim. There will be moments when the perspective of Pilgrim and Poet will diverge. In most cases when this occurs, the reader will probably initially share the reactions of the Pilgrim. In the nineteenth century, Romantic readers of the *Inferno* valued Dante above all for the pathos they found in the passages where Dante the Pilgrim expressed his pity for the damned. The Romantic discovery of Dante viewed him as the master of the poetry of sentiment. Accordingly, Romantic readings of the poem made heroic figures out of the lustful Francesca da Rimini (canto V), the heretical Farinata degli Uberti (canto X), and the silver-tongued Ulysses (canto XXVI).

Dante the Pilgrim certainly is impressed by such people and is fascinated by his conversations with them. He swoons out of pity for Francesca because of his own literary beginnings in the poetry of courtly love. As a citizen of Florence, the Pilgrim is quite naturally interested in Farinata, since he saved his native city from destruction. And as a lover of classical literature, Dante the Pilgrim would have given anything to have read Homer's epic in Greek, and he would never have passed up the opportunity to chat with Ulysses, Homer's most complex character and, in the Poet's view, the archetypal evil counselor. Contemporary critics have managed to agree on at least a general piece of advice about reading the *Inferno*: the judgments of Dante the Pilgrim must be distinguished from those of Dante the Poet. While the Pilgrim may be sentimental and compassionate over souls he encounters, the Poet shares the vantage point of God and the verdict of eternity. The Poet's condemnation of sin is as relentless and as unforgiving as that of God. Unlike Milton in *Paradise Lost*, Dante would never have imagined that the ways of God need to be justified to man, and he would never have conceived of a Lucifer that could even mistakenly be taken as an epic hero. Of crucial importance is the moral development of the Pilgrim as the poem unfolds. Eventually, by the time the Pilgrim spies Lucifer, he has begun to share the vantage point of his maker Dante the Poet, who, in turn, shares that of the Divine Creator. This moral development based on the education and experience of the Pilgrim that Dante the Poet hopes will be replicated in the reader represents the major theme of the entire work.

A second important consideration concerns the vexing issue of allegory in medieval poetry. Dante constantly insists that what he saw in a journey through the afterlife was true. As Charles S. Singleton, one of Dante's greatest American interpreters never tired of emphasizing, the key fiction of *The Divine Comedy* is that the poem is true. Dante wants his readers to believe that what they see, feel, and hear in his poem did actually occur. The work is not just an intellectual pastime for an exiled intellectual. Medieval literature is often described as a literature of allegory. In an allegorical reading of the *Inferno,* the reader would constantly be forced to identify characters with abstract ideas: Dante is Everyman, Virgil is Human Reason, and so forth. Everything in the poem would thus become a vast and impersonal puzzle. The reader's function would involve identifying what each of the characters stood for and observing the relationships and interplay among them. The result would be a lifting of the veil of allegory and a revealing or uncovering of the secret meaning underneath. That concealed meaning would of necessity involve an even more abstract kind of idea: love, death, evil, sin, heresy, treachery, and so forth.

However, such allegorical abstractions are simply not what Dante's great poem is all about. To understand Dante's position on allegory and historical truth, it is first necessary to understand that serious medieval thinkers (theologians, philosophers—not poets) considered poetry to be a fiction that did not tell the truth. Quite rightly, allegorical poems that used characters to represent abstract qualities could not be literally true and were considered "fables" in the pejorative sense. Dante wanted his reader—including serious thinkers—to consider his poem to be a true account of an actual journey. Even if the reader willfully suspends his or her disbelief in the reality of the poem's action and believes that this fantastical journey actually took place, a traditional allegorical poem would simply not serve his purposes. For it would place more emphasis on the abstract ideas contained in the poem than on the characters themselves.

The method that Dante employed in his work, and one that he suggests in a late letter to Cangrande della Scala, is quite different from the traditional allegory typical of works such as *The Romance of the Rose* or *Pilgrim's Progress.* Contrary to the allegory of the poets, Dante accepted at least in part what was known as the allegory of the theologians. This involved bearing in mind four possible senses of a text: the historical or literal; the allegorical; the moral or tropological; and the anagogical. Such a method derived from reading holy scriptures, particularly the relationship between the historical and the allegorical senses. For example, in most Christian services regardless of the denomination, the ritual requires a reading of a passage from the Old Testament followed by, or juxtaposed to, a reading of a passage from the New Testament. In most cases, the Old Testament text prefigures or anticipates that of the New Testament, which fulfills or explains elements of the Old Testament. The classic example of how these four senses operate may be taken from the event that Dante himself refers to in *Purgatory* II: 46–47. There, an angelic boatman (the counterpart to the infernal Charon) delivers souls to the shore of Purgatory. As the souls arrive, they sing in Latin the words from the Vulgate "in exitu Israel de Aegypto" ("When Israel out of Egypt came," a biblical citation from Psalm 114). What are we to make of this moment in the poem? According to the four senses of the allegory of the theologians, we can read the passage in various ways. The event celebrated by the souls about to undergo purgation points us to the Exodus of the Hebrews led by Moses. This event was and is historically and literally true. However, leading the Hebrews out of captivity may be explained allegorically as a prefiguration of Christ's redemption of lost souls, bringing mankind out of bondage to sin. In a real sense, then, Christ fulfills Moses and Moses prefigures or foreshadows Christ. This kind of figural interpretation is common to Christian thought. It explains why Job's suffering might be compared to Christ's passion, why Jonah's three days in the whale's belly was frequently compared to Christ's resurrection three days after the Crucifixion, and why Abraham's sacrifice of Isaac could be viewed as a prefiguration of God's sacrifice of His son, Jesus. In the case of Jonah, Christ even refers to the story in the Bible, Matthew 12: 40, as a prefiguration of what will happen to him, and in the Gospels Christ consciously seeks to fulfill the prophecies of the Old Testament.

Such a "figural" realism, as the literary historian Erich Auerbach has labeled it, makes sense from a Christian point of view, and it is one kind of meaning that Dante certainly understood and employed on occasion in his poem, when another medieval poet might have employed traditional allegory. Another interesting example of this kind of figural realism may be demonstrated by an analysis of why Dante places Cato of Utica, a suicide and a pagan who died before the birth of Christ, in canto I of *Purgatory* rather than either in canto XIII of *Inferno,* the spot reserved for suicides, or in the Limbo of the Virtuous Pagans. Applying the principles of figural realism, Auerbach has argued persuasively that Cato fulfills in the afterlife his historical identity on earth: Once the embodiment of love for political freedom, he now constitutes a figural symbol for the freedom of the immortal soul. Dante's counterintuitive treatments of such pagans as Virgil or Cato point us to the final "house rule" of his poem. Our poet does not concern himself overly much with consistency. He makes the rules to fit his poetic design, not to satisfy logicians, philosophers, theologians, historians, or politicians. Thus it comes as no surprise that Dante damns a pope (Boniface VIII) even before his death. Such is a perfectly logical act of poetic invention (or perhaps revelation) in a Hell created to follow Dante's own fantasy.

Returning to the four senses of a text, the third and fourth senses—the moral, or tropological, and the anagogical sense—always seem more ambiguous. If we take our example from Exodus, the moral sense would refer to the soul of the individual Christian seeking an "exodus" from a life of sin in the present. The anagogical sense would refer to the end of time after the Last Judgment when the saved believe they will arrive in the Promised Land—for Christians, this is Heaven and not the land of Israel. Frankly, Dante infrequently concerns himself with the third and fourth sense of a text, for he is most fascinated by suggesting ways in which historical events, ideas, or characters may suggest (foreshadow, prefigure) other interesting events, ideas, or characters.

The best advice to the reader of *The Divine Comedy* in general and to the *Inferno* in particular is to pay attention to the literal sense of the poem. The greatest poetry in Dante resides in the literal sense of the work, its graphic descriptions of the sinners, their characters, and their punishments. In like manner, the greatest and most satisfying intellectual achievement of the poem comes from the reader's understanding (and not necessarily agreement with) Dante's complex view of morality, or the sinful world that God's punishment is designed to correct. In most cases, a concrete appreciation of the small details of his poem will almost always lead to surprising but satisfying discoveries about the universe Dante's poetry has created.

We read the classics because they offer us different perspectives on timeless questions. Very few people today who encounter *The Divine Comedy,* even Catholics, accept most of Dante's assumptions about the universe. We have gone from the Ptolemaic universe Dante understood through the Newtonian universe that overturned the classical and medieval world views and into the Einsteinian universe of black holes and relativity. In religion, we have experienced the complete schism of a single Christian church after the Reformation into many different Christian churches, and while Western society is clearly more secular in spirit than was the Florence of Dante's day, other non-Christian cultures seem to be returning to a religious fundamentalism not seen in the West for centuries. The confusing politics involving the petty squabbles of Guelf and Ghibelline have long since vanished and have been submerged since Dante's day by various kinds of political systems, most of which are far worse than those he experienced. Perhaps Dante might recognize a similarity between the nascent capitalism of medieval Florence and our own contemporary multinational economic system. Both produced inordinate and unexpected quantities of wealth, although neither ever arrived at a fully equitable means of distributing it, and both economic systems have suffered periodical and frequent cyclical waves of boom and bust that sometimes threaten the lives and fortunes of those who depend on them. Dante would not have been surprised by the many religious, social, political, scientific, intellectual, or economic changes that have taken place since his times. He would only have been surprised if the characters that inhabit his *Inferno* seem dated, almost denizens of another planet. But, of course, Dante's characters are all too contemporary. It would not be difficult to compile a list of our acquaintances or colleagues and to place them in the appropriate places in Hell. More difficult, perhaps, would be a similar assignment of those we know to appropriate places in Purgatory or Paradise.

What explains our contemporary fascination with Dante is his attitude toward his characters. As members of a liberal, diverse, and tolerant culture typical of twenty-first-century democracies, at least in our ideals we tend to see everything and everyone from a variety of positive perspectives. We are asked to respect those with whom we disagree. The French maxim says it all—*tout comprendre, c'est tout pardoner* (to understand all is to forgive all). Dante stands entirely outside such a "civilized," politically correct perspective. For him, understanding does not imply justification, and Dante is the most judgmental of all poets. He believes that civilization involves understanding, an act of the intellect, but for Dante understanding leads inevitably to evaluation, judgment, and the assumption of a moral position based on very simple but immutable ethical and religious precepts. No situational ethics, no "I'm OK, you're OK," no automatic and naive acceptances of every point of view, no matter how ill founded. His energy derives from moral indignation—indignation about the corruption of the Church, about the corruption of Florence and most Italian or European cities, about the weakness of the Holy Roman Empire, and about the general wretched state of humanity. But his genius is based on something even more precious and more unusual—his love for truth and his ability to express it in timeless poetic form.

PETER BONDANELLA is Distinguished Professor of Comparative Literature and Italian at Indiana University and a past President of the American Association for Italian Studies. His publications include a number of translations of Italian classics (Boccaccio, Cellini,

Machiavelli, Vasari), books on Italian Renaissance literature (Machiavelli, Guicciardini) and Italian cinema (postwar Italian cinema, Fellini, Rossellini), and a dictionary of Italian literature. At present, he is completing a book entitled *Hollywood Italians: Dagos, Palookas, Romeos, Wise Guys, and Sopranos,* a history of how Italian Americans have been depicted in American cinema.

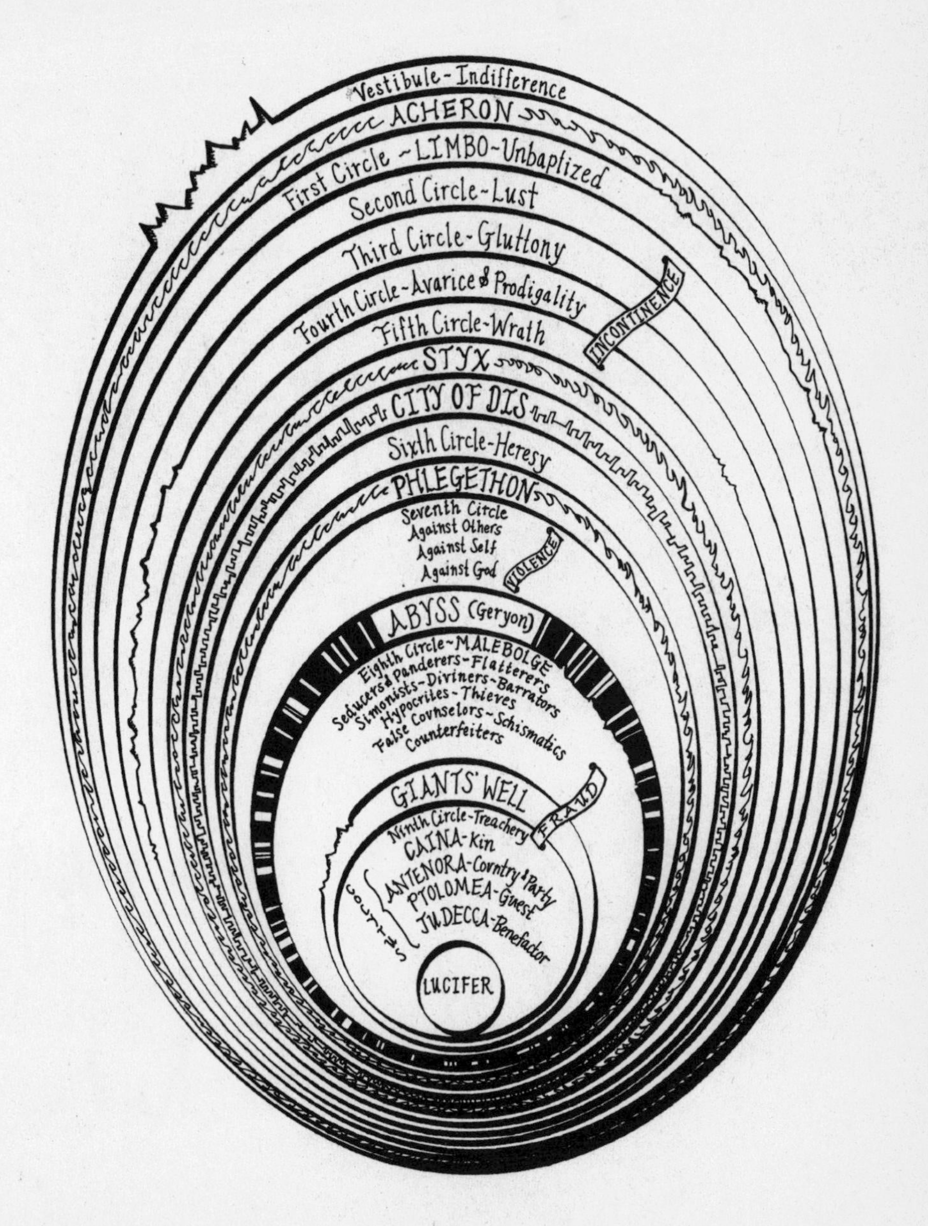
Vestibule - Indifference
ACHERON
First Circle ~ LIMBO ~ Unbaptized
Second Circle ~ Lust
Third Circle ~ Gluttony
Fourth Circle ~ Avarice & Prodigality
Fifth Circle ~ Wrath
INCONTINENCE
STYX
CITY OF DIS
Sixth Circle ~ Heresy
PHLEGETHON
Seventh Circle
Against Others
Against Self
Against God
VIOLENCE
ABYSS (Geryon)
Eighth Circle ~ MALEBOLGE
Seducers & Panderers ~ Flatterers
Simonists ~ Diviners ~ Barrators
Hypocrites ~ Thieves
False Counselors ~ Schismatics
Counterfeiters
GIANTS' WELL
FRAUD
Ninth Circle ~ Treachery
CAINA ~ Kin
ANTENORA ~ Country & Party
PTOLOMEA ~ Guest
JUDECCA ~ Benefactor
LUCIFER

"MAP OF HELL"

THE INFERNO

Canto 1: Dante astray in the Dusky Wood

CANTO I

MIDWAY[1] upon the journey of our life[2]
I found myself[3] within a forest dark,
For the straightforward pathway had been lost.
Ah me! how hard a thing it is to say
What was this forest savage, rough, and stern, 5
Which in the very thought renews the fear.
So bitter is it, death is little more;
But of the good[4] to treat, which there I found,
Speak will I of the other things I saw there.
I cannot well repeat how there I entered, 10
So full was I of slumber at the moment
In which I had abandoned the true way.
But after I had reached a mountain's foot,
At that point where the valley terminated,
Which had with consternation pierced my heart, 15
Upward I looked, and I beheld its shoulders,
Vested already with that planet's rays*
Which leadeth others right by every road.
Then was the fear a little quieted
That in my heart's lake[5] had endured throughout 20
The night, which I had passed so piteously.
And even as he,[6] who, with distressful breath,
Forth issued from the sea upon the shore,
Turns to the water perilous and gazes;
So did my soul, that still was fleeing onward, 25

*The rays of the sun.

Turn itself back to re-behold the pass*
Which never yet a living person left.
After my weary body I had rested,
The way resumed I on the desert slope,
So that the firm foot[7] ever was the lower. 30
And lo! almost where the ascent began,
A panther[8] light and swift exceedingly,
Which with a spotted skin was covered o'er!
And never moved she from before my face,
Nay, rather did impede so much my way, 35
That many times I to return had turned.
The time was the beginning of the morning,
And up the sun was mounting with those stars
That with him were, what time the Love Divine
At first in motion set those beauteous things[9]; 40
So were to me occasion of good hope,
The variegated skin of that wild beast,
The hour of time, and the delicious season;†
But not so much, that did not give me fear
A lion's aspect which appeared to me. 45
He seemed as if against me he were coming
With head uplifted, and with ravenous hunger,
So that it seemed the air was afraid of him;
And a she-wolf, that with all hungerings
Seemed to be laden in her meagreness, 50
And many folk has caused to live forlorn!
She brought upon me so much heaviness,
With the affright that from her aspect came,
That I the hope relinquished of the height.
And as he is who willingly acquires, 55
And the time comes that causes him to lose,
Who weeps in all his thoughts and is despondent,

*The "forest savage" of line 5.
†Springtime.

E'en* such made me that beast withouten† peace,[10]
Which, coming on against me by degrees,
Thrust me back thither where the sun is silent.‡ 60
While I was rushing downward to the lowland,
Before mine eyes did one present himself,
Who seemed from long-continued silence hoarse.
When I beheld him in the desert vast,
"Have pity on me,"[11] unto him I cried, 65
"Whiche'er thou art, or shade or real man!"
He answered me: "Not man; man once I was,[12]
And both my parents were of Lombardy,
And Mantuans by country both of them.
Sub Julio was I born, though it was late, 70
And lived at Rome under the good Augustus,
During the time of false and lying gods.
A Poet was I, and I sang that just
Son of Anchises,§ who came forth from Troy,
After that Ilion** the superb was burned. 75
But thou, why goest thou back to such annoyance?
Why climb'st thou not the Mount Delectable,††
Which is the source and cause of every joy?"
"Now, art thou that Virgilius[13] and that fountain
Which spreads abroad so wide a river of speech?" 80
I made response to him with bashful forehead.
"O, of the other poets honor and light,
Avail me the long study and great love
That have impelled me to explore thy volume!
Thou art my master, and my author thou, 85
Thou art alone the one from whom I took
The beautiful style[14] that has done honor to me.

*Even.

†Without.

‡Toward the darkness.

§Aeneas.

**Troy.

††The mountain of line 13.

Behold the beast, for which I have turned back;
Do thou protect me from her, famous Sage,[15]
For she doth make my veins and pulses tremble." 90
"Thee it behoves to take another road,"
Responded he, when he beheld me weeping,
"If from this savage place thou wouldst escape;
Because this beast, at which thou criest out,
Suffers not any one to pass her way, 95
But so doth harass him, that she destroys him;
And has a nature so malign and ruthless,
That never doth she glut her greedy will,
And after food is hungrier than before.
Many the animals with whom she weds, 100
And more they shall be still, until the Greyhound
Comes, who shall make her perish in her pain.
He shall not feed on either earth or pelf,*
But upon wisdom, and on love and virtue;
'Twixt Feltro and Feltro[16] shall his nation be; 105
Of that low Italy shall he be the saviour,
On whose account the maid Camilla died,
Euryalus, Turnus, Nisus, of their wounds;[17]
Through every city shall he hunt her down,
Until he shall have driven her back to Hell, 110
There from whence envy first did let her loose.
Therefore I think and judge it for thy best
Thou follow me, and I will be thy guide,
And lead thee hence through the eternal place,
Where thou shalt hear the desperate lamentations, 115
Shalt see the ancient spirits disconsolate,
Who cry out each one for the second death;[18]
And thou shalt see those who contented are
Within the fire, because they hope to come,
Whene'er it may be, to the blessed people;[19] 120
To whom, then, if thou wishest to ascend,

*Money.

A soul shall be for that than I more worthy;[20]
With her at my departure I will leave thee;
Because that Emperor,* who reigns above,
In that I was rebellious[21] to his law, 125
Wills that through me none come into his city.
He governs everywhere, and there he reigns;
There is his city and his lofty throne;
O happy he whom thereto he elects!"
And I to him: "Poet, I thee entreat, 130
By that same God whom thou didst never know,
So that I may escape this woe and worse,†
Thou wouldst conduct me there where thou hast said,
That I may see the portal of Saint Peter,[22]
And those thou makest so disconsolate." 135
Then he moved on, and I behind him followed.

*God.

†This present sinful condition and eternal damnation.

CANTO II

DAY was departing[1], and the embrowned air,
Released the animals that are on earth
From their fatigues; and I the only one[2]
Made myself ready to sustain the war,
Both of the way and likewise of the woe,[3] 5
Which memory[4] shall retrace, that erreth not.
O Muses,[5] O high genius,[6] now assist me!
O memory, that didst write down what I saw,
Here thy nobility shall be manifest!
And I began: "Poet, who guidest me, 10
Regard my manhood, if it be sufficient,
Ere to the arduous pass* thou dost confide me.
Thou sayest, that of Silvius the parent,[7]
While yet corruptible, unto the world
Immortal went, and was there bodily. 15
But if the adversary of all evil†
Was courteous, thinking of the high effect
That issue would from him, and who, and what,
To men of intellect unmeet it seems not;
For he was of great Rome, and of her empire 20
In the empyreal heaven[8] as father chosen;
The which and what, wishing to speak the truth,
Were stablished as the holy place, wherein
Sits the successor of the greatest Peter.[9]

*Difficult passage or journey.
†God.

Upon this journey, whence thou givest him vaunt, 25
Things did he hear, which the occasion were
Both of his victory and the papal mantle.
Thither went afterwards the Chosen Vessel,[10]
To bring back comfort thence unto that Faith,
Which of salvation's way is the beginning. 30
But I, why thither come, or who concedes it?
I not Æneas am, I am not Paul,[11]
Nor I, nor others, think me worthy of it.
Therefore, if I resign myself to come,
I fear the coming may be ill-advised; 35
Thou'rt wise, and knowest better than I speak."
And as he is, who unwills what he willed,
And by new thoughts doth his intention change,
So that from his design he quite withdraws,
Such I became, upon that dark hillside, 40
Because, in thinking, I consumed the emprise,[12]
Which was so very prompt in the beginning.
"If I have well thy language understood,"
Replied that shade of the Magnanimous,[13]
"Thy soul attainted is with cowardice, 45
Which many times a man encumbers so,
It turns him back from honored enterprise,
As false sight doth a beast, when he is shy.[14]
That thou mayst free thee from this apprehension,
I'll tell thee why I came, and what I heard 50
At the first moment when I grieved for thee.
Among those was I who are in suspense,[15]
And a fair, saintly Lady[16] called to me
In such wise, I besought her to command me.
Her eyes were shining brighter than the Star; 55
And she began to say, gentle and low,
With voice angelical, in her own language:
'O spirit courteous of Mantua,
Of whom the fame still in the world endures,
And shall endure, long-lasting as the world;[17] 60

A friend of mine,* and not the friend of fortune,
Upon the desert slope is so impeded
Upon his way, that he has turned through terror,
And may, I fear, already be so lost,
That I too late have risen to his succor, 65
From that which I have heard of him in Heaven.
Bestir thee now, and with thy speech ornate,
And with what needful is for this release,
Assist him so, that I may be consoled.
Beatrice am I, who do bid thee go; 70
I come from there, where I would fain return;
Love moved me, which compelleth me to speak.
When I shall be in presence of my Lord,
Full often will I praise thee unto him.'[18]
Then paused she, and thereafter I began: 75
'O Lady of virtue, thou alone through whom
The human race exceedeth all contained
Within the heaven that has the lesser circles,[19]
So grateful unto me is thy commandment,
To obey, if 'twere already done, were late; 80
No farther need'st thou ope† to me thy wish.
But the cause tell me why thou dost not shun
The here descending down into this centre,[20]
From the vast place‡ thou burnest to return to.'
'Since thou wouldst fain so inwardly discern, 85
Briefly will I relate,' she answered me,
'Why I am not afraid to enter here.
Of those things only should one be afraid
Which have the power of doing others harm;
Of the rest, no; because they are not fearful. 90
God in his mercy such created me
That misery of yours attains me not,[21]
Nor any flame assails me of this burning.

*Dante the Pilgrim.
†Make known.
‡The Empyrean, or Heaven proper.

A gentle Lady* is in Heaven, who grieves
At this impediment, to which I send thee, 95
So that stern judgment there above is broken.
In her entreaty she besought Lucía,[22]
And said, "Thy faithful one now stands in need
Of thee, and unto thee I recommend him."
Lucìa, foe of all that cruel is, 100
Hastened away, and came unto the place
Where I was sitting with the ancient Rachel.[23]
"Beatrice," said she, "the true praise of God,
Why succorest thou not him, who loved thee so,
For thee he issued from the vulgar herd?[24] 105
Dost thou not hear the pity of his plaint?
Dost thou not see the death† that combats him
Beside that flood,[25] where ocean has no vaunt?"
Never were persons in the world so swift
To work their weal and to escape their woe, 110
As I, after such words as these were uttered,
Came hither downward from my blessed seat,
Confiding in thy dignified discourse,
Which honors thee, and those who've listened to it.'
After she thus had spoken unto me, 115
Weeping, her shining eyes she turned away;
Whereby she made me swifter in my coming;
And unto thee I came, as she desired;
I have delivered thee from that wild beast,[26]
Which barred the beautiful mountain's short ascent.[27] 120
What is it, then? Why, why dost thou delay?
Why is such baseness bedded in thy heart?
Daring and hardihood why hast thou not,
Seeing that three such Ladies benedight‡
Are caring for thee in the court of Heaven, 125

*The Virgin Mary.
†Both physical and spiritual death.
‡Blessed.

And so much good my speech doth promise thee?"
Even as the flowerets, by nocturnal chill,
Bowed down and closed, when the sun whitens them,
Uplift themselves all open on their stems;
Such I became with my exhausted strength, 130
And such good courage to my heart there coursed,
That I began, like an intrepid person:
"O she compassionate, who succored me,
And courteous thou, who hast obeyed so soon
The words of truth which she addressed to thee! 135
Thou hast my heart so with desire disposed
To the adventure, with these words of thine,
That to my first intent I have returned.
Now go, for one sole will is in us both,
Thou Leader, and thou Lord, and Master thou." 140
Thus said I to him; and when he had moved,
I entered on the deep and savage way.[28]

Canto II: The Darkening Sky of the First Night

CANTO III

THROUGH me the way is to the city dolent;
Through me the way is to eternal dole;
Through me the way among the people lost.*
Justice incited my sublime Creator;
Created me divine Omnipotence, 5
The highest Wisdom and the primal Love.[1]
Before me there were no created things,
Only eterne,† and I eternal last.
All hope abandon, ye who enter in!"
These words in sombre color I beheld 10
Written upon the summit of a gate;
Whence I: "Their sense is, Master, hard‡ to me!"
And he to me, as one experienced:
"Here all suspicion needs must be abandoned,
All cowardice must needs be here extinct. 15
We to the place have come, where I have told thee
Thou shalt behold the people dolorous
Who have foregone the good of intellect."[2]
And after he had laid his hand on mine
With joyful mien, whence I was comforted, 20
He led me in among the secret things.[3]
There sighs, complaints, and ululations loud
Resounded through the air without a star,

*The "city dolent" is the city of woe; "eternal dole" is eternal pain; and the "people lost" are those condemned to Hell.

†Eternal.

‡Both difficult to understand and harsh.

Whence I, at the beginning, wept[4] thereat.
Languages diverse, horrible dialects, 25
Accents of anger, words of agony,
And voices high and hoarse, with sound of hands,[5]
Made up a tumult that goes whirling on
Forever in that air forever black,
Even as the sand doth, when the whirlwind breathes. 30
And I, who had my head with horror bound,
Said: "Master, what is this which now I hear?
What folk is this, which seems by pain so vanquished?"
And he to me: "This miserable mode
Maintain the melancholy souls of those 35
Who lived withouten infamy or praise.[6]
Commingled are they with that caitiff* choir
Of Angels, who have not rebellious been,
Nor faithful were to God, but were for self.[7]
The heavens expelled them, not to be less fair; 40
Nor them the nethermore abyss receives,
For glory none the damned would have from them."
And I: "O Master, what so grievous is
To these, that maketh them lament so sore?"
He answered: "I will tell thee very briefly. 45
These people have not any hope of death;
And this blind life of theirs is so debased,
They envious are of every other fate.
No fame of them the world permits to be;
Misericord† and Justice both disdain them. 50
Let us not speak of them, but look, and pass."
And I, who looked again, beheld a banner,[8]
Which, whirling round, ran on so rapidly,
That of all pause it seemed to me indignant;
And after it there came so long a train 55
Of people, that I ne'er would have believed
That ever Death so many had undone.

*Wicked (from the Italian *cattivo*).
†Mercy, or pity.

When some among them I had recognized,
I looked, and I beheld the shade of him
Who made through cowardice the great refusal.[9] 60
Forthwith I comprehended, and was certain,
That this the sect was of the caitiff wretches
Hateful to God and to his enemies.
These miscreants, who never were alive,
Were naked, and were stung exceedingly 65
By gadflies and by hornets that were there.
These did their faces irrigate with blood,
Which, with their tears commingled, at their feet
By the disgusting worms was gathered up.
And when to gazing farther I betook me, 70
People I saw on a great river's bank;
Whence said I: "Master, now vouchsafe to me,
That I may know who these are, and what law
Makes them appear so ready to pass over,
As I discern athwart the feeble light." 75
And he to me: "These things shall all be known
To thee, as soon as we our footsteps stay.
Upon the dismal shore of Acheron."[10]
Then with mine eyes ashamed and downward cast,
Fearing my words might irksome be to him, 80
From speech refrained I till we reached the river.
And lo! towards us coming in a boat
An old man,[11] hoary with the hair of eld,*
Crying: "Woe unto you, ye souls depraved!
Hope nevermore to look upon the heavens; 85
I come to lead you to the other shore,
To the eternal shades in heat and frost.
And thou, that yonder standest, living soul,
Withdraw thee from these people, who are dead!"
But when he saw that I did not withdraw, 90
He said: "By other ways, by other ports

*White with age.

Thou to the shore shalt come, not here, for passage;
A lighter vessel needs must carry thee."
And unto him the Guide: "Vex thee not, Charon;
It is so willed there where is power to do 95
That which is willed;[12] and ask no further question."
Thereat were quieted the fleecy cheeks
Of him the ferryman of the livid fen,
Who round about his eyes had wheels of flame.
But all those souls who weary were and naked 100
Their color changed and gnashed their teeth together,
As soon as they had heard those cruel words.
God they blasphemed and their progenitors,
The human race, the place, the time, the seed
Of their engendering and of their birth! 105
Thereafter all together they withdrew,
Bitterly weeping, to the accursed shore,
Which waiteth every man who fears not God.
Charon the demon, with the eyes of glede,*
Beckoning to them, collects them all together, 110
Beats with his oar whoever lags behind.
As in the autumn-time the leaves fall off,
First one and then another, till the branch
Unto the earth surrenders all its spoils;
In similar wise the evil seed of Adam 115
Throw themselves from that margin one by one,
At signals, as a bird unto its lure.
So they depart across the dusky wave,
And ere upon the other side they land,
Again on this side a new troop assembles.[13] 120
"My son," the courteous Master[14] said to me,
"All those who perish in the wrath of God
Here meet together out of every land;
And ready are they to pass o'er the river,
Because celestial Justice spurs them on, 125

*Predatory bird, often with red eyes; hence, of red, glowing like coals.

Canto III: The Doomed Souls embarking to cross the Acheron

So that their fear is turned into desire.
This way there never passeth a good soul;
And hence if Charon doth complain of thee,
Well mayst thou know now what his speech imports."
This being finished, all the dusk champaign 130
Trembled so violently, that of that terror
The recollection bathes me still with sweat.[15]
The land of tears gave forth a blast of wind,
And fulminated a vermilion light,
Which overmastered in me every sense, 135
And as a man whom sleep doth seize I fell.[16]

CANTO IV

BROKE the deep lethargy within my head
A heavy thunder, so that I upstarted,
Like to a person who by force is wakened;
And round about I moved my rested eyes,
Uprisen erect, and steadfastly I gazed, 5
To recognize the place wherein I was.
True is it, that upon the verge I found me
Of the abysmal valley dolorous,
That gathers thunder of infinite ululations.
Obscure, profound it was, and nebulous, 10
So that by fixing on its depths my sight
Nothing whatever I discerned therein.
"Let us descend now into the blind world,"
Began the Poet, pallid utterly;[1]
"I will be first, and thou shalt second be." 15
And I, who of his color was aware,
Said: "How shall I come, if thou art afraid,
Who'rt wont to be a comfort to my fears?"
And he to me: "The anguish of the people
Who are below here in my face depicts 20
That pity which for terror thou hast taken.
Let us go on, for the long way impels us."
Thus he went in, and thus he made me enter
The foremost circle[2] that surrounds the abyss.
There, in so far as I had power to hear, 25
Were lamentations none, but only sighs,
That tremulous made the everlasting air.
And this arose from sorrow without torment,

Which the crowds had, that many were and great,
Of infants and of women and of men. 30
To me the Master good: "Thou dost not ask
What spirits these may be, which thou beholdest.
Now will I have thee know, ere thou go farther,
That they sinned not; and if they merit had,
'Tis not enough, because they had not baptism, 35
Which is the portal of the Faith thou holdest;
And if they were before Christianity,
In the right manner they adored not God;
And among such as these am I myself.
For such defects, and not for other guilt, 40
Lost are we, and are only so far punished,
That without hope we live on in desire."[3]
Great grief seized on my heart when this I heard,
Because some people of much worthiness
I knew, who, in that Limbo were suspended.[4] 45
"Tell me, my Master, tell me, thou my Lord,"
Began I, with desire of being certain
Of that Faith which o'ercometh every error,
"Came any one by his own merit hence,
Or by another's, who was blessed thereafter?" 50
And he, who understood my covert speech,
Replied: "I was a novice in this state,
When I saw hither come a Mighty One,[5]
With sign of victory incoronate.
Hence he drew forth the shade of the First Parent,* 55
And that of his son Abel, and of Noah,
Of Moses the lawgiver, and the obedient
Abraham, patriarch, and David, king,
Israel† with his father and his children,
And Rachel, for whose sake he did so much, 60
And others many, and he made them blessed;
And thou must know, that earlier than these

*Adam.
†Jacob.

Never were any human spirits saved."[6]
We ceased not to advance because he spake,
But still were passing onward through the forest, 65
The forest, say I, of thick-crowded ghosts.
Not very far as yet our way had gone
This side the summit, when I saw a fire
That overcame a hemisphere of darkness.[7]
We were a little distant from it still, 70
But not so far that I in part discerned not
That honorable[8] people held that place.
"O thou who honorest every art and science,
Who may these be, which such great honor have,
That from the fashion of the rest it parts them?" 75
And he to me: "The honorable name,
That sounds of them above there in thy life,
Wins grace in Heaven, that so advances them."
In the meantime a voice was heard by me:
"All honor be to the pre-eminent Poet;[9] 80
His shade returns again, that was departed."
After the voice had ceased and quiet was,
Four mighty shades I saw approaching us;
Semblance had they nor sorrowful nor glad.
To say to me began my gracious Master: 85
"Him with that falchion* in his hand behold,
Who comes before the three, even as their lord.
That one is Homer, Poet sovereign;
He who comes next is Horace, the satirist;
The third is Ovid, and the last is Lucan.[10] 90
Because to each of these with me applies
The name† that solitary voice proclaimed,
They do me honor, and in that do well."
Thus I beheld assemble the fair school
Of that lord of the song pre-eminent,[11] 95
Who o'er the others like an eagle soars.

*Broad-bladed sword used in Dante's time.

†That of poet.

When they together had discoursed somewhat,
They turned to me with signs of salutation,
And on beholding this, my Master smiled;
And more of honor still, much more, they did me, 100
In that they made me one of their own band;[12]
So that the sixth was I, 'mid so much wit.
Thus we went on as far as to the light,
Things saying 'tis becoming to keep silent,
As was the saying of them where I was. 105
We came unto a noble castle's foot,
Seven times encompassëd with lofty walls,
Defended round by a fair rivulet;*
This we passed over even as firm ground;
Through portals seven I entered with these
Sages[13] 110
We came into a meadow of fresh verdure.
People were there with solemn eyes and slow,
Of great authority in their countenance;
They spake but seldom, and with gentle voices.
Thus we withdrew ourselves upon one side 115
Into an opening luminous and lofty,
So that they all of them were visible.
There opposite, upon the green enamel,
Were pointed out to me the mighty spirits,
Whom to have seen I feel myself exalted. 120
I saw Electra[14] with companions many,
'Mongst whom I knew both Hector and Æneas[15]
Cæsar in armor with gerfalcon† eyes;[16]
I saw Camilla[17] and Penthesilea[18]
On the other side, and saw the King Latinus, 125
Who with Lavinia his daughter sat;[19]
I saw that Brutus[20] who drove Tarquin forth,
Lucretia, Julia, Marcia, and Cornelia,[21]
And saw alone, apart, the Saladin.[22]
When I had lifted up my brows a little, 130

*Stream.
†Falconlike.

The Master I beheld of those who know,
Sit with his philosophic family.
All gaze upon him, and all do him honor.
There I beheld both Socrates and Plato,[23]
Who nearer him before the others stand; 135
Democritus,[24] who puts the world on chance,
Diogenes, Anaxagoras, and Thales,[25]
Zeno, Empedocles, and Heraclitus;[26]
Of qualities I saw the good collector,
Hight* Dioscorides; and Orpheus[27] saw I, 140
Tully and Livy, and moral Seneca,[28]
Euclid, geometrician, and Ptolemy,[29]
Galen, Hippocrates, and Avicenna,[30]
Averroes[31] who the great Comment made.
I cannot all of them portray in full, 145
Because so drives me onward the long theme,
That many times the word comes short of fact.
The sixfold company in two divides;
Another way my sapient Guide conducts me
Forth from the quiet to the air that trembles; 150
And to a place I come where nothing shines.

*Great.

Canto IV: Homer, the Classic Poets

CANTO V

THUS I descended out of the first circle
Down to the second,[1] that less space begirds,
And so much greater dole,* that goads to wailing.
There standeth Minos horribly, and snarls;
Examines the transgressions at the entrance; 5
Judges, and sends according as he girds him.
I say, that when the spirit evil-born
Cometh before him, wholly it confesses;
And this discriminator of transgressions
Seeth what place in Hell is meet for it; 10
Girds himself with his tail as many times
As grades he wishes it should be thrust down.[2]
Always before him many of them stand;
They go by turns each one unto the judgment;
They speak, and hear, and then are downward hurled. 15
"O thou, that to this dolorous hostelry
Comest," said Minos to me, when he saw me,
Leaving the practice of so great an office,
"Look how thou enterest, and in whom thou trustest;
Let not the portal's amplitude deceive thee." 20
And unto him my Guide: "Why criest thou too?
Do not impede his journey fate-ordained;
It is so willed there where is power to do
That which is willed; and ask no further question."[3]
And now begin the dolesome notes to grow 25

*Pain or suffering.

Audible unto me; now am I come
There where much lamentation strikes upon me.
I came into a place mute of all light,
Which bellows as the sea does in a tempest,
If by opposing winds 'tis combated. 30
The infernal hurricane[4] that never rests
Hurtles the spirits onward in its rapine;
Whirling them round, and smiting, it molests them.
When they arrive before the precipice,[5]
There are the shrieks, the plaints, and the laments, 35
There they blaspheme the puissance divine.*
I understood that unto such a torment
The carnal malefactors were condemned,
Who reason subjugate to appetite.
And as the wings of starlings bear them on 40
In the cold season in large band and full,
So doth that blast the spirits maledict;†
It hither, thither, downward, upward, drives them;
No hope doth comfort them forevermore,
Not of repose, but even of lesser pain. 45
And as the cranes go chanting forth their lays,
Making in air a long line of themselves,
So saw I coming, uttering lamentations,
Shadows borne onward by the aforesaid stress.
Whereupon said I: "Master, who are those 50
People, whom the black air so castigates?"
"The first of those, of whom intelligence
Thou fain wouldst have," then said he unto me,
"The empress was of many languages.
To sensual vices she was so abandoned, 55
That lustful she made licit in her law,
To remove the blame to which she had been led.
She is Semiramis,[6] of whom we read
That she succeeded Ninus, and was his spouse;

*Divine power.
†Cursed.

She held the land which now the Sultan rules. 60
The next is she who killed herself for love,
And broke faith with the ashes of Sichæus;[7]
Then Cleopatra the voluptuous."[8]
Helen I saw, for whom so many ruthless
Seasons revolved;[9] and saw the great Achilles, 65
Who at the last hour combated with Love.[10]
Paris[11] I saw, Tristan;[12] and more than a thousand
Shades did he name and point out with his finger,
Whom Love had separated from our life.
After that I had listened to my Teacher, 70
Naming the dames of eld and cavaliers,*
Pity prevailed, and I was nigh bewildered.
And I began: "O Poet, willingly
Speak would I to those two,[13] who together,
And seem upon the wind to be so light." 75
And he to me: "Thou'lt mark, when they shall be
Nearer to us; and then do thou implore them
By love which leadeth them, and they will come."
Soon as the wind in our direction sways them,
My voice uplift I: "O ye weary souls! 80
Come speak to us, if no one interdicts it."
As turtle-doves, called onward by desire,
With open and steady wings to the sweet nest
Fly through the air by their volition borne,
So came they from the band where Dido is, 85
Approaching us athwart the air malign,
So strong was the affectionate appeal.
"O living creature gracious and benignant,
Who visiting goest through the purple air
Us, who have stained the world incarnadine,† 90
If were the King of the Universe our friend,
We would pray unto him to give thee peace,
Since thou hast pity on our woe perverse.

*Ladies of old and knights.

†With blood.

Of what it pleases thee to hear and speak,
That will we hear, and we will speak to you, 95
While silent is the wind, as it is now.
Sitteth the city, wherein I was born,*
Upon the sea-shore where the Po descends
To rest in peace with all his retinue.
Love, that on gentle heart doth swiftly seize, 100
Seized this man for the person beautiful
That was ta'en from me, and still the mode offends me.
Love, that exempts no one beloved from loving,
Seized me with pleasure of this man so strongly,
That, as thou seest, it doth not yet desert me; 105
Love has conducted us unto one death;
Caïna waiteth him who quenched our life!"[14]
These words were borne along from them to us.
As soon as I had heard those souls tormented,
I bowed my face, and so long held it down 110
Until the Poet said to me: "What thinkest?"
When I made answer, I began: "Alas!
How many pleasant thoughts, how much desires?" 120
Conducted these unto the dolorous pass!"
Then unto them I turned me, and I spake, 115
And I began: "Thine agonies, Francesca,
Sad and compassionate to weeping make me.
But tell me, at the time of those sweet sighs,
By what and in what manner Love conceded,
That you should know your dubious desires." 120
And she to me: "There is no greater sorrow
Than to be mindful of the happy time
In misery, and that thy Teacher knows.
But, if to recognize the earliest root
Of love in us thou hast so great desire, 125
I will do even as he who weeps and speaks.
One day we reading were for our delight

*The city of Ravenna.

Of Launcelot, how Love did him enthrall.
Alone we were and without any fear.
Full many a time our eyes together drew 130
That reading, and drove the color from our faces;
But one point only was it that o'ercame us.
When as we read of the much longed-for smile
Being by such a noble lover kissed,
This man, who ne'er from me shall be divided, 135
Kissed me upon the mouth all palpitating.
Galeotto was the book and he who wrote it.[15]
That day no farther did we read therein."
And all the while one spirit uttered this,
The other one did weep so, that, for pity, 140
I swooned away as if I had been dying,
And fell, even as a dead body falls.[16]

Canto V: The Souls of Paolo and Francesca

CANTO VI

AT the return of consciousness, that closed
Before the pity of those two relations,
Which utterly with sadness had confused me,
New torments I behold, and new tormented
Around me, whichsoever way I move, 5
And whichsoever way I turn, and gaze.
In the third circle[1] am I of the rain
Eternal, maledict, and cold, and heavy;
Its law and quality are never new.
Huge hail, and water sombre-hued, and snow, 10
Athwart the tenebrous air pour down amain;*
Noisome the earth is, that receiveth this.
Cerberus, monster cruel and uncouth,
With his three gullets like a dog is barking,
Over the people that are there submerged. 15
Red eyes he has, and unctuous beard and black,
And belly large, and armed with claws his hands;
He rends the spirits, flays, and quarters them.
Howl the rain maketh them like unto dogs;
One side they make a shelter for the other; 20
Oft turn themselves the wretched reprobates.
When Cerberus perceived us, the great worm![2]
His mouths he opened, and displayed his tusks;
Not a limb had he that was motionless.
And my Conductor, with his spans extended, 25

*With strength or intensity.

Took of the earth, and with his fists well filled,
He threw it into those rapacious gullets.[3]
Such as that dog is, who by barking craves,
And quiet grows soon as his food he gnaws,
For to devour it he but thinks and struggles, 30
The like became those muzzles filth-begrimed
Of Cerberus the demon, who so thunders
Over the souls that they would fain be deaf.
We passed across the shadows,[4] which subdues
The heavy rain-storm, and we placed our feet 35
Upon their vanity that person seems.
They all were lying prone upon the earth,
Excepting one, who sat upright as soon
As he beheld us passing on before him.
"O thou that art conducted through this Hell," 40
He said to me, "recall me, if thou canst;
Thyself wast made before I was unmade."[5]
And I to him: "The anguish which thou hast
Perhaps doth draw thee out of my remembrance,
So that it seems not I have ever seen thee. 45
But tell me who thou art, that in so doleful
A place art put, and in such punishment,
If some are greater, none is so displeasing."
And he to me: "Thy city, which is full
Of envy so that now the sack runs over, 50
Held me within it in the life serene.
You citizens were wont to call me Ciacco;[6]
For the pernicious sin of gluttony
I, as thou seest, am battered by this rain.
And I, sad soul, am not the only one, 55
For all these suffer the like penalty
For the like sin"; and word no more spake he.
I answered him: "Ciacco, thy wretchedness
Weighs on me so that it to weep invites me;[7]
But tell me, if thou knowest, to what shall come 60
The citizens of the divided city;
If any there be just; and the occasion

Tell me why so much discord has assailed it."
And he to me: "They, after long contention,
Will come to bloodshed; and the rustic party 65
Will drive the other out with much offence.
Then afterwards behoves it this one fall
Within three suns, and rise again the other
By force of him who now is on the coast.
High will it hold its forehead a long while, 70
Keeping the other under heavy burdens,
Howe'er it weeps thereat and is indignant.
The just are two, and are not understood there;[8]
Envy and Arrogance and Avarice
Are the three sparks that have all hearts enkindled." 75
Here ended he his tearful utterance;
And I to him: "I wish thee still to teach me,
And make a gift to me of further speech.
Farinata and Tegghiaio, once so worthy,
Jacopo Rusticucci, Arrigo, and Mosca,[9] 80
And others who on good deeds set their thoughts,
Say where they are, and cause that I may know them;
For great desire constraineth me to learn
If Heaven doth sweeten them, or Hell envenom."
And he: "They are among the blacker souls; 85
A different sin downweighs them to the bottom;
If thou so far descendest, thou canst see them.
But when thou art again in the sweet world,
I pray thee to the mind of others bring me;[10]
No more I tell thee and no more I answer." 90
Then his straightforward eyes he turned askance,
Eyed me a little, and then bowed his head;
He fell therewith prone like the other blind.
And the Guide said to me: "He wakes no more
This side the sound of the angelic trumpet; 95
When shall approach the hostile Potentate,
Each one shall find again his dismal tomb,
Shall reassume his flesh and his own figure,
Shall hear what through eternity re-echoes."

So we passed onward o'er the filthy mixture 100
Of shadows and of rain with footsteps slow,
Touching a little on the future life.
Wherefore I said: "Master, these torments here,
Will they increase after the mighty sentence,
Or lesser be, or will they be as burning?" 105
And he to me: "Return unto thy science,[11]
Which wills, that as the thing more perfect is,
The more it feels of pleasure and of pain.
Albeit that this people maledict
To true perfection never can attain, 110
Hereafter more than now they look to be."
Round in a circle by that road we went,
Speaking much more, which I do not repeat;
We came unto the point where the descent is;
There we found Plutus[12] the great enemy. 115

CANTO VII

"Papë Satàn, Papë Satàn, Aleppë!"[1]
Thus Plutus with his clucking voice began;
And that benignant Sage, who all things knew,
Said, to encourage me: "Let not thy fear
Harm thee; for any power that he may have 5
Shall not prevent thy going down this crag."
Then he turned round unto that bloated lip,
And said: "Be silent, thou accursed wolf;
Consume within thyself with thine own rage.
Not causeless is this journey to the abyss; 10
Thus is it willed on high, where Michael wrought
Vengeance upon the proud adultery."[2]
Even as the sails inflated by the wind
Together fall involved when snaps the mast,
So fell the cruel monster to the earth. 15
Thus we descended into the fourth chasm,[3]
Gaining still farther on the dolesome shore
Which all the woe of the universe insacks.
Justice of God, ah! who heaps up so many
New toils and sufferings as I beheld? 20
And why doth our transgression waste us so?
As doth the billow there upon Charybdis,[4]
That breaks itself on that which it encounters,
So here the folk must dance their roundelay.[5]
Here saw I people, more than elsewhere, many, 25
On one side and the other, with great howls,
Rolling weights forward by main-force of chest.
They clashed together, and then at that point

Canto VII: Virgil shows Dante the Souls of the Wrathful

Each one turned backward, rolling retrograde,
Crying, "Why keepest?" and, "Why squanderest thou?" 30
Thus they returned along the lurid circle
On either hand unto the opposite point,
Shouting their shameful metre evermore.
Then each, when he arrived there, wheeled about
Through his half-circle to another joust; 35
And I, who had my heart pierced as it were,
Exclaimed: "My Master, now declare to me
What people these are, and if all were clerks,*
These shaven crowns upon the left of us."
And he to me: "All of them were asquint† 40
In intellect in the first life, so much
That there with measure they no spending made.
Clearly enough their voices bark it forth,
Whene'er they reach the two points of the circle,
Where sunders them the opposite defect. 45
Clerks those were who no hairy covering
Have on the head, and Popes and Cardinals,
In whom doth avarice practise its excess."
And I: "My Master, among such as these
I ought forsooth to recognize some few, 50
Who were infected with these maladies."
And he to me: "Vain thought thou entertainest;
The undiscerning life which made them sordid
Now makes them unto all discernment dim.[6]
Forever shall they come to these two buttings; 55
These from the sepulchre shall rise again
With the fist closed, and these with tresses shorn.[7]
Ill giving and ill keeping the fair world
Have ta'en from them, and placed them in this scuffle;
Whate'er it be, no words adorn I for it. 60
Now canst thou, Son, behold the transient farce
Of goods that are committed unto Fortune,

*Clerics or priests.

†Myopic, or short-sighted in how they spent and saved.

For which the human race each other buffet;
For all the gold that is beneath the moon,
Or ever has been, of these weary souls 65
Could never make a single one repose."
"Master," I said to him, "now tell me also
What is this Fortune which thou speakest of,
That has the world's goods so within its clutches?"
And he to me: "O creatures inbecile,* 70
What ignorance is this which doth beset you?
Now will I have thee learn my judgment of her.
He whose omniscience everything transcends
The heavens created, and gave who should guide them,
That every part to every part may shine, 75
Distributing the light in equal measure;
He in like manner to the mundane splendors
Ordained a general ministress and guide,[8]
That she might change at times the empty treasures
From race to race, from one blood to another, 80
Beyond resistance of all human wisdom.
Therefore one people triumphs, and another
Languishes, in pursuance of her judgment,
Which hidden is, as in the grass a serpent.
Your knowledge has no counterstand against her; 85
She makes provision, judges, and pursues
Her governance, as theirs the other gods.
Her permutations have not any truce;
Necessity makes her precipitate,
So often cometh who his turn obtains. 90
And this is she who is so crucified
Even by those who ought to give her praise,
Giving her blame amiss, and bad repute.
But she is blissful, and she hears it not;
Among the other primal creatures gladsome 95

*Foolish.

She turns her sphere, and blissful she rejoices.
Let us descend now unto greater woe;
Already sinks each star that was ascending
When I set out,[9] and loitering is forbidden."
We crossed the circle to the other bank, 100
Near to a fount* that boils, and pours itself
Along a gully that runs out of it.
The water was more sombre far than perse;
And we, in company with the dusky waves,
Made entrance downward by a path uncouth. 105
A marsh it makes, which has the name of Styx,[10]
This tristful† brooklet, when it has descended
Down to the foot of the malign gray shores.
And I, who stood intent upon beholding,
Saw people mud-besprent‡ in that lagoon, 110
All of them naked and with angry look.
They smote each other not alone with hands,
But with the head and with the breast and feet,
Tearing each other piecemeal with their teeth.
Said the good Master: "Son, thou now beholdest 115
The souls of those whom anger overcame;[11]
And likewise I would have thee know for certain
Beneath the water people are who sigh
And make this water bubble at the surface,
As the eye tells thee wheresoe'er it turns. 120
Fixed in the mire they say, 'We sullen were
In the sweet air, which by the sun is gladdened,
Bearing within ourselves the sluggish reek;
Now we are sullen in this sable mire.'
This hymn do they keep gurgling in their throats, 125
For with unbroken words they cannot say it."

*Spring.
†Dreary, sorry.
‡Sprinkled with mud.

Thus we went circling round the filthy fen
    A great arc 'twixt the dry bank and the swamp,
    With eyes turned unto those who gorge the mire;
Unto the foot of a tower we came at last. 130

CANTO VIII

I say, continuing,[1] that long before
We to the foot of that high tower had come,
Our eyes went upward to the summit of it,
By reason of two flamelets we saw placed there,[2]
And from afar another answer them, 5
So far, that hardly could the eye attain it.
And, to the sea of all discernment turned,
I said: "What sayeth this, and what respondeth
That other fire? and who are they that made it?"
And he to me: "Across the turbid waves 10
What is expected thou canst now discern,
If reek of the morass conceal it not."
Cord never shot an arrow from itself
That sped away athwart the air so swift,
As I beheld a very little boat 15
Come o'er the water tow'rds us at that moment,
Under the guidance of a single pilot
Who shouted, "Now art thou arrived, fell soul?"
"Phlegyas, Phlegyas,[3] thou criest out in vain
For this once," said my Lord; "thou shalt not have us 20
Longer than in the passing of the slough."
As he who listens to some great deceit
That has been done to him, and then resents it,
Such became Phlegyas, in his gathered wrath.
My Guide descended down into the boat, 25
And then he made me enter after him,
And only when I entered seemed it laden.[4]
Soon as the Guide and I were in the boat,

The antique prow goes on its way, dividing
More of the water than 'tis wont with others. 30
While we were running through the dead canal,
Uprose in front of me one full of mire,
And said, "Who'rt thou that comest ere the hour?"
And I to him: "Although I come, I stay not;
But who art thou that hast become so squalid?" 35
"Thou seest that I am one who weeps," he answered.
And I to him: "With weeping and with wailing,
Thou spirit maledict, do thou remain;
For thee I know, though thou art all defiled."
Then stretched he both his hands unto the boat; 40
Whereat my wary Master thrust him back,
Saying, "Away there with the other dogs!"[5]
Thereafter with his arms he clasped my neck;
He kissed my face, and said: "Disdainful soul,
Blessed be she[6] who bore thee in her bosom. 45
That was an arrogant person in the world;
Goodness is none, that decks his memory;
So likewise here his shade is furious.
How many are esteemed great kings up there,
Who here shall be like unto swine in mire, 50
Leaving behind them horrible dispraises!"
And I: "My Master, much should I be pleased,
If I could see him soused into this broth,
Before we issue forth out of the lake."
And he to me: "Ere unto thee the shore 55
Reveal itself, thou shalt be satisfied;
Such a desire 'tis meet thou shouldst enjoy."
A little after that, I saw such havoc
Made of him by the people of the mire,
That still I praise and thank my God for it. 60
They all were shouting, "At Philippo Argenti!"
And that exasperate spirit Florentine
Turned round upon himself with his own teeth.
We left him there, and more of him I tell not;

Canto VIII: Phlegyas ferries Dante and Virgil across the Styx

But on mine ears there smote a lamentation, 65
Whence forward I intent unbar mine eyes.
And the good Master said: "Even now, my son,
The city draweth near whose name is Dis,[7]
With the grave citizens, with the great throng."
And I: "Its mosques[8] already, Master, clearly 70
Within there in the valley I discern
Vermilion, as if issuing from the fire
They were." And he to me: "The fire eternal[9]
That kindles them within makes them look red,
As thou beholdest in this nether Hell." 75
Then we arrived within the moats profound,
That circumvallate that disconsolate city;
The walls appeared to me to be of iron.
Not without making first a circuit wide,
We came unto a place where loud the pilot 80

Cried out to us, "Debark, here is the entrance."
More than a thousand at the gates I saw
Out of the Heavens rained down,[10] who angrily
Were saying, "Who is this that without death
Goes through the kingdom of the people dead?" 85
And my sagacious Master made a sign
Of wishing secretly to speak with them.
A little then they quelled their great disdain,
And said: "Come thou alone, and he begone
Who has so boldly entered these dominions. 90
Let him return alone by his mad road;
Try, if he can; for thou shalt here remain,
Who hast escorted him through such dark regions."
Think, Reader,[11] if I was discomforted
At utterance of the accursed words; 95
For never to return here I believed.
"O my dear Guide, who more than seven times*
Hast rendered me security, and drawn me
From imminent peril that before me stood,
Do not desert me," said I, "thus undone; 100
And if the going farther be denied us,
Let us retrace our steps together swiftly."
And that Lord, who had led me thitherward,
Said unto me: "Fear not; because our passage
None can take from us, it by Such is given.[12] 105
But here await me, and thy weary spirit
Comfort and nourish with a better hope;
For in this nether world I will not leave thee."
So onward goes and there abandons me
My Father sweet, and I remain in doubt, 110
For No or Yes within my head contend.
I could not hear what he proposed to them;
But with them there he did not linger long,
Ere each within in rivalry ran back.
They closed the portals, those our adversaries, 115

*Many times—no precise figure is intended.

On my Lord's breast, who had remained without
And turned to me with footsteps far between.
His eyes cast down, his forehead shorn had he
Of all its boldness, and he said, with sighs,
"Who has denied to me the dolesome houses?" 120
And unto me: "Thou, because I am angry,[13]
Fear not, for I will conquer in the trial,
Whatever for defence within be planned.
This arrogance of theirs is nothing new;
For once they used it at less secret gate,[14] 125
Which finds itself without a fastening still.
O'er it didst thou behold the dead inscription;
And now this side of it descends the steep,
Passing across the circles without escort,
One by whose means the city shall be opened."[15] 130

CANTO IX

THAT hue which cowardice brought out on me,
Beholding my Conductor backward turn,
Sooner repressed within him his new color.[1]
He stopped attentive, like a man who listens,
Because the eye could not conduct him far 5
Through the black air, and through the heavy fog.
"Still it behoveth us to win the fight,"
Began he; "Else . . . Such offered us herself . . .
O how I long that some one here arrive!"
Well I perceived, as soon as the beginning 10
He covered up with what came afterward,
That they were words quite different from the first;
But none the less his saying gave me fear,
Because I carried out the broken phrase,
Perhaps to a worse meaning than he had.[2] 15
"Into this bottom of the doleful conch*
Doth any e'er descend from the first grade,
Which for its pain has only hope cut off?"[3]
This question put I; and he answered me:
"Seldom it comes to pass that one of us 20
Maketh the journey upon which I go.
True is it, once before I here below
Was conjured by that pitiless Erictho,[4]
Who summoned back the shades unto their bodies.
Naked of me short while the flesh had been, 25

*The first circle, or Limbo.

Canto IX: Megaera, Tisiphone and Alecto

Before within that wall she made me enter,
To bring a spirit from the circle of Judas;[5]
That is the lowest region and the darkest,
And farthest from the heaven which circles all.
Well know I the way;[6] therefore be reassured. 30
This fen, which a prodigious stench exhales,
Encompasseth about the city dolent,
Where now we cannot enter without anger."
And more he said, but not in mind I have it;
Because mine eye had altogether drawn me 35
Tow'rds the high tower with the red-flaming summit,
Where in a moment saw I swift uprisen
The three infernal Furies[7] stained with blood,
Who had the limbs of women and their mien,
And with the greenest hydras were begirt; 40
Small serpents and cerastes were their tresses,
Wherewith their horrid temples were entwined.
And he who well the handmaids of the Queen
Of everlasting lamentation[8] knew,
Said unto me: "Behold the fierce Erinnys. 45
This is Megæra, on the left-hand side;
She who is weeping on the right, Alecto;
Tisiphone is between"; and then was silent.
Each one her breast was rending with her nails;
They beat them with their palms, and cried so loud, 50
That I for dread pressed close unto the Poet.
"Medusa[9] come, so we to stone will change him!"
All shouted looking down; "in evil hour
Avenged we not on Theseus his assault!"[10]
"Turn thyself round, and keep thine eyes close shut, 55
For if the Gorgon appear, and thou shouldst see it,
No more returning upward would there be."
Thus said the Master; and he turned me round
Himself, and trusted not unto my hands
So far as not to blind me with his own. 60
O ye who have undistempered intellects,
Observe the doctrine that conceals itself

Beneath the veil of the mysterious verses![11]
And now there came across the turbid waves
The clangor of a sound with terror fraught, 65
Because of which both of the margins trembled;
Not otherwise it was than of a wind
Impetuous on account of adverse heats,
That smites the forest, and, without restraint,
The branches rends, beats down, and bears away; 70
Right onward, laden with dust, it goes superb,
And puts to flight the wild beasts and the shepherds.
Mine eyes he loosed, and said: "Direct the nerve
Of vision now along that ancient foam,
There yonder where that smoke is most intense." 75
Even as the frogs before the hostile serpent
Across the water scatter all abroad,
Until each one is huddled in the earth,
More than a thousand ruined souls I saw,
Thus fleeing from before one who on foot 80
Was passing o'er the Styx with soles unwet.[12]
From off his face he fanned that unctuous air,
Waving his left hand oft in front of him,
And only with that anguish seemed he weary.
Well I perceived one sent from Heaven was he, 85
And to the Master turned; and he made sign
That I should quiet stand, and bow before him.
Ah! how disdainful he appeared to me!
He reached the gate, and with a little rod
He opened it, for there was no resistance. 90
"O banished out of Heaven, people despised!"[13]
Thus he began upon the horrid threshold;
"Whence is this arrogance within you couched?
Wherefore recalcitrate against that will,
From which the end can never be cut off, 95
And which has many times increased your pain?
What helpeth it to butt against the fates?
Your Cerberus, if you remember well,
For that still bears his chin and gullet peeled."[14]

Then he returned along the miry road, 100
And spake no word to us, but had the look
Of one whom other care constrains and goads
Than that of him who in his presence is;
And we our feet directed tow'rds the city,
After those holy words all confident. 105
Within we entered without any contest;
And I, who inclination had to see
What the condition such a fortress holds,
Soon as I was within, cast round mine eye,
And see on every hand an ample plain, 110
Full of distress and torment terrible.
Even as at Arles, where stagnant grows the Rhone,
Even as at Pola near to the Quarnaro,[15]
That shuts in Italy and bathes its borders,
The sepulchres make all the place uneven; 115
So likewise did they there on every side,
Saving that there the manner was more bitter;
For flames between the sepulchres were scattered,
By which they so intensely heated were,
That iron more so asks not any art. 120
All of their coverings uplifted were,
And from them issued forth such dire laments,
Sooth seemed they of the wretched and
tormented.
And I: "My Master, what are all those people
Who, having sepulture within those tombs, 125
Make themselves audible by doleful sighs?"
And he to me; "Here are the Heresiarchs,[16]
With their disciples of all sects, and much
More than thou thinkest laden are the tombs.
Here like together with its like is buried; 130
And more and less the monuments are heated."
And when he to the right[17] had turned, we passed
Between the torments and high parapets.

CANTO X

Now onward goes, along a narrow path
    Between the torments and the city wall,
    My Master, and I follow at his back.
"O power supreme, that through these impious circles
    Turnest me," I began, "as pleases thee, 5
    Speak to me, and my longings satisfy;
The people who are lying in these tombs,
    Might they be seen? already are uplifted
    The covers all, and no one keepeth guard."
And he to me: "They all will be closed up 10
    When from Jehosaphat[1] they shall return
    Here with the bodies they have left above.
Their cemetery have upon this side
    With Epicurus[2] all his followers,
    Who with the body mortal make the soul; 15
But in the question thou dost put to me,
    Within here shalt thou soon be satisfied,
    And likewise in the wish thou keepest silent."
And I: "Good Leader, I but keep concealed
    From thee my heart, that I may speak the less, 20
    Nor only now hast thou thereto disposed me."
"O Tuscan,[3] thou who through the city of fire
    Goest alive, thus speaking modestly,
    Be pleased to stay thy footsteps in this place.
Thy mode of speaking makes thee manifest 25
    A native of that noble fatherland,

Canto X: Farinata degli Uberti addresses Dante

To which perhaps I too molestful* was."
Upon a sudden issued forth this sound
From out one of the tombs; wherefore I pressed,
Fearing, a little nearer to my Leader. 30
And unto me he said: "Turn thee; what dost thou?

*Harmful.

Behold there Farinata who has risen;
From the waist upwards wholly shalt thou see him."
I had already fixed mine eyes on his,
And he uprose erect with breast and front 35
E'en as if Hell he had in great despite.*
And with courageous hands and prompt my Leader
Thrust me between the sepulchres towards him,
Exclaiming, "Let thy words explicit be."
As soon as I was at the foot of his tomb, 40
Somewhat he eyed me, and, as if disdainful,
Then asked of me, "Who were thine ancestors?"
I, who desirous of obeying was,
Concealed it not, but all revealed to him;
Whereat he raised his brows a little upward. 45
Then said he: "Fiercely adverse have they been
To me, and to my fathers, and my party;
So that two several times I scattered them."[4]
"If they were banished, they returned on all sides,"
I answered him, "the first time and the second;[5] 50
But yours have not acquired that art aright."
Then there uprose upon the sight, uncovered
Down to the chin, a shadow at his side;
I think that he had risen on his knees.
Round me he gazed, as if solicitude 55
He had to see if some one else were with me;
But after his suspicion was all spent,
Weeping, he said to me: "If through this blind
Prison thou goest by loftiness of genius,
Where is my son? and why is he not with thee?" 60
And I to him: "I come not of myself;
He who is waiting yonder leads me here,
Whom in disdain perhaps your Guido had."[6]
His language and the mode of punishment
Already unto me had read his name; 65

*Contempt.

On that account my answer was so full.
Up starting suddenly, he cried out: "How
Saidst thou,—he had? Is he not still alive?
Does not the sweet light strike upon his eyes?"
When he became aware of some delay, 70
Which I before my answer made, supine
He fell again, and forth appeared no more.
But the other, magnanimous, at whose desire
I had remained, did not his aspect change,
Neither his neck he moved, nor bent his side. 75
"And if," continuing his first discourse,
"They have that art," he said, "not learned aright,
That more tormenteth me, than doth this bed.
But fifty times shall not rekindled be
The countenance of the Lady who reigns here,[7] 80
Ere thou shalt know how heavy is that art;
And as thou wouldst to the sweet world return,
Say why that people is so pitiless
Against my race in each one of its laws?"
Whence I to him: "The slaughter and great carnage 85
Which have with crimson stained the Arbia,[8] cause
Such orisons* in our temple to be made."
After his head he with a sigh had shaken,
"There I was not alone," he said, "nor surely
Without a cause had with the others moved. 90
But there I was alone, where every one
Consented to the laying waste of Florence,
He who defended her with open face."
"Ah! so hereafter may your seed repose,"
I him entreated, "solve for me that knot,[9] 95
Which has entangled my conceptions here.
It seems that you can see, if I hear rightly,
Beforehand whatsoe'er brings with it,
And in the present have another mode."

*Prayers.

"We see, like those who have imperfect sight, 100
The things," he said, "that distant are from us;
So much still shines on us the Sovereign Ruler.
When they draw near, or are, is wholly vain
Our intellect, and if none brings it to us,
Not anything know we of your human state. 105
Hence thou canst understand, that wholly dead
Will be our knowledge from the moment when
The portal of the future shall be closed."
Then I, as if compunctious for my fault,
Said: "Now, then, you will tell that fallen one, 110
That still his son is with the living joined.
And if just now, in answering, I was dumb,
Tell him I did it because I was thinking
Already of the error you have solved me."
And now my Master was recalling me, 115
Wherefore more eagerly I prayed the spirit
That he would tell me who was with him there.
He said: "With more than a thousand here I lie;
Within here is the second Frederick,
And the Cardinal,[10] and of the rest I speak not." 120
Thereon he hid himself; and I towards
The ancient poet turned my steps, reflecting
Upon that saying, which seemed hostile to me.
He moved along; and afterward, thus going,
He said to me, "Why are thou so bewildered?" 125
And I in his inquiry satisfied him.
"Let memory preserve what thou hast heard
Against thyself," that Sage commanded me,
"And now attend here"; and he raised his finger.
"When thou shalt be before the radiance sweet 130
Of her whose beauteous eyes all things behold,
From her[11] thou'lt know the journey of thy life."
Unto the left hand then he turned his feet;
We left the wall, and went towards the middle,
Along a path that strikes into a valley, 135
Which even up there unpleasant made its stench.

CANTO XI

UPON the margin of a lofty bank
Which great rocks broken[1] in a circle made,
We came upon a still more cruel throng;
And there, by reason of the horrible
Excess of stench the deep abyss throws out, 5
We drew ourselves aside behind the cover
Of a great tomb, whereon I saw a writing,
Which said: "Pope Anastasius[2] I hold,
Whom out of the right way Photinus drew."
"Slow it behoveth our descent to be, 10
So that the sense be first a little used
To the sad blast, and then we shall not heed it."
The Master thus; and unto him I said,
"Some compensation find, that the time pass not
Idly"; and he: "Thou seest I think of that. 15
My son, upon the inside of these rocks,"
Began he then to say, "are three small circles,[3]
From grade to grade, like those which thou art leaving.
They all are full of spirits maledict;
But that hereafter sight alone suffice thee, 20
Hear how and wherefore they are in constraint.
Of every malice that wins hate in Heaven,
Injury is the end; and all such end
Either by force or fraud afflicteth others.[4]
But because fraud is man's peculiar vice, 25
More it displeaseth God; and so stand lowest
The fraudulent, and greater dole assails them.
All the first circle of the Violent is;

But since force may be used against three persons,
In three rounds[5] 'tis divided and constructed. 30
To God, to ourselves, and to our neighbor can we
Use force; I say on them and on their things,
As thou shalt hear with reason manifest.
A death by violence, and painful wounds,
Are to our neighbor given; and in his substance 35
Ruin, and arson, and injurious levies;
Whence homicides, and he who smites unjustly,
Marauders, and freebooters, the first round
Tormenteth all in diverse companies.
Man may lay violent hands upon himself 40
And his own goods; and therefore in the second
Round must perforce without avail repent
Whoever of your world deprives himself,
Who games, and dissipates his property,
And weepeth there, where he should jocund* be 45
Violence can be done the Deity,
In heart denying and blaspheming Him,
And by disdaining Nature and her bounty.
And for this reason doth the smallest round
Seal with its signet Sodom and Cahors;[6] 50
And who, disdaining God, speaks from the heart.
Fraud, wherewithal is every conscience stung,
A man may practice upon him who trusts,
And him who doth no confidence imburse.
This latter mode, it would appear, dissevers 55
Only the bond of love which Nature makes;
Wherefore within the second circle nestle
Hypocrisy, flattery, and who deals in magic,
Falsification, theft, and simony,
Panders, and barrators, and the like filth.[7] 60
By the other mode, forgotten is that love
Which Nature makes, and what is after added,

*Cheerful, happy.

From which there is a special faith engendered.
Hence in the smallest circle,[8] where the point is
Of the Universe, upon which Dis is seated, 65
Whoe'er betrays forever is consumed."
And I: "My Master, clear enough proceeds
Thy reasoning, and full well distinguishes
This cavern and the people who possess it.
But tell me, those within the fat lagoon, 70
Whom the wind drives, and whom the rain doth beat,
And who encounter with such bitter tongues,
Wherefore are they inside of the red city
Not punished, if God has them in his wrath,
And if he has not, wherefore in such fashion?"[9] 75
And unto me he said: "Why wanders so
Thine intellect from that which it is wont?
Or, sooth, thy mind where is it elsewhere looking?
Hast thou no recollection of those words
With which thine Ethics thoroughly discusses 80
The dispositions three, that Heaven abides not,—
Incontinence, and Malice, and insane
Bestiality?[10] and how Incontinence
Less God offendeth, and less blame attracts?
If thou regardest this conclusion well, 85
And to they mind recallest who they are
That up outside are undergoing penance,
Clearly wilt thou perceive why from these felons
They separated are, and why less wroth*
Justice divine doth smite them with its hammer." 90
"O Sun, that healest all distempered vision,
Thou dost content me so, when thou resolvest,
That doubting pleases me no less than knowing!
Once more a little backward turn thee," said I,
"There where thou sayest that usury offends 95
Goodness divine, and disengage the knot."[11]

*Less angry, wrathful.

"Philosophy," he said, "to him who heeds it,
Noteth, not only in one place alone,
After what manner Nature takes her course
From Intellect Divine, and from its art; 100
And if thy Physics carefully thou notest,
After not many pages shalt thou find,
That this your art as far as possible
Follows, as the discipline doth the master;
So that your art is, as it were, God's grandchild. 105
From these two, if thou bringest to thy mind
Genesis at the beginning, it behoves
Mankind to gain their life and to advance;
And since the usurer takes another way,
Nature herself and in her follower 110
Disdains he, for elsewhere he puts his hope.[12]
But follow, now, as I would fain go on,
For quivering are the Fishes on the horizon,
And the Wain wholly over Caurus lies,[13]
And far beyond there we descend the crag." 115

CANTO XII

THE place where to descend the bank we came
Was alpine, and from what was there, moreover,
Of such a kind that every eye would shun it.
Such as that ruin is which in the flank
Smote, on this side of Trent, the Adige,[1] 5
Either by earthquake or by failing stay,
For from the mountain's top, from which it moved,
Unto the plain the cliff is shattered so,
No path 'twould give to him who was above;
Even such was the descent of that ravine, 10
And on the border of the broken chasm
The infamy of Crete[2] was stretched along,
Who was conceived in the fictitious cow;
And when he us beheld, he bit himself,
Even as one whom anger racks within. 15
My Sage towards him shouted: "Peradventure
Thou think'st that here may be the Duke of Athens,
Who in the world above brought death to thee?
Get thee gone, beast, for this one cometh not
Instructed by thy sister, but he comes 20
In order to behold your punishments."
As is that bull who breaks loose at the moment
In which he has received the mortal blow,
Who cannot walk, but staggers here and there,
The Minotaur beheld I do the like; 25
And he, the wary, cried: "Run to the passage;

While he is wroth,* 'tis well thou shouldst descend."
Thus down we took our way o'er that discharge
Of stones, which oftentimes did move themselves
Beneath my feet, from the unwonted burden.[3] 30
Thoughtful I went; and he said: "Thou art thinking
Perhaps upon this ruin, which is guarded
By that brute anger which just now I quenched.
Now will I have thee know, the other time[4]
I here descended to the nether Hell, 35
This precipice had not yet fallen down.
But truly, if I well discern, a little
Before His coming who the mighty spoil
Bore off from Dis, in the supernal circle,[5]
Upon all sides the deep and loathsome valley 40
Trembled so, that I thought the Universe
Was thrilled with love, by which there are who think
The world ofttimes converted into chaos;[6]
And at that moment this primeval crag
Both here and elsewhere made such overthrow. 45
But fix thine eyes below; for draweth near
The river of blood,[7] within which boiling is
Whoe'er by violence doth injure others."
O blind cupidity, O wrath insane,
That spurs us onward so in our short life, 50
And in the eternal then so badly steeps us!
I saw an ample moat bent like a bow,
As one which all the plain encompasseth,
Conformable to what my Guide had said.
And between this and the embankment's foot 55
Centaurs[8] in file were running, armed with arrows,
As in the world they used the chase to follow.
Beholding us descend, each one stood still,
And from the squadron three detached themselves,

*Angry, wrathful.

With bows and arrows in advance selected; 60
And from afar one cried: "Unto what torment
Come ye, who down the hillside are descending?
Tell us from there; if not, I draw the bow."
My Master said: "Our answer will we make
To Chiron, there near by; in evil hour, 65
That will of thine was evermore so hasty."
Then touched he me, and said: "This one is Nessus,
Who perished for the lovely Dejanira,
And for himself, himself did vengeance take.
And he in the midst, who at his breast is gazing, 70
Is the great Chiron, who brought up Achilles;
That other Pholus is,[9] who was so wrathful.
Thousands and thousands go about the moat
Shooting with shafts whatever soul emerges
Out of the blood, more than his crime allots." 75
Near we approached unto those monsters fleet;
Chiron an arrow took, and with the notch
Backward upon his jaws he put his beard.
After he had uncovered his great mouth,
He said to his companions: "Are you ware 80
That he behind moveth whate'er he touches?[10]
Thus are not wont to do the feet of dead men."
And my good Guide, who now was at his breast,
Where the two natures are together joined,
Replied; "Indeed he lives, and thus alone 85
Me it behoves to show him the dark valley;
Necessity, and not delight, impels us.
Some one* withdrew from singing Halleluja,
Who unto me committed this new office;
No thief is he, nor I a thievish spirit. 90
But by that virtue through which I am moving
My steps along this savage thoroughfare,
Give us some one of thine, to be with us,

*This is Beatrice.

Canto XII: The Minotaur on the Shattered Cliff

And who may show us where to pass the ford,
And who may carry this man on his back; 95
For 'tis no spirit that can walk the air."
Upon his right breast Chiron wheeled about,
And said to Nessus: "Turn and do thou guide them,
And warn aside, if other band should meet you."
We with our faithful escort onward moved, 100
Along the brink of the vermilion boiling,
Wherein the boiled were uttering loud laments.
People I saw within up to the eyebrows,
And the great Centaur said: "Tyrants are these,
Who dealt in bloodshed and in pillaging. 105
Here they lament their pitiless mischiefs; here
Is Alexander, and fierce Dionysius[11]
Who upon Sicily brought dolorous years.
That forehead there which has the hair so black
Is Azzolin; and the other who is blond, 110
Obizzo is of Esti, who, in truth,
Up in the world was by his step-son slain."[12]
Then turned I to the Poet; and he said,
"Now he be first to thee, and second I."[13]
A little farther on the Centaur stopped 115
Above a folk, who far down as the throat
Seemed from that boiling stream to issue forth.
A shade he showed us on one side alone,
Saying: "He cleft asunder,[14] in God's bosom
The heart that still upon the Thames is honored." 120
Then people saw I, who from out the river
Lifted their heads and also all the chest;
And many among these I recognized.
Thus ever more and more grew shallower
That blood, so that the feet alone it covered; 125
And there across the moat our passage was.[15]
"Even as thou here upon this side beholdest
The boiling stream, that aye* diminishes,"

*Always, ever.

The Centaur said, "I wish thee to believe
That on this other more and more declines 130
Its bed, until it reunites itself
Where it behoveth tyranny to groan.
Justice divine, upon this side, is goading
That Attila, who was a scourge on earth,
And Pyrrhus, and Sextus; and forever milks 135
The tears which with the boiling it unseals
In Rinier da Corneto and Rinier Pazzo,
Who made upon the highways so much war."[16]
Then back he turned, and passed again the ford.

CANTO XIII

NOT yet had Nessus reached the other side,
When we had put ourselves within a wood,
That was not marked by any path whatever.
Not foliage green, but of a dusky color,
Not branches smooth, but gnarled and intertangled, 5
Not apple-trees were there, but thorns with poison.
Such tangled thickets have not, nor so dense,
Those savage wild-beasts, that in hatred hold
'Twixt Cecina and Corneto[1] the tilled places.
There do the hideous Harpies make their nests, 10
Who chased the Trojans from the Strophades,[2]
With sad announcement of impending doom;
Broad wings have they, and necks and faces human,
And feet with claws, and their great bellies fledged;
They make laments upon the wondrous trees. 15
And the good Master: "Ere thou enter farther,
Know that thou art within the second round,"
Thus he began to say, "and shalt be, till
Thou comest upon the horrible sand-waste;
Therefore look well around, and thou shalt see 20
Things that will credence give unto my speech."
I heard on all sides lamentations uttered,
And person none beheld I who might make them,
Whence, utterly bewildered, I stood still.
I think he thought that I perhaps might think[3] 25
So many voices issued through those trunks
From people who concealed themselves for us;
Therefore the Master said: "If thou break off

Canto XIII: Harpies in the Forest of the Suicides

Some little spray from any of these trees,
The thoughts thou hast will wholly be made vain." 30
Then stretched I forth my hand a little forward,
And plucked a branchlet off from a great thorn;
And the trunk cried, "Why dost thou mangle me?"
After it had become embrowned with blood,
It recommenced its cry: "Why dost thou rend me? 35

Hast thou no spirit of pity whatsoever?
Men once we were, and now are changed to trees;
Indeed, thy hand should be more pitiful,
Even if the souls of serpents we had been."
As out of a green brand, that is on fire 40
At one of the ends, and from the other drips
And hisses with the wind that is escaping;
So from that splinter issued forth together
Both words and blood; whereat I let the tip
Fall, and stood like a man who is afraid. 45
"Had he been able sooner to believe,"
My Sage made answer, "O thou wounded soul,
What only in my verses he has seen,[4]
Not upon thee had he stretched forth his hand;
Whereas the thing incredible has caused me 50
To put him to an act which grieveth me.
But tell him who thou wast, so that by way
Of some amends thy fame he may refresh
Up in the world, to which he can return."
And the trunk said: "So thy sweet words allure me, 55
I can not silent be; and you be vexed not,
That I a little to discourse am tempted.
I am the one who both keys had in keeping
Of Frederick's heart, and turned them to and fro
So softly in unlocking and in locking, 60
That from his secrets most men I withheld;
Fidelity I bore the glorious office
So great, I lost thereby my sleep and pulses.
The courtesan[5] who never from the dwelling
Of Cæsar turned aside her harlot eyes, 65
Death universal and the vice of courts,
Inflamed against me all the other minds,
And they, inflamed, did so inflame Augustus,[6]
That my glad honors to dismal mournings.
My spirit, in disdainful exultation, 70
Thinking by dying to escape disdain,
Made me unjust against myself, the just.

I, by the roots unwonted of this wood,[7]
Do swear to you that never broke I faith
Unto my lord, who was so worthy of honor; 75
And to the world if one of you return,
Let him my memory comfort, which is lying
Still prostrate from the blow that envy dealt it."
Waited awhile, and then: "Since he is silent,"
The Poet said to me, "lose not the time, 80
But speak, and question him, if more may please thee."
Whence I to him: "Do thou again inquire
Concerning what thou think'st will satisfy me;
For I cannot, such pity is in my heart."[8]
Therefore he recommenced: "So may the man 85
Do for thee freely what thy speech implores,
Spirit incarcerate, again be pleased
To tell us in what way the soul is bound
Within these knots; and tell us, if thou canst,
If any from such members e'er is freed." 90
Then blew the trunk amain, and afterward
The wind was into such a voice converted:
"With brevity shall be replied to you.
When the exasperated soul abandons
The body whence it rent itself away, 95
Minos consigns it to the seventh abyss.
It falls into the forest, and no part
Is chosen for it; but where Fortune hurls it,
There like a grain of spelt it germinates.
It springs a sapling, and a forest tree; 100
The Harpies, feeding then upon its leaves,
Do pain create, and for the pain an outlet.
Like others for our spoils shall we return;
But not that any one may them revest,
For 'tis not just to have what one casts off. 105
Here we shall drag them, and along the dismal
Forest our bodies shall suspended be,
Each to the thorn of his molested shade."
We were attentive still unto the trunk,

Thinking that more it yet might wish to tell us, 110
When by a tumult we were overtaken,
In the same way as he is who perceives
The boar and chase approaching to his stand,
Who hears the crashing of the beasts and branches;
And two behold![9] upon our left-hand side, 115
Naked and scratched, fleeing so furiously,
That of the forest every fan they broke.
He who was in advance: "Now help, Death, help!"
And the other one, who seemed to lag too much,
Was shouting: "Lano, were not so alert 120
Those legs of thine at joustings of the Toppo!"
And then, perchance because his breath was failing,
He grouped himself together with a bush.
Behind them was the forest full of black
She-mastiffs, ravenous, and swift of foot 125
As greyhounds, who are issuing from the chain.
On him who had crouched down they set their teeth,
And him they lacerated piece by piece,
Thereafter bore away those aching members.[10]
Thereat my Escort took me by the hand, 130
And led me to the bush, that all in vain
Was weeping from its bloody lacerations.
"O Jacopo," it said, "of Sant' Andrea,
What helped it thee of me to make a screen?
What blame have I in thy nefarious life?" 135
When near him had the Master stayed his steps,
He said: "Who wast thou, that through wounds so many
Art blowing out with blood thy dolorous speech?"
And he to us: "O souls, that hither come
To look upon the shameful massacre 140
That has so rent away from me my leaves,
Gather them up beneath the dismal bush;
I of that city was which to the Baptist
Changed its first patron, wherefore he for this
Forever with his art will make it sad. 145
And were it not that on the pass of Arno

Some glimpses of him are remaining still,[11]
Those citizens, who afterwards rebuilt it
Upon the ashes left by Attila,[12]
In vain had caused their labor to be done. 150
Of my own house I made myself a gibbet."

CANTO XIV

BECAUSE the charity* of my native place
Constrained me, gathered I the scattered leaves,
And gave them back to him, who now was hoarse.
Then came we to the confine, where disparted
The second round is from the third,[1] and where 5
A horrible form of Justice is beheld.
Clearly to manifest these novel things,
I say that we arrived upon a plain,
Which from its bed rejecteth every plant;
The dolorous forest† is a garland to it 10
All round about, as the sad moat to that;
There close upon the edge we stayed our feet.
The soil was of an arid and thick sand,
Not of another fashion made than that
Which by the feet of Cato once was pressed.[2] 15
Vengeance of God, O how much oughtest thou
By each one to be dreaded, who doth read
That which was manifest unto mine eyes!
Of naked souls beheld I many herds,
Who all were weeping very miserably, 20
And over them seemed set a diverse law.
Supine upon the ground some folk were lying;
And some were sitting all drawn up together,
And others went about continually.
Those who were going round were far the more, 25

*Love.

†The grieving forest of the suicides.

Canto XIV: The Violent, tortured in the Rain of fire.

And those were less who lay down to their torment,
But had their tongues more loosed to lamentation.[3]
O'er all the sand-waste, with a gradual fall,
Were raining down dilated flakes of fire,
As of the snow on Alp without a wind. 30
As Alexander, in those torrid parts
Of India, beheld upon his host
Flames fall unbroken till they reached the ground,
Whence he provided with his phalanxes
To trample down the soil, because the vapor 35
Better extinguished was while it was single;
Thus was descending the eternal heat,
Whereby the sand was set on fire,[4] like tinder
Beneath the steel, for doubling of the dole.
Without repose forever was the dance 40
Of miserable hands,[5] now there, now here,

Shaking away from off them the fresh gledes.*
"Master," began I, "thou who overcomest
All things except the demons dire,[6] that issued
Against us at the entrance of the gate, 45
Who is that mighty one who seems to heed not
The fire, and lieth lowering and disdainful,
So that the rain seems not to ripen him?"[7]
And he himself, who had become aware
That I was questioning my Guide about him, 50
Cried: "Such as I was living, am I, dead!
If Jove should weary out his smith, from whom
He seized in anger the sharp thunderbolt,
Wherewith upon the last day I was smitten,
And if he wearied out by turns the others 55
In Mongibello at the swarthy forge,
Vociferating, 'Help, good Vulcan, help!'
Even as he did there at the fight of Phlegra,
And shot his bolts at me with all his might,
He would not have thereby a joyous vengeance." 60
Then did my Leader speak with such great force,
That I had never heard him speak so loud:
"O Capaneus,[8] in that is not extinguished
Thine arrogance, thou punished art the more;
Not any torment, saving thine own rage, 65
Would be unto thy fury pain complete."
Then he turned round to me with better lip,
Saying: "One of the Seven Kings was he
Who Thebes besieged, and held, and seems to hold
God in disdain, and little seems to prize him; 70
But, as I said to him, his own despites†
Are for his breast the fittest ornaments.
Now follow me, and mind thou do not place
As yet thy feet upon the burning sand,
But always keep them close unto the wood." 75

*Predatory birds (the cinders are like the eyes of such birds).
†Insults, acts of defiance, offenses.

Speaking no word, we came to where there gushes
  Forth from the wood a little rivulet,
  Whose redness makes my hair still stand on end.
As from the Bulicamë springs the brooklet,
  The sinful women later share among them,[9] 80
  So downward through the sand it went its way.
The bottom of it, and both sloping banks,
  Were made of stone, and the margins at the side;
  Whence I perceived that there the passage was.
"In all the rest which I have shown to thee 85
  Since we have entered in within the gate
  Whose threshold unto no one is denied,
Nothing has been discovered by thine eyes
  So notable as is the present river,
  Which all the little flames above it quenches." 90
These words were of my Leader; whence I prayed him
  That he would give me largess of the food,
  For which he had given me largess of desire.[10]
"In the mid-sea there sits a wasted land,"
  Said he thereafterward, "whose name is Crete, 95
  Under whose king the world of old was chaste.
There is a mountain there, that once was glad
  With waters and with leaves, which was called Ida;
  Now 'tis deserted, as a thing worn out.
Rhea once chose it for the faithful cradle 100
  Of her own son; and to conceal him better,
  Whene'er he cried, she there had clamors made.[11]
A grand old man stands in the mount erect,
  Who holds his shoulders turned tow'rds Damietta,
  And looks at Rome as if it were his mirror. 105
His head is fashioned of refined gold,
  And of pure silver are the arms and breast;
  Then he is brass as far down as the fork.
From that point downward all is chosen iron,
  Save that the right foot is of kiln-baked clay, 110
  And more he stands on that than on the other.
Each part, except the gold, is by a fissure

Asunder cleft, that dripping is with tears,
Which gathered together perforate that cavern.
From rock to rock they fall into this valley; 115
Acheron, Styx, and Phlegethon they form;
Then downward go along this narrow sluice
Unto that point where is no more descending.
They form Cocytus; what that pool may be
Thou shalt behold, so here 'tis not narrated."[12] 120
And I to him: "If so the present runnel*
Doth take its rise in this way from our world,
Why only on this verge† appears it to us?"
And he to me: "Thou knowest the place is round,
And notwithstanding thou hast journeyed far, 125
Still to the left descending to the bottom,
Thou hast not yet through all the circle turned.
Therefore if something new appear to us,
It should not bring amazement to thy face."
And I again: "Master, where shall be found 130
Lethe and Phlegethon, for of one thou'rt silent,
And sayest the other of this rain is made?"
"In all thy questions truly thou dost please me,"
Replied he; "but the boiling of the red
Water might well solve one of them thou makest. 135
Thou shalt see Lethe, but outside this moat,
There where the souls repair to lave‡ themselves,
When sin repented of has been removed."[13]
Then said he: "It is time now to abandon
The wood; take heed that thou come after me; 140
A way the margins[14] make that are not burning,
And over them all vapors are extinguished."

*Brook, rivulet.
†Rim, edge.
‡Wash, bathe.

CANTO XV

Now bears us onward one of the hard margins,
And so the brooklet's mist o'ershadows it,
From fire it saves the water and the dikes.
Even as the Flemings, 'twixt Cadsand and Bruges,
Fearing the flood that tow'rds them hurls itself, 5
Their bulwarks build to put the sea to flight;
And as the Paduans along the Brenta,
To guard their villas and their villages,
Or* ever Chiarentana feels the heat;[1]
In such similitude had those been made, 10
Albeit not so lofty nor so thick,
Whoever he might be, the master† made them.
Now were we from the forest so remote,
I could not have discovered where it was,
Even if backward I had turned myself, 15
When we a company of souls encountered,
Who came beside the dike, and every one
Gazed at us, as at evening we are wont
To eye each other under a new moon,
And so towards us sharpened they their brows 20
As an old tailor at the needle's eye.[2]
Thus scrutinized by such a family,
By some one I was recognized, who seized
My garment's hem, and cried out, "What a marvel!"
And I, when he stretched forth his arm to me,[3] 25

*Before.
†God.

Canto XV: Brunetto Latini accosts Dante

On his baked aspect fastened so mine eyes,
That the scorched countenance prevented not
His recognition by my intellect;
And bowing down my face unto his own,
I made reply, "Are you here, Ser Brunetto?"[4] 30
And he: "May't not displease thee, O my son,
If a brief space with thee Brunetto Latini
Backward return and let the trail go on."
I said to him: "With all my power I ask it;
And if you wish me to sit down with you, 35
I will, if he please, for I go with him."
"O son," he said, "whoever of this herd
A moment stops, lies then a hundred years,
Nor fans himself when smiteth him the fire.
Therefore go on; I at thy skirts will come, 40
And afterward will I rejoin my band,

Which goes lamenting its eternal doom."
I did not dare to go down from the road
Level to walk with him; but my head bowed
I held as one who goeth reverently. 45
And he began: "What fortune or what fate
Before the last day leadeth thee down here?
And who is this that showeth thee the way?"
"Up there above us in the life serene,"
I answered him, "I lost me in a valley,* 50
Or ever yet my age had been completed.
But yestermorn I turned my back upon it;
This one appeared to me, returning thither,
And homeward leadeth me along this road."
And he to me: "If thou thy star do follow, 55
Thou canst not fail thee of a glorious port,
If well I judged in the life beautiful.
And if I had not died so prematurely,
Seeing Heaven thus benignant unto thee,
I would have given thee comfort in the work 60
But that ungrateful and malignant people,
Which of old time from Fesole descended,[5]
And smacks still of the mountain and the granite,
Will make itself, for thy good deeds, thy foe;
And it is right; for among crabbed sorbs† 65
It ill befits the sweet fig to bear fruit.
Old rumor in the world proclaims them blind;
A people avaricious, envious, proud;
Take heed that of their customs thou do cleanse thee.
Thy fortune so much honor doth reserve thee, 70
One party and the other shall be hungry
For thee; but far from goat shall be the grass.
Their litter let the beasts of Fesole
Make of themselves, nor let them touch the plant,
If any still upon their dunghill rise, 75

*The dark woods of Canto I.

†A tree that bears tart sorb apples.

In which may yet revive the consecrated
Seed of those Romans, who remained there when
The nest of such great malice it became."
"If my entreaty wholly were fulfilled,"
Replied I to him, "not yet would you be 80
In banishment from human nature placed;
For in my mind is fixed, and touches now
My heart the dear and good paternal image
Of you, when in the world from hour to hour
You taught me how a man becomes eternal;[6] 85
And how much I am grateful, while I live
Behoves that in my language be discerned.
What you narrate of my career I write,
And keep it to be glossed with other text
By a Lady[7] who can do it, if I reach her. 90
This much will I have manifest to you;
Provided that my conscience do not chide me,
For whatsoever Fortune I am ready.
Such hansel* is not new unto mine ears;
Therefore let Fortune turn her wheel around 95
As it may please her, and the churl his mattock."†
My Master thereupon on his right cheek
Did backward turn himself, and looked at me;
Then said: "He listeneth well who noteth it."
Nor speaking less on that account, I go 100
With Sir Brunetto, and I ask who are
His most known and most eminent companions.
And he to me: "To know of some is well;
Of others it were laudable to be silent,
For short would be the time for so much speech. 105
Know then, in sum, that all of them were clerks,
And men of letters great and of great fame,
In the world tainted with the selfsame sin.
Priscian goes yonder with that wretched crowd,

*Prophecy.
†The peasant his spade.

And Francis of Accorso; and thou hadst seen there, 110
If thou hadst had a hankering for such scurf,
That one, who by the Servant of the Servants
From Arno was transferred to Bacchiglione,
Where he has left his sin-excited nerves.[8]
More would I say, but coming and discoursing 115
Can be no longer; for that I behold
New smoke uprising yonder from the sand.
A people comes with whom I may not be;
Commended unto thee by my Tesoro,[9]
In which I still live, and no more I ask." 120
Then he turned round, and seemed to be of those
Who at Verona run for the Green Mantle
Across the plain; and seemed to be among them
The one who wins, and not the one who loses.[10]

CANTO XVI

Now was I where was heard the reverberation
Of water falling into the next round,[1]
Like to that humming which the beehives make,
When shadows three together[2] started forth,
Running, from out a company that passed 5
Beneath the rain of the sharp martyrdom.
Towards us came they, and each one cried out:
"Stop, thou; for by thy garb to us thou seemest
To be some one of our depraved city."
Ah me! what wounds I saw upon their limbs, 10
Recent and ancient by the flames burnt in!
It pains me still but to remember it.
Unto their cries my Teacher paused attentive;
He turned his face towards me, and "Now wait,"
He said; "to these we should be courteous. 15
And if it were not for the fire that darts
The nature of this region, I should say
That haste were more becoming thee than them."
As soon as we stood still, they recommenced
The old refrain, and when they overtook us, 20
Formed of themselves a wheel, all three of them.
As champions stripped and oiled are wont to do,
Watching for their advantage and their hold,
Before they come to blows and thrusts between them,
Thus, wheeling round, did every one his visage 25
Direct to me, so that in opposite wise
His neck and feet continual journey made.
And, "If the misery of this soft place

Bring in disdain ourselves and our entreaties,"
Began one, "and our aspect black and blistered, 30
Let the renown of us thy mind incline
To tell us who thou art, who thus securely
Thy living feet dost move along through Hell.
He in whose footprints thou dost see me treading,
Naked and skinless though he now may go, 35
Was of a greater rank than thou dost think;
He was the grandson of the good Gualdrada;[3]
His name was Guidoguerra, and in life
Much did he with his wisdom and his sword.
The other, who close by me treads the sand, 40
Tegghiaio Aldobrandi is, whose fame
Above there in the world should welcome be.
And I, who with them on the cross am placed,
Jacopo Rusticucci was; and truly
My savage wife, more than aught else, doth harm me."[4] 45
Could I have been protected from the fire,
Below I should have thrown myself among them,
And think the Teacher would have suffered it;
But as I should have burned and baked myself,
My terror overmastered my good will, 50
Which made me greedy of embracing them.
Then I began: "Sorrow and not disdain
Did your condition fix within me so,
That tardily it wholly is stripped off,
As soon as this my Lord said unto me 55
Words, on account of which I thought within me
That people such as you are were approaching.
I of your city am; and evermore
Your labors and your honorable names
I with affection have retraced and heard.[5] 60
I leave the gall, and go for the sweet fruits
Promised to me by the veracious Leader;
But to the centre[6] first I needs must plunge."
"So may the soul for a long while conduct
Those limbs of thine," did he make answer then, 65

"And so may thy renown shine after thee,
Valor and courtesy, say if they dwell
Within our city, as they used to do,
Or if they wholly have gone out of it;
For Guglielmo Borsier,[7] who is in torment 70
With us of late, and goes there with his comrades,
Doth greatly mortify us with his words."
"The new inhabitants and the sudden gains,
Pride and extravagance have in thee engendered,
Florence, so that thou weep'st thereat already!" 75
In this wise I exclaimed with face uplifted;
And the three, taking that for my reply,
Looked at each other, as one looks at truth.
"If other times so little it doth cost thee,"
Replied they all, "to satisfy another, 80
Happy art thou, thus speaking at thy will!
Therefore, if thou escape from these dark places,
And come to rebehold the beauteous stars,
When it shall pleasure thee to say, 'I was,'
See that thou speak of us unto the people." 85
Then they broke up the wheel, and in their flight
It seemed as if their agile legs were wings.
Not an Amen could possibly be said
So rapidly as they had disappeared;
Wherefore the Master deemed best to depart. 90
I followed him, and little had we gone,
Before the sound of water[8] was so near us,
That speaking we should hardly have been heard.
Even as that stream which holdeth its own course
The first from Monte Veso tow'rds the East, 95
Upon the left-hand slope of Apennine,
Which is above called Acquacheta, ere
It down descendeth into its low bed,
And at Forlì is vacant of that name,
Reverberates there above San Benedetto 100
From Alps, by falling at a single leap,
Where for a thousand there were room enough;

Thus downward from a bank precipitate,
 We found resounding that dark-tinted water,
 So that it soon the ear would have offended. 105
I had a cord around about me girt,
 And therewithal I whilom* had designed
 To take the panther with the painted skin.[9]
After I this had all from me unloosed,
 As my Conductor had commanded me, 110
 I reached it to him, gathered up and coiled,
Whereat he turned himself to the right side,
 And at a little distance from the verge,
 He cast it down into that deep abyss.
"It must needs be some novelty respond," 115
 I said within myself, "to the new signal
 The Master with his eye is following so."
Ah me! how very cautious men should be
 With those who not alone behold the act,
 But with their wisdom look into the thoughts! 120
He said to me: "Soon there will upward come
 What I await; and what thy thought is dreaming
 Must soon reveal itself unto thy sight."
Aye to that truth which has the face of falsehood,
 A man should close his lips as far as may be, 125
 Because without his fault it causes shame;
But here I can not; and, Reader, by the notes
 Of this my Comedy[10] to thee I swear,
 So may they not be void of lasting favor,
Athwart that dense and darksome atmosphere 130
 I saw a figure swimming upward come,
 Marvellous unto every steadfast heart,
Even as he returns who goeth down
 Sometimes to clear an anchor, which has grappled
 Reef, or aught else that in the sea is hidden, 135
Who upward stretches, and draws in his feet.

*Formerly (archaic).

CANTO XVII

BEHOLD the monster[1] with the pointed tail,
    Who cleaves the hills, and breaketh walls and weapons,
    Behold him who infecteth all the world."
Thus unto me my Guide began to say,
    And beckoned him that he should come to shore, 5
    Near to the confine of the trodden marble;
And that uncleanly image of deceit
    Came up and thrust ashore its head and bust,
    But on the border did not drag its tail.
The face was as the face of a just man, 10
    Its semblance outwardly was so benign,
    And of a serpent all the trunk beside.
Two paws it had, hairy unto the armpits;
    The back, and breast, and both sides it had
    Depicted o'er with nooses and with shields. 15
With colors more, groundwork or broidery
    Never in cloth did Tartars make nor Turks,
    Nor were such tissues by Arachne laid.[2]
As sometimes wherries* lie upon the shore,
    That part are in the water, part on land; 20
    And as among the guzzling Germans there,
The beaver plants himself to wage his war;[3]
    So that vile monster lay upon the border,
    Which is of stone, and shuts the sand-waste in.
His tail was wholly quivering in the void, 25

*Boats.

Canto XVII: The Descent of the Abyss on Geryon's Back

Contorting upwards the envenomed fork,
That in the guise of scorpion armed its point.
The Guide said: "Now perforce must turn aside
Our way a little, even to that beast
Malevolent, that yonder coucheth him." 30
We therefore on the right-hand side[4] descended,

And made ten steps upon the outer verge,
Completely to avoid the sand and flame;
And after we are come to him, I see
A little farther off upon the sand 35
A people sitting near the hollow place.
Then said to me the Master: "So that full
Experience of this round thou bear away,
Now go and see what their condition is.
There let thy conversation be concise; 40
Till thou returnest I will speak with him,
That he concede to us his stalwart shoulders."
Thus farther still upon the outermost
Head of that seventh circle all alone
I went, where sat the melancholy folk.[5] 45
Out of their eyes was gushing forth their woe;
This way, that way, they helped them with their hands
Now from the flames and now from the hot soil.
Not otherwise in summer do the dogs,
Now with the foot, now with the muzzle, when 50
By fleas, or flies, or gadflies, they are bitten.
When I had turned mine eyes upon the faces
Of some, on whom the dolorous fire is falling,
Not one of them I knew; but I perceived
That from the neck of each there hung a pouch, 55
Which certain color had, and certain blazon;*
And thereupon it seems their eyes are feeding.
And as I gazing round me come among them,
Upon a yellow pouch I azure saw
That had the face and posture of a lion. 60
Proceeding then the current of my sight,
Another of them saw I, red as blood,
Display a goose more white than butter is.
And one, who with an azure sow and gravid†
Emblazoned had his little pouch of white, 65

*Heraldic representation of a coat of arms.

†Pregnant.

Said unto me: "What dost thou in this moat?
Now get thee gone; and since thou'rt still alive,
Know that a neighbor of mine, Vitaliano,
Will have his seat here on my left-hand side.
A Paduan am I with these Florentines;[6] 70
Full many a time they plunder in mine ears,
Exclaiming, 'Come the sovereign cavalier,[7]
He who shall bring the satchel with three goats' ";
Then twisted he his mouth, and forth he thrust
His tongue, like to an ox that licks its nose. 75
And fearing lest my longer stay might vex
Him who had warned me not to tarry long,
Backward I turned me from those weary souls.
I found my Guide, who had already mounted
Upon the back of that wild animal, 80
And said to me: "Now be both strong and bold.
Now we descend by stairways such as these;[8]
Mount thou in front, for I will be midway,
So that the tail may have no power to harm thee."
Such as he is who has so near the ague* 85
Of quartan[9] that his nails are blue already,
And trembles all, but looking at the shade;
Even such became I at those proffered words;
But shame in me his menaces produced,
Which maketh servant strong before good master. 90
I seated me upon those monstrous shoulders;
I wished to say, and yet the voice came not
As I believed, "Take heed that thou embrace me."
But he, who other times had rescued me
In other peril, soon as I had mounted, 95
Within his arms encircled and sustained me,
And said: "Now, Geryon, bestir thyself;
The circles large, and the descent be little;[10]
Think of the novel burden which thou hast."

*Recurrent chill or fit of shivering.

Even as the little vessel shoves from shore, 100
Backward, still backward, so he thence withdrew;
And when he wholly felt himself afloat,
There where his breast had been he turned his tail,
And that extended like an eel he moved,
And with his paws drew to himself the air. 105
A greater fear I do not think there was
What time abandoned Phaeton the reins,
Whereby the heavens, as still appears, were scorched;
Nor when the wretched Icarus[11] his flanks
Felt stripped of feathers by the melting wax, 110
His father crying, "An ill way thou takest!"
Than was my own, when I perceived myself
On all sides in the air, and saw extinguished
The sight of everything but of the monster.
Onward he goeth, swimming slowly, slowly; 115
Wheels and descends, but I perceive it only
By wind upon my face and from below.
I heard already on the right the whirlpool
Making a horrible crashing under us;
Whence I thrust out my head with eyes cast downward. 120
Then was I still more fearful of the abyss;
Because I fires beheld, and heard laments,
Whereat I, trembling, all the closer cling.
I saw then, for before I had not seen it,
The turning and descending, by great horrors[12] 125
That were approaching upon divers sides.
As falcon who has long been on the wing,
Who, without seeing either lure or bird,
Maketh the falconer say, "Ah me, thou stoopest,"
Descendeth weary, whence he started swiftly, 130
Thorough a hundred circles, and alights
Far from his master, sullen and disdainful;
Even thus did Geryon place us on the bottom,
Close to the bases of the rough-hewn rock,
And being disencumbered of our persons, 135
He sped away as arrow from the string.[13]

CANTO XVIII

THERE is a place in Hell called Malebolge,[1]
Wholly of stone and of an iron color,
As is the circle that around it turns.
Right in the middle of the field malign
There yawns a well exceeding wide and deep, 5
Of which its place the structure will recount.
Round, then, is that enclosure which remains
Between the well and foot of the high, hard bank,
And has distinct in valleys ten its bottom.
As where for the protection of the walls 10
Many and many moats surround the castles,
The part in which they are a figure forms,
Just such an image those presented there;
And as about such strongholds from their gates
Unto the outer bank are little bridges, 15
So from the precipice's base did crags
Project, which intersected dikes and moats,
Unto the well that truncates and collects them.
Within this place, down shaken from the back
Of Geryon, we found us; and the Poet 20
Held to the left, and I moved on behind.
Upon my right hand I beheld new anguish,
New torments, and new wielders of the lash,
Wherewith the foremost Bolgia was replete.
Down at the bottom were the sinners naked; 25
This side the middle came they facing us,
Beyond it, with us, but with greater steps;
Even as the Romans, for the mighty host,

Canto XVIII: Virgil shows Dante the Shade of Thaïs

The year of Jubilee, upon the bridge,
Have chosen a mode to pass the people over; 30
For all upon one side towards the Castle
Their faces have, and go unto Saint Peter's;
On the other side they go towards the Mountain.[2]
This side and that, along the livid stone

Beheld I hornëd demons with great scourges, 35
Who cruelly were beating them behind.
Ah me! how they did make them lift their legs
At the first blows! and sooth not any one
The second waited for, nor for the third.
While I was going on, mine eyes by one 40
Encountered were; and straight I said: "Already
With sight of this one I am not unfed."*
Therefore I stayed my feet to make him out,
And with me the sweet Guide came to a stand,
And to my going somewhat back assented; 45
And he, the scourged one, thought to hide himself,
Lowering his face, but little it availed him;
For said I: "Thou that castest down thine eyes,
If false are not the features which thou bearest,
Thou art Venedico Caccianimico; 50
But what doth bring thee to such pungent sauces?"
And he to me: "Unwillingly I tell it;
But forces me thine utterance distinct,
Which makes me recollect the ancient world.
I was the one who the fair Ghisola 55
Induced to grant the wishes of the Marquis,[3]
Howe'er the shameless story may be told.
Not the sole Bolognese am I who weeps here;
Nay, rather is this place so full of them,
That not so many tongues to-day are taught 60
'Twixt Reno and Savena to say *sipa;*[4]
And if thereof thou wishest pledge or proof,
Bring to thy mind our avaricious heart."
While speaking in this manner, with his scourge
A demon smote him, and said: "Get thee gone, 65
Pander, there are no women here for coin."[5]
I joined myself again unto mine Escort;
Thereafterward with footsteps few we came

*I have seen this person before.

To where a crag projected from the bank.
This very easily did we ascend, 70
And turning to the right along its ridge,
From those eternal circles we departed.
When we were there, where it is hollowed out
Beneath, to give a passage to the scourged,
The Guide said: "Wait, and see that on thee strike 75
The vision of those others evil-born,
Of whom thou hast not yet beheld the faces,
Because together with us they have gone."[6]
From the old bridge we looked upon the train
Which tow'rds us came upon the other border, 80
And which the scourges in like manner smite,
And the good Master, without my inquiring,
Said to me: "See that tall one who is coming
And for his pain seems not to shed a tear;
Still what a royal aspect he retains! 85
That Jason is, who by his heart and cunning
The Colchians of the Ram made destitute.
He by the isle of Lemnos passed along
After the daring women pitiless
Had unto death devoted all their males. 90
There with his tokens and with ornate words
Did he deceive Hypsipyle, the maiden
Who first, herself, had all the rest deceived.[7]
There did he leave her pregnant and forlorn;
Such sin unto such punishment condemns him, 95
And also for Medea is vengeance done.
With him go those who in such wise deceive;
And this sufficient be of the first valley
To know, and those that in its jaws it holds."
We were already where the narrow path 100
Crosses athwart the second dike, and forms
Of that a buttress for another arch.
Thence we heard people, who are making moan
In the next Bolgia, snorting with their muzzles,
And with their palms beating upon themselves. 105

The margins were encrusted with a mould
By exhalation from below, that sticks there,
And with the eyes and nostrils wages war.
The bottom is so deep, no place suffices
To give us sight of it, without ascending 110
The arch's back, where most the crag impends.
Thither we came, and thence down in the moat
I saw a people smothered in a filth
That out of human privies seemed to flow;
And whilst below there with mine eye I search, 115
I saw one with his head so foul with ordure,*
It was not clear if he were clerk or layman.[8]
He screamed at me: "Wherefore art thou so eager
To look at me more than the other foul ones?"
And I to him: "Because, if I remember, 120
I have already seen thee with dry hair,
And thou'rt Alessio Interminei of Lucca;[9]
Therefore I eye thee more than all the others."
And he thereon, belaboring his pumpkin:†
"The flatteries have submerged me here below, 125
Wherewith my tongue was never surfeited."
Then said to me the Guide: "See that thou thrust
Thy visage somewhat farther in advance,
That with thine eyes thou well the face attain
Of that uncleanly and dishevelled drab, 130
Who there doth scratch herself with filthy nails,
And crouches now, and now on foot is standing.
Thais the harlot[10] is it, who replied
Unto her paramour, when he said, 'Have I
Great gratitude from thee?'—'Nay, marvellous'; 135
And herewith let our sight be satisfied."

*Excrement, dung (*merda* in the original Italian; literally, "shit").
†Head.

CANTO XIX

O Simon Magus,[1] O forlorn disciples,
    Ye who the things of God, which ought to be
    The brides of holiness, rapaciously
For silver and for gold do prostitute,
    Now it behoves for you the trumpet sound,   5
    Because in this third Bolgia ye abide.
We had already on the following tomb*
    Ascended to that portion of the crag
    Which o'er the middle of the moat hangs plumb.
Wisdom supreme, O how great art thou showest   10
    In heaven, in earth, and in the evil world,
    And with what justice doth thy power distribute!
I saw upon the sides and on the bottom
    The livid stone with perforations filled,
    All of one size, and every one was round,   15
To me less ample seemed they not, nor greater
    Than those that in my beautiful Saint John
    Are fashioned for the place of the baptizers,
And one of which, not many years ago,
    I broke for some one, who was drowning in it;   20
    Be this a seal all men to undeceive.
Out of the mouth of each one there protuded
    The feet of a transgressor, and the legs
    Up to the calf, the rest within remained.
In all of them the soles were both on fire;[2]   25

*The next *bolgia.*

Canto XIX: Dante addresses Pope Nicholas III

Wherefore the joints so violently quivered,
They would have snapped asunder withes and bands.
Even as the flame of unctuous things is wont
To move upon the outer surface only,
So likewise was it there from heel to point. 30
"Master, who is that one who writhes himself,
More than his other comrades quivering,"

I said, "and whom a redder flame is sucking?"
And he to me: "If thou wilt have me bear thee
Down there along that bank which lowest lies, 35
From him thou'lt know his errors and himself."
And I: "What pleases thee, to me is pleasing;
Thou art my Lord, and knowest that I depart not
From thy desire, and knowest what is not spoken."
Straightway upon the fourth dike we arrived; 40
We turned, and on the left-hand side descended
Down to the bottom full of holes and narrow.
And the good Master yet from off his haunch
Deposed me not, till to the hole he brought me
Of him who so lamented with his shanks. 45
"Whoe'er thou art, that standest upside down,
O doleful soul, implanted like a stake,"
To say began I, "if thou canst, speak out."
I stood even as the friar who is confessing
The false assassin, who, when he is fixed, 50
Recalls him, so that death may be delayed.
And he cried out: "Dost thou stand there already,
Dost thou stand there already, Boniface?[3]
By many years the record lied to me.
Art thou so early satiate with that wealth, 55
For which thou didst not fear to take by fraud
The beautiful Lady,* and then work her woe?"
Such I became, as people are who stand,
Not comprehending what is answered them,
As if bemocked, and know not how to answer. 60
Then said Virgilius: "Say to him straightway,
I am not he, I am not he thou thinkest."
And I replied as was imposed on me.
Whereat the spirit writhed with both his feet,
Then, sighing, with a voice of lamentation 65
Said to me: "Then what wantest thou of me?

*The Church.

If who I am thou carest so much to know,
That thou on that account hast crossed the bank,
Know that I vested was with the great mantle;*
And truly was I son of the She-bear,[4] 70
So eager to advance the cubs, that wealth
Above, and here myself, I pocketed.
Beneath my head the others are dragged down
Who have preceded me in simony,
Flattened along the fissure of the rock. 75
Below there I shall likewise fall, whenever
That one shall come who I believed thou wast,
What time the sudden question I proposed.
But longer I my feet already toast,
And here have been in this way upside down, 80
Than he will planted stay with reddened feet;
For after him shall come of fouler deed
From tow'rds the west a Pastor without law,
Such as befits to cover him and me.
New Jason will he be, of whom we read 85
In Maccabees;[5] and as his king was pliant,
So he who governs France shall be to this one."
I do not know if I were here too bold,
That him I answered only in this metre:
"I pray thee tell me now how great a treasure 90
Our Lord demanded of Saint Peter first,
Before he put the keys into his keeping?
Truly he nothing asked but 'Follow me.'
Nor Peter nor the rest asked of Matthias
Silver or gold, when he by lot was chosen 95
Unto the place the guilty soul had lost.[6]
Therefore stay here, for thou art justly punished,
And keep safe guard o'er the ill-gotten money,
Which caused thee to be valiant against Charles.[7]
And were it not that still forbids it me 100

*The papacy.

The reverence for the keys superlative
Thou hadst in keeping in the gladsome life,
I would make use of words more grievous still;
Because your avarice afflicts the world,
Trampling the good and lifting the depraved. 105
The Evangelist you Pastors had in mind,
When she who sitteth upon many waters
To fornicate with kings by him was seen;
The same who with the seven heads was born,
And power and strength from the ten horns received, 110
So long as virtue to her spouse was pleasing.[8]
Ye have made yourselves a god of gold and silver;
And from the idolater how differ ye,
Save that he one, and ye a hundred worship?
Ah, Constantine! of how much ill was mother, 115
Not thy conversion, but that marriage-dower
Which the first wealthy Father took from thee!"[9]
And while I sang to him such notes as these,
Either that anger or that conscience stung him,
He struggled violently with both his feet.[10] 120
I think in sooth that it my Leader pleased,
With such contented lip he listened ever
Unto the sound of the true words expressed.
Therefore with both his arms he took me up,
And when he had me all upon his breast, 125
Remounted by the way where he descended.
Nor did he tire to have me clasped to him;
But bore me to the summit of the arch
Which from the fourth dike to the fifth is passage.
There tenderly he laid his burden down, 130
Tenderly on the crag[11] uneven and steep,
That would have been hard passage for the goats:
Thence was unveiled to me another valley.

CANTO XX

OF a new pain behoves me to make verses
And give material to the twentieth canto
Of the first song, which is of the submerged,[1]
I was already thoroughly disposed
To peer down into the uncovered depth, 5
Which bathed itself with tears of agony;
And people saw I through the circular valley,
Silent and weeping, coming at the pace
Which in this world the Litanies assume.[2]
As lower down my sight descended on them, 10
Wondrously each one seemed to be distorted
From chin to the beginning of the chest;
For tow'rds the reins the countenance was turned,
And backward it behoved them to advance,
As to look forward had been taken from them.[3] 15
Perchance indeed by violence of palsy
Some one has been thus wholly turned awry;
But I ne'er saw it, nor believe it can be.
As God may let thee, Reader, gather fruit
From this thy reading, think now for thyself 20
How I could ever keep my face unmoistened,
When our own image near me I beheld,
Distorted so, the weeping of the eyes
Along the fissure bathed the hinder parts.
Truly I wept, leaning upon a peak 25
Of the hard crag, so that my Escort said
To me: "Art thou, too, of the other fools?
Here pity lives when it is wholly dead;

Who is a greater reprobate than he
Who feels compassion at the doom divine?[4] 30
Lift up, lift up thy head, and see for whom
Opened the earth before the Thebans' eyes;
Wherefore they all cried: 'Whither rushest thou,
Amphiaraus?[5] Why dost leave the war?'
And downward ceased he not to fall amain* 35
As far as Minos, who lays hold on all.
See, he has made a bosom of his shoulders!
Because he wished to see too far before him
Behind he looks, and backward makes his way:
Behold Tiresias,[6] who his semblance changed, 40
When from a male a female he became,
His members being all of them transformed;
And afterwards was forced to strike once more
The two entangled serpents with his rod,
Ere he could have again his manly plumes. 45
That Aruns is, who backs the other's belly,
Who in the hills of Luni, there where grubs
The Carrarese who houses underneath,
Among the marbles white a cavern had[7]
For his abode; whence to behold the stars 50
And sea, the view was not cut off from him.
And she there, who is covering up her breasts,
Which thou beholdest not, with loosened tresses,
And on that side has all the hairy skin,
Was Manto,[8] who made quest through many lands, 55
Afterwards tarried there where I was born;
Whereof I would thou list to me a little.
After her father had from life departed,
And the city of Bacchus had become enslaved,
She a long season wandered through the world. 60
Above in beauteous Italy lies a lake
At the Alp's foot that shuts in Germany

*With speed or haste.

Over Tyrol, and has the name Benaco.
By a thousand springs, I think, and more, is bathed,
'Twixt Garda and Val Camonica, Pennino, 65
With water that grows stagnant in that lake.
Midway a place is where the Trentine Pastor,
And he of Brescia, and the Veronese
Might give his blessing,[9] if he passed that way.
Sitteth Peschiera, fortress fair and strong, 70
To front the Brescians and the Bergamasks,[10]
Where round about the bank descendeth lowest.
There of necessity must fall whatever
In bosom of Benaco cannot stay,
And grows a river down through verdant pastures. 75
Soon as the water doth begin to run,
No more Benaco is it called, but Mincio,
Far as Governo, where it falls in Po.[11]
Not far it runs before it finds a plain
In which it spreads itself, and makes it marshy, 80
And oft 'tis wont in summer to be sickly.
Passing that way the virgin pitiless[12]
Land in the middle of the fen* descried,
Untilled and naked of inhabitants;
There to escape all human intercourse, 85
She with her servants stayed, her arts to practise,
And lived, and left her empty body there.
The men, thereafter, who were scattered round,
Collected in that place, which was made strong
By the lagoon it had on every side; 90
They built their city over those dead bones,
And, after her who first the place selected,
Mantua named it, without other omen.
Its people once within more crowded were,
Ere the stupidity of Casalodi 95
From Pinamonte had received deceit.[13]

*Marsh, swamp.

Therefore I caution thee, if e'er thou hearest
Originate my city otherwise,
No falsehood may the verity defraud."[14]
And I: "My Master, thy discourses are 100
To me so certain, and so take my faith,
That unto me the rest would be spent coals.
But tell me of the people who are passing,
If any one note-worthy thou beholdest,
For only unto that my mind reverts." 105
Then said he to me: "He who from the cheek
Thrusts out his beard upon his swarthy shoulders
Was, at the time when Greece was void of males,
So that there scarce remained one in the cradle,
An augur, and with Calchas gave the moment, 110
In Aulis, when to sever the first cable.
Eryphylus his name was,[15] and so sings
My lofty Tragedy[16] in some part or other;
That knowest thou well, who knowest the whole of it.
The next, who is so slender in the flanks, 115
Was Michael Scott,[17] who of a verity
Of magical illusions knew the game.
Behold Guido Bonatti, behold Asdente,[18]
Who now unto his leather and his thread
Would fain* have stuck, but he too late repents. 120
Behold the wretched ones, who left the needle,
The spool and rock, and made them fortune-tellers;
They wrought their magic spells with herb and image.
But come now, for already holds the confines
Of both the hemispheres, and under Seville 125
Touches the ocean-wave, Cain and the thorns,
And yesternight the moon was round already;
Thou shouldst remember well it did not harm thee
From time to time within the forest deep."[19]
Thus spake he to me, and we walked the while.[20] 130

*Gladly, preferably.

CANTO XXI

FROM bridge to bridge thus, speaking other things
Of which my Comedy cares not to sing,[1]
We came along, and held the summit, when
We halted to behold another fissure
Of Malebolge[2] and other vain laments; 5
And I beheld it marvellously dark.
As in the Arsenal of the Venetians[3]
Boils in the winter the tenacious pitch
To smear their unsound vessels o'er again,
For sail they cannot; and instead thereof 10
One makes his vessel new, and one recaulks
The ribs of that which many a voyage has made;
One hammers at the prow, one at the stern,
This one makes oars, and that one cordage twists,
Another mends the mainsail and the mizzen; 15
Thus, not by fire, but by the art divine,
Was boiling down below there a dense pitch
Which upon every side the bank belimed.
I saw it, but I did not see within it
Aught but the bubbles that the boiling raised, 20
And all swell up and resubside compressed,
The while below there fixedly I gazed,
My leader crying out: "Beware, beware!"
Drew me unto himself from where I stood.
Then I turned round, as one who is impatient 25
To see what it behoves him to escape,
And whom a sudden terror doth unman,
Who, while he looks, delays not his departure;

Canto XXI: The Demons threaten Virgil

And I beheld behind us a black devil,
Running along upon the crag, approach. 30
Ah, how ferocious was he in his aspect!
And how he seemed to me in action ruthless,
With open wings and light upon his feet!
His shoulders, which sharp-pointed were and high,
A sinner did encumber with both haunches, 35
And he held clutched the sinews of the feet.
From off our bridge, he said: "O Malebranche,[4]
Behold one of the elders of Saint Zita;[5]
Plunge him beneath, for I return for others
Unto that town, which is well furnished with them. 40
All there are barrators, except Bonturo;[6]
No into Yes for money there is changed."
He hurled him down, and over the hard crag
Turned round, and never was a mastiff loosened

In so much hurry to pursue a thief. 45
The other sank, and rose again face downward;
But the demons, under cover of the bridge,
Cried: "Here the Santo Volto has no place!
Here swims one otherwise than in the Serchio;[7]
Therefore, if for our gaffs thou wishest not, 50
Do not uplift thyself above the pitch."
They seized him then with more than a hundred rakes;
They said: "It here behoves thee to dance covered,
That, if thou canst, thou secretly mayest pilfer."
Not otherwise the cooks their scullions make 55
Immerse into the middle of the caldron
The meat with hooks, so that it may not float.
Said the good Master to me: "That it be not
Apparent thou art here, crouch thyself down
Behind a jag, that thou mayest have some screen; 60
And for no outrage that is done to me
Be thou afraid, because these things I know,
For once before was I in such a scuffle."
Then he passed on beyond the bridge's head,
And as upon the sixth bank he arrived, 65
Need was for him to have a steadfast front.
With the same fury, and the same uproar,
As dogs leap out upon a mendicant,*
Who on a sudden begs, where'er he stops,
They issued from beneath the little bridge, 70
And turned against him all their grappling-irons;
But he cried out: "Be none of you malignant!
Before those hooks of yours lay hold of me,
Let one of you step forward, who may hear me,
And then take counsel as to grappling me." 75
They all cried: "Let Malacoda go";[8]
Whereat one started, and the rest stood still,
And he came to him, saying, "What avails it?"

*Beggar.

"Thinkest thou, Malacoda, to behold me
Advanced into this place," my Master said, 80
"Safe hitherto from all your skill of fence,*
Without the will divine, and fate auspicious?
Let me go on, for it in Heaven is willed
That I another show this savage road."
Then was his arrogance so humbled in him, 85
That he let fall his grapnel at his feet,
And to the others said: "Now strike him not."
And unto me my Guide: "O thou, who sittest
Among the splinters of the bridge crouched down,
Securely now return to me again." 90
Wherefore I started and came swiftly to him;
And all the devils forward thrust themselves,[9]
So that I feared they would not keep their compact.
And thus beheld I once afraid the soldiers
Who issued under safeguard from Caprona, 95
Seeing themselves among so many foes.[10]
Close did I press myself with all my person
Beside my Leader, and turned not mine eyes
From off their countenance, which was not good.
They lowered their rakes, and "Wilt thou have me hit him," 100
They said to one another, "on the rump?"
And answered: "Yes; see that thou nick him with it."
But the same demon who was holding parley
With my Conductor turned him very quickly,
And said: "Be quiet, be quiet, Scarmiglione";[11] 105
Then said to us: "You can no farther go
Forward upon this crag, because is lying
All shattered, at the bottom, the sixth arch.
And if it still doth please you to go onward,
Pursue your way along upon this rock; 110
Near is another crag that yields a path.[12]
Yesterday, five hours later than this hour,

*Hindrance.

One thousand and two hundred sixty-six
Years were complete, that here the way was broken.[13]
I send in that direction some of mine 115
To see if any one doth air himself;
Go ye with them; for they will not be vicious.
Step forward, Alichino and Calcabrina."
Began he to cry out, "and thou, Cagnazzo;
And Barbariccia do thou guide the ten. 120
Come forward, Libicocco and Draghignazzo,
And tuskëd Ciriatto and Graffiacane,
And Farfarello and mad Rubicante;[14]
Search ye all round about the boiling pitch;
Let these be safe as far as the next crag, 125
That all unbroken passes o'er the dens."
"O me! what is it, Master, that I see?
Pray let us go," I said, "without an escort,
If thou knowest how, since for myself I ask none.
If thou art as observant as thy wont is, 130
Dost thou not see that they do gnash their teeth,
And with their brows are threatening woe to us?"[15]
And he to me: "I will not have thee fear;
Let them gnash on, according to their fancy,
Because they do it for those boiling wretches." 135
Along the left-hand dike they wheeled about;
But first had each one thrust his tongue between
His teeth towards their leader for a signal;
And he had made a trumpet of his rump.[16]

CANTO XXII

I HAVE erewhile seen horsemen moving camp,
Begin the storming, and their muster make,
And sometimes starting off for their escape;
Vaunt-couriers* have I seen upon your land,
O Aretines,[1] and foragers go forth, 5
Tournaments stricken, and the joustings run,
Sometimes with trumpets and sometimes with bells,
With kettle-drums, and signals of the castles,
And with our own, and with outlandish things,
But never yet with bagpipe so uncouth 10
Did I see horsemen move, nor infantry,
Nor ship by any sign of land or star.
We went upon our way with the ten demons;
Ah, savage company! but in the church
With saints, and in the tavern with the gluttons! 15
Ever upon the pitch was my intent,
To see the whole condition of that Bolgia,
And of the people who therein were burned.
Even as the dolphins, when they make a sign
To mariners by arching of the back, 20
That they should counsel take to save their vessel,
Thus sometimes, to alleviate his pain,
One of the sinners would display his back,
And in less time conceal it than it lightens.
As on the brink of water in a ditch 25

*Members of an army's advance guard.

Canto XXII: Ciampolo escaping from the Demon Alichino

The frogs stand only with their muzzles out,
So that they hide their feet and other bulk,
So upon every side the sinners stood;
But ever as Barbariccia near them came,
Thus underneath the boiling they withdrew. 30
I saw, and still my heart doth shudder at it,
One waiting thus, even as it comes to pass
One frog remains, and down another dives;
And Graffiacan, who most confronted him,
Grappled him by his tresses smeared with pitch, 35
And drew him up, so that he seemed an otter.
I knew, before, the names of all of them,
So had I noted them when they were chosen,
And when they called each other, listened how.
"O Rubicante, see that thou do lay 40
Thy claws upon him, so that thou mayst flay him,"

Cried all together the accursed ones.
And I: "My Master, see to it, if thou canst,
That thou mayst know who is the luckless wight,*
Thus come into his adversaries' hands." 45
Near to the side of him my Leader drew,
Asked of him whence he was; and he replied:
"I in the kingdom of Navarre was born;
My mother placed me servant to a lord,
For she had borne me to a ribald knave, 50
Destroyer of himself and of his things.
Then I domestic was of good King Tybalt;
I set me there to practise barratry,
For which I pay the reckoning in this heat."[2]
And Ciriatto, from whose mouth projected, 55
On either side, a tusk, as in a boar,
Caused him to feel how one of them could rip.
Among malicious cats the mouse had come;
But Barbariccia clasped him in his arms,
And said: "Stand ye aside, while I enfork him." 60
And to my Master he turned round his face;
"Ask him again," he said, "if more thou wish
To know from him, before some one destroy him."
The Guide: "Now tell then of the other culprits;
Knowest thou any one who is a Latian, 65
Under the pitch?" And he: "I separated
Lately from one who was a neighbor to it;[3]
Would that I still were covered up with him,
For neither claw nor grapnel should I fear."
And Libicocco: "We have borne too much"; 70
And with his grappling-iron seized his arm,
So that, by rending, he tore off a tendon.
Eke† Draghignazzo wished to pounce upon him
Down at the legs; whence their Decurion[4]
Turned round and round about with evil look. 75

*Human being, creature.

†Also (archaic).

When they somewhat were pacified again,
Of him, who still was looking at his wound,
Demanded my Conductor without stay:
"Who was that one, from whom a luckless parting
Thou sayest thou hast made, to come ashore?" 80
And he replied: "It was the Friar Gomita,[5]
He of Gallura, vessel of all fraud,
Who had the enemies of his Lord in hand,
And dealt so with them each exults thereat;
Money he took, and let them smoothly off, 85
As he says; and in other offices
A barrator was he, not mean but sovereign.
Foregathers with him one Don Michael Zanche[6]
Of Logodoro; and of Sardinia
To gossip never do their tongues feel tired. 90
O me! see that one, how he grinds his teeth;
Still farther would I speak, but am afraid
Lest he to scratch my itch be making ready."
And the grand Provost,[7] turned to Farfarello,
Who rolled his eyes about as if to strike, 95
Said: "Stand aside there, thou malicious bird."
"If you desire either to see or hear,"
The terror-stricken recommenced thereon,
"Tuscans or Lombards, I will make them come.
But let the Malebranche cease a little, 100
So that these may not their revenges fear,
And I, down sitting in this very place,
For one that I am will make seven to come,
When I shall whistle, as our custom is
To do whenever one of us emerges." 105
Cagnazzo at these words his muzzle lifted,
Shaking his head, and said: "Just hear the trick
Which he has thought of, down to throw himself!"
Whence he, who snares in great abundance had,
Responded: "I by far too cunning am, 110
When I procure for mine a greater sadness."
Alichin held not in, but running counter

Unto the rest, said to him: "If thou dive,
I will not follow thee upon the gallop,
But I will beat my wings above the pitch; 115
The height be left, and be the bank a shield,
To see if thou alone dost countervail us."
O thou who readest, thou shalt hear new sport![8]
Each to the other side his eyes averted;
He first, who most reluctant was to do it. 120
The Navarrese selected well his time;
Planted his feet on land, and in a moment
Leaped, and released himself from their design.
Whereat each one was suddenly stung with shame,
But he most who was cause of the defeat; 125
Therefore he moved, and cried: "Thou art o'ertaken."
But little it availed, for wings could not
Outstrip the fear; the other one went under,
And, flying, upward he his breast directed.
Not otherwise the duck upon a sudden 130
Dives under, when the falcon is approaching,
And upward he returneth cross and weary.
Infuriate at the mockery, Calcabrina
Flying behind him followed close, desirous
The other should escape, to have a quarrel. 135
And when the barrator had disappeared,
He turned his talons upon his companion,
And grappled with him right above the moat.
But sooth* the other was a doughty sparhawk†
To clapperclaw him well; and both of them 140
Fell in the middle of the boiling pond.
A sudden intercessor was the heat;
But ne'ertheless of rising there was naught,
To such degree they had their wings belimed.
Lamenting with the others, Barbariccia 145
Made four of them fly to the other side

*Really.
†Brave sparrowhawk.

With all their gaffs, and very speedily
This side and that they to their posts descended;
They stretched their hooks towards the pitch-ensnared,
Who were already baked within the crust, 150
And in this manner busied did we leave them.

CANTO XXIII

SILENT, alone, and without company,
We went, the one in front, the other after,
As go the Minor Friars along their way.[1]
Upon the fable of Æsop was directed
My thought, by reason of the present quarrel, 5
Where he has spoken of the frog and mouse;[2]
For *mo* and *issa* are not more alike[3]
Than this one is to that, if well we couple
End and beginning with a steadfast mind.
And even as one thought from another springs, 10
So afterward from that was born another,
Which the first fear within me double made.
Thus did I ponder: "These on our account
Are laughed to scorn, with injury and scoff
So great, that much I think it must annoy them. 15
If anger be engrafted on ill-will,
They will come after us more merciless
Than dog upon the leveret* which he seizes,"
I felt my hair stand all on end already
With terror, and stood backwardly intent, 20
When said I: "Master, if thou hidest not
Thyself and me forthwith, of Malebranche
I am in dread; we have them now behind us;
I so imagine them, I already feel them."
And he: "If I were made of leaded glass,[4] 25

*Young hare.

Thine outward image I should not attract
Sooner to me than I imprint the inner.
Just now thy thoughts came in among my own,
With similar attitude and similar face,
So that of both one counsel sole I made. 30
If peradventure the right bank so slope
That we to the next Bolgia can descend,
We shall escape from the imagined chase."
Not yet he finished rendering such opinion,
When I beheld them come with outstretched wings, 35
Not far remote, with will to seize upon us.
My Leader on a sudden seized me up,
Even as a mother who by noise is wakened,
And close beside her sees the enkindled flames,
Who takes her son, and flies, and does not stop, 40
Having more care of him than of herself,
So that she clothes her only with a shift;
And downward from the top of the hard bank
Supine he gave him to the pendent rock,
That one side of the other Bolgia walls. 45
Ne'er ran so swiftly water through a sluice
To turn the wheel of any land-built mill,[5]
When nearest to the paddles it approaches,
As did my Master down along that border,
Bearing me with him on his breast away, 50
As his own son,[6] and not as a companion.
Hardly the bed of the ravine below
His feet had reached, ere they had reached the hill
Right over us; but he was not afraid;
For the high Providence, which had ordained 55
To place them ministers of the fifth moat,
The power of thence departing took from all.[7]
A painted people there below we found,
Who went about with footsteps very slow,
Weeping and in their semblance tired and vanquished. 60
They had on mantles with the hoods low down
Before their eyes, and fashioned of the cut

Canto XXIII: The Hypocrites address Dante

That in Cologne they for the monks are made.
Without, they gilded are so that it dazzles;
But inwardly all leaden and so heavy 65
That Frederick used to put them on of straw.[8]
O everlastingly fatiguing mantle!
Again we turned us, still to the left hand
Along with them, intent on their sad plaint;
But owing to the weight, that weary folk 70
Came on so tardily, that we were new
In company at each motion of the haunch.[9]
Whence I unto my Leader: "See thou find
Some one who may by deed or name be known,
And thus in going move thine eye about." 75
And one, who understood the Tuscan speech,[10]
Cried to us from behind: "Stay ye your feet,
Ye, who so run athwart the dusky air!

Perhaps thou'lt have from me what thou demandest."
Whereat the Leader turned him, and said: "Wait, 80
And then according to his pace proceed."
I stopped, and two beheld I show great haste
Of spirit, in their faces, to be with me;
But the burden and the narrow way delayed them.
When they came up, long with an eye askance 85
They scanned me without uttering a word.
Then to each other turned, and said together:
"He by the action of his throat seems living;
And if they dead are, by what privilege
Go they uncovered by the heavy stole?" 90
Then said to me: "Tuscan, who to the college
Of miserable hypocrites art come,
Do not disdain to tell us who thou art."
And I to them: "Born was I, and grew up
In the great town on the fair river of Arno, 95
And with the body am I've always had.
But who are ye, in whom there trickles down
Along your cheeks such grief as I behold?
And what pain is upon you, that so sparkles?"
And one replied to me: "These orange cloaks 100
Are made of lead so heavy, that the weights
Cause in this way their balances to creak.[11]
Frati Gaudenti were we, and Bolognese;
I Catalano, and he Loderingo
Named, and together taken by thy city, 105
As the wont is to take one man alone,
For maintenance of its peace; and we were such
That still it is apparent round Gardingo."[12]
"O Friars," began I, "your iniquitous..."[13]
But said no more; for to mine eyes there rushed 110
One crucified with three stakes on the ground.
When me he saw, he writhed himself all over,
Blowing into his beard with suspirations;
And the Friar Catalan, who noticed this,
Said to me: "This transfixed one, who thou seest, 115

Counselled the Pharisees that it was meet
To put one man to torture for the people.
Crosswise and naked is he on the path,
As thou perceivest; and he needs must feel,
Whoever passes, first how much he weighs; 120
And in like mode his father-in-law is punished
Within this moat, and the others of the council,
Which for the Jews was a malignant seed."[14]
And thereupon I saw Virgilius marvel
O'er him who was extended on the cross[15] 125
So vilely in eternal banishment.
Then he directed to the Friar this voice:
"Be not displeased, if granted thee, to tell us
If to the right hand any pass slope down
By which we two may issue forth from here, 130
Without constraining some of the black angels[16]
To come and extricate us from this deep."
Then he made answer: "Nearer than thou hopest
There is a rock, that forth from the great circle
Proceeds, and crosses all the cruel valleys, 135
Save that at this 'tis broken, and does not bridge it;
You will be able to mount up the ruin,
That sidelong slopes and at the bottom rises."
The Leader stood awhile with head bowed down;
Then said: "The business badly he recounted[17] 140
Who grapples with his hook the sinners yonder."
And the Friar: "Many of the Devil's vices
Once heard I at Bologna, and among them,
That he's a liar and the father of lies."
Thereat my Leader with great strides went on, 145
Somewhat disturbed by anger in his looks;[18]
Whence from the heavy-laden I departed
After the prints of his beloved feet.

CANTO XXIV

In that part of the youthful year wherein
The Sun his locks beneath Aquarius tempers,
And now the nights draw near to half the day,
What time the hoar-frost copies on the ground
The outward semblance of her sister white, 5
But little lasts the temper of her pen,
The husbandman, whose forage faileth him,
Rises, and looks, and seeth the champaign
All gleaming white, whereat he beats his flank,
Returns in doors, and up and down laments, 10
Like a poor wretch, who knows not what to do;
Then he returns, and hope revives again,
Seeing the world has changed its countenance
In little time, and takes his shepherd's crook,
And forth the little lambs to pasture drives. 15
Thus did the Master fill me with alarm,
When I beheld his forehead so disturbed,
And to the ailment came as soon the plaster.
For as we came unto the ruined bridge,
The Leader turned to me with that sweet look 20
Which at the mountain's foot I first beheld.[1]
His arms he opened, after some advisement
Within himself elected, looking first
Well at the ruin,[2] and laid hold of me.
And even as he who acts and meditates, 25
For aye it seems that he provides beforehand,
So upward lifting me towards the summit
Of a huge rock, he scanned another crag,

Saying: "To that one grapple afterwards,
But try first if 'tis such that it will hold thee." 30
This was no path for one clothed with a cloak;
For hardly we, he light, and I pushed upward,[3]
Were able to ascend from jag to jag.
And had it not been, that upon that precinct
Shorter was the ascent than on the other, 35
He I know not, but I had been dead beat.
But because Malebolge tow'rds the mouth
Of the profoundest well is all inclining,
The structure of each valley doth import
That one bank rises and the other sinks.[4] 40
Still we arrived at length upon the point
Wherefrom the last stone breaks itself asunder.
The breath was from my lungs so milked away,
When I was up, that I could go no farther,
Nay, I sat down upon my first arrival. 45
"Now it behoves thee thus to put off sloth,"
My Master said; "for sitting upon down,
Or under quilt, one cometh not to fame,
Withouten which whoso his life consumes
Such vestige leaveth of himself on earth, 50
As smoke in air or in the water foam.[5]
And therefore raise thee up, o'ercome the anguish
With spirit that o'ercometh every battle,
If with its heavy body it sink not.
A longer stairway it behoves thee mount; 55
'Tis not enough from these to have departed;
Let it avail thee, if thou understand me."
Then I uprose, showing myself provided
Better with breath than I did feel myself,
And said: "Go on, for I am strong and bold." 60
Upward we took our way along the crag,
Which jagged was, and narrow, and difficult,
And more precipitous far than that before.
Speaking I went, not to appear exhausted;
Whereat a voice from the next moat came forth, 65

Canto XXIV: The Thieves tortured by Serpents

Not well adapted to articulate words.
I know not what it said, though o'er the back
I now was of the arch that passes there;
But he seemed moved to anger who was speaking.
I was bent downward, but my living eyes 70
Could not attain the bottom, for the dark;
Wherefore I: "Master, see that thou arrive
At the next round, and let us descend the wall;
For as from hence I hear and understand not,
So I look down and nothing I distinguish." 75
"Other response," he said, "I make thee not,
Except the doing; for the modest asking
Ought to be followed by the deed in silence."
We from the bridge descended at its head,
Where it connects itself with the eighth bank, 80
And then was manifest to me the Bolgia;

And I beheld therein a terrible throng
Of serpents, and of such a monstrous kind,
That the remembrance still congeals my blood.
Let Lybia boast no longer with her sand; 85
For it Chelydri, Jaculi, and Phareæ
She breeds, with Cenchri and with Amphisbæna,[6]
Neither so many plagues nor so malignant
E'er showed she with all Ethiopia,
Nor with whatever on the Red Sea is! 90
Among this cruel and most dismal throng
People were running naked and affrighted,
Without the hope of hole or heliotrope.[7]
They had their hands with serpents bound behind them;
These riveted upon their reins[8] the tail 95
And head, and were in front of them entwined.
And lo! at one who was upon our side
There darted forth a serpent, which transfixed him
There where the neck is knotted to the shoulders.
Nor *O* so quickly e'er, nor *I* was written,[9] 100
As he took fire, and burned; and ashes wholly
Behoved it that in falling he became.
And when he on the ground was thus destroyed,
The ashes drew together, and of themselves
Into himself they instantly returned. 105
Even thus by the great sages 'tis confessed
The phœnix dies, and then is born again,
When it approaches its five-hundredth year;[10]
On herb or grain it feeds not in its life,
But only on tears of incense and amomum, 110
And nard and myrrh* are its last winding-sheet.†
And as he is who falls, and knows not how,
By force of demons who to earth down drag him,
Or other oppilation[11] that binds man,

*In addition to incense, the three substances are, respectively, balsam, a balm, and a gum resin used in perfumes and incense.
†Shroud.

When he arises and around him looks, 115
Wholly bewildered by the mighty anguish
Which he has suffered, and in looking sighs;
Such was that sinner after he had risen.
Justice of God! O how severe it is,
That blows like these in vengeance poureth down! 120
The Guide thereafter asked him who he was;
Whence he replied: "I rained from Tuscany
A short time since I came into this cruel gorge.
A bestial life, and not a human, pleased me,
Even as the mule I was; I'm Vanni Fucci,[12] 125
Beast, and Pistoia was my worthy den."
And I unto the Guide: "Tell him to stir not,
And ask what crime has thrust him here below,
For once a man of blood and wrath I saw him."
And the sinner, who had heard, dissembled not, 130
But unto me directed mind and face,
And with a melancholy shame was painted.
Then said: "It pains me more that thou hast caught me
Amid this misery where thou seest me,
Than when I from the other life was taken. 135
What thou demandest I cannot deny;
So low am I put down because I robbed
The sacristy of the fair ornaments,
And falsely once 'twas laid upon another;[13]
But that thou mayst not such a sight enjoy, 140
If thou shalt e'er be out of the dark places,
Thine ears to my announcement ope and hear:
Pistoia first of Neri groweth meagre;
Then Florence doth renew her men and manners;
Mars draws a vapor up from Val di Magra, 145
Which is with turbid clouds enveloped round,
And with impetuous and bitter tempest
Over Campo Picen shall be the battle;
When it shall suddenly rend the mist asunder,
So that each Bianco shall thereby be smitten. 150
And this I've said that it may give thee pain."[14]

CANTO XXV

At the conclusion of his words, the thief
Lifted his hands aloft with both the figs,
Crying: "Take that, God, for at thee I aim them."
From that time forth the serpents were my friends;
For one entwined itself about his neck 5
As if it said: "I will not thou speak more";
And round his arms another, and rebound him,
Clinching itself together so in front,
That with them he could not a motion make.[1]
Pistoia, ah, Pistoia![2] why resolve not 10
To burn thyself to ashes and so perish,
Since in ill-doing thou thy seed excellest?
Through all the sombre circles of this Hell,
Spirit I saw not against God so proud,
Not he who fell at Thebes down from the walls![3] 15
He fled away, and spake no further word;
And I beheld a Centaur full of rage
Come crying out: "Where is, where is the scoffer?"
I do not think Maremma has so many
Serpents as he had all along his back,[4] 20
As far as where our countenance begins.
Upon the shoulders, just behind the nape,
With wings wide open was a dragon lying,
And he sets fire to all that he encounters.
My Master said: "That one is Cacus, who 25
Beneath the rock upon Mount Aventine
Created oftentimes a lake of blood.
He goes not on the same road with his brothers,

By reason of the fraudulent theft he made
Of the great herd,[5] which he had near to him; 30
Whereat his tortuous actions ceased beneath
The mace of Hercules, who peradventure
Gave him a hundred, and he felt not ten."
While he was speaking thus, he had passed by,
And spirits three had underneath us come, 35
Of which nor I aware was, nor my Leader,
Until what time they shouted: "Who are you?"
On which account our story made a halt,
And then we were intent on them alone.
I did not know them; but it came to pass, 40
As it is wont to happen by some chance,
That one to name the other was compelled,
Exclaiming: "Where can Cianfa[6] have remained?"
Whence I, so that the Leader might attend,
Upward from chin to nose my finger laid.[7] 45
If thou art, Reader, slow now to believe
What I shall say, it will no marvel be,
For I who saw it hardly can admit it.
As I was holding raised on them my brows,
Behold! a serpent with six feet darts forth 50
In front of one, and fastens wholly on him.[8]
With middle feet it bound him round the paunch,
And with the forward ones his arms it seized;
Then thrust its teeth through one cheek and the other;
The hindermost it stretched upon his thighs, 55
And put its tail through in between the two,
And up behind along the reins[9] outspread it.
Ivy was never fastened by its barbs
Unto a tree so, as this horrible reptile
Upon the other's limbs entwined its own. 60
Then they stuck close, as if of heated wax
They had been made, and intermixed their color;
Nor one nor other seemed now what he was;
E'en as proceedeth on before the flame
Upward along the paper a brown color, 65

Canto XXV: Agnello changing into a Serpent

Which is not black as yet, and the white dies.
The other two looked on, and each of them
Cried out: "O me, Agnello, how thou changest!
Behold, thou now art neither two nor one."
Already the two heads had one become, 70
When there appeared to us two figures mingled

Into one face, wherein the two were lost.
Of the four lists were fashioned the two arms,
The thighs and legs, the belly and the chest
Members became that never yet were seen. 75
Every original aspect there was cancelled;
Two and yet none did the perverted image
Appear, and such departed with slow pace.
Even as a lizard,[10] under the great scourge
Of days canicular, exchanging hedge, 80
Lightning appeareth if the road it cross;
Thus did appear, coming towards the bellies
Of the two others, a small fiery serpent,
Livid and black as is a peppercorn.
And in that part whereat is first received 85
Our ailment,[11] it one of them transfixed;
Then downward fell in front of him extended.
The one transfixed looked at it, but said naught;
Nay, rather with feet motionless he yawned,
Just as if sleep or fever had assailed him. 90
He at the serpent gazed, and it at him;
One through the wound, the other through the mouth
Smoked violently, and the smoke commingled.
Henceforth be silent Lucan, where he mentions
Wretched Sabellus and Nassidius, 95
And wait to hear what now shall be shot forth.
Be silent Ovid,[12] of Cadmus and Arethusa;
For if him to a snake, her to a fountain,
Converts he fabling, that I grudge him not;
Because two natures never front to front 100
Has he transmuted, so that both the forms
To interchange their matter ready were.
Together they responded in such wise,
That to a fork the serpent cleft his tail,
And eke* the wounded drew his feet together. 105

*Also (archaic).

The legs together with the thighs themselves
Adhered so, that in little time the juncture
No sign whatever made that was apparent.
He with the cloven tail assumed the figure
The other one was losing, and his skin 110
Became elastic, and the other's hard.
I saw the arms draw inward at the armpits,
And both feet of the reptile, that were short,
Lengthen as much as those contracted were.
Thereafter the hind feet, together twisted, 115
Became the member that a man conceals,*
And of his own† the wretch had two created.
While both of them the exhalation veils
With a new color, and engenders hair
On one of them and depilates the other, 120
The one uprose and down the other fell,
Though turning not away their impious lamps,[13]
Underneath which each one his muzzle changed.
He who was standing drew it tow'rds the temples,
And from excess of matter, which came thither, 125
Issued the ears from out the hollow cheeks;
What did not backward run and was retained
Of that excess made to the face a nose,
And the lips thickened far as was befitting.
He who lay prostrate thrusts his muzzle forward, 130
And backward draws the ears into his head,
In the same manner as the snail its horns;
And so the tongue, which was entire and apt
For speech before, is cleft, and the bi-forked
In the other closes up, and the smoke ceases. 135
The soul, which to a reptile had been changed,
Along the valley hissing takes to flight,
And after him the other speaking sputters.
Then did he turn upon him his new shoulders,

*The penis.
†Of his own penis.

And said to the other: "I'll have Buoso run, 140
Crawling as I have done,[14] along this road."
In this way I beheld the seventh ballast[15]
Shift and reshift, and here be my excuse
The novelty, if aught my pen transgress.[16]
And notwithstanding that mine eyes might be 145
Somewhat bewildered, and my mind dismayed,
They could not flee away so secretly
But that I plainly saw Puccio Sciancato;[17]
And he it was who sole of three companions,
Which came in the beginning, was not changed; 150
The other was he whom thou, Gaville, weepest.[18]

CANTO XXVI

REJOICE, O Florence, since thou art so great,
That over sea and land thou beatest thy wings,[1]
And throughout Hell thy name is spread abroad!
Among the thieves five citizens of thine
Like these I found, whence shame comes unto me, 5
And thou thereby to no great honor risest.
But if when morn is near our dreams are true,[2]
Feel shalt thou in a little time from now
What Prato, if none other, craves for thee.
And if it now were, it were not too soon; 10
Would that it were, seeing it needs must be,
For 'twill aggrieve me more the more I age.[3]
We went our way, and up along the stairs
The bourns[4] had made us to descend before,
Remounted my Conductor and drew me. 15
And following the solitary path
Among the rocks and ridges of the crag,
The foot without the hand sped not at all.
Then sorrowed I, and sorrow now again,
When I direct my mind to what I saw, 20
And more my genius curb than I am wont,
That it may run not unless virtue guide it;
So that if some good star, or better thing,
Have given me good, I may myself not grudge it.
As many as the hind* (who on the hill 25

*Peasant.

Canto XXVI: The Flaming Spirits of the evil Counsellors

Rests at the time when he who lights the world
His countenance keeps least concealed from us,
Whileas the fly gives place unto the gnat)*

*At dusk (Longfellow translates *la zanzara* as "gnat" rather than "mosquito").

Seeth the glow-worms* down along the valley,
Perchance there where he ploughs and makes his vintage;
With flames as manifold resplendent all 31
Was the eighth Bolgia, as I grew aware
As soon as I was where the depth appeared.
And such as he who with the bears avenged him
Beheld Elijah's chariot at departing,[5] 35
What time the steeds to heaven erect uprose,
For with his eye he could not follow it
So as to see aught else than flame alone,
Even as a little cloud ascending upward,
Thus each along the gorge of the intrenchment 40
Was moving; for not one reveals the theft,
And every flame a sinner steals away.[6]
I stood upon the bridge uprisen to see,
So that, if I had seized not on a rock,
Down had I fallen without being pushed. 45
And the Leader, who beheld me so attent,
Exclaimed: "Within the fires the spirits are;
Each swathes himself with that wherewith he burns."
"My Master," I replied, "by hearing thee
I am more sure; but I surmised already 50
It might be so, and already wished to ask thee
Who is within that fire, which comes so cleft
At top, it seems uprising from the pyre
Where was Eteocles with his brother placed."[7]
He answered me: "Within there are tormented 55
Ulysses and Diomed,[8] and thus together
They unto vengeance run as unto wrath.
And there within their flame do they lament
The ambush of the horse, which made the door
Whence issued forth the Romans' gentle seed; 60
Therein is wept the craft, for which being dead
Deidamia still deplores Achilles,

*Fireflies.

And pain for the Palladium there is borne."[9]
"If they within those sparks possess the power
To speak," I said, "thee, Master, much I pray, 65
And re-pray, that the prayer be worth a thousand,
That thou make no denial of awaiting
Until the hornëd flame shall hither come;
Thou seest that with desire I lean towards it."
And he to me: "Worthy is thy entreaty 70
Of much applause, and therefore I accept it;
But take heed that thy tongue restrain itself.
Leave me to speak, because I have conceived
That which thou wishest; for they might disdain
Perchance, since they were Greeks, discourse of thine."[10] 75
When now the flame had come unto that point,
Where to my Leader it seemed time and place,
After this fashion did I hear him speak:
"O ye, who are twofold within one fire,
If I deserved of you, while I was living, 80
If I deserved of you or much or little
When in the world I wrote the lofty verses,[11]
Do not move on, but one of you declare
Whither, being lost, he went away to die."
Then of the antique flame the greater horn,[12] 85
Murmuring, began to wave itself about
Even as a flame doth which the wind fatigues.
Thereafterward, the summit to and fro
Moving as if it were the tongue that spake,
It uttered forth a voice, and said: "When I 90
From Circe had departed,[13] who concealed me
More than a year there near unto Gaëta,
Or ever yet Æneas named it so,
Nor fondness for my son, nor reverence
For my old father, nor the due affection 95
Which joyous should have made Penelope,
Could overcome within me the desire
I had to be experienced of the world,
And of the vice and virtue of mankind;

But I put forth on the high open sea 100
With one sole ship, and that small company
By which I never had deserted been.
Both of the shores I saw as far as Spain,
Far as Morocco, and the isle of Sardes,
And the others which that sea bathes round about. 105
I and my company were old and slow
When at that narrow passage we arrived
Where Hercules his landmarks set as signals,
That man no farther onward should adventure.
On the right hand behind me left I Seville, 110
And on the other already had left Ceuta.
'O brothers, who amid a hundred thousand
Perils,' I said, 'have come unto the West,
To this so inconsiderable vigil
Which is remaining of your senses still, 115
Be ye unwilling to deny the knowledge,
Following the sun, of the unpeopled world.
Consider ye the seed from which ye sprang;
Ye were not made to live like unto brutes,
But for pursuit of virtue and of knowledge.'[14] 120
So eager did I render my companions,
With this brief exhortation, for the voyage,
That then I hardly could have held them back.
And having turned our stern unto the morning,
We of the oars made wings for our mad flight, 125
Evermore gaining on the larboard side.
Already all the stars of the other pole
The night beheld, and ours so very low
It did not rise above the ocean floor.
Five times rekindled and as many quenched[15] 130
Had been the splendor underneath the moon,
Since we had entered into the deep pass,
When there appeared to us a mountain,[16] dim
From distance, and it seemed to me so high
As I had never any one beheld. 135
Joyful were we, and soon it turned to weeping;

For out of the new land a whirlwind rose,
And smote upon the fore part of the ship.
Three times it made it whirl with all the waters,
At the fourth time it made the stern uplift, 140
And the prow downward go, as pleased Another,
Until the sea above us closed again."

CANTO XXVII

ALREADY was the flame erect and quiet,
To speak no more, and now departed from us
With the permission of the gentle Poet;
When yet another, which behind it came,
Caused us to turn our eyes upon its top 5
By a confusëd sound that issued from it.
As the Sicilian bull (that bellowed first
With the lament of him, and that was right,
Who with his file had modulated it[1])
Bellowed so with the voice of the afflicted, 10
That, notwithstanding it was made of brass,
Still it appeared with agony transfixed;
Thus, by not having any way or issue
At first from out the fire, to its own language
Converted were the melancholy words. 15
But afterwards, when they had gathered way
Up through the point, giving it that vibration
The tongue had given them in their passage out,
We heard it said: "O thou, at whom I aim
My voice, and who but now wast speaking Lombard,[2] 20
Saying, 'Now go thy way, no more I urge thee,'
Because I come perchance a little late,
To stay and speak with me let it not irk thee;
Thou seest it irks me not, and I am burning.
If thou but lately into this blind world 25
Hast fallen down from that sweet Latian* land,

*Italian.

Wherefrom I bring the whole of my transgression,
Say, have the Romagnuoli* peace or war,
For I was from the mountains there between
Urbino and the yoke whence Tiber bursts."[3] 30
I still was downward bent and listening,
When my Conductor touched me on the side,
Saying: "Speak thou: this one a Latian is."
And I, who had beforehand my reply
In readiness, forthwith began to speak: 35
"O soul, that down below there art concealed,
Romagna thine is not and never has been
Without war in the bosom of its tyrants;
But open war I none have left there now.
Ravenna stands as it long years hath stood; 40
The Eagle of Polenta there is brooding,
So that she covers Cervia with her vans.
The city which once made the long resistance,
And of the French a sanguinary heap,
Beneath the Green Paws finds itself again; 45
Verrucchio's ancient Mastiff and the new,
Who made such bad disposal of Montagna,
Where they are wont make wimbles† of their teeth.
The cities of Lamone and Santerno
Governs the Lioncel of the white lair, 50
Who changes sides 'twixt summer-time and winter;
And that of which the Savio bathes the flank,
Even as it lies between the plain and mountain,
Lives between tyranny and a free state.[4]
Now I entreat thee tell us who thou art; 55
Be not more stubborn than the rest have been,
So may thy name hold front there in the world."[5]
After the fire a little more had roared
In its own fashion, the sharp point it moved
This way and that, and then gave forth such breath: 60

*People living in the Romagna area of Italy.
†Augurs, used for boring holes in wood.

Canto XXVII: The Mutilated Shade of Mahomet

"If I believed that my reply were made
	To one who to the world would e'er return,
	This flame without more flickering should stand still;
But inasmuch as never from this depth
	Did any one return, if I hear true, 65
	Without the fear of infamy I answer,[6]

I was a man of arms, then Cordelier,[7]
Believing thus begirt to make amends;
And truly my belief had been fulfilled
But for the High Priest,[8] whom may ill betide, 70
Who put me back into my former sins;
And how and wherefore I will have thee hear.
While I was still the form of bone and pulp
My mother gave to me, the deeds I did
Were not those of a lion, but a fox.[9] 75
The machinations and the covert ways
I knew them all, and practised so their craft,
That to the ends of earth the sound went forth.
When now unto that portion of mine age
I saw myself arrived, when each one ought 80
To lower the sails, and coil away the ropes,
That which before had pleased me then displeased me;
And penitent and confessing I surrendered,
Ah woe is me! and it would have bestead me.
The Leader of the modern Pharisees 85
Having a war near unto Lateran,
And not with Saracens nor with the Jews,
For each one of his enemies was Christian,
And none of them had been to conquer Acre,
Nor merchandising in the Sultan's land,[10] 90
Nor the high office, nor the sacred orders,
In him regarded, nor in me that cord
Which used to make those girt with it more meagre;
But even as Constantine sought out Sylvester
To cure his leprosy, within Soracte,[11] 95
So this one sought me out as an adept
To cure him of the fever of his pride.
Counsel he asked of me, and I was silent,
Because his words appeared inebriate.
And then he said: 'Be not thy heart afraid; 100
Henceforth I thee absolve; and thou instruct me
How to raze Palestrina to the ground.
Heaven have I power to lock and to unlock,

As thou dost know; therefore the keys are two,
The which my predecessor held not dear.'[12] 105
Then urged me on his weighty arguments
There, where my silence was the worst advice;
And said I: 'Father, since thou washest me
Of that sin into which I now must fall,
The promise long with the fulfilment short[13] 110
Will make thee triumph in thy lofty seat.'
Francis came afterward, when I was dead,
For me; but one of the black Cherubim
Said to him: 'Take him not; do me no wrong;[14]
He must come down among my servitors, 115
Because he gave the fraudulent advice[15]
From which time forth I have been at his hair;
For who repents not cannot be absolved,
Nor can one both repent and will at once,
Because of the contradiction which consents not.' 120
O miserable me! how I did shudder
When he seized on me, saying: 'Peradventure*
Thou didst not think that I was a logician!'
He bore me unto Minos, who entwined
Eight times his tail[16] about his stubborn back, 125
And after he had bitten it in great rage,
Said: 'Of the thievish fire a culprit this';
Wherefore, here where thou seest, am I lost,
And vested thus in going I bemoan me."
When it had thus completed its recital, 130
The flame departed uttering lamentations,
Writhing and flapping its sharp-pointed horn.
Onward we passed, both I and my Conductor,
Up o'er the crag above another arch,
Which the moat covers, where is paid the fee 135
By those who, sowing discord, win their burden.[17]

*Perhaps (archaic).

CANTO XXVIII

WHO ever could, e'en* with untrammelled words,
Tell of the blood and of the wounds in full
Which now I saw, by many times narrating?
Each tongue would for a certainty fall short,
By reason of our speech and memory, 5
That have small room to comprehend so much.
If were again assembled all the people
Which formerly upon the fateful land
Of Puglia were lamenting for their blood
Shed by the Romans and the lingering war[1] 10
That of the rings made such illustrious spoils,
As Livy has recorded,[2] who errs not,
With those who felt the agony of blows
By making counterstand† to Robert Guiscard,[3]
And all the rest, whose bones are gathered still 15
At Ceperano, where a renegade
Was each Apulian, and at Tagliacozzo,
Where without arms the old Alardo conquered,[4]
And one his limb transpierced, and one lopped off,
Should show, it would be nothing to compare 20
With the disgusting mode of the ninth Bolgia.
A cask by losing centre-piece or cant
Was never shattered so, as I saw one
Rent from the chin to where one breaketh wind.

*Even.
†Confronting, opposing.

Between his legs were hanging down his entrails; 25
His heart was visible, and the dismal sack
That maketh excrement of what is eaten.
While I was all absorbed in seeing him,
He looked at me, and opened with his hands
His bosom, saying: "See now how I rend me; 30
How mutilated, see, is Mahomet;[5]
In front of me doth Ali weeping go,
Cleft in the face from forelock unto chin;[6]
And all the others whom thou here beholdest,
Sowers of scandal and of schism[7] have been 35
While living, and therefore are thus cleft asunder.
A devil is behind here, who doth cleave us
Thus cruelly, unto the falchion's edge*
Putting again each one of all this ream
When we have gone around the doleful road; 40
By reason that our wounds are closed again
Ere any one in front of him repass.
But who art thou, that musest on the crag,
Perchance to postpone going to the pain
That is adjudged upon thine accusations?" 45
"Nor death has reached him yet, nor guilt doth lead him,"
My Master made reply, "to be tormented;
But to procure him full experience,
Me, who am dead, behoves it to conduct him
Down here through Hell, from circle unto circle; 50
And this is true as that I speak to thee."
More than a hundred were there when they heard him,
Who in the moat stood still to look at me,
Through wonderment oblivious of their torture.
"Now say to Fra Dolcino,[8] then, to arm him, 55
Thou, who perhaps wilt shortly see the sun,
If soon he wish not here to follow me,
So with provisions, that no stress of snow

*Sword's edge.

May give the victory to the Novarese,[9]
Which otherwise to gain would not be easy." 60
After one foot to go away he lifted,
This word did Mahomet say unto me,
Then to depart upon the ground he stretched it.
Another one, who had his throat pierced through,
And nose cut off close underneath the brows, 65
And who had left him but a single ear,
Staying to look in wonder with the others,
Before the others did his gullet open,
Which outwardly was red in every part,
And said: "O thou, whom guilt doth not condemn, 70
And whom I once saw up in Latian land,
Unless too great similitude deceive me,
Call to remembrance Pier da Medicina,
If e'er thou see again the lovely plain
That from Vercelli slopes to Marcabò, 75
And make it known to the best two of Fano,
To Messer Guido and Angiolello likewise,
That if foreseeing here be not in vain,
Cast over from their vessel shall they be,
And drowned near unto the Cattolica, 80
By the betrayal of a tyrant fell.
Between the isles of Cyprus and Majorca
Neptune ne'er yet beheld so great a crime,
Neither of pirates nor Argolic people.[10]
That traitor, who sees only with one eye, 85
And holds the land,[11] which some one here with me
Would fain be fasting from the vision of,
Will make them come unto parley with him;
Then will do so, that to Focara's wind
They will not stand in need of vow or prayer."[12] 90
And I to him: "Show to me and declare,
If thou wouldst have me bear up news of thee,
Who is this person of the bitter vision."
Then did he lay his hand upon the jaw
Of one of his companions, and his mouth 95

Canto XXVIII: The Severed Head of Bertrand de Born speaks

Oped, crying: "This is he, and he speaks not.
This one, being banished, every doubt submerged
In Cæsar by affirming the forearmed
Always with detriment allowed delay."
O how bewildered unto me appeared, 100

With tongue asunder in his windpipe slit,
Curio,[13] who in speaking was so bold!
And one, who both his hands dissevered had,
The stumps uplifting through the murky air,
So that the blood made horrible his face, 105
Cried out: "Thou shalt remember Mosca also,
Who said, alas! 'A thing done has an end!'
Which was an ill seed for the Tuscan people";[14]
"And death unto thy race," thereto I added;
Whence he, accumulating woe on woe, 110
Departed, like a person sad and crazed.
But I remained to look upon the crowd;
And saw a thing which I should be afraid,
Without some further proof, even to recount,
If it were not that conscience reassures me, 115
That good companion which emboldens man
Beneath the hauberk* of its feeling pure.
I truly saw, and still I seem to see it,
A trunk without a head walk in like manner
As walked the others of the mournful herd. 120
And by the hair it held the head dissevered,
Hung from the hand in fashion of a lantern,
And that upon us gazed and said: "O me!"
It of itself made to itself a lamp,
And they were two in one, and one in two; 125
How that can be, He knows who so ordains it.
When it was come close to the bridge's foot,
It lifted high its arm with all the head,
To bring more closely unto us its words,
Which were: "Behold now the sore penalty, 130
Thou, who dost breathing go to the dead beholding;
Behold if any be as great as this.
And so that thou may carry news of me,
Know that Bertram de Born am I, the same
Who gave to the Young King the evil comfort. 135

*Tunic armor made from chain mail.

I made the father and the son rebellious;
Achitophel not more with Absalom[15]
And David did with his accursed goadings.
Because I parted persons so united,
Parted do I now bear my brain, alas! 140
From its beginning, which is in this trunk.
Thus is observed in me the counterpoise."[16]

CANTO XXIX

THE many people and the diverse wounds
These eyes of mine had so inebriated,
That they were wishful to stand still and weep;
But said Virgilius: "What dost thou still gaze at?
Why is thy sight still riveted down there 5
Among the mournful, mutilated shades?
Thou hast not done so at the other Bolge;
Consider, if to count them thou believest,
That two-and-twenty miles the valley winds,[1]
And now the moon is underneath our feet;[2] 10
Henceforth the time allotted us is brief,
And more is to be seen than what thou seest."
"If thou," I thereupon made answer, "hadst
Attended to the cause for which I looked,
Perhaps a longer stay thou wouldst have pardoned." 15
Meanwhile my Guide departed, and behind him
I went, already making my reply,
And superadding: "In that cavern where
I held mine eyes with such attention fixed,
I think a spirit of my blood laments, 20
The sin which down below there costs so much."
Then said the Master: "Be no longer broken
Thy thought from this time forward upon him;
Attend elsewhere, and there let him remain;
For him I saw below the little bridge, 25
Pointing at thee, and threatening with his finger
Fiercely, and heard him called Geri del Bello.[3]
So wholly at that time wast thou impeded

By him who formerly held Altaforte,[4]
Thou didst not look that way; so he departed." 30
"O my Conductor, his own violent death,
Which is not yet avenged for him," I said,
"By any who is sharer in the shame,
Made him disdainful; whence he went away,
As I imagine, without speaking to me, 35
And thereby made me pity him the more."
Thus did we speak as far as the first place
Upon the crag, which the next valley shows
Down to the bottom, if there were more light.
When we were now right over the last cloister 40
Of Malebolge,[5] so that its lay-brothers
Could manifest themselves unto our sight,
Divers lamentings pierced me through and through,
Which with compassion had their arrows barbed,
Whereat mine ears I covered with my hands. 45
What pain would be, if from the hospitals
Of Valdichiana, 'twixt July and September,
And of Maremma and Sardinia[6]
All the diseases in one moat were gathered,
Such was it here, and such a stench came from it 50
As from putrescent limbs is wont to issue.
We had descended on the furthest bank
From the long crag, upon the left hand still,
And then more vivid was my power of sight
Down tow'rds the bottom, where the ministress 55
Of the high Lord, Justice infallible,
Punishes forgers, which she here records.
I do not think a sadder sight to see
Was in Ægina the whole people sick,
(When was the air so full of pestilence, 60
The animals, down to the little worm,
All fell, and afterwards the ancient people,
According as the poets have affirmed,
Were from the seed of ants restored again,)[7]
Than was it to behold through that dark valley 65

Canto XXIX: Virgil reproves Dante's Curiosity

The spirits languishing in divers heaps.
This on the belly, that upon the back
One of the other lay, and others crawling
Shifted themselves along the dismal road.

We step by step went onward without speech, 70
Gazing upon and listening to the sick
Who had not strength enough to lift their bodies.
I saw two sitting leaned against each other,
As leans in heating platter against platter,
From head to foot bespotted o'er with scabs; 75
And never saw I plied a currycomb
By a stable-boy for whom his master waits,
Or him who keeps awake unwillingly,
As every one was plying fast the bite
Of nails upon himself, for the great rage 80
Of itching which no other succor had.
And the nails downward with them dragged the scab,
In fashion as a knife the scales of bream,
Or any other fish that has them largest.
"O thou, that with thy fingers dost dismail thee," 85
Began my Leader unto one of them,
"And makest of them pincers now and then,
Tell me if any Latian is with those
Who are herein; so may thy nails suffice thee
To all eternity unto this work." 90
"Latians are we, whom thou so wasted seest,
Both of us here," one weeping made reply;
"But who art thou, that questionest about us?"
And said the Guide: "One am I who descends
Down with this living man from cliff to cliff, 95
And I intend to show Hell unto him."
Then broken was their mutual support,
And trembling each one turned himself to me.
With others who had heard him by rebound.
Wholly to me did the good Master gather, 100
Saying: "Say unto them whate'er thou wishest."
And I began, since he would have it so:
"So may your memory not steal away
In the first world from out the minds of men,
But so may it survive 'neath many suns, 105

Say to me who ye are, and of what people;
Let not your foul and loathsome punishment
Make you afraid to show yourselves to me."
"I of Arezzo was," one made reply;
"And Albert of Siena had me burned;[8] 110
But what I died for does not bring me here.
'Tis true I said to him, speaking in jest,
That I could rise by flight into the air,
And he who had conceit, but little wit,
Would have me show to him the art; and only 115
Because no Dædalus I made him, made me
Be burned by one who held him as his son.
But unto the last Bolgia of the ten,
For alchemy, which in the world I practised,
Minos, who cannot err, has me condemned." 120
And to the Poet said I: "Now was ever
So vain a people as the Sienese?
Not for a certainty the French by far."[9]
Whereat the other leper, who had heard me,
Replied unto my speech: "Taking out Stricca, 125
Who knew the art of moderate expenses,
And Niccolò, who the luxurious use
Of cloves discovered earliest of all
Within that garden where such seed takes root;
And taking out the band, among whom squandered 130
Caccia d' Ascian his vineyards and vast woods,
And where his wit the Abbagliato proffered!
But, that thou know who thus doth second thee
Against the Sienese, make sharp thine eye
Tow'rds me, so that my face well answers thee, 135
And thou shalt see I am Capocchio's shade,
Who metals falsified by alchemy;
Thou must remember, if I well descry thee,
How I a skilful ape of nature was."[10]

CANTO XXX

'TWAS at the time when Juno was enraged,
For Semele, against the Theban blood,
As she already more than once had shown,
So reft of reason Athamas became,
That, seeing his own wife with children twain 5
Walking encumbered upon either hand,
He cried: "Spread out the nets, that I may take
The lioness and her whelps upon the passage";
And then extended his unpitying claws,
Seizing the first, who had the name Learchus, 10
And whirled him round, and dashed him on a rock;
And she, with the other burthen,* drowned herself;—[1]
And at the time when fortune downward hurled
The Trojans' arrogance, that all things dared,
So that the king was with his kingdom crushed, 15
Hecuba sad, disconsolate, and captive,
When lifeless she beheld Polyxena,
And of her Polydorus on the shore
Of ocean was the dolorous one aware,
Out of her senses like a dog did bark, 20
So much the anguish had her mind distorted;[2]
But not of Thebes the furies nor the Trojan
Were ever seen in any one so cruel
In goading beasts, and much more human members,
As I beheld two shadows pale and naked, 25

*Burden.

Who, biting, in the manner ran along
That a boar does, when from the sty turned loose.
One to Capocchio came, and by the nape
Seized with its teeth his neck, so that in dragging
It made his belly grate the solid bottom.[3] 30
And the Aretine, who trembling had remained,
Said to me: "That mad sprite is Gianni Schicchi,[4]
And raving goes[5] thus harrying other people."
"O," said I to him, "so may not the other
Set teeth on thee, let it not weary thee 35
To tell us who it is, ere it dart hence."
And he to me: "That is the ancient ghost
Of the nefarious Myrrha,[6] who became
Beyond all rightful love her father's lover.
She came to sin with him after this manner, 40
By counterfeiting of another's form;
As he who goeth yonder undertook,
That he might gain the lady of the herd,
To counterfeit in himself Buoso Donati,
Making a will and giving it due form." 45
And after the two maniacs had passed
On whom I held mine eye, I turned it back
To look upon the other evil-born.
I saw one made in fashion of a lute,
If he had only had the groin cut off 50
Just at the point at which a man is forked.
The heavy dropsy, that so disproportions
The limbs with humors, which it ill concocts,
That the face corresponds not to the belly,
Compelled him so to hold his lips apart 55
As does the hectic,* who because of thirst
One tow'rds the chin, the other upward turns.
"O ye, who without any torment are,
And why I know not, in the world of woe,"

*Consumptive.

He said to us, "behold, and be attentive 60
Unto the misery of Master Adam;
I had while living much of what I wished,
And now, alas! a drop of water crave.
The rivulets, that form the verdant hills
Of Cassentin descend down into Arno, 65
Making their channel-courses cool and soft,
Ever before me stand, and not in vain;
For far more doth their image dry me up
Than the disease which strips my face of flesh.
The rigid justice that chastises me 70
Draweth occasion from the place in which
I sinned, to put the more my sighs in flight.
There is Romena, where I counterfeited
The currency imprinted with the Baptist,
For which I left my body burned above.[7] 75
But if I here could see the tristful soul
Of Guido, or Alessandro, or their brother,
For Branda's fount I would not give the sight.
One is within already,[8] if the raving
Shades that are going round about speak truth; 80
But what avails it me, whose limbs are tied?
If I were only still so light, that in
A hundred years I could advance one inch,
I had already started on the way,
Seeking him out among this squalid folk, 85
Although the circuit be eleven miles,
And be not less than half a mile across.[9]
For them am I in such a family;
They did induce me into coining florins,
Which had three carats of impurity." 90
And I to him: "Who are the two poor wretches
That smoke like unto a wet hand in winter,
Lying there close upon thy right-hand confines?"
"I found them here," replied he, "when I rained
Into this chasm, and since they have not turned, 95
Nor do I think they will for evermore.

One the false woman is who accused Joseph,
The other the false Sinon, Greek of Troy;[10]
From acute fever they send forth such reek."
And one of them, who felt himself annoyed 100
At being, peradventure, named so darkly,
Smote with the fist upon his hardened paunch.
It gave a sound, as if it were a drum;
And Master Adam smote him with his arm
Upon the face, that did not seem less hard, 105
Saying to him: "Although be taken from me
All motion, for my members that are heavy,
I have an arm unfettered for such need."
Whereat he answer made: "When thou didst go
Unto the fire, thou hadst it not so ready;[11] 110
But hadst it so and more when thou wast coining."
The dropsical: "Thou sayest true in that;
But thou wast not so true a witness there,
Where thou wast questioned of the truth at Troy."
"If I spake false, thou falsifiedst the coin," 115
Said Sinon; "and for one fault I am here,
And thou for more than any other demon."[12]
"Remember, perjurer, about the horse,"
He made reply who had the swollen belly,
"And rueful be it thee the whole world knows it." 120
"Rueful to thee the thirst be wherewith cracks
Thy tongue," the Greek said, "and the putrid water
That hedges so thy paunch before thine eyes."
Then the false-coiner: "So is gaping wide
Thy mouth for speaking evil, as 'tis wont; 125
Because if I have thirst, and humor stuff me,[13]
Thou hast the burning and the head that aches,
And to lick up the mirror of Narcissus[14]
Thou wouldst not want words many to invite thee."
In listening to them was I wholly fixed, 130
When said the Master to me: "Now just look,
For little wants it that I quarrel with thee."
When him I heard in anger speak to me,

I turned me round towards him with such shame
That still it eddies through my memory. 135
And as he is who dreams of his own harm,
Who dreaming wishes it may be a dream,
So that he craves what is, as if it were not;
Such I became, not having power to speak,
For to excuse myself I wished, and still 140
Excused myself, and did not think I did it.
"Less shame doth wash away a greater fault,"
The Master said, "than this of thine has been;
Therefore thyself disburden of all sadness,
And make account that I am aye* beside thee, 145
If e'er it come to pass that fortune bring thee
Where there are people in a like dispute;
For a base wish it is to wish to hear it."[15]

*Always, ever.

CANTO XXXI

ONE and the self-same tongue first wounded me,
So that it tinged the one cheek and the other,
And then held out to me the medicine;
Thus do I hear that once Achilles' spear,[1]
His and his father's, used to be the cause 5
First of a sad and then a gracious guerdon.*
We turned our backs upon the wretched valley,
Upon the bank that girds it round about,
Going across it without any speech.
There it was less than night, and less than day, 10
So that my sight went little in advance;
But I could hear the blare of a loud horn,
So loud it would have made each thunder faint,
Which, counter to it following its way,
Mine eyes directed wholly to one place. 15
After the dolorous discomfiture
When Charlemagne the holy emprise† lost,
So terribly Orlando sounded not.[2]
Short while my head turned thitherward‡ I held
When many lofty towers I seemed to see, 20
Whereat I: "Master, say, what town is this?"
And he to me: "Because thou peerest forth
Athwart§ the darkness at too great a distance,

*Reward.
†Enterprise or adventure.
‡In that direction.
§From side to side.

Canto XXXI: The Giant Antaeus lowering Dante and Virgil

It happens that thou errest in thy fancy.
Well shalt thou see, if thou arrivest there, 25
How much the sense deceives itself by distance;
Therefore a little faster spur thee on."
Then tenderly he took me by the hand,
And said: "Before we farther have advanced,

That the reality may seem to thee 30
Less strange, know that these are not towers, but giants,[3]
And they are in the well, around the bank,
From navel downward, one and all of them."
As, when the fog is vanishing away,
Little by little doth the sight refigure 35
Whate'er the mist that crowds the air conceals,
So, piercing through the dense and darksome air,
More and more near approaching tow'rd the verge,
My error fled, and fear came over me;
Because as on its circular parapets 40
Montereggione crowns itself with towers,
E'en thus the margin which surrounds the well
With one half of their bodies turreted[4]
The horrible giants, whom Jove menaces[5]
E'en now from out the heavens when he thunders. 45
And I of one already saw the face,
Shoulders, and breast, and great part of the belly,
And down along his sides both of the arms.
Certainly Nature, when she left the making
Of animals like these, did well indeed, 50
By taking such executors from Mars;
And if of elephants and whales she doth not
Repent her, whosoever looketh subtly
More just and more discreet will hold her for it;
For where the argument of intellect 55
Is added unto evil will and power,
No rampart can the people make against it.[6]
His face appeared to me as long and large
As is at Rome the pine-cone of Saint Peter's[7]
And in proportion were the other bones; 60
So that the margin, which an apron was
Down from the middle,[8] showed so much of him
Above it, that to reach up to his hair
Three Frieslanders[9] in vain had vaunted them;
For I beheld thirty great palms of him 65
Down from the place where man his mantle buckles.[10]

"Raphel mai amech izabi almi,"[11]
Began to clamor the ferocious mouth,
To which were not befitting sweeter psalms.
And unto him my Guide: "Soul idiotic, 70
Keep to thy horn, and vent thyself with that,
When wrath or other passion touches thee.
Search round thy neck, and thou wilt find the belt
Which keeps it fastened, O bewildered soul,
And see it, where it bars thy mighty breast." 75
Then said to me: "He doth himself accuse;
This one is Nimrod, by whose evil thought
One language in the world is not still used.
Here let us leave him and not speak in vain;
For even such to him is every language 80
As his to others, which to none is known."[12]
Therefore a longer journey did we make,
Turned to the left, and a crossbow-shot off
We found another far more fierce and large.
In binding him, who might the master be 85
I cannot say; but he had pinioned close
Behind the right arm, and in front the other,
With chains, that held him so begirt about
From the neck down, that on the part uncovered
It wound itself as far as the fifth gyre.[13] 90
"This proud one wished to make experiment
Of his own power against the Supreme Jove,"
My Leader said, "whence he hath such deserts.
Ephialtes[14] is his name; he showed great prowess,
What time the giants terrified the Gods; 95
The arms he wielded never more he moves."
And I to him: "If possible, I should wish
That of the measureless Briareus[15]
These eyes of mine might have experience."
Whence he replied: "Thou shalt behold Antæus[16] 100
Close by here, who can speak and is unbound,
Who at the bottom of all crime shall place us.

Much farther yon is he whom thou wouldst see,
  And he is bound, and fashioned like to this one,
  Save that he seems in aspect more ferocious." 105
There never was an earthquake of such might
  That it could shake a tower so violently,
  As Ephialtes suddenly shook himself.
Then was I more afraid of death than ever,
  For nothing more was needful than the fear, 110
  If I had not beheld the manacles.
Then we proceeded farther in advance,
  And to Antæus came, who, full five ells[17]
  Without the head, forth issued from the cavern.
"O thou, who in the valley fortunate, 115
  Which Scipio the heir of glory made,
  When Hannibal turned back with all his hosts,
Once brought'st a thousand lions for thy prey,[18]
  And who, hadst thou been at the mighty war
  Among thy brothers, some it seems still think 120
The sons of Earth the victory would have gained;
  Place us below, nor be disdainful of it,
  There where the cold doth lock Cocytus[19] up.
Make us not go to Tityus nor Typhœus;[20]
  This one can give of that which here is longed for; 125
  Therefore stoop down, and do not curl thy lip.
Still in the world can he restore thy fame;
  Because he lives, and still expects long life,
  If to itself Grace call him not untimely."
So said the Master; and in haste the other 130
  His hands extended and took up my Guide,—
  Hands whose great pressure Hercules once felt.
Virgilius, when he felt himself embraced,
  Said unto me: "Draw nigh, that I may take thee";
  Then of himself and me one bundle made. 135
As seems the Carisenda, to behold
  Beneath the leaning side, when goes a cloud
  Above it so that opposite it hangs;[21]

Such did Antæus seem to me, who stood
Watching to see him stoop, and then it was 140
I could have wished to go some other way.
But lightly in the abyss, which swallows up
Judas with Lucifer, he put us down;[22]
Nor thus bowed downward made he there delay,
But, as a mast doth in a ship, uprose. 145

CANTO XXXII

If I had rhymes both rough and stridulous,
As were appropriate to the dismal hole
Down upon which thrust all the other rocks,
I would press out the juice of my conception
More fully; but because I have them not, 5
Not without fear I bring myself to speak;
For 'tis no enterprise to take in jest,
To sketch the bottom of all the universe,
Nor for a tongue that cries Mamma and Babbo.[1]
But may those Ladies[2] help this verse of mine, 10
Who helped Amphion in enclosing Thebes,
That from the fact the word be not diverse.
O rabble ill-begotten above all,
Who're in the place to speak of which is hard,
'Twere better ye had here been sheep or goats! 15
When we were down within the darksome well,
Beneath the giant's feet, but lower far,
And I was scanning still the lofty wall,[3]
I heard it said to me[4]: "Look how thou steppest!
Take heed thou do not trample with thy feet 20
The heads of the tired, miserable brothers!"
Whereat I turned me round, and saw before me
And underfoot a lake, that from the frost
The semblance had of glass, and not of water.
So thick a veil ne'er made upon its current 25
In winter-time Danube in Austria,
Nor there beneath the frigid sky the Don,
As there was here; so that if Tambernich

Had fallen upon it, or Pietrapana,[5]
E'en at the edge 'twould not have given a creak. 30
And as to croak the frog doth place himself
With muzzle out of water,—when is dreaming
Of gleaning oftentimes the peasant-girl,—
Livid, as far down as where shame appears,[6]
Were the disconsolate shades within the ice, 35
Setting their teeth unto the note of storks.[7]
Each one his countenance held downward bent;
From mouth the cold, from eyes the doleful heart
Among them witness of itself procures.
When round about me somewhat I had looked, 40
I downward turned me, and saw two so close,
The hair upon their heads together mingled.
"Ye who so strain your breasts together, tell me,"
I said, "who are you"; and they bent their necks,
And when to me their faces they had lifted, 45
Their eyes, which first were only moist within,
Gushed o'er the eyelids, and the frost congealed
The tears between, and locked them up again.
Clamp never bound together wood with wood
So strongly; whereat they, like two he-goats, 50
Butted together, so much wrath o'ercame them.
And one, who had by reason of the cold
Lost both his ears, still with his visage downward,
Said: "Why dost thou so mirror thyself in us?
If thou desire to know who these two are, 55
The valley whence Bisenzio descends
Belonged to them and to their father Albert.
They from one body came, and all Caïna
Thou shalt search through, and shalt not find a shade
More worthy to be fixed in gelatine; 60
Not he in whom were broken breast and shadow
At one and the same blow by Arthur's hand;
Focaccia not; not he who me encumbers
So with his head I see no farther forward,
And bore the name of Sassol Mascheroni;[8] 65

Canto XXXII: Ugolino gnawing the Head of Ruggieri

Well knowest thou who he was, if thou art Tuscan.
And that thou put me not to further speech,
Know that I Camicion de' Pazzi was,
And wait Carlino to exonerate me."[9]
Then I beheld a thousand faces,[10] made 70
Purple with cold; whence o'er me comes a shudder,
And evermore will come, at frozen ponds.
And while we were advancing tow'rds the middle,
Where everything of weight unites together,
And I was shivering in the eternal shade, 75
Whether 'twere will, or destiny, or chance,
I know not; but in walking 'mong the heads
I struck my foot hard in the face of one.
Weeping he growled: "Why dost thou trample me?
Unless thou comest to increase the vengeance 80
Of Montaperti,[11] why dost thou molest me?"

And I: "My Master, now wait here for me,
That I through him may issue from a doubt;
Then thou mayst hurry me, as thou shalt wish."
The Leader stopped; and to that one I said 85
Who was blaspheming vehemently still:
"Who art thou, that thus reprehendest others?"
"Now who art thou, that goest through Antenora
Smiting," replied he, "other people's cheeks,
So that, if thou wert living, 'twere too much?" 90
"Living I am, and dear to thee it may be,"
Was my response, "if thou demandest fame,
That 'mid the other notes thy name I place."
And he to me; "For the reverse I long;
Take thyself hence, and give me no more trouble; 95
For ill thou knowest to flatter in this hollow."
Then by the scalp behind I seized upon him,
And said: "It must needs be thou name thyself,
Or not a hair remain upon thee here."
Whence he to me: "Though thou strip off my hair, 100
I will not tell thee who I am, nor show thee,
If on my head a thousand times thou fall."
I had his hair in hand already twisted,
And more than one shock of it had pulled out,
He barking, with his eyes held firmly down, 105
When cried another: "What doth ail thee, Bocca?[12]
Is't not enough to clatter with thy jaws,
But thou must bark? what devil touches thee?"
"Now," said I, "I care not to have thee speak,
Accursed traitor; for unto thy shame 110
I will report of thee veracious news."
"Begone," he answered, "and tell what thou wilt,
But be not silent, if thou issue hence,
Of him who had just now his tongue so prompt;
He weepeth here the silver of the French; 115
'I saw,' thus canst thou phrase it, 'him of Duera[13]
There where the sinners stand out in the cold.'
If thou shouldst question be who else was there,

Thou hast beside thee him of Beccaria,
Of whom the gorget* Florence slit asunder; 120
Gianni del Soldanier, I think, may be
Yonder with Ganellon, and Tebaldello
Who oped† Faenza[14] when the people slept."
Already we had gone away from him,
When I beheld two frozen in one hole,[15] 125
So that one head a hood was to the other;
And even as bread through hunger is devoured,
The uppermost on the other set his teeth,
There where the brain is to the nape united.
Not in another fashion Tydeus gnawed 130
The temples of Menalippus in disdain,[16]
Than that one did the skull and the other things.
"O thou, who showest by such bestial sign
Thy hatred against him whom thou art eating,
Tell me the wherefore," said I, "with this compact, 135
That if thou rightfully of him complain,
In knowing who ye are, and his transgression,
I in the world above repay thee for it,
If that wherewith I speak be not dried up."[17]

*Figuratively, the throat; literally, armor over the throat.
†Opened up.

CANTO XXXIII

His mouth uplifted from his grim repast,
That sinner, wiping it upon the hair
Of the same head that he behind had wasted.
Then he began: "Thou wilt that I renew
The desperate grief, which wrings my heart already 5
To think of only, ere I speak of it;
But if my words be seed that may bear fruit
Of infamy to the traitor whom I gnaw,
Speaking and weeping shalt thou see together.
I know not who thou art, nor by what mode 10
Thou hast come down here; but a Florentine
Thou seemest to me truly, when I hear thee.
Thou hast to know I was Count Ugolino,[1]
And this one was Ruggieri the Archbishop;
Now I will tell thee why I am such a neighbor. 15
That, by effect of his malicious thoughts,
Trusting in him I was made prisoner,
And after put to death, I need not say;
But ne'ertheless what thou canst not have heard,
That is to say, how cruel was my death, 20
Hear shalt thou, and shalt know if he has wronged me.
A narrow perforation in the mew,*
Which bears because of me the title of Famine,
And in which others still must be locked up,
Had shown me through its opening many moons[2] 25

*Cage for hawks when molting, often in a tower.

Already, when I dreamed the evil dream
Which of the future rent for me the veil.
This one appeared to me as lord and master,
Hunting the wolf and whelps upon the mountain
For which the Pisans cannot Lucca see. 30
With sleuth-hounds gaunt, and eager, and well trained,
Gualandi with Sismondi and Lanfranchi[3]
He had sent out before him to the front.
After brief course seemed unto me forespent*
The father and the sons, and with sharp tushes† 35
It seemed to me I saw their flanks ripped open.
When I before the morrow was awake,
Moaning amid their sleep I heard my sons
Who with me were, and asking after bread.[4]
Cruel indeed art thou, if yet thou grieve not, 40
Thinking of what my heart foreboded me,
And weep'st thou not, what art thou wont to weep at?[5]
They were awake now, and the hour drew nigh
At which our food used to be brought to us,
And through his dream was each one apprehensive; 45
And I heard locking up the under door
Of the horrible tower; whereat without a word
I gazed into the faces of my sons.
I wept not, I within so turned to stone;
They wept; and darling little Anselm mine[6] 50
Said: 'Thou dost gaze so, father, what doth ail thee?'
Still not a tear I shed, nor answer made.
All of that day, nor yet the night thereafter,
Until another sun rose on the world.
As now a little glimmer made its way 55
Into the dolorous‡ prison, and I saw
Upon four faces my own very aspect,
Both of my hands in agony I bit;

*Flagging, tiring.
†Tusks, sharp teeth.
‡Grieving, full of pain and sorrow.

And, thinking that I did it from desire
Of eating, on a sudden they uprose, 60
And said they: 'Father, much less pain 'twill give us
If thou do eat of us; thyself didst clothe us
With this poor flesh, and do thou strip it off.'
I calmed me then, not to make them more sad.
That day we all were silent, and the next. 65
Ah! obdurate earth, wherefore didst thou not open?
When we had come unto the fourth day, Gaddo
Threw himself down outstretched before my feet,
Saying, 'My father, why dost thou not help me?'[7]
And there he died; and, as thou seest me, 70
I saw the three fall one by one, between
The fifth day and the sixth; whence I betook me,
Already blind, to groping over each,
And three days called them after they were dead;
Then hunger did what sorrow could not do."[8] 75
When he had said this, with his eyes distorted,
The wretched skull resumed he with his teeth,
Which, as a dog's, upon the bone were strong.
Ah! Pisa,[9] thou opprobrium* of the people
Of the fair land there where the *Sì* doth sound,[10] 80
Since slow to punish thee thy neighbors are,
Let the Capraia and Gorgona[11] move,
And make a hedge across the mouth of Arno,
That every person in thee it may drown!
For if Count Ugolino had the fame 85
Of having in thy castles thee betrayed,
Thou shouldst not on such cross have put his sons.
Guiltless of any crime, thou modern Thebes![12]
Their youth made Uguccione and Brigata,[13]
And the other two my song doth name above! 90
We passed still farther onward, where the ice
Another people ruggedly enswathes,

*A thing that brings disgrace.

Not downward turned, but all of them reversed.
Weeping itself there does not let them weep,
And grief that finds a barrier in the eyes 95
Turns itself inward to increase the anguish;
Because the earliest tears a cluster form,
And, in the manner of a crystal visor,
Fill all the cup beneath the eyebrow full.[14]
And notwithstanding that, as in a callus, 100
Because of cold all sensibility
Its station had abandoned in my face,
Still it appeared to me I felt some wind;
Whence I: "My Master, who sets this in motion?
Is not below here every vapor quenched?" 105
Whence he to me: "Full soon shalt thou be where
Thine eye shall answer make to thee of this,
Seeing the cause which raineth down the blast."[15]
And one of the wretches of the frozen crust
Cried out to us: "O souls so merciless 110
That the last post is given unto you,
Lift from mine eyes the rigid veils, that I
May vent the sorrow which impregns my heart
A little, e'er the weeping recongeal."
Whence I to him: "If thou wouldst have me help thee, 115
Say who thou wast; and if I free thee not,
May I go to the bottom of the ice."[16]
Then he replied: "I am Friar Alberigo;
He am I of the fruit of the bad garden,
Who here a date am getting for my fig."[17] 120
"O," said I to him, "Now art thou, too, dead?"
And he to me: "How may my body fare
Up in the world, no knowledge I possess.
Such an advantage has this Ptolomæa,
That oftentimes the soul descendeth here 125
Sooner than Atropos in motion sets it.
And, that thou mayest more willingly remove
From off my countenance these glassy tears,
Know that as soon as any soul betrays

As I have done, his body by a demon 130
Is taken from him,[18] who thereafter rules it,
Until his time has wholly been revolved.
Itself down rushes into such a cistern;
And still perchance above appears the body
Of yonder shade, that winters here behind me. 135
This thou shouldst know, if thou hast just come down;
It is Ser Branca d'Oria, and many years
Have passed away since he was thus locked up."
"I think," said I to him, "thou dost deceive me;
For Branca d'Oria is not dead as yet, 140
And eats, and drinks, and sleeps, and puts on clothes."
"In moat above," said he, "of Malebranche,
There where is boiling the tenacious pitch,
As yet had Michael Zanche not arrived,
When this one left a devil in his stead 145
In his own body and one near of kin,
Who made together with him the betrayal.[19]
But hitherward stretch out thy hand forthwith,
Open mine eyes";—and open them I did not,
And to be rude to him was courtesy.[20] 150
Ah, Genoese! ye men at variance
With every virtue, full of every vice!
Wherefore are ye not scattered from the world?
For with the vilest spirit of Romagna[21]
I found of you one such, who for his deeds 155
In soul already in Cocytus bathes,
And still above in body seems alive!

CANTO XXXIV

VEXILLA *Regis prodeunt Inferni*[1]
Towards us; therefore look in front of thee,"
My Master said, "If thou discernest him."
As, when there breathes a heavy fog, or when
Our hemisphere is darkening into night, 5
Appears far off a mill the wind is turning,[2]
Methought that such a building then I saw;
And, for the wind, I drew myself behind
My Guide, because there was no other shelter.[3]
Now was I, and with fear in verse I put it, 10
There where the shades were wholly covered up,[4]
And glimmered through like unto straws in glass.
Some prone are lying, others stand erect,
This with the head, and that one with the soles;
Another, bow-like, face to feet inverts. 15
When in advance so far we had proceeded,
That it my Master pleased to show to me
The creature who once had the beauteous semblance,[5]
He from before me moved and made me stop,
Saying: "Behold Dis,[6] and behold the place 20
Where thou with fortitude must arm thyself."
How frozen I became and powerless then,
Ask it not, Reader, for I write it not,
Because all language would be insufficient.
I did not die, and I alive remained not;[7] 25
Think for thyself now, hast thou aught of wit,
What I became, being of both deprived.

The Emperor of the kingdom dolorous*
From his mid-breast forth issued from the ice;
And better with a giant I compare[8] 30
Than do the giants with those arms of his;
Consider now how great must be that whole,
Which unto such a part conforms itself.
Were he as fair once, as he now is foul,
And lifted up his brow against his Maker, 35
Well may proceed from him all tribulation.
O, what a marvel it appeared to me,
When I beheld three faces on his head!
The one in front, and that vermilion was;
Two were the others, that were joined with this 40
Above the middle part of either shoulder,
And they were joined together at the crest;
And the right-hand one seemed 'twixt white and yellow;
The left was such to look upon as those
Who come from where the Nile falls valley-ward.[9] 45
Underneath each came forth two mighty wings,
Such as befitting were so great a bird;
Sails of the sea I never saw so large.
No feathers had they, but as of a bat
Their fashion was; and he was waving them, 50
So that three winds proceeded forth there-from.[10]
Thereby Cocytus wholly was congealed.
With six eyes did he weep, and down three chins
Trickled the tear-drops and the bloody drivel.
At every mouth he with his teeth was crunching 55
A sinner, in the manner of a brake,
So that he three of them tormented thus.
To him in front the biting was as naught
Unto the clawing, for sometimes the spine
Utterly stripped of all the skin remained. 60
"That soul up there which has the greatest pain,"

*Hell, the kingdom of pain and sorrow.

Canto XXXIV: Lucifer, King of Hell

The Master said, "is Judas Iscariot;
With head inside, he plies his legs without.
Of the two others, who head downward are,
The one who hangs from the black jowl is Brutus; 65
See how he writhes himself, and speaks no word.
And the other, who so stalwart seems, is Cassius.[11]
But night is reascending, and 'tis time[12]
That we depart, for we have seen the whole."
As seemed him good, I clasped him round the neck, 70
And he the vantage seized of time and place,
And when the wings were opened wide apart,
He laid fast hold upon the shaggy sides;
From fell to fell descended downward then
Between the thick hair and the frozen crust. 75
When we were come to where the thigh revolves

Exactly on the thickness of the haunch,
The Guide, with labor and with hard-drawn breath,
Turned round his head where he had had his legs,[13]
And grappled to the hair, as one who mounts, 80
So that to Hell I thought we were returning.
"Keep fast thy hold, for by such stairs as these,"
The Master said, panting as one fatigued,
"Must we perforce depart from so much evil."
Then through the opening of a rock he issued, 85
And down upon the margin seated me;
Then tow'rds me he outstretched his wary step.
I lifted up mine eyes and thought to see
Lucifer in the same way I had left him;
And I beheld him upward hold his legs. 90
And if I then became disquieted,
Let stolid people think who do not see
What the point is beyond which I had passed.[14]
"Rise up," the Master said, "upon thy feet;
The way is long, and difficult the road, 95
And now the sun to middle-tierce returns."[15]
It was not any palace corridor
There where we were, but dungeon natural,
With floor uneven and unease of light.
"Ere from the abyss I tear myself away, 100
My Master," said I when I had arisen,
"To draw me from an error speak a little;
Where is the ice? and how is this one fixed
Thus upside down? and how in such short time
From eve to morn has the sun made his transit?"[16] 105
And he to me: "Thou still imaginest
Thou art beyond the centre, where I grasped
The hair of the fell* worm,[17] who mines the world.
That side thou wast, so long as I descended;
When round I turned me, thou didst pass the point 110
To which things heavy draw from every side,

*Fierce.

And now beneath the hemisphere, art come
Opposite that which overhangs the vast
Dry-land, and 'neath whose cope* was put to death
The Man† who without sin was born and lived. 115
Thou hast thy feet upon the little sphere
Which makes the other face of the Judecca.[18]
Here it is morn when it is evening there;
And he who with his hair a stairway made us
Still fixed remaineth as he was before. 120
Upon this side he fell down out of heaven;
And all the land, that whilom‡ here emerged,
For fear of him made of the sea a veil,
And came to our hemisphere; and peradventure
To flee from him, what on this side appears 125
Left the place vacant here, and back recoiled."[19]
A place there is below, from Beelzebub[20]
As far receding as the tomb extends,
Which not by sight is known, but by the sound
Of a small rivulet, that there descendeth 130
Through chasm within the stone, which it has gnawed
With course that winds about and slightly falls.
The Guide and I into that hidden road
Now entered,[21] to return to the bright world;
And without care of having any rest 135
We mounted up, he first and I the second,
Till I beheld through a round aperture
Some of those beauteous things which Heaven doth bear;
Thence we came forth to rebehold the stars.[22]

*Canopy.
†Christ.
‡Once.

Endnotes

CANTO I

1. (p. 3) *Midway:* According to biblical tradition (Psalms 90:10), man's lifespan covers "three score and ten," or seventy years. Born in 1265, Dante would be midway in his life's journey in 1300, also the year of a papal jubilee proclaimed by Dante's nemesis, Pope Boniface VIII. There is general agreement that the actual day of Dante's descent into Hell is Friday, March 25. In 1300, March 25 was Good Friday; March 25 was also considered the birth date of Adam, the day of Christ's Incarnation, and therefore also the day of the Annunciation.

2. (p. 3) *the journey of our life:* Medieval Christians saw life as a journey or a pilgrimage, the final goal of which was God. The fact that Dante the Poet refers to this journey as that of "our life" rather than "my life" invites the reader to consider Dante the Pilgrim as Everyman.

3. (p. 3) *I found myself:* Dante's discovery that his life is lost to sin comes as a sudden shock. By mixing first-person plural ("our life" in l. 1) with a first-person singular ("I found myself"), Dante the Poet links the personal journey of Dante the Pilgrim with that taken by all of humanity.

4. (p. 3) *of the good:* In spite of the fear that struck Dante the Pilgrim upon entering the dark wood and the bitterness of remembering this experience, Dante the Poet feels compelled to describe the good he found there—God's mercy in allowing him to experience the vision of salvation through his journey.

5. (p. 3) *in my heart's lake:* In Dante's time, the "lake" of the heart, where blood gathered, was also considered to be the seat of the emotion of fear in the body.

6. (p. 3) *as he:* This is the first of the hundreds of celebrated epic similes in *The Divine Comedy*. It is based on lines in Virgil's *Aeneid*, Book I, where the Poet describes an exhausted Aeneas landing

on the coast of Carthage after a shipwreck. In canto II: 32, Dante will protest to his guide Virgil that he is neither Aeneas nor Saint Paul (both of whom supposedly visited the other world), but, in fact, Dante the Poet presents Dante the Pilgrim as following in the tracks of both the classical hero and the Christian apostle.

7. (p. 4) *the firm foot:* Literally, Dante refers to the left, or bottom, foot being employed to anchor the Pilgrim on the hill as he advances with the right foot. According to Christian tradition, the left foot was identified with the will and the right foot with the intellect. Man was defined as *homo claudus* (limping man), his wounds being the result of Adam's original sin.

8. (p. 4) *A panther:* Dante calls this first of three threatening beasts a *lonza* in Italian, which Longfellow translates as "panther" but which most recent translators render as "leopard." According to medieval lore, the *lonza* was the fruit of crossbreeding between a lion and a leopard. No more vexing textual problem appears in the *Inferno* than the identification of the three beasts that confront Dante the Pilgrim. Early Dante commentators interpreted the three animals that appear—the spotted panther/leopard, the lion, and the she-wolf—as representing three of the seven deadly sins (respectively lust, pride, and avarice). Others link the beasts to envy, pride, and avarice. Still others associate the three beasts with qualities that Virgil, when outlining the system of Hell's punishment of sins, describes in canto XI: 81–82: Incontinence, Malice, and insane Bestiality. What is clear in all discussions of these puzzling animals is that the three beasts represent three different categories of human sin, and that they all threaten to terminate the journey of Dante the Pilgrim.

9. (p. 4) *those beauteous things:* It was thought that when God (described as "the Love Divine" in l. 39) created the universe and the heavenly bodies ("those beauteous things"), the sun was in conjunction with the constellation of Aries. This supposedly happened on March 25, the same day Dante and his contemporaries believed the Annunciation, the Incarnation, and the Crucifixion occurred.

10. (p. 5) *E'en such made me that beast withouten peace:* Dante's second simile compares his stomach-wrenching fear upon seeing the beasts to the feeling experienced by a merchant or gambler who risks

a profit or a bet and in an instant realizes that he has lost his chance of gain.

11. (p. 5) *"Have pity on me":* In the original Italian, Dante the Pilgrim's first spoken words are in Latin, *Miserere di me.*

12. (p. 5) *"Not man; man once I was":* The shade is of Virgil, the Roman epic poet. He was born in 70 B.C. in the era of Julius Caesar (referred to as "Sub Julio" in l. 70) and died in 19 B.C. during the reign of Augustus Caesar. In Virgil's epic poem, the *Aeneid,* the Poet describes the foundation of the Roman Empire by refugees from Troy, and the work contains a famous journey to the underworld of the classical Hell by its protagonist, Aeneas. While many commentators have interpreted Virgil as the symbol, or the allegory, of human reason, Dante presents his guide as the shade of a specific historic individual and not an abstraction. He is a real person born near the northern Italian town of Mantua.

13. (p. 5) *"art thou that Virgilius":* Dante chooses Virgil (or, in Latin, Publius Vergilius Maro) as his guide through Hell for a variety of important reasons. As author of the *Aeneid,* he too created a literary figure who visits Hell. Virgil thus knows the way. Secondly, he was both a poet and an Italian poet: Dante is not above considerations of Italian patriotism, and he certainly believed that a great poet (particularly a classical poet) represented one of humanity's highest repositories of learning. Christians interpreted Virgil's Fourth Eclogue incorrectly as predicting the birth of Christ, and because of this, Virgil represents for Dante the perfect mediator between the classical world before the arrival of Christ and the postclassical, Christian era in which he lived. Finally, in the Middle Ages, Virgil was also considered something of a necromancer, or magician, and while he guides Dante the Pilgrim through Hell, Virgil will need all of the superhuman powers he can summon up. No stranger to the sin of pride, Dante the Poet could imagine no other individual but the greatest epic poet of Roman antiquity as the man he deserved as the guide for his alter ego, Dante the Pilgrim.

14. (p. 5) *The beautiful style:* While some of Dante's more serious poems composed before *The Divine Comedy* may well reflect the high-tragic style of Virgil's epic poetry, in general Dante's poetic style is diametrically opposed to the constant drive in Virgil's work to main-

tain a "high" style. Dante's epic style is original precisely because he mixes levels of style, both the noble and tragic, as well as the humble and comic.

15. (p. 6) *famous Sage:* Dante and his contemporaries considered classical poets not only to be literary figures but also learned men, paragons of wisdom—that is, sages. Farther on in the poem (in canto IV: 110), Dante will call Homer, Virgil, Horace, Ovid, and Lucan "sages," and he uses this term again in *Purgatory* XXIII: 8 to describe Virgil and Statius.

16. (p. 6) *'Twixt Feltro and Feltro:* Virgil's prediction that a greyhound (*veltro* in Italian) will come to save Italy is one of the most controversial passages in the *Inferno*. Most commentators identify the greyhound with Cangrande della Scala, who ruled the northern Italian city of Verona between 1308 and 1329. Cangrande's birthplace of Verona is located between the towns of Feltro and Montefeltro. Two other such political prophecies are to be found in *Purgatory* XXXIII: 37–45; and *Paradise* XXVII: 142–148.

17. (p. 6) *Euryalus, Turnus, Nisus, of their wounds:* In Virgil's *Aeneid*, Camilla was the daughter of King Metabus, who was killed fighting against the Trojans. Turnus also died fighting the Trojans, while Euryalus and Nisus were young Trojans killed in the invasion of Italy. See the *Aeneid*, Books IX and XII.

18. (p. 6) *second death:* For Dante, the first death is that of the physical body, while the second death—that of the soul after it is condemned during the Last Judgment—is far more horrifying.

19. (p. 6) *"those who contented are . . . to the blessed people":* Hell's punishments are eternal, while Purgatory's are temporary. Thus souls condemned only to the purifying punishments of Purgatory are "contented" because they know their eventual salvation is guaranteed.

20. (p. 7) *"A soul shall be for that than I more worthy":* Virgil alludes to the fact that Beatrice will eventually replace him as Dante the Pilgrim's guide, since, as a pagan poet, Virgil is only able to understand a part of God's divine plan of salvation.

21. (p. 7) *rebellious:* While it is difficult to conceive of Virgil rebelling against a Christ he could not have known, as a pagan he was guilty of original sin and in spite of his many personal merits, he will be forever denied the blessedness known by the souls who

reach Paradise. It should be remembered that Dante the Poet has created a fiction bordering on heresy by placing Virgil and other classical poets he admired in a Christian Limbo, an act of poetic license that the Catholic Church would never have sanctioned.

22. (p. 7) *portal of Saint Peter:* There is no gate guarded by Saint Peter in Dante's Paradise. Most commentators believe this line refers, instead, to the gate of Purgatory, since in Purgatory IX: 104–128, we learn that a gate is guarded by an angel who received the keys to it from Saint Peter. It is, of course, possible that Dante does also refer here to the popular belief that Saint Peter guards the "pearly gates."

CANTO II

1. (p. 8) *Day was departing:* An entire day has passed since Dante the Pilgrim began the futile attempt to climb the mountain.

2. (p. 8) *I the only one:* Since Dante the Pilgrim is a living human being and Virgil is a shade, Dante can technically describe himself as alone.

3. (p. 8) *Made myself ready to sustain the war, both of the way and likewise of the woe:* Dante the Pilgrim must first overcome both the physical dangers along the way of his journey but even more important, he must also learn to overcome the pity (*pietade,* a term Longfellow renders as "woe") he will feel when he observes the sufferings of the damned. As shall become clearer in later sections of the poem, one of the most important lessons Dante the Pilgrim needs to learn in Hell is that God's punishments are perfectly just. Human pity for the damned is a sure sign of spiritual weakness. Dante the Poet, of course, has already learned this lesson and is merciless to the damned, since his superior and subsequent perspective is derived from completing the journey to Paradise that he reports in the poem.

4. (p. 8) *memory:* By claiming that Dante the Pilgrim remembers a real journey, Dante the Poet rejects the notion that the journey through the three realms of the afterlife is merely a vision or a dream. The fiction of the entire poem is that the journey is real.

5. (p. 8) *O Muses:* This invocation of the poetic muses imitates Dante's model, the classic epic of Virgil and others. The fact that Dante invokes the Muses in canto II rather than in canto I (unlike

similar invocations in canto I of *Purgatory* and canto I of *Paradise*) suggests to most critics that Dante considers *Inferno* I as a kind of prologue to the entire poem. In fact, the *Inferno* contains 34 cantos (one prologue and 33 others), while both *Purgatory* and *Paradise* contain 33 cantos. The total number is 100, a figure Dante and his contemporaries considered a perfect number.

6. (p. 8) *O high genius:* This refers either to Dante's own genius as a poet or, as some critics claim, to Virgil's genius or even to the genius of God Himself. If the praise refers to a request for God's assistance, Dante thus invokes help from both classical and Christian forces.

7. (p. 8) *of Silvius the parent:* The parent of Silvius was Aeneas (*Aeneid,* Book VI). According to Virgil, Aeneas descended into the Underworld while still alive ("while yet corruptible," as Longfellow renders the original Italian in l. 14).

8. (p. 8) *the empyreal heaven:* In the Ptolemaic system of the universe, the Empyrean Heaven is the tenth, or outermost, sphere. Dante and his contemporaries considered this place to be the residence of God.

9. (p. 8) *the holy place, wherein sits the successor of the greatest Peter:* As the founder of ancient Rome, Aeneas also served to found "the holy place" of the Eternal City, the residence of the Christian popes, the successors to Saint Peter.

10. (p. 9) *the Chosen Vessel:* Saint Paul is called "the Chosen Vessel" in the Bible, Acts 9:15. In II Corinthians 12: 2–4, Paul recounts his ascent to Heaven while still alive. Dante and other medieval readers would also have been familiar with the *Visio Sancti Pauli,* an account of Paul's journey to the kingdom of the dead.

11. (p. 9) *I not Aeneas am, I am not Paul:* While Dante the Pilgrim complains that he is neither Aeneas nor Paul (both of whom supposedly visited Hell before him), Dante the Poet in fact implies that his protagonist is precisely the successor to both Aeneas and Paul, combining some characteristics of both the classical hero and the Christian saint.

12. (p. 9) *And by new thoughts doth his intention change . . . because, in thinking, I consumed the emprise:* In other words, "I undid the enterprise": Dante is saying that the time that elapsed between the mo-

ment he decided to undertake the journey to the moment he became afraid to do so was instantaneous—it was as rapid as thought itself.

13. (p. 9) *the Magnanimous:* Here Dante the Poet calls Virgil magnanimous (meaning courageous) to contrast his apparent courage to Dante the Pilgrim's cowardice.

14. (p. 9) *"As false sight doth a beast, when he is shy":* Dante is referring to the way a beast shies away from a shadow.

15. (p. 9) *"Among those... who are in suspense":* As we shall learn in canto IV, the virtuous pagan souls, such as Virgil, dwell in Limbo in a kind of suspension—suspended or set apart physically from the rest of Hell proper, and suspended spiritually from the damned undergoing punishment.

16. (p. 9) *a fair, saintly Lady:* Beatrice, Dante's beloved muse who died in 1290 and, the Poet believes, surely dwells in Heaven, takes pity on the Pilgrim's plight and begins a chain of events to rescue him that will involve not only Saint Lucìa or Lucy, but also the Virgin Mary. To Dante, Beatrice is indeed saintly, and in his *La Vita Nuova* (*The New Life*), he celebrates her as a woman who brings salvation.

17. (p. 9) *long-lasting as the world:* This the first of many incidences in the *Inferno* in which its inhabitants consider earthly fame to be their only means of immortality, since their souls will never reach the realm of the blessed in Paradise.

18. (p. 10) *"Full often will I praise thee unto him":* It is unclear why Beatrice promises to praise Virgil to God, since there is no chance of salvation for him, just as it is puzzling that Virgil immediately recognizes Beatrice in Limbo, where we shall subsequently discover he resides—he died in 19 B.C., many centuries before Beatrice's earthly existence.

19. (p. 10) *"O Lady of virtue... the lesser circles":* Virgil is claiming that Beatrice has a universal importance for all mankind and influences human affairs in the sublunary and sinful world of earth, where Fortune controls human destiny through divine guidance.

20. (p. 10) *"tell me why thou dost not shun the here descending down into this centre":* Inhabitants of Paradise, like Beatrice, follow the Ptolemaic system and consider Earth to be the center of the universe.

Hell, in the center of Earth, is therefore a place that they desire to avoid.

21. (p. 10) *"That misery of yours attains me not":* As part of God's divine plan and His generosity, the blessed in Paradise are not capable of feeling pity for the souls of the damned or the shades in Limbo. Dante the Pilgrim, however, must be purged of the weak emotion of pity during his journey through Hell.

22. (p. 11) *Lucìa:* Saint Lucy of Syracuse was a Christian martyr considered to be the patron saint of eye ailments. Her name means "light," and Beatrice will refer significantly to her "shining eyes" in l. 116, "her shining eyes she turned away." Lucìa returns in *Purgatory* IX: 52–63 and again in *Paradise* XXXII: 137–138.

23. (p. 11) *the ancient Rachel:* In Genesis, Rachel is the sister of Leah and the wife of Jacob. According to Christian tradition, Rachel is a symbol of the contemplative life and Leah is a symbol of the active life. Rachel is seated near Beatrice when Dante the Pilgrim reaches Paradise.

24. (p. 11) *the vulgar herd:* Lucìa reminds Beatrice that in Dante's life on Earth as a poet, her influence as a real, living woman raised him above his contemporaries. Dante's *Vita Nuova* recounts this influence.

25. (p. 11) *"Beside that flood, where ocean has no vaunt":* This is the same river, or flood, that Dante calls a sea in canto I: 22–27. Since this water does not flow into the ocean, the ocean has no vaunt, or claim, over it.

26. (p. 11) *that wild beast:* This is the she-wolf of canto I: 49–60 that initially prevented Dante the Pilgrim from climbing the mountain.

27. (p. 11) *the beautiful mountain's short ascent:* Unable to climb the mountain by the easy, short path, Dante the Pilgrim (along with the reader of the poem) will be forced to follow the more arduous, difficult path, enabling him to understand fully the organization of Hell and the system of its punishments.

28. (p. 12) *the deep and savage way:* This is a reference to the "forest dark" of canto I: 2 and the "arduous pass" of canto II: 12. The journey proper may now commence, and it will be both a literal passage through the physical territory of Hell and a spiritual journey through the dark forest of human sin.

CANTO III

1. (p. 14) *"Created me divine Omnipotence, the highest Wisdom and the primal Love":* Omnipotence (or Power), Wisdom, and Love are qualities traditionally associated with the three persons of the Holy Trinity.

2. (p. 14) *the good of intellect:* This is ultimately God, defined as the source of all truth. Aristotle, in his *Ethics,* defines truth as the good of the intellect.

3. (p. 14) *the secret things:* These things are secret because they are hidden from the living, since few mortals have ever visited Hell before Dante's arrival.

4. (p. 15) *Whence I, at the beginning, wept:* The first sensory impressions of Hell derive from the sound of the wailing souls, and the pilgrim's tearful reaction demonstrates that he has yet to learn to disregard the human sentiment of pity and to consider the punishments the damned receive as just.

5. (p. 15) *with sound of hands:* Sinners strike themselves with open palms in their misery, beating their breasts.

6. (p. 15) *"those who lived withouten infamy or praise":* Entering what is the Vestibule of Hell, the Pilgrim first encounters the souls of sinners who in life were neither horrible nor meritorious—they were merely neutral or lukewarm. Dante found such neutrality over important questions so reprehensible that he leaves these sinners unworthy even of a special place in Hell.

7. (p. 15) *"Of Angels, who have not rebellious been, nor faithful were to God, but were for self":* This group of sinners represents the neutral angels, who refused to take sides when Lucifer rebelled against God.

8. (p. 15) *a banner:* The rebel angels from Heaven and the lukewarm on Earth are punished according to the nature of their sin. They are condemned for eternity to chase aimlessly after a banner without an insignia. As their sin involved taking no position, now they are condemned forever to follow a neutral cause (the lack of insignia underlining the emptiness of their hellish fate). This first punishment represents a perfect example of the governing principle

behind Hell's punishments, the famous *contrapasso* of canto XXVIII: 142, which Longfellow renders as "counterpoise." Punishments either resemble the sin (as in this case) or may even be exactly the opposite of a sin. At any rate, they are always appropriate to the sin, are punished in quite specific ways, and are always strikingly graphic.

9. (p. 16) *Who made through cowardice the great refusal:* Most commentators identify this figure with Pope Celestine V, who resigned the papacy five months after his election in 1294. It was rumored that another of Dante's least favorite figures, Cardinal Benedetto Caetani, who succeeded Celestine as Pope Boniface VIII, had hidden in Celestine's bedroom and pretended to be an angel urging the aged pope to abdicate! One obstacle to identifying this figure with Celestine is the fact that Celestine was renowned for his humility and canonized in 1313. Other suggestions include Esau, who in Genesis renounces his rights to Jacob, and Pontius Pilate, whose refusal to pronounce a sentence on Christ indirectly led to his Crucifixion.

10. (p. 16) *the dismal shore of Acheron:* In classical mythology and literature, this is one of the five rivers of Hades, the others being Styx, Phlegethon, Cocytus, and Lethe (all of which Dante will eventually include in his poem). Dante discusses the Acheron in canto XIV: 112–120, and Virgil describes it in the *Aeneid,* Book VI.

11. (p. 16) *An old man:* In Greek mythology, Charon is the boatman who ferries the souls of the dead across the river Styx to Hades. In the *Inferno,* Charon fulfills this task across the Acheron from the Vestibule of Hell to Hell proper.

12. (p. 17) *"By other ways, by other ports . . . there where is power to do that which is willed":* Charon recognizes that unlike the other shades, Dante is alive and a physical being. He initially refuses him passage until Virgil informs Charon that Dante's journey is ordered by God in Heaven ("there where is power to do that which is willed"). The fact that Charon declares the pilgrim will come "by other ports" is a prophecy that Dante will eventually reach Purgatory and ultimately Paradise.

13. (p. 17) *As in the autumn-time . . . a new troop assembles:* This majestic simile combines two references to Virgil's poetry: *Aeneid,* Book VI, and *Georgics,* Book II.

14. (p. 17) *the courteous Master:* Virgil is courteous because he answers the Pilgrim's questions before they are posed, explaining that the damned actually desire their punishments.

15. (p. 18) *The recollection bathes me still with sweat:* Here Dante the Poet interjects his personal memory of the event when he, as Dante the Pilgrim, encountered this frightful scene in a real journey, not in a dream. It is always important to bear in mind that Dante presents the events he relates as real, as opposed to something remembered from a dream vision—this is the key to Dante's poetics in the *Inferno.*

16. (p. 18) *And as a man whom sleep doth seize I fell:* Dante the Poet remains unable to explain why he swooned into unconsciousness, and the reader is not given a precise description of exactly how he crossed the river. The pilgrim will swoon again at the conclusion of *Inferno* V.

CANTO IV

1. (p. 19) *"Let us descend now into the blind world," began the Poet, pallid utterly:* The world of Limbo, where Virgil resides, is "blind," or dark, without the benefit of the sun. Virgil's pallor reflects his compassion for his companions in Limbo, not pity for the souls undergoing harsher punishments in Hell proper.

2. (p. 19) *The foremost circle:* Limbo is the first circle of Hell.

3. (p. 20) *"without hope we live on in desire":* According to Church doctrine, only infants who were not baptized inhabited Limbo after Christ harrowed Hell, when, after his death and before his earthly resurrection, he took the Hebrew patriarchs and matriarchs out of Hell and up to Paradise with him. Dante's addition of the virtuous pagans to Limbo is a bold invention rooted in his love for classical antiquity. Nevertheless, the virtuous pagans are denied the vision of God, the goal toward which their thwarted desire is directed.

4. (p. 20) *in that Limbo were suspended:* The virtuous pagans are literally suspended, or separated, from the geographical location of Hell proper and are figuratively suspended from its tortures. The word Limbo is derived from the Latin *limbus,* meaning edge, hem, or border.

5. (p. 20) *a Mighty One:* The reference is to Christ during the Harrowing of Hell. In medieval and Renaissance art, the Harrowing

of Hell was a popular theme. In the period between the Crucifixion and the Resurrection, Christ—usually represented carrying a white banner with a red cross—descended into Hell to rescue certain souls held there since the beginning of the world. There is little basis in scripture for this event, but by the fourth century A.D. it had become an article of Catholic faith. During the course of *The Divine Comedy,* the following Old Testament figures are mentioned as having been saved: Adam, Eve, Abel, Noah, Moses, Abraham, David, Jacob, Jacob's twelve sons, Rachel, Sarah, Rebecca, Judith, Ruth, Samuel, Rahab, Solomon, Joshua, Judas Maccabeus, and Ezechiel.

6. (p. 21) *"Never were any human spirits saved":* This line basically affirms Church dogma that no one without baptism can be saved. The souls that Christ removed from Hell during the Harrowing of Hell were saved by a special and theologically exceptional dispensation.

7. (p. 21) *I saw a fire that overcame a hemisphere of darkness:* The light, which in line 106 we will learn emanates from "a noble castle's foot," overcomes Hell's darkness, because it is from the place where the virtuous pagans of Limbo reside.

8. (p. 21) *honorable:* The encounter of the Pilgrim and the great pagan poets continuously plays upon variants of the word "honor," underlying the fact that Dante considered poetry to be the highest human vocation.

9. (p. 21) *"All honor be to the pre-eminent Poet":* The reader ultimately realizes that this address is actually intended for Virgil, but this line suggests it is also meant for Dante. This ambiguity is surely intentional, underscoring Dante's high regard for his own poem.

10. (p. 21) *Four mighty shades . . . the last is Lucan:* Although Dante was unable to read Greek, he shared Virgil's opinion that Homer represented the greatest achievement in classical poetry. Here Homer is pictured with a sword, underlining the bellicose content of his two epics, the *Iliad* and the *Odyssey*. Dante celebrates Horace for his satirical poetry. In Dante's time and afterward, Ovid's *Metamorphoses* represented the most popular treatment of classical mythology. Lucan's *Pharsalia,* an epic poem about the Roman civil wars between Caesar and Pompey, was popular in Dante's time but is not widely read today.

11. (p. 21) *of the song pre-eminent:* Dante believed that epic poetry was the noblest form of poetry.

12. (p. 22) *one of their own band:* While few poets have ever dared to compare themselves with the likes of Homer or Virgil, as Dante does here, subsequent estimations of Dante's accomplishments in *The Divine Comedy* would affirm the Florentine poet's high estimation of his genius. However, the works he completed before his Christian epic would not have stood comparison with Homer, Virgil, Horace, or Ovid (Lucan is perhaps a borderline case).

13. (p. 22) *We came unto a noble castle's foot . . . through portals seven I entered with these Sages:* The picture of a noble castle with seven walls and seven gates, with a surrounding stream over which the great poets walk as if it were dry land, invites an allegorical interpretation. Medieval allegory, in which things represent abstract ideas, is extremely rare in Dante's poetry. The castle itself seems to reflect the highest degree of noble life possible without the benefit of Christian illumination. A number of suggestions have been made to explain the seven walls and gates: the seven liberal arts (the *quadrivium* of music, arithmetic, geometry, and astronomy and the *trivium* of grammar, logic, and rhetoric) or perhaps the seven virtues (the three Christian virtues of faith, hope, and charity and the four cardinal, or classical, virtues of justice, prudence, fortitude, and temperance).

14. (p. 22) *Electra:* This is the mother of Dardanus, founder of Troy, and not the female protagonist of several classic Greek tragedies.

15 (p. 22) *Hector and Aeneas:* Two Trojan warrior heroes: In the *Iliad,* Hector is the champion who Achilles kills in battle; according to Virgil's *Aeneid,* Aeneas founded Rome with other refugees from the destroyed Trojan capital.

16. (p. 22) *Caesar in armor with gerfalcon eyes:* Dante considered Julius Caesar (101–44 B.C.) to be Rome's first emperor; the Roman biographer Suetonius described Caesar as falcon-eyed.

17. (p. 22) *Camilla:* See canto 1, note 17.

18. (p. 22) *Penthesilea:* This warrior maiden and Queen of the Amazons came to the aid of Troy in the Trojan War and was killed by Achilles.

19. (p. 22) *King Latinus, who with Lavinia his daughter sat:* In the

Aeneid, Lavinia, daughter of Latinus, king of Latium, marries Aeneas after the Trojan champion defeats the forces of Turnus.

20. (p. 22) *Brutus:* Lucius Junius Brutus, called the "first Brutus" to distinguish him from the Brutus who assassinated Julius Caesar many years later, roused Rome against Tarquin the Proud after Tarquin had violated Lucretia's honor. As a result, the monarchy was abolished and the Roman Republic established. Dante's source is Livy's history of republican Rome, *Ab urbe condita.*

21. (p. 22) *Lucretia, Julia, Marcia, and Cornelia:* Julia, daughter of Julius Caesar, married Pompey in 54 B.C. to further her father's political ambitions; Marcia was the second wife of Cato of Utica; Cornelia was the daughter of Scipio Africanus. These three Roman matrons, plus the previously mentioned Lucretia, who committed suicide after losing her honor, symbolize the maternal virtues of ancient Rome.

22. (p. 22) *the Saladin:* Completely breaking with Church dogma, Dante places this famous "infidel" opponent of the Christian Crusaders (c.1138–1193) in Limbo, accepting the medieval reputation Saladin enjoyed for courtesy, clemency, and tolerance. Saladin's great antagonist in the Holy Land was Richard the Lion-Hearted, king of England.

23. (p. 23) *the Master I beheld of those who know.... There I beheld both Socrates and Plato:* Aristotle (384–322 B.C.), called the master philosopher, was the most important thinker for Dante's time. As a result of the Scholastic philosophy of Thomas of Aquinas, Aristotle's works were reconciled, in large measure, with Christian philosophy. It is significant that Dante has both Socrates and Plato pay homage to Aristotle, recognizing his preeminence.

24. (p. 23) *Democritus:* This Greek philosopher from Thrace (c.460–c.370 B.C.), a contemporary of Socrates, proposed a theory that explained the formation of the universe by the random encounter of atoms.

25. (p. 23) *Diogenes, Anaxagoras, and Thales:* The Greek philosopher Diogenes the Cynic (c.412–323 B.C.) believed in attaining virtue through self-control and scorned normal social conventions. Anaxagoras (500–428 B.C.) is a Greek pre-Socratic philosopher; in *Il Convivio* (*The Banquet*), Dante contrasts his explanations about the creation of the universe with theories of the Pythagoreans. Thales (born c.640 B.C.) founded the Greek Ionian school of philosophy and believed that water was the basis of all things.

26. (p. 23) *Zeno, Empedocles, and Heraclitus:* The three are Greek philosophers. Zeno (c.336–264 B.C.) was one of the founders of Stoic philosophy; Empedocles (c.490–430 B.C.) proposed that the four basic elements of the world are fire, air, earth, and water; and Heraclitus (c.540–480 B.C.) believed that fire was the basic form of matter.

27. (p. 23) *the good collector, Hight Dioscorides; and Orpheus:* Dioscorides, a Greek scientist (first century B.C.), wrote *De materia medica,* which until 1500 or so remained the authoritative work on the medicinal properties of herbs and plants. Orpheus is a mythical Greek poet who uses his lyre to charm men and animals; he descended into the Underworld in a futile attempt to rescue his wife, Eurydice.

28. (p. 23) *Tully and Livy, and moral Seneca:* Tully is the celebrated Roman orator, writer, and statesman Marcus Tullius Cicero (106–43 B.C.). Linus is a mythical Greek poet who Virgil identifies as the inventor of pastoral poetry. Lucias Annaeus Seneca (died A.D. 65), Roman philosopher, dramatist, and tutor to the Emperor Nero, wrote moral essays as well as dramatic works; Dante clearly indicates a preference for Seneca's moral essays by calling him "moral Seneca."

29. (p. 23) *Euclid, geometrician, and Ptolemy:* Euclid (fourth and third centuries B.C.) is a Greek mathematician from Alexandria whose *Elements* forms the basis of geometry. Ptolemy (active in Alexandria, A.D. 127–c.170) is a Greek mathematician and astronomer whose *Almagest* provided the dominant interpretation of the heavenly bodies and the universe's structure until overtaken by the Copernican system in the late Renaissance. Dante's views of the cosmos are heavily indebted to Ptolemy's theories, particularly the view that the planets and the sun revolve around the earth.

30. (p. 23) *Galen, Hippocrates, and Avicenna:* Galen (A.D. 129–c.201), a Greek physician who practiced in Alexandria and Rome, wrote numerous medical treatises that formed an important body of medical knowledge. Hippocrates (c.460–377 B.C.), the Greek physician, is considered to be the founder of the medical profession. Avicenna, or Ibn Sina (A.D. 980–1037), the best-known philosopher and physician of Islam in the Middle Ages, wrote numerous treatises in

Persian and Arabic, including important commentaries on the works of Galen and Aristotle.

31. (p. 23) *Averroes:* Also known as Ibn Rushd, this twelfth-century Arab scholar (c.1126–1198) from Moorish Spain wrote commentaries on Aristotle that were key texts for the medieval Christian, or Scholastic, understanding of the Greek philosopher; Thomas Aquinas, for instance, wrote important commentaries on his interpretations of Aristotle. Dante's inclusion of three "infidels"—Saladin, Avicenna, and Averroës—in Limbo represents a courageous intellectual choice, one that did not reflect the opinion of the Catholic Church. Nevertheless, Dante does not hesitate to condemn Muhammad (c.570–632), the founder of Islam, to the punishments of Hell (canto XXVIII: 22–31) with the sowers of religious discord. So, even though Dante was generous with his intellectual tolerance, there were limits to his religious tolerance.

CANTO V

1. (p. 25) *Down to the second:* As Virgil and Dante the Pilgrim descend, they enter the second circle of Hell, where, properly speaking, the real punishments begin. Carnal lust and sins of the flesh are punished here, and it is important to remember that although Dante considers these sins to be the least serious (because they are punished in a location that is closest to the top of Hell), they are still heinous enough to merit eternal damnation. The second circle occupies, or "begirds," less space, because the pit of Hell is shaped like an inverted funnel that gets smaller and smaller the farther down one descends.

2. (p. 25) *There standeth Minos. . . . as grades he wishes it should be thrust down:* As is frequently the case in the *Inferno,* Dante employs a figure from classical mythology—here Minos, the son of Europa and Zeus—to supply the monsters that populate his Christian Hell. Minos was supposedly so just that he was made judge of the dead, a function he serves in the *Aeneid,* Book VI. However, Dante has transformed him from a human being into a frightening monster who serves as Hell's gatekeeper and determines the circle of Hell in which a sinner belongs. He wraps his tail around the sinner the number of times equivalent to the circle in which the sinner must be con-

demned, then flings the unfortunate wretch to the appropriate location. Like Charon, he is splendidly depicted in Michelangelo's *Last Judgment* in the Sistine Chapel.

3. (p. 25) *"Look how thou enterest, and in whom thou trustest. . . . and ask no further question":* Minos is trying to shake the Pilgrim's trust in his guide. Meanwhile, in rebuking Minos, Virgil employs the same words that he used earlier with Charon in canto III: 95–96.

4. (p. 26) *The infernal hurricane:* The punishment of the "carnal malefactors" in the second circle involves a hellish wind that blows the sinners about as they wail, just as their subjugation of reason to lust in life tossed them around like the birds (starlings and cranes) Dante mentions in the famous similes just below, in ll. 40–48.

5. (p. 26) *before the precipice:* In the orignal Italian, the term that Longfellow translates as "precipice" is *ruina,* which usually means "ruin"; this term and its interpretation have provoked a great deal of critical discussion. Later, in canto XII, Dante uses the word to refer to the crack in the wall of Hell caused by the earthquake that accompanied Christ's Crucifixion and Harrowing of Hell. Similar results of that unique event can also be seen in cantos XXI and XXIV.

6. (p. 26) *Semiramis:* This legendary and lustful Queen of Assyria assumed power upon the death of her husband, Ninus; her territory encompassed the lands governed in Dante's times by Islamic sultans.

7. (p. 27) *"The next is she who killed herself for love, and broke faith with the ashes of Sichaeus":* In the *Aeneid,* Dido, the founder and Queen of Carthage, vows to remain faithful to the memory of her dead husband, Sichaeus. Her passion for Aeneas, however, leads to her suicide when he abandons her to continue his journey. Dante offers no reason for not including Dido with the other suicides he mentions in canto XIII.

8. (p. 27) *Cleopatra the voluptuous:* The daughter of the last king of Egypt before Rome conquered that territory, Cleopatra was famous for her lustful liaisons with Julius Caesar and Mark Antony. When her charms failed to move the much colder Octavianus (later Emperor Augustus), Cleopatra committed suicide. Again, Dante offers no reason why he does not include her with his other suicides in canto XIII.

9. (p. 27) *Helen I saw, for whom so many ruthless seasons revolved:* According to Greek mythology and Homer's *Iliad,* Helen, wife of King Menelaus of Sparta, launched the Trojan War when Paris carried her off to Troy.

10. (p. 27) *the great Achilles, who at the last hour combated with Love:* Dante could not read Greek and therefore did not read Homer's *Iliad* or any of the Greek tragedies dealing with the aftermath of the Trojan War. His knowledge of the Trojan War comes primarily from the *Aeneid* (which contains far more information about what happened in the aftermath of the war than the *Iliad* does). He also knew a number of sources that were popular in the medieval period, such as Dictys the Cretan's *Diary of the Trojan War* (a Latin version of what was supposedly a Greek diary written by a soldier in the war) and Dares Phrygian's Latin *History of the Destruction of Troy,* which presents a personal account of the conflict from the Trojan side. Both works appeared during the fourth through the sixth centuries and were based upon earlier Greek originals. Based on these works, Dante understood Achilles to be a knight fatally in love with Polyxena, Priam's daughter. According to the non-Homeric and non-Virgilian sources Dante followed, Achilles died because of lust and his place here is appropriate. Thinking he was to meet Polyxena in the Temple of Apollo, Achilles was lured into an ambush by Paris, who killed him by shooting an arrow into the only place he was vulnerable, his heel.

11. (p. 27) *Paris:* The son of Priam, king of Troy, Paris is more famous for his way with women than for his skills as a warrior, and the fact that his passion for Helen, wife of the King of Sparta, began the Trojan War is more than sufficient reason to place him in this second circle.

12. (p. 27) *Tristan:* According to a number of Old French romances with versions in both German and Italian, this courtly knight and nephew of King Mark of Cornwall, has a love affair with Mark's betrothed, Iseut, or Isolt.

13. (p. 27) *"O Poet, willingly speak would I to those two":* Thus begins what is the most famous and most misunderstood encounter Dante the Pilgrim experiences in his journey toward Paradise. Francesca da Polenta, daughter of the ruler of Ravenna, was the wife of Gianciotto

Malatesta, second son of the Lord of Rimini. However, she carried on a love affair for years after her marriage with Paolo Malatesta, Gianciotto's brother, before Gianciotto discovered this and killed them. The highly rhetorical style of Francesca's speech to the pilgrim is clearly designed to win his sympathy, just as her references to Love in three different tercets make reference to Dante's own lyric poetry composed before *The Divine Comedy*. Like generations of readers afterward (especially in the Romantic period), Dante the Pilgrim forgets the righteous indignation he should feel for any sin—no matter how attractively it is presented, as in Francesca's monologue—and he is carried away by his feelings for her plight. Perhaps the Pilgrim should have asked himself why Paolo, the other unhappy lover of the pair, says nothing and only wails during their encounter—unlike Francesca, who wants to win the pilgrim's sympathy, Paolo acts as miserable as she pretends not to be, no doubt because Francesca may be lying and he knows the bitter truth.

14. (p. 28) *"Caïna waiteth him who quenched our life!":* Gianciotto Malatesta is still alive when Dante supposedly takes his journey in 1300. As one who betrayed and murdered his kin, there is already a spot reserved for him in Caïna, one of the four parts of Cocytus, the lowest part of Hell. Malatesta died in 1304.

15. (p. 29) *"Galeotto was the book and he who wrote it.":* Because of this verse, *galeotto* came to mean "panderer" in Italian. In the Old French romance *Lancelot du Lac,* Galeotto, or Galehot, was a go-between in the love affair of Queen Guinevere and Lancelot. Thus both the book Paolo and Francesca read and its author were panderers in the passion that sprung up between the couple.

16. (p. 29) *And fell, even as a dead body falls:* While Francesca's seductive words cause Dante the Pilgrim to faint from pity, Dante the Poet is unswayed by her rhetoric and has placed her where she belongs—in Hell. However, the Poet is not above using this reaction on the Pilgrim's part as a convenient transitional device to the first line of the next canto, "At the return of consciousness."

CANTO VI

1. (p. 31) *the third circle:* In the third circle of Hell, the gluttons are punished. Like the people they once were on Earth who thought

of nothing but wallowing in food and drink and producing nothing but garbage and offal, they are now condemned to wallow in filth for eternity.

2. (p. 31) *Cerberus, monster cruel and uncouth . . . the great worm:* Dante's model is the three-headed dog guarding the entrance to the underworld in Virgil's *Aeneid,* Book VI. Dante has given his Cerberus some human features (in particular, a beard). Three heads with three mouths make an appropriate guardian of the gluttons, but the number three also prefigures the appearance of Lucifer in canto XXXIV, where in l. 108 Dante refers to the ruler of Hell as a "fell," or evil worm, just as he calls Cerberus "the great worm." Lucifer has one head with three faces, thus resembling the physical appearance of the three-headed infernal guard dog.

3. (p. 32) *Took of the earth . . . threw it into those rapacious gullets:* In the *Aeneid,* Book VI, the Sibyl leading Aeneas through the underworld tosses Cerberus some honey cakes. Now Virgil, the author of that poem, manages the same feat with simple dirt.

4. (p. 32) *We passed across the shadows:* The physical laws governing Hell are often strange. While the shades, or shadows, of the damned are not material, they can nevertheless suffer physical punishment or, as here, support the Pilgrim's weight (Virgil, of course, is weightless). It is also important to remember that although Dante passes through a number of hideous punishments (such as the terrible rain in the third circle), he and Virgil do not usually feel this or any other punishment during the journey. In other words, the physics of Hell follow laws that Dante himself invents to suit his poetic purposes.

5. (p. 32) *"Thyself wast made before I was unmade":* That is to say, "You were born before I died." The shade expects Dante the Pilgrim to recognize him, since they were both alive at the same time in Florence.

6. (p. 32) *Ciacco:* We know little about this figure, except that he was a Florentine and Dante's contemporary. The name is probably a nickname for "pig" or "hog" and, by implication, "filthy" or "swinish." Boccaccio's *Decameron,* Day IX, Story 8, contains a character by the same name, but he was probably inspired by Dante.

Several dozen Florentines appear in *The Divine Comedy*, and most of them are in Hell.

7. (p. 32) *"thy wretchedness . . . to weep invites me":* Apparently, the Pilgrim has not yet learned that showing compassion in the face of sin and sinners provides evidence of moral weakness. In canto V, Dante was moved to weep and to swoon over two self-professed "tragic" lovers. Now, his human compassion and patriotism are aroused by meeting one of his fellow Florentine citizens, and he inquires if any Florentines are just and asks why Florence has always been torn by internecine strife. When the subject of Florentine politics is brought up, the Pilgrim seems to forget all about the scene at hand—the nature and punishment of gluttony.

8. (p. 33) *And he to me . . . "The just are two, and are not understood there":* This is the first of some nine prophecies about events that touch Dante's personal life. There are three other such prophecies delivered by three characters in the *Inferno* (Farinata, canto X: 79–81; Brunetto Latini, canto XV: 55–57; and Vanni Fucci, canto XXIV: 143–150); four characters in *Purgatory* (Currado Malaspina, canto VIII: 133–139; Oderisi, canto XI: 139–141; Bonagiunta da Lucca, canto XXIV: 37–38; and Forese, canto XXIV: 82–90); and one in *Paradise* (Cacciaguida, XVII: 46–93). During Dante's era, there was a struggle between forces owing allegiance to the pope (the Guelphs) and those supporting the Holy Roman Emperor (the Ghibellines). In fact, however, these allegiances usually only reflected the struggle of factions with the various Italian city-states who sought allies outside their communes to continue their struggle. After defeating the Ghibellines in 1289, the Florentine Guelphs split into warring factions: the Whites, led by the Cerchi family (called the "rustic" party in l. 65, because many of them lived in the wooded outskirts of Florence), and the Blacks, led by the Donati family. In May of 1300, only a few weeks after the date of the Pilgrim's journey, the two parties collided, resulting in the expulsion of the Blacks from the city in 1301. However, the Blacks returned in 1302 ("within three suns," as the Poet writes in l. 68, meaning "within three years"). They were assisted by the inaction of Pope Boniface VIII ("by force of him who now is on the coast," as noted in l. 69), and they drove the Whites (including Dante) into exile. The two just men are never

identified in Dante's poem, but many critics believe Dante refers to himself and to some other as yet unidentified person.

9. (p. 33) *"Farinata and Tegghiaio . . . Jacopo Rusticucci, Arrigo, and Mosca":* Forgetting about the instruction he should be receiving about the nature of the sin of gluttony and warming to talk of his native Florence, the Pilgrim asks the fates of a number of Florentines of his day and learns that "they are among the blacker souls" (l. 85), in various locations in Hell. Farinata degli Uberti will appear in canto X with the heretics. Tegghiaio Aldobrandini and Jacopo Rusticucci are among the sodomites in canto XVI. Mosca dei Lamberti is among the sowers of discord in canto XXVIII. Arrigo does not reappear later in the poem and has never been successfully identified by scholars.

10. (p. 33) *"But when thou art again in the sweet world, I pray thee to the mind of others bring me":* Ciacco's prophecy in ll. 64–75 (see note 8) and his conversation with the Pilgrim reveal another strange rule of Hell: Its inhabitants may foretell the future (such as the expulsion of Dante and the Whites from Florence within three years of the fictional date of the poem), and they may know or remember the past, but they know nothing about the present. It is part of their eternal punishment that they know nothing of their present reputation on earth, and, since earthly fame and family pride are two of the most characteristic qualities sought by the Florentines and Italians of Dante's time, the damned souls are eager for Dante the Pilgrim to return to the land of the living and report favorably on them. Conversely, they dread any truthful account of their sins.

11. (p. 34) *"Return unto thy science":* The Pilgrim's seemingly innocent question about whether punishments increase or decrease after the Last Judgment is answered sternly by Virgil, who orders him to return to his "science," which for that day could have meant only Aristotle. It has been suggested that the source of this idea is a commentary by Thomas Aquinas on Aristotle's *De anima.* The gist of the discussion about the souls after the Last Judgment is that the damned will feel more pain while the blessed will feel more pleasure as they are both, in a sense, "perfected."

12. (p. 34) *There we found Plutus:* The mythological figure overseeing the punishments in the next layer, the fourth circle, is the classical god of wealth (not to be confused with Pluto, ruler of the underworld). He is the perfect choice to preside over the torture of the avaricious and the prodigal.

CANTO VII

1. (p. 35) *"Papë Satàn, Papë Satàn, Aleppë!":* The first words Plutus speaks are generally considered to be gibberish. Though Virgil, "who all things knew" (l. 3), understands this strange language, no one else has managed to make any sense of it, although a number of interpretations have been advanced to explain their meaning. "Aleppë" might seem to suggest "aleph," the first letter in the Hebrew alphabet; "Papë" seems to suggest "papa" or "pope"; and "Satàn" obviously brings "Satan" to mind. But taken together these words make little sense. Perhaps the most amusing explanation comes from Benvenuto Cellini's *My Life* (II: 27). The sixteenth-century Florentine sculptor knew Dante's poem quite well and while living in Paris claimed that Dante must have learned this strange language from the howling judges and screaming magistrates in the Parisian courts, who entangled him in endless lawsuits.

2. (p. 35) *the proud adultery:* Longfellow takes the original Italian (*del superbo stupor*) to mean a sexual assault, while most other translators render the words to mean a generic attack, referring to the battle between the rebel angels and the Archangel Michael, who defeated them.

3. (p. 35) *the fourth chasm:* Virgil and the Pilgrim continue their descent into the abyss of the fourth circle, which is devoted to the punishment of two different but integrally related sins: avarice, or miserliness, and prodigality, or wastefulness. Both categories of sinners thought of nothing but money, albeit in different ways, and as a result, their humanity was distorted by their perversity. As a fitting punishment, they are encumbered by dead weights and are forced to participate in a parody of an earthy dance. In this canto, for the first time, two different circles of Hell will be introduced, since the canto also introduces the sins of the fifth circle, where the wrathful and the sullen reside.

4. (p. 35) *Charybdis:* In classical mythology, this is the name given to a whirlpool in the Strait of Messina between Italy and Sicily.

5. (p. 37) *their roundelay:* The popular dance to which the movement of the sinners is compared is, in Italian, a *ridda,* a dance that includes the reversal of circular movement as each strophe begins. The circular movement of the dance of the sinners is directly related to the concept of Fortune discussed in great detail later in canto VII, ll. 59–96, since the power of Fortune was traditionally represented in the medieval and Renaissance periods by the classical image of a turning wheel.

6. (p. 37) *"unto all discernment dim":* Virgil explains why the Pilgrim is unable to recognize anyone in the group of the avaricious and the prodigal, many of whom are men of the Church: Since they accomplished nothing in their lives except thinking about money, here their sordid earthly nature renders them anonymous. Avarice is completely contrary to the directives of Christ to embrace poverty, a virtue exemplified by that most remarkable Italian saint of the Middle Ages, Saint Francis of Assisi, whose mendicant order took vows of poverty in imitation of Christ. For a religious person to practice avarice was the negation of his vocation. Dante's remarks, and his placement of unnamed popes and cardinals in Hell, imply that the churchmen even outnumber others in their practice of avarice.

7. (p. 37) *"With the fist closed, and these with tresses shorn":* At the Last Judgment, the avaricious will have their outstretched hands closed forever, while the prodigal (who have spent their last cent) will be shaved bald, perhaps recalling an old Italian proverb that describes the wasteful as spending "down to their last hair."

8. (p. 38) *"He . . . ordained a general ministress and guide":* Asked to elaborate on Fortune, Virgil explains that this force (which in mythology and other classical literature is often personified as a fickle woman or as a turning wheel that determines human fates by its random movements) is actually delegated by God. In other words, Dante has Christianized a pagan deity and has changed it from a fickle and irrational force into something that ultimately has purpose and direction within a Christian mission. Fortune is thus transformed into a kind of angel.

9. (p. 39) *"Already sinks each star that was ascending when I set out":* It is now after midnight on Good Friday evening, and approximately

six hours have passed since the Pilgrim and Virgil set out in the morning. The stars that are now setting in the West were rising in the East at the beginning of the journey.

10. (p. 39) *A marsh it makes, which has the name of Styx:* The Styx is one of the five rivers in the classical underworld and the second of Dante's four rivers in Hell. Dante turns the river into a filthy marsh, but it first appears as a boiling spring. Ultimately all of the rivers in Dante's Hell derive from the tears pouring from a crack in the statue of the Old Man of Crete (canto XIV: 94–120). The geographical division of Hell between the rivers Acheron and the Styx delineates the portion of Upper Hell where the sins of the she-wolf, or Incontinence, are punished. Beyond the Styx, the Pilgrim will soon spy the flaming walls of the City of Dis, inside of which the sins of the lion and the leopard, or violence and fraud, will be encountered and described.

11. (p. 39) *The souls of those whom anger overcame:* Now in the fifth circle proper, the Pilgrim and Virgil come upon the wrathful (which would seem to be a sin of violence, not of Incontinence) and the sullen. Most commentators believe that Dante was influenced by Thomas Aquinas's commentary on Aristotle's *Ethics,* which attempted to distinguish various types of anger. In his depiction of the sinners in the fifth circle, Dante concentrates upon the wrathful who express their anger actively and those who are more sullenly wrathful ("We sullen were," Dante writes in l. 121) and brood over their anger.

CANTO VIII

1. (p. 41) *I say, continuing:* Here, for the first time in the poem, Dante the Poet breaks into the narrative and relates what happened between the time the travelers encountered the wrathful being punished in the Styx and when they reached the foot of the tower of the walled city of Dis. The belief that this interruption might represent an actual break in the composition of the poem is difficult to prove or disprove, since there are no autograph manuscripts of Dante's works extant.

2. (p. 41) *the foot of that high tower . . . two flamelets we saw placed there:* The tower of Dis functions as a point from which the boatman of the Styx may be summoned by the "two flamelets."

3. (p. 41) *"Phlegyas, Phlegyas":* Phlegyas was the mythological King of Boeotia. The son of Mars and a human mother, he set fire to one of Apollo's temples after the god seduced his daughter. Apollo killed him and condemned him to eternal punishment in the Underworld. Because Phlegyas was sentenced to the other world for an act of wrath, he is the appropriate guardian of the wrathful. As a rebel against one of the Greek gods, he also suggests a parallel with the rebel angels, who will soon be revealed as the guards at the gates of the City of Dis.

4. (p. 41) *only when I entered seemed it laden:* The boat piloted by Phlegyas sinks lower into the water when Dante the Pilgrim steps into it, because his body has material weight, while the shade of Virgil is weightless.

5. (p. 42) *"thou art all defiled. . . . Away there with the other dogs!":* Dante recognizes the damned soul arising from the marsh, but the reader only learns later, in l. 61, that his name is Philippo (Filippo) Argenti—a member of the Admiari family and a Black Guelph, therefore one of Dante's sworn political enemies. Note the dramatic difference in Dante's reaction to this soul. No longer does the Pilgrim weep out of compassion for the sinner (the sinner weeps now), and he curses Argenti ("Away there with the other dogs").

6. (p. 42) *"Blessed be she":* When Virgil detects the first note of righteous indignation in the Pilgrim's reaction to the damned, he uses words reminiscent of Christ's words in the Bible, Luke 11: 29–32. The Pilgrim's desire to have Argenti punished more than is the norm (a desire that is satisfied) certainly borders on the vindictive and is thus a reflection of the wrath punished in this area of Hell. So, while the Pilgrim has progressed morally from his swooning at the words of Francesca in canto V, now his act of moral indignation is tainted with the very sin that is being punished where he stands.

7. (p. 43) *Dis:* The King of the classical underworld, Pluto, was also called Dis. The City of Dis is the citadel of Lower Hell, where the most serious sins are punished and where Lucifer resides at its very bottom and center.

8. (p. 43) *Its mosques:* By characterizing the City of Dis as having buildings shaped like mosques—the worship places of the most dan-

gerous enemies of medieval Christendom—Dante renders the city much more frightening.

9. (p. 43) *fire eternal:* The reader of the *Inferno* should note that contrary to popular ideas about Hell as a place characterized by fire and brimstone, this is the first time in the poem that Dante associates infernal punishment with fire. Dante's imagination creates many other suitable punishments in his depiction of the afterworld.

10. (p. 44) *More than a thousand at the gates I saw out of the Heavens rained down:* These are the rebel angels who, led by Lucifer, turned against God. These rebels will prove to be the greatest obstacle Virgil and the Pilgrim have encountered up to this point in the journey through Hell. Because of the Angels' rank—though fallen, they are still higher in importance than the classical monsters Dante has recycled in other places—Virgil is forced to negotiate with them, something that proves fruitless without higher intervention.

11. (p. 44) *Think, Reader:* Dante's many addresses to his reader (seven in the *Inferno*; seven in *Purgatory*; five in *Paradise*) are crucial in creating an intimate relationship between author and audience. Moreover, in these addresses, Dante the Poet often asks his reader to consider a particular emotion that Dante the Pilgrim is experiencing—thereby underlining the distinction between Poet and Pilgrim that is so important to the overall structure and dramatic unfolding of the poem.

12. (p. 44) *"it by Such is given":* Virgil is referring either to God or to the three ladies in Heaven (the Virgin Mary, Lucy, and Beatrice) who have sent Virgil to guide Dante the Pilgrim.

13. (p. 45) *"because I am angry":* Because of the unexpected resistance of the rebel angels, who have closed the gates of Dis to the travelers, even Virgil shares the sin of the canto and expresses anger.

14. (p. 45) *less secret gate:* When Christ harrowed Hell and descended into Limbo to release the patriarchs and matriarchs of the Old Testament, he broke the main entrance gate (the principal entrance was thus "less secret"), and it will now remain open for all eternity. Because Virgil witnessed the Harrowing of Hell by Christ, he has reason to believe that he too may prevail in his contest with the rebel angels, as Christ did. This particular gate is the one men-

tioned in the service for Mass on Holy Saturday (the day in question).

15. (p. 45) *"One by whose means the city shall be opened":* A Divine Messenger sent by God to open the gates of the City of Dis is on the way to help the two beleaguered travelers.

CANTO IX

1. (p. 46) *his new color:* While the Pilgrim has turned white with fright, his guide, Virgil, is probably red-faced, because of his anger at the end of canto VIII.

2. (p. 46) *"Because I carried out the broken phrase, perhaps to a worse meaning than he had":* In ll. 7–9, Virgil expresses doubt as to the outcome of their contest with the inhabitants of Hell and even for a moment wonders if Beatrice's promised assistance will materialize. When Virgil interrupts his train of thought, the Pilgrim wonders for a moment if they will be abandoned in Hell.

3. (p. 46) *"Doth any e'er descend from the first grade, which for its pain has only hope cut off?":* This is a reference to canto IV: 42, in which Virgil defines the punishment of the virtuous heathen in Limbo, the "first grade," as "without hope we live on in desire."

4. (p. 48) *Erictho:* In Lucan's *Pharsalia,* Book VI, Erictho, or Erichtho, is a sorceress who conjures up dead spirits.

5. (p. 48) *the circle of Judas:* Judecca, the ninth circle of Hell, is named for Judas, the betrayer of Christ.

6. (p. 48) *"That is the lowest region and the darkest.... Well know I the way":* Dante seems to have entirely invented the story about Virgil being conjured up by Erictho and visiting the lower extremities of Hell (Judecca), the region farthest from the Primum Mobile ("the heaven which circles all"). By this literary fiction, the Pilgrim is convinced that Virgil, his guide, knows the way through Hell from past personal experience, not just because he invented a fictional visit in his own epic poem, the *Aeneid.*

7. (p. 48) *The three infernal Furies:* In Greek mythology, the Three Furies (or Erinyes)—Megaera, Alecto, and Tisiphone—are the traditional avengers of bloody crimes.

8. (p. 48) *the Queen of everlasting lamentation:* This is Hecate, or Persephone, wife of Pluto, classical god of the Underworld.

9. (p. 48) *Medusa:* In classical mythology, Medusa is one of the three Gorgons; her gaze turns mortal men into stone.

10. (p. 48) *"Avenged we not on Theseus his assault!":* The Furies complain that Theseus, hero of Athens, was not put to death when he came to Hell to rescue Proserpina, Pluto's queen. Dante's sources for this story from classical mythology were Virgil's *Aeneid,* Book VI, and Statius's *Thebiad,* Book VIII.

11. (p. 49) *of the mysterious verses:* This is the second address to the reader in the poem (the first begins in canto VIII: 94) and has puzzled commentators. Some readers of the poem believe the "mysterious verses" allude to the Furies and Medusa, previously mentioned in this canto. Medusa would thus represent some form of fear or despair. The Three Furies might suggest the three categories of sin punished in Hell. Other scholars believe the "mysterious verses" refer us forward to the angel that arrives at the Gates of Dis to clear the obstruction from the path of the Pilgrim and his guide. While commentators have not arrived at one single satisfying explanation of the lines, all modern interpreters of Dante agree that there are no secret doctrines concealed under the "veil" of Dante's poetry. Such notions were common in the nineteenth century: Some Rosicrucians, for example, believed that Dante's entire poem contained hidden doctrines that corresponded to their beliefs and even that Dante himself was a Rosicrucian.

12. (p. 49) *Was passing o'er the Styx with soles unwet:* The angelic messenger walks on water in imitation of Christ.

13. (p. 49) *"O banished out of Heaven, people despised!":* These are the rebel angels, who have been thrown out of heaven and guard the City of Dis.

14. (p. 49) *"For that still bears his chin and gullet peeled":* The angelic messenger reminds Cerberus that when he was dragged out of Hell by Hercules, the chain employed by the Greek hero rubbed his throat raw; the source of this anecdote is Virgil's *Aeneid,* Book VI.

15. (p. 50) *Even as at Arles . . . near to the Quarnaro:* Here Dante refers to two ancient Roman cemeteries, one near the Rhone River at Arles, France, and one near the Quarnaro Gulf at Pola in Istria (Croatia). The physical shape of these sarcophagi—raised, stone

monuments containing the dead—sets the stage for the scene to follow in the sixth circle of Hell.

16. (p. 50) *the Heresiarchs:* The Arch Heretics are enclosed in various kinds of sepulchers, all of which will be closed forever after the Last Judgment. For Dante, heretics denied the immortality of the soul. Their sin was one of pride and obstinate refusal to accept the Christian conception of the world. Heresy is thus a sin of the intellect: more serious than simple sins of the flesh but less serious than some other violent sins involving action. The punishment of heretics fits the crime, for those who believed that the soul perished with the body now have their souls entombed for eternity where their bodies were laid to rest.

17. (p. 50) *to the right:* Normally Virgil and the Pilgrim move to the left, but on two occasions in the poem (here and in canto XVII: 32) they head in the opposite direction.

CANTO X

1. (p. 51) *Jehosaphat:* A valley in the Holy Land where, according to the Old Testament, Joel 3: 2, souls will gather for the Last Judgment.

2. (p. 51) *Epicurus:* This Greek philosopher and founder of the Epicurean school (342–270 B.C.) taught that the highest good was happiness. Dante believed Epicurus denied the immortality of the soul, a belief that many pious pagans shared with Christians.

3. (p. 51) *"O Tuscan":* Recognizing the Pilgrim by his Florentine speech, Farinata degli Uberti (d. 1264) rises up from his tomb (thereby in his action, ironically negating his disbelief in the Resurrection) and asks the Pilgrim to pause and speak to him. Farinata was the head of the Ghibelline faction that expelled the Guelphs from Florence in 1248. The Guelphs returned in 1251 and eventually expelled Farinata in 1258. Led by Farinata, the Ghibellines routed their opponents at the disastrous battle of Montaperti in 1260 and subsequently proposed razing of the city of Florence. By his objections, Farinata saved Dante's native city from destruction. However, the Florentines showed little appreciation for Farinata's deeds. In 1266 the Guelphs once again returned to power and crushed the

Ghibellines and the Uberti family, razing their homes in the city's center to the ground.

4. (p. 53) *"So that two several times I scattered them":* As the leader of the Florentine Ghibellines, Farinata took part in driving the Guelphs out of Florence in 1248 (although the Ghibellines were themselves expelled three years later). Subsequently, Farinata led Tuscan Ghibellines to a great military victory over their Guelf adversaries at the battle of Montaperti in 1260.

5. (p. 53) *"the first time and the second":* The Guelphs returned twice, in 1251 and again in 1266.

6. (p. 53) *"Whom in disdain perhaps your Guido had":* The soul who rises out of Farinata's tomb to interrogate the Pilgrim is Cavalcante de' Cavalcanti (d. c.1280), a Florentine Guelph and father of the poet Guido Cavalcanti, one of Dante's best friends. Guido was betrothed to Beatrice degli Uberti, Farinata's daughter, in 1267. Thus two in-laws from Florence on different sides of the internecine political struggles of the times are being punished in the same location in Hell. Guido Cavalcanti does not appear in the poem because he has not yet died at the time of the action (March 1300); he will die in exile in August 1300, banished from Florence by the city's government during the period (June–August 1300) Dante served in the communal government. Dante the Poet, of course, writes about all this in exile himself. The "disdain," or scorn, the Pilgrim says Guido expresses is a problematic reference. Some scholars believe Guido, according to Dante, held the works of Virgil in contempt. Others feel Guido disapproved of Dante's love for Beatrice, his poetic muse and the woman who is assisting him in his journey in the afterlife (and, of course, not to be confused with the Beatrice mentioned above).

7. (p. 54) *"But fifty times . . . the countenance of the Lady who reigns here":* Farinata predicts that in fifty moons, or months, Dante himself will be exiled. Dante actually first went into exile in January 1302, but his banishment became virtually final in July 1304, approximately fifty months from March 1300. This length of time is established by the face of the lady reigning in Hell (Hecate, or Proserpina), who is also the goddess of the moon.

8. (p. 54) *the Arbia:* A river near the site of the battle of Montaperti, in which the Ghibellines defeated the Guelphs.

9. (p. 54) *"solve for me that knot":* Realizing that Cavalcanti does not know that his son Guido is still alive while Farinata, seemingly in contrast, knows Dante's distant future, the Pilgrim asks for clarification. He is told that the condemned souls are ignorant of the present or the near future and know only distant things, like those who suffer from "imperfect sight" (l. 100). After the Final Judgment, their minds will be completely void in timelessness. While some commentators believe this condition is ubiquitous in Hell, others believe it refers only to the heretics.

10. (p. 55) *the second Frederick, and the Cardinal:* Dante places Frederick II (1194–1250), king of Sicily and Naples and known in his time as the "wonder of the world," in Hell because he was reputed to be an Epicurean. Cardinal Ottaviano degli Ubaldini (d. 1272), a member of an important Ghibelline family, was reputed to have declared that "if I have a soul, I have lost it a thousand times for the Ghibellines," thereby qualifying him for membership in the region where heretics are punished. Other relatives of the Cardinal who appear in the afterlife are his nephew, Archbishop Ruggieri (*Inferno* XXXIII: 14), and his brother, Ubaldino della Pila (*Purgatory* XXIV: 29).

11. (p. 55) *From her:* Although Virgil tells Dante the Pilgrim that he will learn about his future life from Beatrice (as he points his finger upward to where Beatrice resides), in fact the Pilgrim learns about his future career from Cacciaguida in *Paradise* XVII: 46–75. This is yet another case of Virgil's fallibility, undermining the thesis that he represents pure Reason in the poem. His mistakes become more frequent as the action of the *Inferno* develops.

CANTO XI

1. (p. 56) *great rocks broken:* This is more evidence of the change in Hell's geography after the earthquake that followed the death of Christ and during upheavals caused by the Harrowing of Hell.

2. (p. 56) *"Pope Anastasius I hold, whom out of the right way Photinus drew":* Dante probably confused Pope Anastasius II, who held the office between 496 and 498, with Emperor Anastasius I of Byzantium, who ruled between 491 and 518. This period coincides with the schism between the Roman and the Byzantine churches. Photinus was either a deacon of Thessalonica or the bishop of Sirmium who held the heretical belief that Jesus was born from a natural union of Mary and Joseph, thus denying the divine paternity of Christ. It was the emperor, not the pope, who was persuaded of this heretical position.

3. (p. 56) *three small circles:* Standing on the cliff that marks off the sixth circle, the two travelers can see three smaller circles below them—the seventh, the eighth, and the ninth—that make up the structure of lower Hell. The first part of the Pilgrim's journey took him through Limbo and the first six circles, where the sins of the she-wolf, based on Incontinence, were punished in cantos IV–XI. The second major division involves sins of the lion, based upon force or violence: violence against others, against oneself, or against God. These sins are punished in the seventh circle in cantos XII–XVII. In the third section, the sins of fraud (the sins of the leopard) are punished. Here, in the eighth circle, there are ten additional subdivisions of the area called Malebolge (literally "evil pockets"), where so-called simple fraud is punished (fraud against people who have no special trusting relationship to the defrauder). This section comprises cantos XVIII through XXXI. In the ninth circle, itself divided into four sections—Caïna, Antenora, Ptolomaea, and Judecca—a more complex fraud against people who have a special trusting relationship to the sinner is punished. The Pilgrim visits this region in cantos XXXII through XXXIV, concluding the *Inferno.*

4. (p. 56) *"Of every malice . . . either by force or fraud":* All sins in Lower Hell are sins of malice (*malizia*), since the sin is committed by a sinner who willfully intends to do injury or harm to others. Dante found a distinction between injury by force or by violence and fraud (l. 24) in Cicero's *De Officiis,* Book I.

5. (p. 57) *In three rounds:* Sins involving force or violence against others, oneself, or God are grouped into three different *gironi* ("rounds" or "circles"; the singular is *girone*).

6. (p. 57) *Sodom and Cahors:* Sodom is the biblical city identified with perverse sexual activity, while Cahors is a city in southern France that was once notorious for its usury. The two cities represent

the Sodomites and Usurers punished in the smallest *girone* of the seventh circle.

7. (p. 57) *within the second circle nestle . . . and the like filth:* Virgil provides a list of eight of the ten sins punished in the ten Malebolge, leaving out two of the specific sins punished there that the reader will encounter later. He refers to these unspecified sins as "the like filth."

8. (p. 58) *in the smallest circle:* In the Ptolomaic system of the universe, Earth is at the center of the universe, and the bottom of Hell is located at the center of Earth, which makes it the "smallest circle."

9. (p. 58) *"Wherefore are they inside of the red city . . . wherefore in such fashion?":* Even though the Pilgrim initially claims to have understood Virgil's explanation ("My Master, clear enough proceeds thy reasoning," ll. 67–69), he is puzzled by why those being punished for the sins of Incontinence (such as the angry, the gluttons, the avaricious and prodigal, and the others in the first six circles of Hell) are not inside the City of Dis.

10. (p. 58) *"Incontinence, and Malice, and insane Bestiality?":* In Aristotle's *Nicomachean Ethics,* VII: 1 (a book the Pilgrim is supposed to know so well that Virgil refers to it as "thine Ethics" in l. 79), the Greek philosopher discusses Incontinence, Malice (Dante's *malizia*), and "insane Bestiality" (what Dante calls in the original *matta bestialitade*). Malice in Aristotle would correspond to the sins of the lion in Dante's seventh and eighth circles—those involving violence or force and simple fraud. "Insane Bestiality" does not really correspond to Dante's divisions and may be best understood as another name for treachery, the complex sort of fraud punished in the ninth circle. It might console the general reader who is confused by this system to know that the problem has vexed scholarly commentators for years. What is most interesting about the system of punishments in Hell as outlined by Virgil to Dante here is that the ideas are based on thinking from the classical world (Aristotle and Cicero) and not the traditional notion of the seven deadly sins.

11. (p. 58) *"There where thou sayest that usury offends goodness divine, and disengage the knot":* While claiming to understand perfectly, the Pilgrim once again asks his guide to clarify why usury offends divine goodness. Such a question was of great importance to a man from Florence, since one of the main sources of the city's wealth was banking and, therefore, usury.

12. (p. 59) *"And if thy Physics... for elsewhere he puts his hope":* Virgil describes the sins of usury. Referring to Aristotle's *Physics,* II: 2, where the imitation of Nature by Art is described, he argues that Art (that is, craft or human industry) is the child of Nature and thus the grandchild of God. By doing violence to human industry, usurers do violence indirectly to God. "Genesis at the beginning" (l. 107) refers to the biblical dictum in Genesis 3: 19, that man must earn his bread by the sweat of his brow.

13. (p. 59) *"wholly over Caurus lies":* Virgil usually tells time by the heavens, although it is not clear how he does this, since the stars are not visible from Hell. Pisces, the Fish, is on the horizon, while the Great Bear, or Great Dipper (the "Wain"), is in the northwestern part of the heavens (Caurus is the northwest wind). We know from canto I that the sun is rising in Aries, and since each Zodiac sign comprises about two hours, it should be roughly two hours before sunrise, or 4:00 A.M. on Holy Saturday.

CANTO XII

1. (p. 60) *Such as that ruin... on this side of Trent, the Adige:* Dante compares the way down the cliff to the seventh circle to the remains of a huge landslide (in Italian called the Slavini di Marco) that took place in the late ninth century near the city of Trent in northern Italy. It changed the course of the Adige River. The landscape here in Hell is the result of the earthquake that struck Hell after the death of Christ and just before the Harrowing of Hell.

2. (p. 60) *The infamy of Crete:* The Minotaur of Crete (identified by name in l. 25), the half-man, half-bull was born as the result of the union between the wife of King Minos of Crete, Pasiphaë (who crawled inside a wooden cow), and a bull. The Minotaur lived in the labyrinth constructed by Daedalus, where it was given a yearly human sacrifice. It was finally killed by Theseus, the Duke of Athens mentioned in l. 17, with the assistance of Ariadne, Pasiphaë's daughter (and therefore the half-sister of the Minotaur).

3. (p. 61) *the unwonted burden:* Once again, the Pilgrim's weight

is underlined by his effect on the physical structure of Hell and is contrasted to the weightlessness of the damned.

4. (p. 61) *the other time:* See canto IX: 22–30 for Virgil's account of his earlier visit through the Underworld. It should be recalled that Virgil witnessed the Harrowing of Hell after he reached Limbo (see canto IV: 52–63), so he is able to compare the geography in Hell before and after the Harrowing of Hell and the earthquake that changed the landscape.

5. (p. 61) *"who the mighty spoil bore off from Dis, in the supernal circle":* Christ carried off the virtuous pagans and the patriarchs ("the mighty spoil") from Dis (here meaning Lucifer, not the city of Dis) to the Empyrean ("the supernal circle").

6. (p. 61) *converted into chaos:* Because he is a pagan, Virgil must explain the Harrowing of Hell by Christ in a non-Christian manner. According to Empedocles (mentioned in canto IV: 138), the universe is constructed not only by the four basic elements but by two opposing forces—Hate and Love—that operate in a circular fashion. This timeless view of the universe is diametrically opposed to the Christian vision of the universe as dominated by God's love and controlled by an eschatological theory that foresees an end to history after the Last Judgment takes place.

7. (p. 61) *The river of blood:* Phlegethon (later identified by name in canto XIV: 116) is a river of boiling blood that runs through the first *girone,* of the seventh circle, then through the second round, and finally through the third round before pouring over the Great Cliff into the eighth circle then to the bottom of Hell (Cocytus).

8. (p. 61) *Centaurs:* The Centaurs, which Dante takes from classical mythology, guard the tyrants and murderers punished in this section of Hell. Like the Minotaur, the centaurs are a mixture of the bestial and the human (half-human, half-horse) and are therefore appropriate for the sins in question.

9. (p. 62) *"Our answer will we make to Chiron. . . . That other Pholus is":* Dante mentions three Centaurs by name. Chiron, in classical mythology the son of Saturn and Philyra and supposedly the tutor of Achilles, is the leader of the Centaurs. According to Ovid's *Metamorphoses,* IX, Nesus tries to rape Dejanira, the wife of Hercules, and Hercules kills him with a poison arrow. Before Nesus dies, he

gives Dejanira a shirt stained with his poisoned blood, telling her that it will cause whoever wears it to fall in love with her. Later, when Hercules falls in love with Iole, Dejanira gives Hercules the shirt and it causes his death. Little is known of Pholus, except that he was involved with the attack of the drunken Centaurs against the Lapiths during the wedding of Pirithous and Hippodamia.

10. (p. 62) *"Are you ware that he behind moveth whate'er he touches?"*: Once again, the fact that the Pilgrim's body has weight amazes the denizens of Hell.

11. (p. 64) *"Is Alexander, and fierce Dionysius"*: This Alexander is either Alexander the Great (356–323 B.C.), the Macedonian conqueror of most of the ancient world, or Alexander, the tyrant of Pherae (ruled 369–359 B.C.). Dionysius may be either of two tyrants of Syracuse, Dionysius the Elder (ruled 405–367 B.C.), or his son, Dionysius the Younger (ruled 367–356 B.C. and 354–343 B.C.). Both father and son had well-deserved reputations for bloodthirsty cruelty.

12. (p. 64) *"Azzolin... Obizzo is of Esti, who, in truth, up in the world was by his step-son slain"*: Azzolino, or Ezzelino III da Romano (1194–1259), was the cruel Ghibelline tyrant who became famous for his actions while he ruled in Padua for Frederick II of Sicily. Obizzo II d'Este (1264–1293), Marquis of Ferrara, was said to have been murdered by his own son, who Dante here calls "step-son" *(figliastro)*, possibly suggesting he was illegitimate.

13. (p. 64) *"Now he be first to thee, and second I"*: In cantos X and XI, the Pilgrim has been warned to pay attention and not to waste words, and it has become clear that Virgil even answers unanswered questions. Here he responds to the unspoken question of which of the three (the Pilgrim, his guide, or the Centaur, who will carry the Pilgrim) should go first.

14. (p. 64) *"He cleft asunder... the heart that still upon the Thames is honored"*: Guy de Montfort (1243–1298) murdered Henry, earl of Cornwall, cousin of King Edward I of England, reportedly while Henry attended Mass at a church in Viterbo, Italy. (De Montfort was avenging his father's death at the hands of Edward.) Henry's heart was apparently returned to England and, according to Dante, at the time of the poem still drips blood from a column on the

Thames Bridge in London, because the murder has not yet been avenged.

15. (p. 64) *there across the moat our passage was:* Dante is actually crossing the river of blood on the back of the Centaur Nessus, and they cross at the place where the river is most shallow. Sinners in this area are punished according to the gravity of their violence: Tyrants lie in deeper blood than murderers, who directed their crimes against individuals rather than entire nations.

16. (p. 65) *"That Attila . . . in Rinier da Corneto and Rinier Pazzo, who made upon the highways so much war":* Dante names five individuals here. Three are ancient rulers: Attila the Hun (c.405–453), known as the "scourge of God," conquered much of Italy; King Pyrrhus of Epirus (319–272 B.C.) opposed the Romans in a number of wars (some commentators believe this figure is, instead, Pyrrhus, the son of Achilles); and Sextus, the son of Pompey the Great, engaged in piracy that endangered the food supply of Rome, according to Lucan's *Pharsalia,* Book VI; others believe this Sextus is the Sextus Tarquinius Superbus who raped Lucretia, thus bringing about the expulsion of the tyrannical Tarquin kings from Rome and the establishment of the Roman Republic. Rinier da Coreto and Rinier Pazzo were highwaymen who lived during Dante's day.

CANTO XIII

1. (p. 66) *'Twixt Cecina and Corneto:* Dante compares this part of Hell, where the suicides are punished, to the wild, marshy, and forested area in the Maremma district of Tuscany between the river of Cecina in the north and the town of Corneto in the south.

2. (p. 66) *the hideous Harpies . . . who chased the Trojans from the Strophades:* Harpies are birds with the faces of women and claws who, according to Virgil's *Aeneid,* Book III, lived in the islands of the Strophades and befouled the food of the Trojans. Like so many other monsters in this region of Hell, they are half-animal, half-human.

3. (p. 66) *I think he thought that I perhaps might think:* This famous and complex line (*cred'io ch'ei credette ch'io credesse,* in the original) is the kind of verse that medieval rhetoricians and poets of the Sicilian School would appreciate. Indeed, shortly after the Pilgrim utters it

to himself, we meet an important representative of the Sicilian School (ll. 54–78). He is not identified specifically by name but is obviously Pier della Vigne (1190–1249), minister to Frederick II of Sicily, who imprisoned and blinded Pier, driving him to suicide. Pier's literary talents (reflected in the style of this canto) included not only Italian poetry but a highly ornate Latin employed in the government chancery.

4. (p. 68) *"What only in my verses he has seen":* The talking trees of this canto are obviously inspired by a similar passage in Virgil's *Aeneid,* Book III, where Aeneas pulls a leaf off a myrtle tree, causing it to bleed, and as he does so hears the voice of one of his friends who has been treacherously killed. In Dante's version of the episode, the Harpies attack the plants, tearing off the leaves and torturing the souls within in them. But as Virgil instructs the Pilgrim to tear off a piece of the plant to hear an explanation for the punishment (ll. 28–30), it is also clear that the only way the souls have of speaking is to be torn asunder.

5. (p. 68) *The courtesan:* She is the personification of Envy, the force that helped turn Frederick (called "Caesar" in l. 65) against Pier.

6. (p. 68) *"And they, inflamed, did so inflame Augustus":* This is another line typical of the style of the Sicilian School; Augustus is Frederick.

7. (p. 69) *"I, by the roots unwonted of this wood":* Here "unwonted" means not "unwanted" but "new," referring to the fact that since Pier della Vigne committed suicide only a few years earlier, the roots of his plant are not yet very deep.

8. (p. 69) *"such pity is in my heart":* Dante's pity here is for the fact that Pier claims to have been wrongly accused of theft, not for Pier's just punishment as a suicide. Some modern commentators claim that Pier was actually guilty of the crime for which he was imprisoned, but Dante apparently thought him innocent.

9. (p. 70) *And two behold!:* The two souls who appear represent the profligates, who did violence to their material goods by not placing sufficient value upon them, just as the suicides did not value their earthly bodies. The first figure is believed to be a certain Lano from Siena, who went into battle at Pieve al Toppo near Arezzo in

1287, apparently intending to die at what Dante calls the "joustings of the Toppo" (l. 121) because he had wasted his fortune. The second figure is Jacopo da Sant'Andrea from Padua, who jeers at Lano (ll. 120–121) and accuses him of not running as fast at the battle where he was killed as he does now in Hell. Jacopo was famous for being a spendthrift.

10. (p. 70) *As greyhounds . . . him they lacerated piece by piece, thereafter bore away those aching members:* These hounds of Hell are also found in Giovanni Boccaccio's *Decameron,* Day V, Story 6, a scene illustrated by Botticelli. The punishment of the Profligates is to be driven naked through the thorny wood by the hounds that tear them apart, carrying off their limbs. Implicit in this punishment is the fact that the body recomposes in order that the punishment may be repeated over and over for eternity.

11. (pp. 70–71) *"I of that city was which to the Baptist . . . some glimpses of him are remaining still":* The anonymous soul whose leaves are being rent asunder is a Florentine; the city was first dedicated to the god Mars, then afterward to the patronage of John the Baptist. A piece of what was supposed to be the statue of Mars (pieces of which "are remaining still") stood on the Ponte Vecchio ("the pass of the Arno") until the flood of 1333. One explanation of why the anonymous suicide claims that the change from Mars to John the Baptist was "sad" is that the change in patron implies a passage from a skill in arms to a skill in business (since the picture of John the Baptist was on the most famous coin of the medieval period, the Florentine gold florin).

12. (p. 71) *"Upon the ashes left by Attila":* It was not Atilla but King Totila of the Ostrogoths (d. 552) who attacked Florence in 542.

CANTO XIV

1. (p. 72) *Because the charity of my native place . . . second round is from the third:* We have now reached the border between the second ring (*girone*) of the seventh circle (violence against oneself) and the third ring of the eighth circle (violence against God). While Dante often concludes an action at the end of a canto, he also frequently carries action through from the end of one canto to the opening of the

next canto, as he does here, showing the Pilgrim gathering up the remains of the anonymous suicide because of their common Florentine heritage.

2. (p. 72) *The soil was of an arid and thick sand... which by the feet of Cato once was pressed:* Cato of Utica, also known as Cato the Younger (95–46 B.C.), supported Pompey against Julius Caesar in the Roman civil wars, and after he and his allies lost the battle of Pharsalus (48 B.C.), he killed himself to avoid capture. According to Lucan's *Pharsalia,* Book IX, rather than let himself be carried across the barren sands of Libya by slaves, as was the custom for Roman generals, Cato set out on foot with his enlisted men. Dante places Cato in *Purgatory,* canto I (and not in the region of the suicides of Hell), because of his selfless devotion to Roman republican liberty.

3. (pp. 72–73) *Supine upon the ground... had their tongues more loosed to lamentation:* Here Dante neatly summarizes the different punishments of the three kinds of sinners being tortured in the third round of the seventh circle. Blasphemers lie supine, are the smallest group, and cry the loudest because they cursed God. Usurers, the next largest group, are crouching or sitting hunched up. The largest group is made up of homosexuals, who move about constantly.

4. (p. 73) *As Alexander... whereby the sand was set on fire:* According to the *De Meteoris,* I:IV, of Albertus Magnus, thirteenth-century philosopher and theologian, Alexander the Great encountered a heavy snowstorm and then a rain of fire in India and ordered his men to march on the snow. Following Albertus's error in reporting this event, Dante has Alexander marching over the fire. The rain of fire may also suggest the similar downpour inflicted on Sodom and Gomorrah, cities identified with unnatural sexual practices, in the Bible, Genesis 19:24.

5. (p. 73) *Without repose forever was the dance of miserable hands:* Dante compares the movements of the tortured sinners to a Neapolitan dance called the *tresca.* In this dance, a leader touches a part of the body and is imitated by the other dancers, a process that becomes more and more complicated as more and more body parts are indicated and imitated rapidly by the dancers.

6. (p. 74) *"All things except the demons dire":* While praising his guide, the Pilgrim is not above reminding Virgil that he was unsuc-

cessful in overcoming the demons that obstructed their path at the gate of Dis.

7. (p. 74) *"seems not to ripen him":* While many translators and editors of the text construe the Italian word here to mean "ripen" or "soften," it may also mean "torture."

8. (p. 74) *"O Capaneus":* One of the seven kings who warred against Thebes, Capaneus scaled the walls of the city and blasphemed Jove by daring the god to protect the city, and he was struck by a thunderbolt. Still arrogant, Capaneus boasted that Jove would be unable to overcome him if he employed the entire production of thunderbolts made by Vulcan in his forge in Mount Etna (at the battle of Phlegra, Jove used Vulcan's supply of thunderbolts to overcome the rebellious Titans attempting to storm Mount Olympus).

9. (p. 75) *a little rivulet . . . the sinful women later share among them:* This little stream of boiling, blood-red water derives from the overflow of Phlegethon that descends the Wood of the Suicides and the Burning Plain to fall over a great cliff into the eighth circle and into frozen Cocytus (we learn this later, in ll. 115–117). Dante compares the rivulet to the Bulicamë, a hot sulphur spring near Viterbo, Italy, that prostitutes (the "sinful women") employed, since they were not permitted to use the other public baths. Because of its mineral content, the Bulicamë was also reddish in color.

10. (p. 75) *That he would give me . . . largess of desire:* Virgil has piqued the Pilgrim's appetite ("largess of desire") about the rivers of Hell, and now the Pilgrim begs Virgil to supply him with additional information about them ("largess of food").

11. (p. 75) *"Rhea . . . had clamors made":* Wife of Cronos and mother of Zeus in Greek mythology (Saturn and Jupiter, respectively, in Roman mythology), Rhea hid Zeus on Mount Ida in Crete to save him from being killed by her husband, who had received the prophecy that one of his children would depose him. The Bacchantes served as guards and their loud celebratory screams ("clamors made") covered up the infant's cries to prevent Cronos from hearing them.

12. (pp. 75–76) *"A grand old man . . . so here 'tis not narrated":* Dante's *gran veglio,* or the Old Man of Crete, is one of his most unusual poetic inventions. From Ovid's *Metamorphoses,* Book I, Dante borrows the Roman poet's outline of four ages following the creation of the world: the Golden Age, the Silver Age, the Bronze Age, and the Iron Age. The Old Man himself is taken from Nebuchadnezzar's dream in the biblical book of Daniel, 2: 31–35. The Old Man turns toward the West and Rome (the center of Christian and Roman civilization) and away from Damietta (a city in Egypt), symbolizing the East. The parts of the Old Man of Crete are made up of the different metals described in part by Ovid. This appears to be one of the few instances in the *Inferno* where some kind of allegorical interpretation is demanded to make sense of the image. It has been suggested that the golden head represents the Golden Age of man (in Christian terms, the Eden before the Fall of Man; in classical terms, the Golden Age celebrated by pastoral poets). The other metals (silver, bronze, and iron) may represent the three deteriorating ages of man. Some see the invention of the clay foot as a representation of the weakness of the Roman Catholic Church. The tears of the Old Man form the rivers of Hell called Acheron, Styx, and Phlegethon, and they eventually pool to form Cocytus at the bottom of Hell. Virgil informs the pilgrim that he will not describe Cocytus because Dante will eventually see that for himself.

13. (p. 76) *"Lethe and Phlegethon . . . sin repented of has been removed":* Because of Dante's knowledge of classical literature and mythology, he naturally inquires about the locations of two rivers in Hell he recalls from his readings. He is told that Lethe, the famous river of forgetfulness mentioned by Plato, Ovid, Lucan, and, of course, by Virgil in his *Aeneid,* Book VI, will be seen elsewhere—atop the mountain of Purgatory in the Earthly Paradise. Since the Phlegethon has not actually been named until this point in the poem, the Pilgrim and perhaps the Poet's contemporary readers do not realize that the river of blood and Phlegethon are the same, but Virgil says that the Pilgrim should have realized this by the fact that the river of blood was boiling, as it is described in his own poem (*Aeneid,* Book VI).

14. (p. 76) *the margins:* The Pilgrim and his guide walk on paths that run alongside the stream to protect themselves from the hellish environment in this section of the *Inferno.*

CANTO XV

1. (p. 77) *Even as the Flemings, 'twixt Cadsand and Bruges... or ever Chiarentana feels the heat:* In a double simile, Dante compares the paths alongside the stream of Phlegethon to the dikes the Flemish built to hold back the sea between Wissant (Cadsand) and Bruges, as well as to those the Paduans built to hold back the Brenta River when it floods during the spring snow melt in the Chiarentana area north of the city.

2. (p. 77) *Gazed at us... at the needle's eye:* In another double simile, Dante compares the gaze of the people he encounters in this region of Hell to the intense gaze of people looking at each other under a new moon (and therefore in the dark of a medieval city) and to the gaze of a tailor looking through the eye of a needle to thread it.

3. (p. 77) *stretched forth his arm to me:* The reader should remember that Dante the Pilgrim is walking above the sodomites on the path alongside the stream, so the soul being punished there must reach upward to touch his garment.

4. (p. 78) *Ser Brunetto:* This is Brunetto Latini (1220–1294), a Guelph notary (thus the honorific title "Ser," from "Messer") and Florentine writer. His *Tesoretto* (*Little Treasure*), written in the 1260s, was a long narrative poem that influenced Dante. Because of this impact upon Dante's work, the Pilgrim bows in homage to Latini (ll. 29 and 44) and also uses a respectful form of address, "voi" rather than "tu"; this distinction has been lost in contemporary English but is used by Longfellow, who employs "thou" or "thy" frequently in his translation.

5. (p. 79) *from Fesole descended:* Brunetto provides a prophecy about Dante's future that is related to the town of Fiesole (which Dante spells as "Fesole"), on a hillside overlooking Florence. He claims both political factions, the Guelphs and the Ghibellines, will hunger to destroy Dante (l. 71), since trees bearing bitter fruit (the "crabbed sorbs" of l. 65) will not permit the sweet fig tree to bear good fruit. The reference to Fiesole explains part of Dante's problem, since during a power struggle in Rome, Catiline fled the capital and went to Fiesole, where Caesar destroyed Catiline's forces but allowed the Fiesolan survivors to intermingle with the Roman inhabitants of Florence. Dante thus implies that he, descended from

the original Florentine Romans, will be constantly harassed in the city by those who are related to the less noble Fiesolans descended from Catiline.

6. (p. 80) *"You taught me how a man becomes eternal":* What Brunetto Latini taught Dante was that literary fame grants a certain kind of immortality, or earthly fame, but certainly not the kind of immortality that one earns in the afterlife.

7. (p. 80) *"To be glossed . . . by a Lady":* From what is said in canto X: 130–132, we know that Dante believes that Beatrice will reveal his future and will "gloss," or explain, the prophecies of Ciacco (canto VI: 64–75) and Farinata (canto X: 79–81). In fact, it will be Dante's great-great-grandfather, Cacciaguida, who performs this function, in *Paradise* cantos XV–XVIII.

8. (pp. 80–81) *"All of them were clerks . . . where he has left his sin-excited nerves":* Brunetto Latini lists three sodomites punished with him, all of whom are men of letters ("clerks"). Priscian was a famous sixth-century Latin grammarian. Francis of Accorso, or Francesco d'Accursio (1225–1293), was a well-known Florentine jurist who taught law at Bologna and Oxford. The third man, not identified precisely by name, may be Andrea de' Mozzi, Bishop of Florence from 1287 to 1295. He was, in fact, transferred by Pope Boniface VIII—"the Servant of the Servants" (*servus servorum* was a medieval expression for the pope) from Florence ("from Arno") to Bacchiglione (Vicenza, on the River Bacchiglione) because of his sexual transgressions. There he died and thus abandoned his "sin-excited nerves" (his erections). Some scholars deny that Dante punishes homosexuality in this and the next canto, arguing that Dante is really attacking other, even more subtle vices. Dante is not a politically correct contemporary poet. For him, homosexuality is simply a sin, and as much as he liked and admired Latini in life, Dante the Poet places his friend where he believes he belongs, no matter how much sympathy Dante the Pilgrim may feel for his lost friend.

9. (p. 81) *"my Tesoro":* While some commentators on Dante believe this is a reference to Latini's encyclopedic treatise written in French (*Li Livres dou trésor*), others (more correctly) claim that it must refer instead to the long narrative poem Latini wrote in Italian, the *Tesoretto* (but referred to within the poem several times as the *Tesoro*). Since the *Tesoretto* was the longest narrative poem written in the

vernacular that Dante could have read before he wrote his *Comedy*, the second interpretation is most likely.

10. (p. 81) *Who at Verona . . . not the one who loses:* During Dante's time, the city of Verona held a footrace on the first Sunday of Lent. The first prize was a green cloth, while the runner who finished last was given a rooster that he had to carry around the city. The runners were completely naked, and, in like manner, the fate of the sodomites is to run naked through this region of Hell.

CANTO XVI

1. (p. 82) *water falling into the next round:* This is the sound of the waterfall plunging over the Great Cliff into the eighth circle, as we shall discover later in the canto.

2. (p. 82) *three together:* Dante now encounters three shades who are natives of Florence (they recognize Dante by his garb, not his speech, as was the case with Farinata in canto X). Earlier, when speaking with another Florentine, Ciacco, in canto VI, Dante mentions two of the three as men he would like to meet because of their positive qualities. The first man to appear is Guido Guerra (c.1220–1272), a Guelph political leader who was instrumental in leading the Guelphs after their defeat at Montaperti in 1260 to their final victory over the Ghibellines at Benevento (1266). Tegghiaio Aldobrandini of the Adimari family (l. 41) is one of the two men cited earlier in canto VI. Like Guerra, he advised the Guelphs of Florence not to wage war against Siena, ending in the disastrous battle of Montaperti. The other figure, the speaker, is Jacopo Rusticucci (l. 44), another Guelph (dates unknown but mentioned in city records as being active between 1235 and 1266).

3. (p. 83) *the grandson of the good Gualdrada:* The good Gualdrada was the daughter of Bellincione Berti of Florence and, according to medieval legend, was married to Guido Guerra at the suggestion of Emperor Otto IV. In fact, she married in 1180, before Otto IV became emperor. She was the grandmother of Guido Guerra, mentioned in the preceding note.

4. (p. 83) *"My savage wife . . . doth harm me":* Jacopo implies that his wife drove him to sodomy.

5. (p. 83) *"Sorrow and not disdain . . . I with affection have retraced and* *heard":* In spite of the fact that the sinners are sodomites, Dante respects their love for their common native city of Florence and honors them. His pity for them, however, is quite different from that uncritical pity that caused him to swoon over Francesca da Rimini in canto V.

6. (p. 83) *to the centre:* This is the center of the Earth, the lowest part of Hell: Cocytus.

7. (p. 84) *Guglielmo Borsier:* Guglielmo Borsier (better known as Borsiere) was possibly a purse maker, given his name (*borsa* means "purse" in Italian). Boccaccio mentions him in Day I, Story 8 of the *Decameron.* As he has died very recently (his arrival is reported in l. 71 as "of late"), he has disturbed the other Florentine sodomites with his opinion that the "good old days" in Florence, when "valor and courtesy" (l. 67) were still valued, are finished. Nowhere better in his verse does Dante the Poet reveal himself to be a conservative social thinker as he does when he has Dante the Pilgrim declare in l. 73 that *"the new inhabitants and the sudden gains" (in the original Italian, la gente nuova e i subiti guadagni*) have ruined the old city values. In fact, it is more likely that the opposite is true: The great migration toward Florence of new citizens and the huge profits made by the banking and textile industries that supported the city's prosperity provided the economic basis of the Florentine Renaissance.

8. (p. 84) *the sound of water:* The sound of the water falling into the eighth circle that opened the canto is heard again. In ll. 94–101, Dante compares the fall of the water in the Phlegethon to the fall of the Montone River (called in Dante's day the Acquacheta as far as Forlì, then the Montone—the name for the entire river today).

9. (p. 85) *a cord . . . to take the panther with the painted skin:* The cord that Dante produces from around his waist has not been mentioned previously, and he claims that he equipped himself with it to capture the panther in canto I (leopard in most other translations—the original Italian is *la lonza*; see canto I, note 8). It has been claimed, with little evidence, that Dante became a member of the Franciscan order and the cord is part of his habit, but he does not use the specific term for the cord worn by the Franciscans. Perhaps the best we can say here is that Dante needed his Pilgrim to signal Geryon,

the monster of fraud that appears in l. 97 of the next canto, and the cord was as good a signal as any he could devise.

10. (p. 85) *Reader, by the notes of this my Comedy to thee I swear:* For the first time in the poem, Dante provides us with a title for his work. The word—pronounced in Dante's day as *comedìa* and not as it is pronounced today in contemporary Italian, *commèdia*—is repeated again in canto XXI: 1–2. The word *divina* (divine) was added to Dante's title by the Venetian edition of 1555, printed by Gabriele Giolito and edited under the supervision of Ludovico Dolce. It was never Dante's intention to use *divina* as part of the title. For Dante, comedy implied that the work had a happy ending, but he expanded greatly the other conception of comedy popular with his day—that comedy was connected to only a low, humble style. Dante's comedy is unique precisely because it encompasses all levels of style, not only the low comic style of classical theatrical comedy but also the middle style identified with classical satire and the high, tragic style of serious dramatic works. In this passage, Dante the Poet makes an important address to his reader, swearing by his very poetic work that the sight the reader of his poem is about to share with Dante the Pilgrim—the arrival of Geryon—is a literally true image remembered from a literally real journey to Hell, and not a figure to be construed as a theological or philosophical allegory that is not derived from concrete human experience.

CANTO XVII

1. (p. 86) *the monster:* Virgil drops Dante's cord into the abyss, summoning the monster Geryon (identified by name only in l. 97). In classical mythology, Geryon is a three-headed giant Hercules kills during one of his Twelve Labors. He is mentioned by a number of classical authors (including Virgil, Pliny, and Ovid), and is usually identified with the number three, perhaps to suggest a perversion of the Christian Trinity. Dante's description of Geryon may also have been influenced by any number of monsters described in the biblical book of Revelation. Dante makes Geryon the personification of fraud, since his face is "the face of a just man" (l. 10), but his poisoned tail is compared to a scorpion's stinger (l. 27).

2. (p. 86) *Never in cloth did Tartars make nor Turks, nor were such* *tissues by Arachne laid:* Arachne was a Lydian woman who was so skilled in weaving that she challenged Minerva to a contest; when Minerva lost, she changed Arachne into a spider (Ovid, *Metamorphoses,* Book VI). The Tartars and Turks were regarded in Dante's day as the best weavers in the world.

3. (p. 86) *And as among the guzzling Germans there, the beaver plants himself to wage his war:* According to medieval bestiaries, the beaver (an animal more common in Germanic lands than in Italy) fished with its tail—a position similar to the one Geryon assumes. Identifying Germans with drunkenness ("guzzling Germans") was a common idea that had classical as well as medieval Italian roots.

4. (p. 87) *on the right-hand side:* As in canto IX: 132, Virgil and Dante the Pilgrim move to the right, but their normal motion is to the left. Here they can only move to the right, since the river of blood is on their left, viewed from the spot where they are standing. After Geryon flies them to the other side of the waterfall, they will continue to move to the left.

5. (p. 88) *the melancholy folk:* These sinners are the usurers, described in canto XI: 105 as having sinned against Art, God's grandchild, since they make money increase against Nature by charging interest. They crouch, staring at the pouches or purses hanging around their necks, each of which bears the emblem or coat of arms of a different family. In life they have been obsessed with material goods, so, in death, they have lost their individuality. Their position duplicates their position in life, crouched over a desk thinking about money. The yellow purse with the blue lion (ll. 59–60) probably refers to the Gianfigliazzi family, Florentine Guelphs; the red purse with the white goose (ll. 62–63) represents the Ubriachi, or Obriachi, family, Florentine Ghibellines; and the third purse with the blue sow (ll. 64–65) belongs to the Scrovegni family from Padua.

6. (p. 89) *"Know that a neighbor of mine, Vitaliano . . . a Paduan am I with these Florentines":* The only usurer to speak is usually identified as Reginaldo degli Scrovegni, whose son used some of his father's ill-gotten gains to commission Giotto to paint the Scrovegni Chapel in Padua, the work of art that marks the birth of Renaissance painting and the use of realism in the depiction of the human form. Scrovegni reports the name of another sinner being punished with

him, Vitaliano, so the Pilgrim will take news of him back to the living. Vitaliano has been identified as another Paduan usurer, Vitaliano del Dente.

7. (p. 89) *"Come the sovereign cavalier":* This is probably Giovanni Buiamonte, of the Becchi family in Florence, who apparently had been knighted by 1298. The Becchi family's coat of arms contained three black goats on a gold field (in Italian, *becchi* is the plural form of a word for "goat").

8. (p. 89) *"by stairways such as these":* Virgil notes that from this point on, they will travel in Hell assisted by other "stairways"—these are infernal monsters, like Geryon. Later in the poem Antaeus (canto XXXI) and Lucifer himself (canto XXXIV) will assist the Pilgrim and his guide in moving over gaps in the geography of Hell that they cannot walk across.

9. (p. 89) *So near the ague of quartan:* Quartan fever is a chill (ague) that is associated with malaria and has a four-day cycle.

10. (p. 89) *"the descent be little":* Dante and Virgil mount on Geryon's back and fly down in slow, gradual circles. Geryon must be careful not to drop the Pilgrim, who is a "novel" burden (l. 99) because he has actual weight, unlike Virgil and the shades of Hell.

11. (p. 90) *Phaeton . . . the wretched Icarus:* Dante the Pilgrim compares the fear he experiences while riding on the back of Geryon to classical precursors who were unsuccessful in their flights. In Ovid's *Metamorphoses,* Book II, Phaeton persuades his father, Apollo, to allow him to drive the chariot of the sun, but he loses control and Zeus kills him to prevent the Earth from catching fire. In Book VIII of the *Metamorphoses,* Daedalus fashions wings for his son, Icarus, and fastens them with wax, which melts when the boy flies too close to the sun, causing him to fall into the Aegean Sea.

12. (p. 90) *The turning and descending, by great horrors:* This is the first moment that the Pilgrim sees that Geryon is descending in a spiral like a falcon.

13. (p. 90) *As falcon who has long been on the wing . . . sped away as arrow from the string:* Geryon's flight resembles that of a falcon, because hunting birds of prey are trained not to land until they have taken their prey or are called down by the falconer, who uses a lure to signal the recall. Geryon's uncooperative attitude is underlined by

the simile, for he lands before he is called and apparently in a place of his own choosing. Nevertheless, he has been forced to obey Virgil and fulfill his role. His slow descent is contrasted to the manner in which he speeds off like an arrow shot from a bow.

CANTO XVIII

1. (p. 91) *Malebolge:* By putting two words together—*malo*, meaning "evil," and *bolge*, plural of *bolgia*, meaning "ditch" or "pouch"—Dante invents an original name for the eighth circle. This circle contains ten concentric, sloping ditches, inside of which are punished ten different kinds of simple fraud. Dante and Virgil walk above the *bolge* along dikes and observe the sinners below them.

2. (pp. 91–92) *Even as the Romans . . . towards the Mountain:* When Pope Boniface VIII declared 1300 a Jubilee Year in the Eternal City, crowd control was handled by sending all those heading toward St. Peter's basilica to one side of the street that passed by the Castel Sant'Angelo, while those returning from St. Peter's headed toward Monte Giordano, a low hill across the River Tiber from the Castel Sant'Angelo. The sinners below Dante and Virgil walk on either side of the dike below them, each group going in a different direction as the hundreds of thousands of pilgrims did in Rome during the Jubilee. Three groups of sinners are punished together in the first Bolgia: panderers, along with seducers and flatterers.

3. (p. 93) *Venedico Caccianimico . . . to grant the wishes of the Marquis:* Venedico Caccianimico, a Guelph nobleman of Bologna, was active in the last half of the thirteenth century and, according to popular belief, sold his sister, Ghisola, to Marquis Opizzo d'Este of Ferrara to win his favor. Venedico actually died in 1303, although Dante believed he died before 1300, the date of his fictional journey.

4. (p. 93) *"Not the sole Bolognese . . . to say* sipa*": Sipa* is Bolognese dialect for *sì*, or "yes." The city of Bologna is located between the Savena and the Reno Rivers, and Venedico is saying that there are more procurers and pimps from Bologna in Hell than there are Bolognese alive and living still in their native city. Even today, Bologna has a reputation among Italians for sexual prowess (particularly fellatio).

5. (p. 93) *"there are no women here for coin":* For the term that

Longfellow translates as "coin," Dante uses the word *conio,* which means fraudulent deception and also refers to the steel die used to stamp coins. Thus Venedico is being told by a demon that there are no women in Hell whom he can exploit for fraudulent purposes as well as for money.

6. (p. 94) *From those eternal circles we departed. . . . "Because together with us they have gone":* The "eternal circles" may well refer not only to the ditches of Malebolge but also to the Florentine practice of whipping a condemned man along the path to his execution. Dante now leaves behind one group of sinners engaged in eternal circling (the panderers) and encounters another circling group (the seducers). He and Virgil have not yet been able to see the faces of this group, since the sinners are hurrying ahead of the two poets with their backs turned to them ("Because together with us they have gone").

7. (p. 94) *That Jason is . . . had all the rest deceived:* Jason, the leader of the Argonauts, carried off the Golden Fleece (the Ram of the Colchians). He seduced and betrayed Medea, daughter of the King of Colchis, in order to capture the Fleece, and he also seduced Hypsipyle, daughter of the King of the island of Lemnos. Hypsipyle and other women on Lemnos were cursed by a terrible smell when they stopped worshiping Aphrodite, making them unattractive to their husbands or lovers. The women responded by murdering all their males. Hypsipyle "all the rest deceived" because she lied about killing her father, King Thoas.

8. (pp. 94–95) *In the next Bolgia, snorting with their muzzles . . . clerk or layman:* Flatterers in both Italian and in English are often called "ass kissers," and the source of the delicately translated *ordure* (l. 116) is, in the original Italian, literally "shit," derived naturally from the area of the body where flatterers generally congregate. Everything about the second Bolgia, the part of Hell where the flatterers are punished, is disgusting: There is the foul smell, caked-on crust from human excrement has formed along the embankments (the "margins" of l. 106), and the sinners immersed in excrement snort with their muzzles in animal-like fashion (l. 104). All of this constitutes one of the most graphic images of punishment in the entire *Inferno.*

9. (p. 95) *Alessio Interminei of Lucca:* According to documents, Alessio Interminei, or Interminelli, of Lucca, a member of a White

Guelph family, was still alive in 1295 but probably died shortly thereafter. Dante refers to his head as a *zucca*, a "pumpkin" (l. 124)—a word often employed by Florentines to indicate a slow-witted person.

10. (p. 95) *Thaïs the harlot:* In act 3, scene 1, of the play *Eunuchus*, by the Roman playwright Terence, Thaïs is associated with flattery: Her lover first sends her a slave, then later sends a servant to ask her if he deserved her thanks. According to the servant, she makes an immoderately flattering reply. Dante most likely knew of this example not from Terence, whom he probably did not read, but from a source he certainly did know—Cicero, who in his *De amicitia*, XXVI, cites Thaïs as an example of immoderate flattery.

CANTO XIX

1. (p. 96) *Simon Magus:* The third Bolgia of the eighth circle punishes the simonists, those who sold ecclesiastical offices or favors (simony). The term derives from Simon Magus, who in the Bible, Acts 8: 9–24, tries to purchase the power of the Holy Spirit from the Apostles John and Peter.

2. (p. 96) *The livid stone with perforations filled . . . the soles were both on fire:* In this passage Dante describes a physical structure resembling a baptismal font with round holes out of which the feet of the simonists protrude, burning with an oily fire (l. 28). This is an ironic reference to the sacrament of Extreme Unction as well as to the Pentecost—when, in the Bible, Acts 2: 1–4, after the Ascension of Christ the apostles were invested with the Holy Spirit and spoke in tongues, always represented in the religious art of Dante's day as tongues of fire. Dante claims here that he once broke the baptismal font in the church of San Giovanni in Florence (his "beautiful Saint John" of l. 17) in order to save a child who was drowning in the water; unlike those who sold church offices, Dante commits what might seem to some to be a sacrilegious act out of kindness.

3. (p. 98) *"Dost thou stand there already, Boniface?":* We learn later in the canto (ll. 69–72) that the figure to whose feet Dante is speaking is Giovanni Gaetano degli Orsini, elevated to the papacy in 1277 as Pope Nicholas III. He was infamous for his simony and the promotion of his relatives to church offices, even though he only

ruled as supreme pontiff for a few years, until 1280. Since the damned know the distant future, Nicholas knows that Pope Boniface VIII will take his place in Hell too, but when he hears the Pilgrim's voice, he mistakes him for Boniface and wonders if he miscalculated, since the date is 1300, not 1303, when he knows Boniface will die. Not one to be impressed by powerful prelates, Dante the Poet has thus consigned a living pope to the punishments of Hell while he is still alive (at least still alive in the fictional time of 1300, during which the Poet's action takes place). Boniface VIII, born Benedetto Caetani c.1235, was elected to succeed Pope Celestine V in 1294 and died in 1303. Dante loathed him and believed the often-told story of how Boniface persuaded Celestine to give up the papacy, making what Dante calls in canto III: 59 the "great refusal" (see canto III, note 9).

4. (p. 99) *son of the She-bear:* Pope Nicholas's family name, degli Orsini, literally means "of the bear cubs."

5. (p. 99) *"a Pastor without law . . . Jason will he be, of whom we read in Maccabees":* Not content with condemning one living pope to Hell, Dante has Nicholas predict the eminent arrival of yet another pontiff, Clement V, born Bertrand de Got in France around 1264 and pope from 1305 to 1314. Clement began the so-called Babylonian Captivity of the Catholic Church, moving the papacy to Avignon, France, in 1309, where it remained for more than seventy years, thanks to the influence of Philip the Fair, king of France, who engineered Clement's election. Dante compares Clement to Jason, who in the Apocrypha of the Bible, 2 Maccabees 4: 7–27, becomes High Priest of the Jewish Temple by bribing King Antiochus IV of Syria and introduces Greek and pagan elements into Judaism, actions that lead to the uprising of the Jews under the Maccabees.

6. (p. 99) *"I pray thee tell me now how great a treasure . . . the place the guilty soul had lost":* According to the Bible, Acts 1: 15–26, after Judas betrays Christ and commits suicide, lots are cast to determine who will replace him as one of the apostles, and the lot falls to Matthias. What is most relevant about this story here, in this section of Hell, is that the office was not sold—no one "asked of Matthias silver or gold." Meanwhile, Christ did not demand a great treasure when

he chose Peter to receive the keys of the church, but asked only his willingness to follow him as the Son of God.

7. (p. 99) *"valiant against Charles":* Dante believes Nicholas III helped to instigate the 1282 uprising against Charles I of Anjou, king of Naples and Sicily, known as the Sicilian Vespers. Actually the Sicilian Vespers was a spontaneous popular uprising that destroyed French power on the island, and Nicholas III had been dead for a couple of years when the revolt occurred.

8. (p. 100) *"When she who sitteth upon many waters . . . to her spouse was pleasing":* In the biblical Book of Revelation: 17, Saint John the Evangelist pictures a woman who embodies a vision of Pagan Rome. Dante employs the same image to represent the Roman Church—the seven heads are the seven Holy Sacraments and the ten horns are the Ten Commandments.

9. (p. 100) *"Ah, Constantine! . . . which the first wealthy Father took from thee":* Dante believed that the "Donation of Constantine"—a document in which Emperor Constantine (ruled 306–337) supposedly gave temporal power to Pope Sylvester I (314–335)—marked the disastrous beginning of Church corruption. He did not know that the Donation was also a forgery, a fact that was not brought to light until the fifteenth century by Italian humanist Lorenzo Valla.

10. (p. 100) *with both his feet:* The feet are those of Nicholas III.

11. (p. 100) *with both his arms he took me up . . . tenderly on the crag:* Overcome by pleasure with the fact that Dante the Pilgrim has understood the essence of simony almost without taking any cues from his guide, Virgil lifts him up bodily and carries him back out of the *bolgia,* holding him against his breast; when Virgia carried the Pilgrim down into the *bolgia,* he clasped him to his side, or "haunch" (l. 43). Placed on the bridge overlooking the fourth Bolgia, the Pilgrim will now encounter fortune-tellers and diviners.

CANTO XX

1. (p. 101) *to the twentieth canto . . . of the submerged:* For the first time, Dante actually assigns a number to a canto, and he calls the entire *Inferno* the "first song" (*canzone* in Italian). He does not employ the technical term "canticle" (*cantica*) that we use today and that he employs in *Purgatory* XXXIII: 140 to refer to the three separate di-

visions of his *Comedy* that conform to the three regions of the afterlife.

2. (p. 101) *at the pace which in this world the Litanies assume:* The diviners are walking in the same slow-paced procession that is used when litanies, in which the priest chants an invocation and the congregation responds, are performed.

3. (p. 101) *to look forward had been taken from them:* Dante has found the perfect punishment for those who presumed to tell the future (thus implicitly denying God's power to control and know the future). Their faces have been twisted so that they cannot stare forward but must always look backward, and their tears run down their backs and through the buttocks ("the hinder parts" of l. 24).

4. (pp. 101–102) *Truly I wept.... "Who feels compassion at the doom divine?":* Dante the Pilgrim again falls into the trap of feeling compassion for the tortured souls, causing Virgil to rebuke him indignantly and to remind him that true pity cannot be wasted on those who justly deserve punishment. Feeling compassion for the damned reflects an imperfect understanding of God's plan or may even, as if often suggested by Dante's critics, mark the Poet's recognition that he, himself, is guilty of the sins for which he feels compassion.

5. (p. 102) *"Opened the earth before the Thebans' eyes... Amphiaraus":* This legendary king was one of the Seven Against Thebes, seven kings who attacked Thebes in classical antiquity (another king, Capaneus, appears in canto XIV). In the *Thebaid,* Books VII–VIII, Statius recounts how Amphiaraus tries to hide to avoid going off to war, since he foresees that he will die. Indeed, he is swallowed up in an earthquake at Thebes and is transformed into an oracle.

6. (p. 102) *Tiresias:* In Ovid's *Metamorphoses,* Book III, this Theban soothsayer changes into a woman when he finds a staff with two coupled serpents; seven years later, he (now a she) finds the same staff, and she becomes a he again. Jupiter and Juno argue about who derives the most pleasure from sex, the man or the woman, and ask Tiresias to decide. He agrees with Jupiter that women have the most pleasure. Angry with his response (and for revealing women's secret), Juno blinds Tiresias, but Jupiter gives him the gift of prophecy to compensate for his lost sight.

7. (p. 102) *"Aruns . . . among the marbles white a cavern had":* In Lucan's *Pharsalia,* Book I, this Etruscan soothsayer Aruns foretells the triumph of Caesar in the Roman civil wars. Luni is an ancient Etruscan city near Carrara, where the Carrarese quarry the famous marble that Michelangelo used in his greatest stone sculptures.

8. (p. 102) *Manto:* This is a Theban prophetess and the daughter of Tiresias who abandoned Thebes, which had been enslaved by the tyrant Creon, and went to Italy. Virgil's claim that Manto founded Mantua directly contradicts the explanation he offers for the origins of his native city in the *Aeneid,* Book X. Moreover, in *Purgatory* XXII: 113, the poet Statius points out that the daughter of Tiresias (Manto) resides in Limbo. Virgil's explanation here for the origins of his birthplace of Mantua represents another example of the classical poet's fallibility, since Dante the Poet has Virgil silently correct the remarks he made in the *Aeneid.* Like Virgil, Dante the Poet is not fallible: He seems to have forgotten that he placed Manto in Hell when later in *Purgatory* he has Statius say that Manto is in Limbo!

9. (p. 103) *"Benaco . . . might give his blessing":* Lake Benaco is now called Lake Garda, which is near Mantua. The three dioceses of Trent, Brescia, and Verona converge in an island in the lake ("midway a place," l. 67), and Dante notes that here the three bishops of those dioceses (Dante calls them pastors) could bestow their blessings in the same spot. He locates the island between the city of Garda, the Val Camonica (a valley west of Garda), and the town of Pennino.

10. (p. 103) *"Peschiera, fortress fair and strong, to front the Brescians and the Bergamasks":* The town of Peschiera del Garda is on the southeastern shore of Lake Garda. In Dante's time, the Scaliger family, rulers of Verona, controlled the town's fortress, designed to protect the area from attacks by Brescia and Bergamo.

11. (p. 103) *"No more Benaco . . . it falls in Po":* The waters of the river that becomes the Mincio flow southward toward Mantua, then, reaching a town called Govérnolo (which Dante calls "Governo"), join the Po and flow toward the Adriatic Sea.

12. (p. 103) *the virgin pitiless:* This is a reference to the Theban prophetess Manto (canto XX, note 8), described as pitiless or cruel because she has no interest in men.

13. (p. 103) *"From Pinamonte had received deceit":* Pinamonte de' Buonaccorsi, a Ghibelline who ruled Mantua between 1272 and 1291, expelled Count Alberto da Casalodi, a Guelph leader, from the city is a deceitful fashion. He persuaded Alberto to banish most of the nobility (his supporters), then turned around and drove the weakened Alberto out of the city and ruled it himself.

14. (p. 104) *"may the verity defraud":* Virgil has just delivered his longest speech in the *Inferno*: He has been talking about Manto and Mantua to Dante since l. 27. What is remarkable about his explanation is that it directly contradicts what Virgil himself wrote in the *Aeneid,* Book X, where the Roman poet makes it very clear that Mantua was founded by Ocnus, the son of Manto. Nevertheless, the Pilgrim asserts that his guide's discourses are so true, and he believes them so firmly, that any other explanation would be useless—like the spent, or burnt, coals of l. 103. Of course, Virgil has just negated his own explanation in the *Aeneid,* and so Dante the Poet is enjoying teasing his acknowledged poetic master, perhaps implying that without the light of Christian revelation, even the greatest of the classical poets may sometimes make a mistake. But there is also a more serious motive. During the Middle Ages, Virgil acquired the reputation of a magician and a necromancer. People would find a random passage in the *Aeneid,* just as they often did in the Bible, and assign to it some divinatory or predictive power over the future. Therefore, Dante's readers might well think that Virgil was a necromancer and deserving of punishment here in this section of Hell rather than living a much quieter and less stressful life in Limbo. Dante, therefore, makes Virgil explain that Mantua was founded *after* Manto's death by people who had left Thebes (men who were "scattered round," l. 88) but who returned to found the city "without other omen" (l. 93; the Italian original reads *senz'altra sorte*)—meaning without the powers of divination associated with Thebes. In short, Dante wants to remove any possible link between his beloved Virgil and the sin expiated in this region of Hell.

15. (p. 104) *"Was, at the time when Greece was void of males . . . : Eryphylus his name was":* At a time when so many men were away at the Trojan War that there were virtually no males left in Greece, Eryphylus was sent to the oracle of Apollo to obtain a prophecy about how the Greeks should leave Troy after the war was won. Calchas, the augur,

interpreted the message that Eryphylus delivered: Since the war began with the sacrifice of Iphigenia, there must be another sacrifice before the Greeks could return. Aulis is the port from which the Greek ships set sail, or severed their cables.

16. (p. 104) *"My lofty Tragedy":* Here Virgil refers to his *Aeneid,* which Dante would have understood to be a work of the high, lofty style ending in unhappiness. The death of the noble Turnus at the hands of the Trojan hero Aeneas, who thereafter sets the stage for the foundation of Rome, is certainly a tragic conclusion.

17. (p. 104) *Michael Scott:* This Scottish scholar and necromancer (c.1175–c.1235) translated a number of important astronomical works from Arabic into Latin, including the commentaries of Averroës, the twelfth-century Arab scholar also known as Ibn Rushd, on Aristotle. He probably served as the astrologer for Emperor Frederick II of Sicily.

18. (p. 104) *"Behold Guido Bonatti, behold Asdente":* Bonatti, a famous astrologer and soothsayer from Forlì, was a roofer, covering houses with tiles by trade, but he apparently served Guido da Montefeltro (who appears in canto XXVII). Asdente (whose name means "Toothless" in Italian) was even humbler, a shoemaker from Parma who lived during the second half of the thirteenth century and was reputed to have powers to tell the future; Dante (ll. 119–120) remarks that he should have stuck to his original shoemaking trade. Note that the cultural level of the diviners is becoming increasingly lower and lower. Finally, we come to anonymous witches who mix magic potions and make images of those upon whom they wish to cast spells.

19. (p. 104) *"But come now . . . within the forest deep":* This puzzling passage presents several difficulties, not the least of which is how Virgil manages to tell time by gazing at the heavens, which are not visible from Hell. Medieval tradition held that Cain had been banished to the moon for his killing of Abel: The reference to "Cain and the thorns" is the equivalent of our own Man in the Moon. The moon is setting in the ocean west of Seville over a point that divides the hemisphere of the land from that of the water, and scholars have calculated that the time is therefore 6:00 A.M. on Holy Saturday, 1300. What Dante means when he writes that the moon

assisted the Pilgrim "within the forest deep"—this would have been in canto I, when he was lost and confused in the dark forest—is simply unclear.

20. (p. 104) *we walked the while:* It is interesting that Dante employs a word for "meanwhile" or "the while" (*introcque,* in Italian, from the Latin *inter hoc*) that he specifically criticized in his *De vulgari eloquentia* and banished from the illustrious vernacular language, considering it too typical of the Florentine vulgar tongue. But since his conception of "comedy" includes the permissible use of the low style, it is perhaps not surprising that he employs such language here. Alternatively, after maneuvering his literary character Virgil into correcting something that the historical Virgil wrote in the *Aeneid* (see canto XX, note 8), perhaps Dante the Poet is doing the same thing to himself, reversing in his own poem the advice he gave in an earlier work.

CANTO XXI

1. (p. 105) *of which my Comedy cares not to sing:* This is the second reference to the title of Dante's poem (the first was in canto XVI, l. 128). It is not clear which subjects Dante could have discussed at this point that he decides not to include in his poem.

2. (p. 105) *another fissure of Malebolge:* This is the fifth Bolgia, where barrators (those who sell offices to make money) are punished in boiling pitch and guarded by demons who tear them into pieces with claws and hooks if the souls venture above the surface. These are important sins to Dante, since a false accusation of barratry was employed to exile him from his native Florence. Note that barratry is the lay equivalent of selling church offices, the simony punished in the third Bolgia.

3. (p. 105) *the Arsenal of the Venetians:* Perhaps the most highly developed industrial complex in medieval and Renaissance Europe, the Arsenal (founded in 1104 and expanded over the years) could eventually produce a complete warship in a single day, applying advanced industrial techniques to the process of shipbuilding that approximated the modern assembly line. The description of the sticky pitch used in the Venetian Arsenal provides the perfect symbol and punishment for the barrators, who sell public offices behind

the scenes hidden from human sight, just as the sinners are out of our sight under the boiling pitch. Their sticky fingers remind us of how money once stuck to their evil hands.

4. (p. 106) *"O Malebranche":* The devil addresses his colleagues by a name that may be translated into English as "Evil Claws."

5. (p. 106) *"Behold one of the elders of Saint Zita":* The patron saint of Lucca, a Tuscan city, died in the last part of the thirteenth century and was canonized in the seventeenth century. Dante would have known her to be not an official saint but merely a woman who was reputed to be very holy. One of her elders would be an alderman of the city; scholars have tried to identify this Luccan barrator as Martino Bottario, who died in 1300.

6. (p. 106) *except Bonturo:* Bonturo Dati (d. 1325), a politician active during the beginning of the fourteenth century, was reputedly the most corrupt man in all of Lucca. Dante's contemporaries would have taken the devil's remark that everyone in Lucca except Bonturo is corrupt to be humorously ironic.

7. (p. 107) *"Here the Santo Volto has no place! Here swims one otherwise than in the Serchio":* The Serchio River is near Lucca. The mention of the Santo Volto (literally "Sacred Face"), a dark-wood crucifix venerated since the early Middle Ages in the cathedral of Lucca, implies that the sinner is floating in a cruciform position with the face up. Since he is covered with pitch, he may be said to resemble the dark wood crucifix.

8. (p. 107) *"Let Malacoda go":* This devil, whose name means "Evil Tail," seems to be the leader of the Malebranche in Malebolge.

9. (p. 108) *Then was his arrogance so humbled in him ... all the devils forward thrust themselves:* Malacoda has won Virgil's confidence by dropping his grapple hook ("grapnel" of l. 86) and told him that his fellow devils will not advance. This proves not to be the case, and Virgil's self-assurance that he can handle the devils is proven to be mistaken. Virgil's all-too-human fallibility once again underscores why he cannot be considered to be an allegorical symbol for human reason.

10. (p. 108) *beheld I once afraid the soldiers ... seeing themselves among so many foes:* An army composed of men from Florence and Lucca attacked the fortress of Caprona near Pisa in August of 1289, only a

brief time after the victory Dante's Guelph faction won at Campaldino in June 1289. Dante was apparently present at both battles. At Caprona, the Pisans were given safe conduct through the besieging army's lines, but Dante asks us to imagine what their fear must have been like while they marched between their enemies on either side of them with their arms drawn.

11. (p. 108) *Scarmiglione:* This is the first of the twelve devils who now make an appearance.

12. (p. 108) *"Near is another crag that yields a path":* Malacoda is lying about this bridge, or "crag," being intact, since all bridges but the one Virgil and the Pilgrim have already crossed are down, destroyed by the great earthquake that shook Hell after the death of Christ. Other such ruins caused by the same earthquake are to be found in cantos V and IX, but Dante does not discover this information until Virgil is so informed by Fra Catalano in canto XXIII: 133–138.

13. (pp. 108–109) *"Yesterday, five hours later than this hour . . . that here the way was broken":* It is therefore 7:00 A.M. on the morning of Holy Saturday.

14. (p. 109) *"some of mine . . . and mad Rubicante":* Malacoda calls ten of the Malebranche devils, some of whose names seem to underline bestial qualities. Barbariccia may be translated roughly as "Curley Beard," Graffiacane may be rendered literally as "Scratch Dog," and Draghignazzo may mean "Evil Dragon." But other names seem only to be intended to sound amusing when pronounced. Needless to say, Malacoda's statement that the devils "will not be vicious" is another lie.

15. (p. 109) *"their brows are threatening woe to us?":* Dante the Pilgrim is far more suspicious of Malacoda and his colleagues than is his guide. Virgil may embody some of the aspects of reason and learning, but from his performance in various places in Hell, it is clear that he cannot represent Human Reason in any strict allegorical sense, since he is so often quite fallible.

16. (p. 109) *each one thrust his tongue . . . made a trumpet of his rump:* The Italian is a bit more explicit, "rump" being Longfellow's more polite word for what Dante really intended in the original—"ass" or "asshole." Malacoda farts toward his troops as a signal, and they seem prepared to respond with a counter signal, a "Bronx cheer" or

a "raspberry." The depiction of the devils in this section of Hell contains, as shall be evident from the next canto as well, some of the more comic action in the entire poem.

CANTO XXII

1. (p. 110) *O Aretines:* Most commentators believe this remark about the Aretines (residents of the city of Arezzo) refers to the battle of Campaldino (1289), where forces from Arezzo were defeated by Florentines and troops from Lucca. Dante fought at this battle.

2. (p. 112) *"I in the kingdom of Navarre was born... pay the reckoning in this heat":* The identity of this barrater is not known. We learn from Dante that he served King Thibault II of Navarre, who ruled this kingdom in northern Spain from 1253 to 1270. Most commentators have identified him as a certain Ciampolo, or Giampolo. Almost any courtier would serve Dante's purpose here.

3. (p. 112) *"Latian... was a neighbor to it":* In the original, Dante uses the word *latino,* which can mean "Latin" but also "Italian," referring particularly to Italians who come from what was ancient Latium (modern Lazio), the region around Rome. When Ciampolo says he knows of a sinner "who was a neighbor," he means someone from Italy. He will identify that individual in l. 82 as Friar Gomita (see note 5).

4. (p. 112) *their Decurion:* This is a reference to Barbariccia, who, in canto XXI: 120, Dante describes as the leader of the ten devils (he calls them there a *decina,* from the Latin military term *decuria,* meaning a squad of ten soldiers). He is therefore in rank a decurion, just as a centurion was in charge of 100 Roman soldiers.

5. (p. 113) *Friar Gomita:* Around 1294, this friar was appointed deputy to the Pisan chancellor of Gallura, one of the four administrative districts into which the island of Sardinia was divided. He was hanged for his outrageous acceptance of bribes to allow prisoners to escape.

6. (p. 113) *Don Michael Zanche:* He served as governor of another administrative district in Sardinia, Logodoro, during the thirteenth century. When King Enzo of Sardinia, the son of Frederick II, was captured, Don Michael married his wife, Adelasia, and ruled Sardinia

until around 1290, when his son-in-law, Branca d'Oria of Genoa, murdered him. Branca will appear in canto XXXII: 137–147, in the lowest region of Hell. Don Michael apparently surpassed even Friar Gomita in barratry.

7. (p. 113) *the grand Provost:* The grand provost, or marshal, is Barbariccia (see note 4).

8. (p. 114) *thou shalt hear new sport!:* The events in this passage seem like an infernal game. In fact, Dante the Poet refers to what he witnesses as the "new sport," and we must remember that these antics will be repeated for all eternity. The speaker is the sinner who scholars have identified as Ciampolo. During this conversation with the two poets and the Malebranche devils, he proves that he is cleverer than his torturers. Basically, he tricks the devils into allowing him to escape their claws, thereby deceiving his captors with the cleverness that is involved in the sins connected with fraud. Earlier Dante the Pilgrim seemed to understand the devils better than did his guide Virgil. Here Cagnazzo understands that Ciampolo is lying to the devils, while Alichino does not.

CANTO XXIII

1. (p. 116) *As go the Minor Friars along their way:* Franciscans (known as Friars Minor) usually walked in single file, led by the most highly ranked member of the group.

2. (p. 116) *the fable of Æsop . . . of the frog and mouse:* This fable (probably not by Aesop) recounts that a mouse asks a frog to carry him across a stream, and the frog agrees and ties the mouse to his leg, but once in the water he dives to drown the mouse. Meanwhile, a hawk swoops down on them both and carries them away, killing the frog. The mouse tied to the frog is either killed along with the frog (according to a version of the fable included in a collection attributed to Romulus, a writer of the Carolingian period) or is freed by accident while the frog dies (according to a twelfth-century version told by Marie de France). Dante compares this fable (and it is unclear which ending he intends) to the events we have witnessed in canto XXII, where Ciampolo tricks the devils. Ciampolo would be the mouse, Alichino the frog, and Calcabrina the rapacious bird. It may also refer to the situation in which the two poets find

themselves: In this case, Dante would be the mouse, Virgil the frog, and the Malebranche devils the hawk. Whatever meaning Dante intended to assign to this story, he has certainly presented a puzzle that will continue to bemuse his critics.

3. (p. 116) *For* mo *and* issa *are not more alike:* Both words are dialect terms meaning "now" and are derived respectively from the Latin *modo* and *ipsa hora.* Dante the Poet continues to pique our curiosity by saying, in effect, that the story from the fable and the action we have just witnessed are as alike as the two words. But again the puzzle continues, since their meanings (like the content of the stories) are the same, while their spellings and Latin origins are different.

4. (p. 116) *of leaded glass:* Dante means a mirror, as mirrors were made with clear glass backed by lead.

5. (p. 117) *any land-built mill:* Dante distinguishes this mill, the kind operated by running water diverted from its source by a sluice, from water mills that actually floated on a raft in a stream or river.

6. (p. 117) *As his own son:* Dante underlines the close affection Virgil has begun to feel for his pupil, who is no longer just a guest in Hell but is like a son to him. Earlier in the canto (l. 40), Dante compares Virgil's act of grabbing the Pilgrim to his breast to escape the attacking devils to the maternal action of a woman seeking to save a child from a house fire.

7. (p. 117) *The power of thence departing took from all:* We learn another of Hell's rules—the beings assigned to torture the souls in each section of Hell are not permitted by God to leave the region to which they have been assigned. Virgil has now brought the Pilgrim to the sixth Bolgia, the region of the hypocrites.

8. (pp. 117–118) *They had on mantles . . . of straw:* Hypocrites dress as monks (so proverbial was the hypocrisy of the clergy in Dante's time and afterward). Longfellow has followed a textual reading here that has been rejected by contemporary Dante scholars, for he translates the city as Cologne, in Germany, while the texts accepted today use Cluny, the town in France where the famous Benedictine abbey was located. This seems to make more sense in the context of the passage. The mantles are gilded, recalling the biblical story in Matthew 23:27, in which hypocritical scribes and Pharisees are described

as being, on the outside, like beautiful sepulchers that contain bones and corruption within. Dante's mantles are made of lead and are so heavy that the ones employed by Frederick II (the ruler already mentioned in canto X: 119) weigh no more than straw in comparison. According to medieval tradition, Frederick executed traitors by wrapping them in capes of lead, using fire to melt the metal and killing the traitors in a slow, horribly painful manner.

9. (p. 118) *we were new in company at each motion of the haunch:* The hypocrites move so slowly with the weight of their mantles that each time the two poets take a step (that is, move their hips, or haunches), they pass on to another slow-moving sinner.

10. (p. 118) *the Tuscan speech:* Once again, Dante's Tuscan dialect (today standard Italian) causes the denizens of Hell to recognize him immediately. Needless to say, Dante did not mean this to be a complement to his fellow citizens, since so many of them populate the *Inferno.*

11. (p. 119) *their balances to creak:* The friars resemble creaking balances, or scales, because the weight they support is so great. Dante refers, of course, to the medieval balance—in which two pans hang from each end of a bar balanced on a central support, a shape that resembles the hypocrites wearing their mantles.

12. (p. 119) *"Frati Gaudenti were we . . . round Gardingo":* The Frati Gaudenti (Jovial Friars) was a military and conventual order that was officially called the Knights of the Blessed Virgin Mary. Formed in Bologna in 1261, the order was dedicated, under the patronage of Pope Urban IV, to peacemaking between the warring factions in Italian cities. Obviously, given their informal name, the Jovial Friars were not too interested in the aesthetic life. Catalano Catalani (1210–1285), a Bolognese Guelph, and Loderingo degli Andalò, a Bolognese Ghibelline, were elected in 1266 to serve jointly in Florence as *podestà* (something like a mayor, an office held by noncitizens to maintain impartiality among the warring factions of the city). In fact, their support of the Guelph party resulted in the expulsion, with the assistance of Pope Clement IV, of the Ghibellines from Florence in 1266 and the destruction of many of the most famous Ghibelline residences in the city, including that of Farinata, the Florentine

Dante encountered in canto X. This area near the Palazzo Vecchio was then called the Gardingo.

13. (p. 119) *"O Friars," began I, "your iniquitous . . .":* The Pilgrim is probably about to lower the boom on the two hypocrites who caused so much damage to his native city, but he is interrupted by a more startling sight—that of crucified men upon whom people are walking.

14. (pp. 119–120) *"This transfixed one . . . for the Jews was a malignant seed":* Catalano's explanation enables us to identify the "transfixed one" as Caiaphas, leader of the Pharisees who condemned Jesus to death (as told in the Bible, John 11: 49–52). Here too is his father-in-law, Annas, who delivered Jesus to Caiaphas for judgment (John 18: 13). Since Dante believed the Jews shed the innocent blood of Christ, that "malignant seed" bore bitter fruit when the Romans, led by Titus, son of the Emperor Vespasian, destroyed the Temple and brought about the Diaspora of the Hebrews in A.D. 70. Obviously Dante had not yet been enlightened by the pronouncement of Pope John Paul II that the Roman Catholic Church no longer holds the Jews responsible for the death of Jesus!

15. (p. 120) *I saw Virgilius marvel o'er him who was extended on the cross:* This is the first time that Virgil marvels at a punishment in Hell. He has seen not Caiaphas on the cross before, because his previous visit to Hell was before Christ's Crucifixion. As a Roman, he would not likely marvel at the type of punishment, since crucifixion was the Roman punishment par excellence. It is more likely that Virgil cannot understand why anyone who knew Christ could have done such a thing, since his experience after Christ's death has obviously revealed to the Roman poet how the powers of the Christian God control the universe and the afterlife.

16. (p. 120) *the black angels:* These are the winged devils from the last *bolgia.*

17. (p. 120) *"badly he recounted":* Virgil is now told that Malacoda lied to him about the crossings on the road ahead—the bridge Malacoda said was still in operation cannot be used.

18. (p. 120) *by anger in his looks . . . after the prints of his beloved feet:* Virgil is angry that Malacoda has tricked him and also because, in l. 44, Catalano has cited the Bible to him—a passage from John 8:

44, which states that the Devil is a liar and the father of lies. Virgil is well aware that the devil is a liar and is annoyed to be told so by the shade of a sinner, and he rushes angrily off the scene. In spite of Virgil's human failings, the Pilgrim respects his "beloved guide."

CANTO XXIV

1. (p. 121) *beneath Aquarius tempers . . . at the mountain's foot I first beheld:* We are now in the seventh Bolgia, where thieves are punished. The simile that opens the canto places the stars in the zodiacal sign of Aquarius, between January 21 and February 21. In the first part of the simile, a peasant erroneously believes hoarfrost to be snow and is unhappy, but when he sees that the frost is gone, "the world has changed its countenance," he realizes that he can indeed drive his sheep to pasture. Like the peasant, Dante is relieved when he sees that Virgil is returning to his former self-confidence and realizes that things will be as they once were when Virgil met the Pilgrim at the foot of the mountain in canto I.

2. (p. 121) *at the ruin:* This is more evidence of the earthquake that followed the Crucifixion of Christ.

3. (p. 122) *no path for one clothed with a cloak . . . he light, and I pushed upward:* Dante is saying that a hypocrite wearing one of the mantles of lead described in canto XXIII could not have made this climb. Virgil has no body mass and therefore is immune to the force of gravity ("he light"), but as a human being affected by gravity's pull, the Pilrgim is hard pressed to make the ascent.

4. (p. 122) *one bank rises and the other sinks:* Because Malebolge slopes toward a pit in the center (Cocytus), each *bolgia* is like a step on a conical, or funnel-shaped, staircase, with a steep bank on one side and a drop-off on the other.

5. (p. 122) *As smoke in air or in the water foam:* Virgil's remarks echoes the view of the damned in Hell that only earthly fame will keep their memory alive. This is a comment that no true Christian should make.

6. (p. 124) *a terrible throng of serpents . . . and with Amphisbæna:* Dante took the list of the frightening serpents he sees torturing the thieves in the seventh Bolgia from Lucan's *Pharsalia,* Book IX. The Chelydri leave smoke in their wake; the Jaculi fly; the Phareae make tracks

with their tails; the Cenchri wiggle from side to side; and the Amphisbaena have a head at each end. The appropriateness of the punishments here is clear. Thievery is a sneaky, reptilian operation. Since the thieves used their hands to steal, their hands are now bound; since thieves took property away, they are now made to disappear, only to reform again to repeat the entire process eternally.

7. (p. 124) *Without the hope of hole or heliotrope:* Heliotrope is a mythical stone reputed to have the power to make its owner invisible, as in Boccaccio's comic story about Calandrino in the *Decameron,* Day VIII, Story 3. The sinners have no place to hide or no power to make them disappear.

8. (p. 124) *upon their reins:* Longfellow uses a literal translation of the Italian *le rene* (kidneys), but the word here refers to the lower back. Therefore the serpents are between the legs of the sinners.

9. (p. 124) *Nor* O *so quickly e'er, nor* I *was written:* Both these letters of the alphabet can be written quite quickly with a single stroke.

10. (p. 124) *The phœnix dies . . . its five-hundredth year:* According to Ovid, *Metamorphoses,* Book XV, this rare Arabian bird burned itself on a funeral pyre containing perfumes and was reborn from the ashes every five hundred years. Dante compares the thief he is about to meet to the bird's eternal burning and rebirth.

11. (p. 124) *by force of demons . . . or other oppilation:* An oppilation, an obstruction in a vein from the heart to the brain, may trigger the mysterious fainting spells Dante describes, but such fits may also be caused by the devils.

12. (p. 125) *"a short time since I came into this cruel gorge . . . I'm Vanni Fucci":* A Tuscan from the city of Pistoia, Fucci was the illegitimate son of Fuccio de' Lazzari, the leader of the Black faction in that city. Vanni died some time around 1300 and is thus a fresh arrival. Dante is surprised to see him here, since he knew him as a violent, angry man who might have been expected to turn up in the River Phlegethon in the seventh circle.

13. (p. 125) *I robbed the sacristy of the fair ornaments . . . 'twas laid upon another:* Unlike the devils or monsters that punish them, tortured souls are obliged to confess when asked about their sins (another rule of Hell). They do, however, try to dissemble or place a positive

interpretation on what they say. In 1293 Vanni Fucci robbed the treasury of San Jacopo in the cathedral of San Zeno in Pistoia with several accomplices. Another man was almost executed for the crime before the truth emerged; Fucci was exiled from Pistoia and one of his confederates hanged.

14. (p. 125) *"Thine ears to my announcement ope.... And this I've said that it may give thee pain":* To take revenge on the Pilgrim for forcing him to confess his crime, Vanni Fucci provides an unpleasant prophecy about the future: The Whites of Pistoia will banish the Neri (the Blacks) from the city, and they will go to Florence. In 1301 Pistoian Blacks went to Florence and joined the Florentine Black faction to take control of the city, exiling the Whites with the support of Charles of Valois. As a result of these events, Dante was banished from his native city. So even though Vanni Fucci has been condemned to Hell for theft, he nevertheless knows the future and understands that Dante will soon be exiled from Florence, never to return home. Vanni also prophesizes other political events that would be of interest to the Pilgrim. The "vapor" drawn by Mars from the Val di Magra refers to Moroello Malaspina, a Black Guelph leader from that area who soldiered for Florence against the Ghibellines; "Campo Picen" is near a White Guelph fortress that the Black Guelphs of Pistoia captured in 1302.

CANTO XXV

1. (p. 126) *with both the figs... he could not a motion make:* Vanni Fucci's gesture consists of inserting a thumb between the index and the middle finger of the hand and closing the fist, thus combining an image of the female vulva with a male phallus. (The gesture could be translated into the English vernacular as "Fuck you!" or "Up your ass!") Since he points the gesture toward God (and, in fact, says, "Take that, God"), Fucci succeeds in being both obscene and blasphemous and is attacked by the snakes for his impertinence.

2. (p. 126) *Pistoia, ah, Pistoia!:* Pistoia was supposedly founded after 62 B.C. by the defeated soldiers in Catiline's army, a group of Roman rebels for whom Dante had little use (see canto XV: 61–78).

3. (p. 126) *Spirit I saw not against God so proud... at Thebes down from the walls!:* Fucci's blasphemy surpasses even that of Capaneus,

who blasphemed Jove while warring against Thebes and who we have already encountered among the blasphemers in the seventh circle (canto XIV: 63).

4. (p. 126) *I do not think Maremma has so many serpents as he had all along his back:* The Maremma (also mentioned in canto XIII: 8–9 and canto XXIX: 48–49) is a marshy, malaria-ridden section of Tuscany along the coast that was once infested with snakes.

5. (pp. 126–127) *That one is Cacus . . . the fraudulent theft he made of the great herd:* Cacus is Vulcan's son. Dante follows long but perhaps mistaken literary tradition to represent him as a centaur covered with snakes and carrying a fire-belching dragon on his back, but in the *Aeneid*, Book VIII, Virgil says only that he is half-human. Cacus was a thief, since he stole some of Hercules' cattle that had been brought into Italy. Because of this theft, Cacus "goes not on the same road with his brothers"—he is not assigned to guard Phlegethon with the other centaurs in the seventh circle (canto XII). The cave into which Cacus tried to hide the cattle stolen from Hercules was located on one of the seven hills of ancient Rome (Mount Aventine); the reference to a "lake of blood" comes from a hint in Dante's Virgilian source that Cacus devoured human flesh inside his cave.

6. (p. 127) *Cianfa:* This is a Florentine thief who died toward the end of the thirteenth century and who has been identified with the Donati family by early commentators on Dante. Soon, in l. 50, he will appear in the form of a serpent.

7. (p. 127) *from chin to nose my finger laid:* Dante the Pilgrim bids Virgil to remain silent.

8. (p. 127) *Behold! A serpent with six feet . . . fastens wholly on him:* The treatment of the thieves allows Dante to try his hand at the poetry of metamorphosis and to challenge the poets identified with this subject matter, Ovid and Lucan, with his own skill. Vanni Fucci was the first metamorphosis in the poem (canto XXIV: 97–120), since he is struck by a serpent at the base of the neck, turns to ash, and is resurrected from the pile of ashes, only to undergo this punishment for eternity. The second and even more complicated metamorphosis involves Cianfa, who here attaches himself in the form of a six-footed serpent to another sinner (we discover that he is a Florentine named Agnello). The two sinners merge, like ivy attached

to a tree (ll. 58–60); or like two pieces of heated wax melting together (ll. 61–63); or in the way a flame on a piece of white paper becomes intermixed with the brown color of the paper burning before it turns to black ash (ll. 64–66).

9. (p. 128) *the reins:* See canto XXIV, note 8; here Dante refers to the buttocks.

10. (p. 129) *Even as a lizard:* This is the beginning of a third complex metamorphosis (ll. 79–141) that Dante describes as taking place during the hot, dog days of July and August—the "days canicular," when Sirius, the Dog Star, rises up with the sun. The first sinner appears as a "small fiery serpent" (l. 83) and is only identifiable in the last line of the canto as Francesco de' Cavalcanti (see note 18). He attaches himself to the navel of another sinner—Buoso (identified in l. 140)—and they basically exchange, or transmute, their natures, as Dante says in ll. 100–103. The lizard to which Dante refers (*il ramarro*) is the kind of green lizard that is commonly found in Italy and most Mediterranean locations on rocks or walls during the hot summer days. They are extremely quick in their movements, and thus the poet compares the speed of such common reptiles to that of the "small, fiery serpent" he sees.

11. (p. 129) *that part whereat is first received our ailment:* The navel.

12. (p. 129) *Henceforth be silent Lucan . . . Be silent Ovid:* Employing a theme of traditional classical and medieval rhetoric to crow over his triumph, Dante points to famous classical versions of metamorphoses and attacks by serpents that he believes he has surpassed. In the *Pharsalia,* Book IX, Lucan describes the horrible deaths of Sabellus and Nassidius, soldiers marching across the desert in Cato's army. After being bitten by a deadly serpent, Sabellus turned into a puddle of corruption and Nassidius swelled up until he burst his armor. In *Metamorphoses,* Ovid describes how Cadmus was changed into a snake (Book IV) and how Arethusa was changed into a fountain (Book V). Dante is quick to note that Ovid never transmuted two different natures and, as a result, his poetic skill surpasses that of the Roman poet (ll. 100–102).

13. (p. 129–130) *Together they responded in such wise. . . . The one uprose and down the other fell, though turning not away their impious lamps:* Francesco de' Cavalcanti is being transformed from a snake into human form

and stands upright, while the other sinner, Buoso, falls down because he is being transformed into a snake. Each stares into the other's eyes ("their impious lamps"; in the Bible, Matthew 6: 22, the eye is described as the lamp of the body). Francesco's changes from a snake into human form are as follows: The tail becomes human legs; the front paws become human arms; the rear legs become a penis; the snake hide becomes human skin; his prone posture as a snake becomes human erect posture; his snake nose becomes a face; and his snake hiss becomes a human voice. Exactly the opposite transformation takes place in Buoso: human legs to tail; human arms to front paws; penis to rear legs; human skin to snake hide; erect human posture to prone snake posture; human face into a snake nose; and human voice to a snake hiss.

14. (p. 131) *"I'll have Buoso run, crawling as I have done":* Still unidentified himself, Francesco de' Calvacanti names Buoso. Now that Francesco has been changed from a serpent into a human being, with the power to speak rather than merely to hiss, he hopes that Buoso will be made to crawl for a while before the next transformation, as he has been forced to do.

15. (p. 131) *the seventh ballast:* Dante implies that the seventh circle is like the hold of a cargo ship filled with worthless materials of ballast, used to balance the weight inside a ship. The mention of a ship provides a hint of the next major figure and theme to appear in the poem—Ulysses and his epic sea voyages, which Dante discusses in canto XXVI.

16. (p. 131) *if aught my pen transgress:* It has been suggested that in this passage Dante may offer an excuse for spending so much time on the metamorphoses—the sights were so marvelous that his pen strayed. It has also been argued that Dante may be suggesting that the incredible sights he was reporting caused him to work hurriedly, blotching the manuscript with ink in the process. The interpretation of the passage hinges upon the meaning of a rather unusual verb, *abborracciare,* which combines the idea of doing something badly and hurriedly as well as that of wandering or of being confused.

17. (p. 131) *Puccio Sciancato:* This is the third sinner who appeared with the other two in l. 35 ("spirits three had underneath us come"). Puccio is the only one of the three Florentine thieves who

does not assume a different shape. He was a member of a Ghibelline family, the Galigai, and was exiled from Florence in 1268. Little of his career as a thief is known to us, but Dante undoubtedly knew some story of his transgression that has not come down to us in detail.

18. (p. 131) *he whom thou, Gaville, weepest:* The final line of the canto finally provides the identification of the soul who first appeared earlier as a little snake (l. 83). Francesco de' Cavalcanti, known as Guercio, was murdered by the people of Gaville, a town in the Val d'Arno in Tuscany, and in turn the Cavalcanti family avenged his death so ferociously that they practically depopulated the town, hence the townspeople's weeping.

CANTO XXVI

1. (p. 132) *over sea and land thou beatest thy wings:* Dante's ironic apostrophe to his native city underscores his bitterness at the corruption and the political strife causing his exile. It is possible that the reference to Florence's dominion over sea and land refers to a Latin inscription on the Palazzo del Podestà boasting that the city rules over land, sea, and the entire world.

2. (p. 132) *our dreams are true:* In Dante's time, as during the classical period, it was believed that dreams experienced in the early morning just before waking were prophetic. During the Pilgrim's journey through Purgatory, he will experience three such waking dreams—in cantos IX, XIX, and XXVII.

3. (p. 132) *What Prato . . . the more I age:* Commentators and scholars have advanced several interpretations of this passage. It may refer to the 1309 revolt in Prato (a Tuscan town just outside of Florence) against the Black Guelphs. Or it may refer to Cardinal Niccolò da Prato, who failed in his attempts in 1304 to bring peace to Florence's warring factions after Pope Benedict IV sent him there as papal legate. The cardinal became angry and placed the city under an interdict. A number of disasters that ensued in Prato (the collapse of a bridge during a religious ceremony, the strife between Black and White Guelphs, a large fire) were attributed to the negative effects of the cardinal's interdict.

4. (p. 132) *bourns:* Scholars have argued on Dante's intention

in the Italian original here, accepting either *i borni* (the boundaries formed by the outcroppings of the rocks), the more traditional reading that Longfellow follows, or *iborni* (referring to the pallid color of the Pilgrims as they descend the stairs). I believe Longfellow's reading is the correct one.

5. (p. 134) *Elijah's chariot at departing:* In the Bible, the prophet Elisha sees Elijah carried off to Heaven in a fiery chariot (2 Kings 2: 11).

6. (p. 134) *every flame a sinner steals away:* We are now in the eighth Bolgia, where evil counselors are punished inside a flame that is perhaps a parody of their glib tongues, the instrument of their sin.

7. (p. 134) *"it seems uprising from the pyre where was Eteocles with his brother placed":* Dante compares the divided flame he sees to the flame that arose from the funeral pyre of Eteocles and Polynices, sons of Oedipus, who fought over the Kingdom of Thebes (Polynices led the group of allies who formed against Eteocles, known as Seven Against Thebes). They killed each other in combat and were buried together. Dante's sources are Statius, *Thebaid,* Book XII, and Lucan, *Pharsalia,* Book I.

8. (p. 134) *Ulysses and Diomed:* In the Trojan War, Ulysses (King of Ithaca) and Diomedes (King of Argos) fought on the victorious Greek side (not the side Dante favored, since the offspring of the Trojans founded Rome). It is important to remember that Dante never read Homer's *Iliad* and knew about the Trojan War only through what he had read in Virgil's *Aeneid* and the works of a number of lesser authors, including Dicyts the Cretan and Dares the Phrygian. Basically, much of what he recounts about Ulysses is a fiction of his own invention, although he accurately captures the shrewd, calculating personality of Homer's protagonist.

9. (pp. 134–135) *"The ambush of the horse . . . there is borne":* Ulysses and Diomedes are punished as evil counselors in Hell. Ulysses proposed the Trojan horse and also tricked Achilles into joining the campaign against Troy, during which he was killed. Deidamia, daughter of the King of Sykros, bore Achilles a son and died of grief when she learned of his death in battle (in the *Purgatory,* canto XXII, we learn she is in Limbo). Dante's source here is the *Achilleid,*

by Statius. Both Ulysses and Diomedes stole the Palladium, a wooden image of Athena that the goddess entrusted to Troy; the theft ensured a Greek victory over the Trojans.

10. (p. 135) *"they might disdain . . . discourse of thine":* Virgil's refusal to allow Dante to address the two Greeks directly has provoked a great deal of critical debate. Dante knew no Greek and his native tongue, Italian, was derived from Latin. While Latin was the classical language of the Roman Republic and Empire, and surpassed Greek in the realms of politics and economics, Greek remained the language of culture, and all educated Romans spoke Greek fluently. Perhaps Virgil mediates the encounter with the Greek heroes because his poetry was one of the most important means of transmitting Greek culture to Latin Rome and medieval Italy.

11. (p. 135) *"If I deserved of you . . . the lofty verses":* Virgil's mention of his "lofty verses" brings to mind canto XX, line 113, where he describes his epic poem as "my lofty Tragedy." Virgil does mention Ulysses and Diomed in his *Aeneid,* but does not do so favorably, since his poem celebrates the Trojan origins of ancient Rome. Western culture was prejudiced against the Greeks (for example, Shakespeare famously admonishes us to beware Greeks bearing gifts) right up to the Romantic period, when Homer was rediscovered and Greece, for the first time in Western culture, was raised above Rome.

12. (p. 135) *"of the antique flame the greater horn":* The larger part of the horn-shaped flame represents Ulysses, since he was the most important of the two Greek warriors.

13. (p. 135) *"When I from Circe had departed. . . .":* Ulysses' speech (ll. 90–142) represents one of the high points of Dante's epic poetry. After escaping from the enchantress Circe, who had transformed Ulysses' sailors into swine, Ulysses claims to have visited Gaëta on the coast of Italy above Naples—and to have arrived there before Aeneas, who does so in Virgil's *Aeneid,* Book VII; "or ever yet Aeneas named it so," l. 93, is a reference to "Caieta," as Aeneas called the place, after his nurse, who died there. Ulysses admits to abandoning the ties of family and his love for his son (Telemachus), wife (Penelope), and father (Laertes) in favor of a hubristic desire to know the world. This was exactly the opposite course taken by Virgil's pious hero Aeneas, who revered his son Ascanius, his wife Creusa, and his father Anchises, and who always obeyed the commands of the gods, to the point of sometimes annoying his modern readers. Ulysses' adventuresome voyage in a single ship took him beyond the known world, the Strait of Gibraltar, then called the Pillars of Hercules (l. 108). His mention of Seville (l. 110) simply refers to the fact that he has left Spain behind, just as his mention of Ceuta (l. 111), a city on the North African coast opposite Gibraltar, signifies Africa. Some recent commentators have suggested that the voyage of Ulysses beyond the boundaries of the medieval world might reflect an expedition of the Vivaldi brothers, who in 1291 set out from Italy to reach India by sailing through the Strait of Gibraltar and were never heard from again. For the post-Renaissance reader of Dante, there is certainly a touch of Christopher Columbus in Dante's Ulysses.

14. (p. 136) *"but for pursuit of virtue and of knowledge":* One of the most famous and appealing of all of Dante's lines (*ma per seguir virtute e canoscenza*) has been as misunderstood as the equally famous lines uttered by Francesca da Rimini in canto V. Ulysses is being punished in Hell because of his treacherous words. The beautiful speech he gives to his men to convince them to sail to their deaths (ll. 112–120) may give the impression that Dante has created a Romantic hero, but in point of fact, Dante considers Ulysses to be a paragon of pride; even the glib Ulysses admits that his voyage was "our mad flight" (l. 125). In Homer's *Odyssey* (a poem Dante could not have known, though he captures the spirit of the work in his depiction of Ulysses), the protagonist, Odysseus, indirectly kills his men off in adventure after adventure, usually motivated by instincts that Dante would not have admired if he had had access to the poem.

15. (p. 136) *"on the larboard side . . . five times rekindled and as many quenched":* After passing through the Strait of Gibraltar, Ulysses' ship turns left toward the Equator, where the men can see that night beholds "the other pole"—that is, the Antarctic—and "ours," a reference to the stars of "our" hemisphere, probably the North Star. Ulysses and his men sail for five months ("five times rekindled").

16. (p. 136) *a mountain:* Ulysses has no way of knowing it, but he and his men have sighted the Mount of Purgatory that rises from the sea in the Southern Hemisphere at a point exactly opposite the holy city of Jerusalem. Why a Mount of Purgatory existed in the

time of Ulysses, before Christ appeared to redeem the world and the idea of purgation was born, is never addressed. Naturally, Dante treats the Mount of Purgatory at great length in *Purgatory*, the second canticle of his epic.

CANTO XXVII

1. (p. 138) *As the Sicilian bull . . . with his file had modulated it:* Phalaris, the tyrant who ruled the Sicilian city of Agrigentum from c.570 B.C.–c.554 B.C., had an artist named Perillus construct a bronze bull into which a victim could be placed. The bull was heated, roasting the victim, whose screams sounded like the roar of a bellowing animal. Phalaris tested this device of torture on Perillus. Dante compares the manner in which the bull's roar was produced to the way the sinners in this region of Hell can speak through the tongue-shaped flame.

2. (p. 138) *now wast speaking Lombard:* The sinner has overheard Virgil dismissing Ulysses, and apparently he recognizes the language Virgil speaks as the Lombard dialect of Italian. "Lombard" may also be employed here simply to mean "Italian." Although the sinner's name is not identified here and is only later revealed in an indirect manner (ll. 67–78), there is no doubt that he is Guido da Montefeltro (1223–1298), the most important Ghibelline leader in the Romagna district of northern Italy.

3. (p. 139) *"between Urbino and the yoke whence Tiber bursts":* This refers to the Montefeltro region, between the city of Urbino and Monte Coronaro, where the Tiber River begins.

4. (p. 139) *Ravenna stands . . . and a free state:* In his eager attempt to answer the question posed by the tortured sinner in l. 28—whether the peoples of the Romagna are at war or not—the Pilgrim mentions cities and forts in the Romagna, all governed by different rulers. The city of Ravenna on the Adriatic coast was then ruled by Guido Vecchio (d. 1310), head of the powerful Polenta family, who controlled the city from the thirteenth century to 1441, when it was taken over by Venice. Guido, whose coat of arms bore the insignia of an eagle, was the father of Francesca da Rimini (see canto V). Cervia, a town a few miles below Ravenna, was valuable because of the revenue its salt generated. In ll. 43–44, Dante is referring to the

town of Forlì ("the city which one made the long resistance"): Guido da Montefeltro defended the city against a French attack in 1282, during which time the French suffered heavy losses ("of the French a sanguinary heap"); the city then came under the rule of the Ordeleffi family, whose coat of arms contained a green lion (the "Green Paws" of l. 45). "Verrucchio's ancient Mastiff" (l. 46) refers to Malatesta da Verrucchio (d. 1312), the lord of Rimini who captured the city from the Ghibellines in 1295. (One of his sons was the husband of the aforementioned Francesca da Rimini of canto V.) The "new" mastiff is Malatestino, who succeeded his father as lord of Rimini in 1312 and ruled until 1317. Dante refers to the men as dogs, or mastiffs, because of their cruelty, and he describes them as fashioning "wimbles," or augurs, of their teeth, the better to bite into their beleaguered subjects (l. 48). The "bad disposal of Montagna" (l. 47) refers to the fact that in 1295, after Malatesta captured the leader of the Ghibellines of Rimini, Montagna de' Parcitati, he had him murdered by his son Malatestino. The towns of Faenza on the Lamone River and Imola on the Santerno River were governed by a ruler Dante calls the "Lioncel of the white lair" (l. 50); the so-called "little lion" was Maghinardo Pagani da Susinna, whose coat of arms bore a blue lion on a white field. Dante describes him as changing sides, since he was Ghibelline in Romagna but supported the Guelphs in Tuscany. The city "of which the Savio bathes the flank" (l. 52) is Cesena, which is located between Forlì and Rimini; it "lives between tyranny and a free state," because it was not ruled by a tyrant like the other cities of the Romagna, and its affairs were controlled by a cousin of Guido da Montefeltro named Galasso da Montefeltro.

5. (p. 139) *"so may thy name hold front there in the world":* The Pilgrim knows that the tortured souls cannot resist the chance to have justification of their lives delivered to the world of the living, but he is also aware that they hate the idea of any notice of their damnation being brought back to earth.

6. (p. 140) *"If I believed . . . without the fear of infamy I answer":* The Pilgrim manages to persuade a famous soul, Guido da Montefeltro, to discuss his fate, something Guido only says he does because he does not think his words will ever be reported—Guido mistakenly

believes Dante to be a damned soul who can never repeat what he says to the world of the living.

7. (p. 141) *"I was a man of arms, then Cordelier":* Guido was a soldier, but in 1296 he joined the Franciscan order of friars (and therefore wore the cord typical of that order, calling himself a Cordelier, or "cord wearing friar").

8. (p. 141) *the High Priest:* This is a reference to Pope Boniface VIII. In ll. 85–111, Guido blames his fraudulent counseling upon Boniface. Several chronicles of the period collaborate the account Dante provides here, but it is possible that the authors of these chronicles took the story to be true after reading the *Comedy.*

9. (p. 141) *"the deeds I did were not those of a lion, but a fox":* Guido was frequently referred to during his lifetime as a crafty, astute fox. No doubt Dante knew the metaphor of the lion and the fox from Cicero's *De officiis,* Book I, in which the author declares that injustice may be done in two ways, through force (the aspect of the lion) or through deceit (the aspect of the fox), and that while both of these sources of injustice are alien to human nature, that of deceit is more despicable. Niccolò Machiavelli, the great Renaissance Florentine philosopher, picked up Cicero's metaphor again in his famous description of the ideal prince's qualities as those of the lion and the fox in *The Prince,* Book XVIII. Unlike either Cicero or Dante, Machiavelli praises the qualities of force and deceit Cicero and Dante identified with these two animals, since he believed that without such qualities, a ruler could never survive.

10. (p. 141) *"of the modern Pharisees... in the Sultan's land":* In 1297 Pope Boniface (compared here to the evil Pharisees who killed Christ) was at odds with the powerful Colonna family, who lived near the Lateran palace in Rome. Rather than attending to the proper business of the papacy and attacking the traditional enemies of the Church (Muslims and Jews, l. 87), Pope Boniface made war upon Christians who had neither helped the Muslims reconquer Acre (the last Crusader stronghold in the Holy Land, l. 89), nor engaged in commerce with the infidel, as did the Jews (l. 90).

11. (p. 141) *as Constantine sought out Sylvester... within Soracte:* Guido compares the advice he was asked to give Pope Boniface to the fourteenth-century deal made between Emperor Constantine and

Pope Sylvester I. According to legend, after persecuting the Christians, Constantine was struck with leprosy as a punishment. He went to visit the pope, who was in hiding near Rome on Monte Soracte, was converted and cured, and, as a sign of his gratitude, supposedly made the famous "Donation of Constantine." This document gave the papacy the city of Rome and temporal power in the West (and was proven to be a forgery in the fifteenth century by Lorenzo Valla, who served as papal secretary).

12. (pp. 141–142) *"I thee absolve... which my predecessor held not dear":* Boniface promises Guido absolution for his evil counsel, declaring that he has the power to bind and unbind on Earth because of the two keys given symbolically by Christ to the first pope, the Apostle Peter—and which Celestine V gave up, "he held not dear," when he renounced the papacy in 1294. Guido advises the pope on how to take control of Palestrina, a Colonna stronghold outside of Rome, by fraud. Boniface promised the Colonna complete amnesty if they surrendered the fortress, then, following Guido's advice, destroyed it completely.

13. (p. 142) *"The promise long with the fulfilment short":* This is an apt description of Boniface's false promise to the Colonna of Palestrina (see note above).

14. (p. 142) *"Francis came afterward... 'Take him not; do me no wrong'":* According to Dante's account (obviously invented), Saint Francis comes to claim the soul of Guido, who is a Franciscan monk, but since Guido has never repented of his sin and has trusted in the fraudulent promises of an evil pope, Francis is denied possession of his soul and a black Cherubim carries it to Hell. The Cherubim were the second most important rank of the nine orders of angels; some of them rebelled against God with Lucifer and were placed in Hell with him. In *Purgatory* V: 104–105, Guido's son Bonconte experiences a similar struggle between a devil and an angel contesting for his soul, but Bonconte is saved and the devil is thwarted. Such interrelated narrative episodes across Canticles make up one of the most interesting structural devices holding Dante's poem together.

15. (p. 142) *the fraudulent advice:* In canto XI: 52–60, Virgil does not specifically name the sin punished in the eight and ninth Bolge. In fact, after listing hypocrisy, flattery, magic, falsification, theft, si-

mony, pandering, and barratry, Virgil concludes the list with the phrase "and the like filth." Here, for the first time, the reader learns what that sin punished in the eight Bolgia is and what "like filth" means in part: *consigilo frodolente,* false or evil counseling.

16. (p. 142) *unto Minos, who entwined eight times his tail:* After the black Cherubim wins the contest with Saint Francis, he follows the rules of Hell and delivers Guido to Minos, who performs his normal function by wrapping his tail around the sinner the number of times (eight) that signifies the location of his punishment (the eighth Bolgia).

17. (p. 142) *the moat ... win their burden:* The "moat" is the ditch of the ninth Bolgia, where the sowers of discord are punished—where they pay the "fee" and take on the burden of their guilt.

CANTO XXVIII

1. (p. 143) *Assembled all the people.... the lingering war:* Dante opens his description of the ninth Bolgia with a long simile. The Pilgrim declares that the horribly mutilated souls he sees here far outnumber those killed in various military actions that took place in Puglia, called Apuglia in Roman times, a southeastern section of the Italian peninsula. First, he mentions the blood shed by the Trojans when Aeneas invaded Italy. Longfellow translates the original Italian *Troiani* as "Romans," and other commentators and scholars have accepted the translation and interpreted the word to refer to the Romans killed in the wars between the Samnites and the Romans in 343–290 B.C. ("blood shed by the Romans"). But "Trojans" may well be the correct translation here. Second, Dante refers to the "lingering war," which can only refer to the huge number of Romans killed in the Second Punic War against Hannibal in 218–201 B.C.

2. (p. 143) *That of the rings ... as Livy has recorded:* In his history of Rome, Livy noted that so many Romans were killed by Hannibal at the disastrous battle of Cannae (216 B.C.) that Hannibal delivered several bushels filled with gold rings cut from Roman fingers to the Carthaginian Senate.

3. (p. 143) *Robert Guiscard:* This Norman warrior and duke of Apulia and Calabria fought the Byzantines and the Saracens in south-

ern Italy c.1060–1080. Dante places him in *Paradise* XVIII: 48, in the Heaven of Mars, for his efforts as a Christian warrior.

4. (p. 143) *At Ceperano . . . the old Alardo conquered:* In 1266 Manfred, king of Sicily, commanded troops at the pass of Ceperano against the soldiers of Charles of Anjou, but his Apulian troops allowed the French to force the pass without opposition. Shortly thereafter, at the battle of Benevento, Charles defeated Manfred, who was killed during the combat. Two years later, at the battle of Tagliacozzo, Charles employed a ruse suggested to him by Érard de Valéry ("old Aloardo"—Longfellow employs an Italian version of this French soldier's name) to defeat the remainder of Manfred's followers in Italy. At Tagliacozzo, Ghibelline forces opposing Charles of Anjou were led by Conradin, grandson of Emperor Frederick II. After the defeat, Conradin was executed, and his death effectively ended Hohenstaufen aspirations to rule over Italy.

5. (p. 144) *"See now how I rend me; how mutilated, see, is Mahomet":* Dante thought of Mohammed (c.570–632) not as the founder of a new, Islamic religion, but as a Christian schismatic. His punishment literally embodies the sin of discord by having his body torn apart from chin to buttocks.

6. (p. 144) *"Ali . . . cleft in the face from forelock unto chin":* Mohammed's adopted son and son-in-law, husband of his daughter Fatima, assumed the caliphate in 656 until his death by assassination in 661. Arguments over Ali's succession caused the followers of Islam to split into two factions—Sunni and Shiite—that remain disunited today. While Mohammed is split from the chin down, Ali is split from the chin up.

7. (p. 144) *"Sowers of scandal and of schism":* Here Dante describes the sinners being punished in the ninth Bolgia as sowers of discord. "Scandal" was understood in Dante's theology as any doctrine that causes others to stumble and lose their path to truth. Schism is distinguished from heresy, in that schism cuts off a person from the unity of the Church, while heresy opposes faith itself. In the ninth Bolgia, Dante meets schismatic groups associated with both religion and politics.

8. (p. 144) *"say to Fra Dolcino":* The leader of a religious sect known as the Apostolic Brothers preached a return to apostolic

simplicity, as well as the sharing of property and women. Declared heretical by Pope Clement V in 1305, the sect was eradicated by a crusade at Novara, in nothern Italy. Dolcino and his mistress, Margaret of Trent, were burned at the stake in 1307.

9. (pp. 144–145) *"If soon he wish not here to follow me . . . the victory to the Novarese":* Souls in Hell, it must be remembered, have knowledge of events that occur some time ahead of the present. So when Mohammed learns from Virgil that Dante the Pilgrim is a living being who will return to the world, he seeks to send a message to Fra Dolcino (see note above) concerning his death, which will actually occur after the fictional date of the poem (1300). Mohammed warns Dolcino to stock plenty of provisions so he will not be forced to surrender for lack of them, as he actually would do during his last stand at Novara.

10. (p. 145) *Pier da Medicina . . . nor Argolic people:* Medicina is a small town between Vercelli and Marcabò, near Bologna. Little is known of Pier, but Dante must have known him. Early commentators considered him to be an instigator of political strife. Pier now provides another of the prophecies that various sinners along the Pilgrim's path through Hell have revealed—the prediction of a double murder near Fano. The victims are Guido del Cassero and Angiolello di Carignano, leading figures in Fano, a small town on the Adriatic south of Rimini. The tyrant of Rimini, Malatestino Malatesta (already mentioned in canto XXVII: 46) invites them to meet him at the town of Cattolica, another small town on the same coastal area, where he greets their ship and has them drowned. This treacherous assassination will take place some time after 1312, more than a decade after the fictional date of the poem (1300). Pier claims that Malatestino's murder of the two men is unmatched by any crime in the entire Mediterranean, even those atrocities committed by pirates or by the inhabitants of Greece (the "Argolic people").

11. (p. 145) *"who sees only with one eye . . . and holds the land":* Malatestino had only one eye; the land he "holds" is Rimini.

12. (p. 145) *"to Focara's wind they will not stand in need of vow or prayer":* Pier's prophecy concludes that the two assassinated men from Fano will not need any protection from the Focara's wind, a famous gale that destroyed many ships off that particular coast.

13. (pp. 145–147) *"this person of the bitter vision" . . . Curio:* Dante asks Pier the identity of the soul who he described earlier (ll. 86–87) as one who would have preferred not to have had the bitter sight of the land around Rimini. Pier identifies the soul as Gaius Scribonius Curio, a Roman tribune who reportedly advised Caesar to cross the Rubicon River. This body of water formed the boundary line that the republican government forbad Roman armies and their commanders to cross. When Caesar crossed the Rubicon, he went on to overthrow the Roman Republic and begin a period of civil war leading to the formation of the Roman Empire. Curio reportedly told Caesar that when forewarned, to delay is fatal (ll. 98–99). The Rubicon is associated with the city of Rimini because it empties into the Adriatic near there. Curio has apparently lost the use of his tongue by the sword of the devil who administers punishment in this region, so Pier is forced to pry open his mouth to show the Pilgrim.

14. (p. 147) *"remember Mosca also . . . an ill seed for the Tuscan people":* This is Mosca dei Lamberti, a Ghibelline from Florence. He advised the murder of Buondelmonte dei Buondelmonti, who was engaged to a girl from the Amidei family but married one of the Donati family instead. This murder, carried out in 1215, was reportedly the origin of the bitter internecine strife in Florence between the Guelphs and Ghibellines, since the Amidei family (the assassins) were Ghibellines while the Donati were Guelphs. By his advice—"A thing done has an end" (l. 107)—Mosca means that since anything less than murder would provoke the same violent reaction, it is better to kill than to undertake a milder form of vendetta. The story, including Mosca's advice, is reported in Giovanni Villani's fourteenth-century history of Florence. The reader should remember that the Pilgrim asked Ciacco about Mosca and other Florentines earlier, in canto VI: 80.

15. (p. 147–148) *"Bertram de Born . . . Achitophel not more with Absalom":* One of the most famous of all Provençal poets, Bertran de Born (whom Dante calls "Bertram") lived in the second half of the twelfth century. While Dante praises his poetry in other works, here he places Bertran in Hell for supporting the rebellion of Prince Henry ("the Young King," l. 135) against his father, Henry II of

England. Bertran's advice to Prince Henry is compared to that given by Achitophel the Gilonite, who instigated Absalom's rebellion against King David, his father, in the Bible, 2 Samuel 15–17.

16. (p. 148) *the counterpoise:* Dante finally names the principle of punishment in Hell, divine retribution that is exemplified in Bertran de Born's frightening punishment: His head is severed from his body, because in life he divided father and son. Longfellow is one of the few translators of Dante to have rendered Dante's term for this principle of punishment, *contrapasso,* into a precise English term: A counterpoise is any force or influence that balances or equally counteracts another force or influence. Therefore, in almost all cases in Hell, the punishment the sinners receive fits their crimes. The punishment is counterpoised to the sin in some fashion, often an extremely ingenious one. The principle of "counterpoise" owes something to the *lex talionis* of the Old Testament (see Exodus 23: 23–27: the proverbial "eye for an eye, a tooth for a tooth") and to the medieval Latin translation of a term in Aristotle's *Nicomachean Ethics,* Book V—*contrapassum*—that means "retaliation." Thomas Aquinas discusses this term at some length in his *Summa Theologica.*

CANTO XXIX

1. (p. 149) *two-and-twenty miles the valley winds:* This is the first precise measurement we are offered of an area in Hell, the circumference of the next Bolgia, the ninth. In canto XXX: 86, Dante tells us that the tenth Bolgia is exactly half this size, or 11 miles in circumference. If it has not already been obvious to the reader up to this point, it is now clear that Hell is a huge inverted cone, becoming narrower and narrower as the two poets travel down toward its center.

2. (p. 149) *underneath our feet:* If the moon is underneath, then the sun is directly overhead, and it is therefore midday in Jerusalem on Holy Saturday.

3. (p. 149) *Geri del Bello:* This character was a first cousin to Dante's father and was murdered by a member of the Sacchetti family around the time of the poem's fictional action. His death was avenged by a member of the Alighieri family only around 1310—therefore long after the time Dante meets Geri in Hell.

4. (p. 150) *him who formerly held Altaforte:* Dante was so engaged

in his conversation with Bertran de Born (the lord of Altaforte, as Dante refers to him) that he failed to notice Geri earlier.

5. (p. 150) *the last cloister of Malebolge:* Cantos XXIX and XXX are devoted to falsifications: Dante discusses alchemists, who falsify metals and other materials, in canto XXIX, and evil impersonators, counterfeiters, and false witnesses in canto XXX.

6. (p. 150) *From the hospitals of Valdichiana . . . and Sardinia:* The Valdichiana and the Maremma are two districts in Tuscany that were once known for summertime cases of malaria, as was the island of Sardinia.

7. (p. 150) *a sadder sight to see was in Ægina . . . the seed of ants restored again:* Dante compares the sufferings in this *bolgia* to those recounted in Ovid's *Metamorphoses,* Book VII. Ovid describes how Juno sent a plague to the island of Aegina, killing everyone there except Aeacus. Aeacus asked Jupiter to repopulate the island, and the god did so by turning ants into human beings.

8. (p. 153) *"I of Arezzo was . . . Albert of Siena had me burned":* Since the earliest commentaries on Dante, this figure has been identified as an alchemist named Griffolino from the town of Arezzo, who pretended to teach Albero da Siena how to fly like Icarus. When this fraud was uncovered, Albero exacted his revenge by having the bishop (whose son he may have been) condemn Griffolino to be burned at the stake as a magician.

9. (p. 153) *"So vain a people as the Sienese? Not for a certainty the French by far":* Florence and Siena were natural rivals, and inhabitants of each city habitually poked fun at those of the other. Florentines considered both the Sienese and the French to be extremely vain people.

10. (p. 153) *"Taking out Stricca . . . a skilful ape of nature was":* This speech concerns sinners from Siena who were members of an infamous Spendthrifts Brigade (the "band" of l. 130) and went through their fortunes giving lavish banquets, eating outrageously exotic foods, and generally misbehaving as the period's most conspicuous consumers. Dante suggests their behavior is typical of Siena, "a garden where such seed takes root." Almost nothing is known of Stricca. Niccolò (l. 127) has been identified as one of the Salimbeni family who invented unusual meals based upon cloves. Caccia

d'Asciano (l. 131) is Caccia of Asciano, who squandered away his vineyards and lands, while Abbagliato (l. 32) may be a certain Bartolomeo dei Folcacchieri. (The identities of all these men are uncertain and really matter very little, since what concerns Dante is the sin they exemplify, not their personalities.) Near the end of the speech the speaker identifies himself as Capocchio, a Florentine Dante may have known as a young student and who was burned at the stake for alchemy in Siena in 1293.

CANTO XXX

1. (p. 154) *'Twas at the time . . . drowned herself:* Dante opens the canto with two complicated similes derived from Ovid's poetry. The first simile recounts how Semele, the daughter of Cadmus, king of Thebes, bore a son named Bacchus to Jupiter, thus enraging his wife, Juno. Juno took revenge by causing the death of Semele and her sister, Ino. Juno drove Ino's husband, Athamas, mad, and he killed their son, Learchus (l. 10), driving Ino to drown her other son, Melicertes ("the other burthen" of l. 12), and herself. See *The Metamorphoses,* Book IV, for the Ovidian source.

2. (p. 154) *Hecuba sad . . . the anguish had her mind distorted:* Dante's second simile concerns Hecuba, the wife of King Priam of Troy, who was carried back to Greece after the destruction of her homeland. There she witnessed the slaughters of her daughter, Polyxena, on the grave of Achilles (l. 17) and her son, Polydorus, killed by the king of Thrace, Polymnestor, and left unburied on the Thracian beach (l. 18). As a result, Hecuba became insane (ll. 20–21) but was still able to kill Polymnestor. See *The Metamorphoses,* Book XIII, for the Ovidian source.

3. (pp. 154–155) *But not of Thebes . . . made his belly grate the solid bottom:* Dante now declares that the insanity of Athamas and Hecuba was not as bestial as the two shades that arrive like two Furies, running on all fours like a hog freed from its sty (l. 27). One of the two shades attacks Capocchio and drags him away.

4. (p. 155) *And the Aretine . . . "That mad sprite is Gianni Schicchi":* The Aretine speaker (l. 31) is Griffolino of Arezzo who appeared earlier in canto XXIX: 109–120. He identifies the raving "mad sprite" as Gianni Schicchi, a member of Cavalcanti family of Florence who

died around 1280. Gianni was famous for his talents as a mimic, and Dante now tells the famous story of how he was reputed to have impersonated Buoso di Donati (l. 44) in a deathbed confession. Posing as Buoso—who had already died, without having left his fortune to his son, Simone—Gianni first gave himself some bequests, including a very handsome mare ("the lady of the herd," l. 43), then made sure that Simone inherited most of Buoso's fortune. This story is the source of Giacomo Puccini's opera *Gianni Schicchi.*

5. (p. 155) *and raving goes:* Gianni, who we soon learn is guilty of the sin of impersonation, is "raving," the curse of sinners of his type. The punishment of each of the four types of falsifiers resembles a terrible disease. The alchemists seem to have leprosy; the impersonators are rabid; the counterfeiters have dropsy; and the liars have a fever that makes them smell badly. Each of these horrible diseases was very common in Dante's time and would have conjured up to his readers a very precise image of pain and suffering, as well as of hideousness.

6. (p. 155) *the nefarious Myrrha:* Griffolino explains that the other shade is Myrrha, the daughter of the king of Cyprus, who disguised herself in order to sleep with her father. See Ovid, *Metamorphoses,* Book X.

7. (p. 156) *"the misery of Master Adam . . . my body burned above":* The Counts Guidi of the town of Romena (l. 73), located in the Casentino region (l. 65; Longfellow uses a double "s" in the spelling) near Florence, ordered Master Adam to strike counterfeit florins, the internationally accepted currency of medieval business that contained a legal standard of 24 carats of gold and bore the image of John the Baptist (l. 74), the patron saint of Florence. The florins Master Adam struck contained only 21 carats of gold mixed with 3 carats of alloy ("three carats of impurity," l. 90), enough to cause the zealous Florentine authorities to burn him alive in 1281.

8. (p. 156) *"Of Guido, or Alessandro . . . one is within already":* Of the four Guidi brothers—Guido, Alessandro, and the unnamed Aghinolfo and Ildebrando—who caused Master Adam to sin, Guido (d. 1292) is the only one who has died before 1300 and is already in Hell. "Branda's fount" (l. 78) is a spring near Romena.

9. (p. 156) *"a hundred years I could advance one inch . . . less than half a*

mile across": Dante provides precise details about the physical size of the tenth Bolgia, which is 11 miles in the circumference and a full half-mile across (making it difficult to envision a bridge across the space). Master Adam reveals that he is so angry with Guido Guidi that he is willing to inch toward him for revenge, even though he can only advance one inch every hundred years. Since souls in Hell have eternity on their hands, perhaps this journey (calculated by scrupulous Dante scholars to require more than 700,000 years) is a good way to pass infernal time.

10. (p. 157) *One the false woman . . . the other the false Sinon, Greek of Troy:* The woman who accused Joseph is Potiphar's wife. In the Bible, Genesis 39: 7–23, she falsely accuses Joseph of trying to seduce her, when in reality she has made the sexual advances. Sinon is the Greek who persuaded the Trojans to bring the so-called Trojan Horse inside the city, causing its downfall and destruction. Dante's source is Virgil, the *Aeneid,* Book II.

11. (p. 157) *And one of them . . . thou hadst it not so ready:* Sinon exchanges blows with Master Adam ("the dropsical" of l. 112) and insults Adam by telling him that his arm was not quite so ready to strike out when he was burned alive (because he was bound hand and foot at the time). The insulting give-and-take between the two characters presents a comic scene in Hell that may owe something to the medieval poetic genre called the *tenzone,* a poetic debate usually filled with invective. Dante himself exchanged such poems with a number of his contemporaries, including Dante da Maiano, Cecco Angiolieri, and Forese Donati.

12. (p. 157) *"for one fault I am here, and thou for more than any other demon":* While Sinon committed only one sin at Troy, Master Adam falsified numerous counterfeit florins. Since each coin could be counted as a separate sin (Florentines were deadly serious about the purity of their money), Master Adam could be guilty of thousands of individual transgressions.

13. (p. 157) *"I have thirst, and humor stuff me":* The "humor" Adam refers to is not wit but the liquid that dropsy causes the body to retain; ironically, the condition is accompanied by a terrible thirst.

14. (p. 157) *the mirror of Narcissus:* Adam refers to a pool of water that would reflect Sinon's image, like the one that reflected that of

Narcissus in the Greek myth. In love with his own image reflected in a pond, Narcissus stared at it until he died and was turned into the flower bearing his name. Dante's source is Ovid's *Metamorphoses*, Book III.

15. (pp. 157–158) *When him I heard in anger speak to me.... "A base wish it is to wish to hear it":* Once again, Virgil rebukes the Pilgrim sternly, because he has lost his focus and has been enjoying the comic scene in Hell between Master Adam and Sinon. Virgil reminds the Pilgrim that he should be standing above the scene with the requisite moral indignation of a judge.

CANTO XXXI

1. (p. 159) *Thus do I hear that once Achilles' spear:* The Poet compares Virgil's words to him at the end of the last canto (first rebuking, then comforting) to the legendary spear of Achilles, formerly the property of his father Peleus, that could heal the wounds it inflicted.

2. (p. 159) *the blare of a loud horn... so terribly Orlando sounded not:* Dante compares the horn blast to that famous sound in *The Song of Roland.* In this epic, Roland blows his oliphant (a horn made from elephant tusk) to summon Charlemagne after Ganellon (also often spelled "Ganelon") betrays the emperor's rear guard to the Saracens in the pass of Roncesvalles. Dante probably did not know the text we read today as *The Song of Roland,* but the story was proverbial and a version of it was recounted in a number of French and Italian narratives Dante could have read.

3. (pp. 159–161) *many lofty towers I seemed to see... "not towers, but giants":* Virgil and Dante now approach the ninth and final circle of Hell, having left Malebolge behind. The Pilgrim mistakenly believes he is staring at the towers of a great city. In fact, the towers are the upper halves of giants who are keeping guard around the pit, with their upper bodies rising above the rim. These giants may be compared to the rebel angels who guarded the City of Dis, and both groups of figures—one pagan and classical in origin, the other Judeo-Christian in origin—may be said to represent the evil effects of pride that moved both groups to rebel against their respective gods.

4. (p. 161) *Montereggione... with one half of their bodies turreted:* Montereggione, a fortified town a few miles northwest of Siena, was

constructed between 1213 and 1260. In Dante's time the town was enclosed by a high wall with fourteen towers (the walls and some of the towers still stand today). The upper torsos of the giants surrounding the pit of Hell resemble these towers distributed along the wall of the fortress.

5. (p. 161) *The horrible giants, whom Jove menaces:* As Dante noted in canto XIV: 51–62, Jove (another name for the god Jupiter) struck the giants down with lightning bolts when they rebelled against Heaven, and he still menaces them with thunder bolts now that they are condemned to guard the worst sinners in Hell.

6. (p. 161) *Certainly Nature . . . can the people make against it:* In this passage Dante remarks that Nature did well to discontinue producing a race of giants such as the Titans, for if they had allied themselves with Mars (l. 51), the god of War, they could have destroyed the world. While Nature produces such strange animals as elephants and whales (l. 52), they lack the power of intellect that, combined with physical strength, could make them dangerous to human beings.

7. (p. 161) *the pine-cone of Saint Peter's:* There is a bronze pinecone in the garden of the Vatican Palace that originally stood near the Campus Martius in ancient Rome. Dante most likely saw the pinecone, which is some 4 yards in height, when he was a member of a papal delegation.

8. (p. 161) *so that the margin, which an apron was down from the middle:* The "margin" (bank) cuts the anatomy of the Titans off from the Pilgrim's view and acts as a kind of apron. In the original, Dante uses a word that literally means "fig leaf"—*perizoma*—bringing to mind the fig leaves that Adam and Eve donned after their sin made them aware of their nakedness in the Garden of Eden.

9. (p. 161) *Three Frieslanders:* In Dante's time, the inhabitants of Friesland were considered to be extremely tall. Dante is saying that the giant is so tall that three Frieslanders would not reach from his waist to his hair.

10. (p. 161) *down from the place where man his mantle buckles:* From the neck to the waist.

11. (p. 162) *"Raphel mai amech izabi almi":* Gibberish issues forth from the giant's mouth. There seems to be no possibility of understanding what Dante has this creature say, since the words are meant

to be incomprehensible because of the giant's association with the Tower of Babel; in the Bible, Genesis 11: 1–9, the Lord confounds the language of the builders of the Tower to punish their pride.

12. (p. 162) *"this one is Nimrod . . . every language as his to others, which to none is known":* Nimrod is described in the Bible, Genesis 10: 9, as a hunter, not a giant. Medieval tradition, however, identified Nimrod with the builders of the infamous Tower of Babel, hence the gibberish he speaks. Even though Virgil declares that Nimrod cannot understand him, and he and the Pilgrim can not understand Nimrod, he converses with him anyway!

13. (p. 162) *It wound itself as far as the fifth gyre:* The chains imprisoning this second giant are wrapped around his upper torso (the only part of his body that is visible) five times.

14. (p. 162) *Ephialtes:* The son of Neptune and Iphimedia, Ephialtes, with his brother Otus, tried to make war on the gods and was killed by Apollo.

15. (p. 162) *measureless Briareus:* The son of Uranus and Gaea or Earth, this Titan also rebelled against the Olympian gods. Virgil's *Aeneid*, Book X, describes him with a hundred arms and fifty heads, the source of Dante's "measureless Briareus."

16. (p. 162) *Antæus:* The son of Neptune and Gaea or Earth, Antaeus did not rebel against the gods and is not chained like the other Titans in Hell. He was invincible in combat so long as he remained in contact with the ground, and when Hercules discovered this, he managed to hold him off the ground and kill him. Dante's source is Lucan's *Pharsalia*, Book IV.

17. (p. 163) *full five ells:* This medieval measurement differed in length from country to country, but was generally the length from the elbow to the tip of the middle finger. In England an ell was 45 inches, while in Flanders it was 27 inches.

18. (p. 163) *"who in the valley fortunate . . . for thy prey":* Virgil must flatter Antaeus into helping the two voyagers reach their next destination in their journey—Cocytus, the final pit at the very bottom of Hell. So he notes that Antaeus killed a large number of lions in the same spot where Scipio Africanus defeated Hannibal at the North African battle of Zama in 202 B.C.

19. (p. 163) *Cocytus:* This is the frozen lake in the ninth circle

of Hell, which the Pilgrim and Virgil will explore in the final cantos of the *Inferno.*

20. (p. 163) *Tityus nor Typhoeus:* Both of these Titans offended Jupiter. The god buried Typhoeus under Mount Aetna (the volcano's eruptions were supposedly caused by his attempts to free himself) and ordered Tityus to be bound and stretched out on a plain in Hell while a vulture devoured his liver.

21. (p. 163) *"the Carisenda ... so that opposite it hangs":* The Garisenda tower in Bologna (Dante refers to the tower as the "Carisenda") was built at the beginning of the twefth century. It is one of two remaining towers in that city that are leaning (most of the rest of these medieval towers were destroyed in the nineteenth century). The Garisenda is the shorter of the two towers (163 feet high, as opposed to the 320 feet of the Asinelli tower), though it was higher when Dante wrote the *Inferno* (it was shortened in the fourteenth century) and it leans the most. Dante notes that if a cloud passes the leaning side of the tower, the structure appears to be falling.

22. (p. 164) *watching to see him stoop ... he put us down:* Like Geryon of canto XVII, who sets the two poets down on the bottom of the eighth circle, Antaeus stoops down and places the Pilgrim and Virgil on the very bottom of Hell. Here the abyss "swallows up" Judas Iscariot and Lucifer, a concept that will mean more to us when Dante provides details about the punishment of these two figures in the next canto.

CANTO XXXII

1. (p. 165) *a tongue that cries Mamma and Babbo:* Dante describes the rock-bottom pit of Hell, as the "bottom of all the universe," since, following the Ptolemaic system, Earth is in the center of the universe and Hell is in the center of Earth. He then introduces the theme of modesty, as practiced by all good classical and medieval poets, and protests that he lacks verses harsh enough to capture the scene he is about to describe—especially if he must do so in the vernacular, a tongue that "cries" Mommy and Daddy (*Babbo* is a Tuscan word for "Daddy"). But, of course, like the classical poets before Dante who employed such a topos, his modesty is false, and

Dante the Poet is more than prepared to provide such an unusual description for his readers.

2. (p. 165) *those Ladies:* The ladies are the Muses, who helped Jupiter's son Amphion build defenses in Thebes by playing a lyre to compel the stones to form themselves into a wall. Dante's first invocation of the Muses is in canto II: 7.

3. (p. 165) *beneath the giant's feet, but lower far, and I was scanning still the lofty wall:* Many commentators have discussed the exact position of the two poets at this point in the narrative. It seems that they are looking up at the high wall, implying that Antaenus set them down on the icy floor of Cocytus but is not standing on it himself.

4. (p. 165) *I heard it said to me:* It is unclear who the Pilgrim is hearing.

5. (pp. 165–166) *if Tambernich had fallen upon it, or Pietrapana:* While it is unclear which mountain Dante meant by the Tambernich, the Pietrapana is usually identified as a peak in Tuscany known as Pania della Croce.

6. (p. 166) *where shame appears:* This is the face, the only part of the sinner's body that emerges from the ice. We are now in Caïna, named after Cain, the first human murderer, who in the Bible, Genesis 4: 8, kills his brother, Abel. Caïna is the first of four parts of Cocytus and contains those who were treacherous to their kin. In canto V: 107, Francesca da Rimini has mentioned this part of Hell as the place where her murderous husband will be punished.

7. (p. 166) *setting their teeth unto the note of storks:* Storks clack their bills (at least according to literary tradition and medieval bestiaries), and they make the kind of brittle sound that fits into an ice-dominated universe.

8. (p. 166) *If thou desire to know . . . Sassol Mascheroni:* The as yet unnamed speaker identifies two souls who are locked together as Alessandro and Napoleone, sons of Count Alberto of Mangona, who owned part of the Bisenzio valley in Tuscany. They killed each other in the 1280s over a dispute about their inheritance. The speaker goes on to inform the Pilgrim about others in Caïna. Mordred (ll. 61–62) was King Arthur's evil nephew, who both killed Arthur and was killed by him—Arthur pierced him with a lance that let a ray of light through to pierce his shadow as well (l. 61); Dante found this

story in the Old French *Morte d'Arthur* or perhaps in the French romance *Lancelot du Lac*, the book Francesca da Rimini blames for placing her in Hell (*Inferno* V). Focaccia (l. 63) was the nickname of Vanni de' Cancellieri from Pistoia, who at the end of the thirteenth century murdered his cousin. Sassol Mascheroni (l. 65) was a Florentine of the Toschi family who murdered a nephew.

9. (p. 167) *"I Camicion de' Pazzi was, and wait Carlino to exonerate me":* The speaker finally identifies himself; it is possible that he may also be the unidentified speaker of ll. 19–21 who warns the Pilgrim not to step on the heads of the two "miserable brothers," Alessandro and Napoleone degli Alberti. Little is known about Camicione de' Pazzi except for the fact that he murdered a relative named Ubertino. Another of his relatives, Carlino (l. 69), died only in 1302, so he was alive during the fictitious date that the Pilgrim's journey through Hell took place. Camicione foretells a bit of the future here, for he predicts that Carlino will "exonerate" him—commit an even greater sin, making Camicione's crime seem much less important. In fact, in 1302 Carlino de' Pazzi was commanding the fortress of Piantravigne in the Arno valley for the Florentine Whites and betrayed the fortress to the Florentine Blacks and their Lucchese allies. Thus while Camicione is in Caïna for murdering his kin, Carlino will apparently be sent to the next level down, to the second ring of Cocytus (Antenora), where traitors to their party, country, or city are punished.

10. (p. 167) *a thousand faces:* The passage from Caïna to Antenora occurs abruptly, signaled only by the fact that the faces Dante sees look straight ahead and are not bent down as they are in Caïna. Antenora is named for a Trojan warrior, Antenor, who, according to some accounts (but not Virgil's), betrayed Troy to the Greeks after Paris refused to give Helen back to them and subsequently went on to found the city of Padua in Italy.

11. (p. 167) *Montaperti:* On September 4, 1260, the Florentine Guelphs met disaster at the hands of the Florentine and Sienese Ghibellines in this village in Tuscany east of Siena (referred to earlier, in canto X: 85–86).

12. (p. 168) *"What doth ail thee, Bocca?":* The soul who the Pilgrim kicks hard (l. 78), who seeks not fame in the world of the living

but oblivion (l. 94), and whose hair the Pilgrim pulls to force him, without success, to identify himself (l. 101), is identified by another sinner as Bocca degli Abati. Bocca was blamed for the disastrous defeat of the Guelphs at Montaperti, where he cut off the arm of the standard-bearer at the crucial moment in the battle, causing the Florentine Guelphs to panic and to be slaughtered. In revenge for this misdeed, Dante promises to tell the living about Bocca's punishment in Hell.

13. (p. 168) *"the silver of the French . . . 'him of Duera . . .' ":* Bocca names the soul who identified him to the Pilgrim as Buoso da Duera, a Ghibelline from the city of Cremona. Bribed by the French, Buoso allowed Guelph forces commanded by Charles of Anjou in 1265 to enter a pass near Parma and capture the city uncontested. Bocca also identifies a number of other souls in Antenora.

14. (p. 169) *"Beccaria . . . Ganellon, and Tebaldello who oped Faenza":* We now learn the identities of other sinners in Antenora. Tesauro de' Beccheria of Pavia, a legate in Tuscany for Pope Alexander, was beheaded by the Florentine Guelphs in 1258 on a charge of conspiring with the Ghibellines. Gianni del Soldanier, a Florentine Ghibelline, deserted his party and supported a popular Florentine uprising favorable to the Guelphs after Manfred, the Ghibelline leader, was killed at the battle of Benevento in 1266. Ganellon (also often spelled "Ganelon") betrayed Charlemagne's rear guard and its commander Roland at the pass of Roncesvalles in 778 (see canto XXXI: 16–18). Tebaldello Zambrasi (d. 1282), a Ghibelline, opened up the city gates of Faenza in 1280 to the Bolognese Guelphs in order to take revenge on some of the Bolognese Ghibellines who had taken refuge in the town.

15. (p. 169) *two frozen in one hole:* These two sinners will be identified by name only in canto XXXIII: 13–14.

16. (p. 169) *even as bread . . . Tydeus gnawed the temples of Menalippus in disdain:* Dante compares the as yet unidentified sinner who is gnawing upon the other's head to Tydeus, one of the Seven Against Thebes, the mythical expedition against Eteocles, king of Thebes. Tydeus slew Menalippus in battle but was mortally wounded by him. Tydeus asked his men to cut off the head of Menalippus, and he chewed upon it as he died. It is Capaneus (see canto XIV) who

brings the head to Tydeus, according to Dante's source, Statius's *Thebaid*, Book VIII.

17. (p. 169) *if that wherewith I speak be not dried up:* Dante promises to present the sinner's story so that the living may judge if his actions are justified (something the Poet does in the following canto, XXXIII). The last line of the canto has been interpreted in a number of ways, but ultimately Dante is simply emphasizing that he will fulfill his promise no matter what happens—whether or not his tongue fails him, whether or not he is frozen in Cocytus, whether or not he is paralyzed, and whether or not he survives his journey.

CANTO XXXIII

1. (p. 170) *Count Ugolino:* Ugolino della Gherardesca (c.1220–1289) was a Ghibelline from Pisa who joined the Guelph Visconti family to take control of the city but instead was banished. He returned to Pisa and conspired with Archbishop Ruggieri degli Ubaldini (l. 14), a Ghibelline, against his own grandson, Nino Visconti, a Guelph judge. When Visconti was forced to leave the city, Ugolino and Ruggieri had a falling out, and the Archbishop falsely accused Ugolino of surrendering the Pisan fortresses to their Florentine and Lucchese enemies. In 1288 Ugolino was imprisoned with two sons and two grandsons, and they all died by starvation in 1289. Ugolino is in Antenora primarily because he betrayed his Ghibelline party and probably not for the false accusation of surrendering Pisa's fortresses.

2. (p. 170) *"A narrow perforation in the mew . . . many moons":* Ugolino was able to peer out of a tiny slit in the mew, or molting loft, in a tower that became known as the Torre della Fame ("Tower of Hunger") because of the fate of Ugolino and the others. Some six months (moons) passed between the time of Ugolino's imprisonment and his death.

3. (p. 170) *"I dreamed the evil dream . . . Sismondi and Lanfranchi":* Ugolino's dream was prophetic: In it, the hunter is the Archbishop (l. 28), who is hunting Ugolino and his offspring (the wolf and his whelps of l. 29) on the mountain that hides Lucca from Pisa, Monte San Giuliano (l. 30). In ambush are waiting the leading Ghibelline

families of Pisa (the Gualandi, Sismondi, and the Lanfranchi of l. 32), as well as the Pisan populace (the gaunt sleuth-hounds of l. 31).

4. (p. 171) *"before the morrow... asking after bread":* According to medieval tradition, waking dreams (those that occur just before awakening in the morning) were prophetic. Here Ugolino awakens in the morning to be confronted by the instant materialization of his dream, not just a prophecy of what might occur: His offspring (sons and grandsons) are standing before him asking for food.

5. (p. 171) *"what art thou wont to weep at?":* Ugolino's question underlines the fact that this time, the Pilgrim has not been provoked to a sympathetic reaction—he sheds no tears for this traitor, even though his tale (like that of Francesca da Rimini in canto V, for example) seems heartrending. Near the end of his journey through Hell, the Pilgrim has learned something about the proper reaction to evil.

6. (p. 171) *"little Anselm mine":* Anselmuccio (diminutive of Anselmo) was the younger of Ugolino's grandsons and about fifteen at the time of his imprisonment.

7. (p. 172) *"Gaddo... 'Why dost thou not help me?' ":* The accusing words of Ugolino's son may recall Christ's last words on the cross, as told in the Bible, Matthew 27: 46: "My God, my God, why hast thou forsaken me?" Gaddo was actually a young man at the time, not a child, but the effect is more shocking on the reader if his age is left unmentioned. Besides Anselmo and Gaddo, the other two relatives of Ugolino who died were his son Uguccione and his grandson Nino. The time that elapses from the moment the prison door is sealed until the deaths of the four children totals seven days.

8. (p. 172) *"Then hunger did what sorrow could not do":* The simplest and most obvious explanation for this line is that three days after the death of the last boy, Ugolino died of starvation. In other words, hunger killed him when sorrow was unable to achieve that result. After delivering his remarks, Ugolino returns to gnawing upon Ruggieri's skull ("the wretched skull" of l. 77). This fact has led some commentators to interpret Ugolino's remark as an admission that he ate his own offspring to prolong his life.

9. (p. 172) *Ah! Pisa:* Pisa's shame is not to have executed Ug-

olino (who is rightfully condemned in Hell) but to have executed his offspring (who, again rightfully, are not in Hell with him).

10. (p. 172) *where the* Sì *doth sound:* In his *De vulgari eloquentia,* Book I, Dante divides various European Romance languages into groups by their words for "yes"—therefore, this is Dante's unusual way of saying "Italy."

11. (p. 172) *the Capraia and Gorgona:* These islands in the Mediterranean belonged to Pisa at the time Ugolino was executed.

12. (p. 172) *thou modern Thebes!:* Classical literature and mythology contain many references to violent episodes in the history of the city of Thebes, some of which are mentioned in the *Inferno*: Jupiter's killing of Capaneus (canto XIV: 49–72); the slaying of the sons of Oedipus (canto XXVI: 52–54); King Athamas's insane killing of his son (canto XXX: 1–12). Ugolino's tale thus makes modern Pisa fit to be compared to this ancient city.

13. (p. 172) *Uguccione and Brigata:* Uguccione was the youngest son of Count Ugolino and brother to Gaddo (mentioned earlier in l. 68). The eldest son of Count Ugolino was named Nino but was known as "Il Brigata," the nickname Dante employs.

14. (pp. 172–173) *Another people . . . beneath the eyebrow full:* The brief phrase "another people" alerts the reader to the fact that Virgil and the Pilgrim are now in Ptolomaea (also spelled "Ptolomea" by modern scholars), the third zone of Cocytus in the ninth circle, the part reserved for traitors of the host-guest relationship. The name has occasioned some comment, since it may either be a reference to Ptolemy, the captain of Jericho who had his father-in-law and two sons killed while dining with him (as told in the Apocrypha of the Bible, 1 Maccabees 16:11–17), or to Ptolemy XII, the king of Egypt who gave hospitality to Pompey, who was fleeing Caesar after the battle of Pharsalus (48 B.C.), then arranged to have him murdered to curry favor with the Roman victor. Most ancient civilizations and many modern ones (such as Dante's) believed that the relationship between guest and host was sacred and violating it was extremely serious. Here the sinners suffer with their heads thrown back so that their tears freeze in their eye sockets (ll. 94–99).

15. (p. 173) *I felt some wind . . . "the cause which raineth down the blast":* Feeling a wind on his frozen face, Dante is puzzled: According to

the scientific theory of his time, the sun created wind by heat striking moisture (the "vapor" of l. 105), and there is no sun in Hell. Virgil promises him that the answer is soon to be revealed (in the next canto, XXXIV: 46–51).

16. (p. 173) *"Say who thou wast . . . to the bottom of the ice"*: Armed now with the kind of righteous indignation for sin necessary to protect himself from false sentimentalism, the Pilgrim lies to the sinner, vowing he will free him or be sent to Judecca, the bottom section of Cocytus and the worst place in Hell. Of course, the Pilgrim knows that he is already going to Judecca as a guest, not to be tortured, and his lie encourages the speaker to identify himself in spite of the usual reluctance in Hell to have one's sins and name remembered among the living.

17. (p. 173) *"Friar Alberigo . . . a date am getting for my fig"*: Alberigo was a Guelph from Faenza and a member of the previously mentioned Frati Gaudenti, or "Jovial Friars" (see canto XXIII, note 12). In 1285, he invited several relatives to dinner and had them murdered as he called out for the fruit course to end the meal. Now, he claims he is suffering more than he should, because he is receiving a date for his fig—at that time, dates were more expensive than figs, so he is saying that his crime (the fig) does not warrant the high level of punishment (the more expensive date) he is receiving.

18. (pp. 173–174) *"an advantage has this Ptolomæa . . . his body by a demon is taken from him"*: Alberigo presents one of Dante's most ingenious inventions. Sinners who qualify for occupancy in this part of Cocytus suffer the death of their souls immediately, when they are still living. The souls go directly to Hell, quicker than Atropos, the third of the Three Fates in classical mythology, can perform her usual deed, snipping off the thread of human existence. The souls thus abandon the bodies on earth. Until the physical death of the bodies, a devil inhabits the shells, but those who are so cursed are unaware of the fact that their bodies have no souls.

19. (p. 174) *"Of yonder shade . . . with him the betrayal"*: In order to prove his point about Ptolomaea's unique manner of punishment, Alberigo offers the Pilgrim an example of a soul "wintering" in Ptolomaea while the body still walks the earth—a soulless person Dante must have encountered in the world of the living. Branca

Doria or d'Oria (c.1233–c.1325) was a Ghibelline nobleman from a famous family in Genoa who murdered his father-in-law, Michael Zanche, after inviting him to dinner. The murder took place in 1275, but Branca lived on in his earthly body, inhabited by a demon, until his death. His soul (and that of a co-conspirator, ll. 146–147) fell to Ptolomaea even before Michael Zanche's soul reached the fifth Bolgia of the eighth circle (l. 144), where the reader has already encountered him (canto XXII: 88) being punished for barratry. Since Branca lived for almost a century and survived Dante, it is tempting to wonder what his reaction might have been if and when he read a manuscript of the *Comedy* (as he very well might have done) and found himself condemned to Hell.

20. (p. 174) *to be rude to him was courtesy:* Following the proper procedure toward rightfully condemned souls in Hell, Dante the Pilgrim now has no patience with them whatsoever, refusing even to open the frozen eyes of the sinner as he had promised to do earlier. The Pilgrim now, in short, is much closer in perspective to Dante the Poet. It was generally agreed in Dante's day (although somewhat contrary to Christian notions of charity and forgiveness) that one need not keep one's word with a traitor.

21. (p. 174) *Ah, Genoese . . . the vilest spirit of Romagna:* Along with Florence, Lucca, Siena, Arezzo, and Pisa (to mention only a few of the Italian cities that Dante tells us throughout the *Inferno* are full of sin), Genoa now joins the list of dens of iniquity on the peninsula. Its despicable nature is underscored by the fact that Genoa's Branca Doria can be found in the same place as the "vilest spirit of Romagna," Friar Alberigo (he was from Faenza, which is in the Romagna region). It must be said about Dante that his love for his native city of Florence, for Italy, and for his mother tongue of Italian do not blind him to the faults of his fellow citizens and those who share his beautiful language where "sì" means "yes"!

CANTO XXXIV

1. (p. 175) "Vexilla Regis prodeunt Inferni": Dante modifies the opening lines of a Latin hymn by Venantius Fortunatus, a bishop in Poitiers (c.530–610), by adding *Inferni* ("of Hell") to it: "The

banners of the King of Hell are advancing." The hymn is sung in celebration of the mystery of the Cross during processions.

2. (p. 175) *a mill the wind is turning:* In the distance, Virgil points out an object that the Pilgrim will discover is Lucifer. From a distance, Lucifer's wings (the banners to which the Latin song that opens the canto ironically refers) seem like a windmill in the thick fog.

3. (p. 175) *no other shelter:* It is notable here that the Pilgrim's fear is so great that he tries to take shelter behind Virgil, a weightless shade who essentially provides no shelter.

4. (p. 175) *wholly covered up:* The two travelers have passed into the final and fourth section of Hell, Judecca—named after Judius Iscariot, who betrayed Christ—where those who have been treacherous to their masters are punished. Here the sinners are completely immersed in ice, so it is not possible to speak to them.

5. (p. 175) *The creature who once had the beauteous semblance:* Before the Fall, Lucifer was the fairest of all the angels in Heaven. After his overweening pride caused him to rebel against God, he was cast down as the arch-traitor of all time and sits fixed in the ice, weeping.

6. (p. 175) *"Behold Dis":* Twice before in the poem, in canto XI: 65 and canto XII: 39, Dante has referred to Lucifer as Dis, a name used in classical antiquity for Pluto, god of the Underworld.

7. (p. 175) *Ask it not, Reader.... and I alive remained not:* This last of the seven addresses Dante makes to his reader in the *Inferno* is a perfect example of what is known as the "classical inexpressibility topos": by declaring how impossible it is to describe some amazing sight, the writer provides a fitting description of the sight. In effect, the sight of Lucifer renders the Pilgrim half dead and half alive.

8. (p. 176) *And better with a giant I compare:* Dante's height is closer to that of the giants we have observed earlier in the poem than a giant's height is to Lucifer's. In other words, Lucifer's length is enormous, even when half of it is buried in the ice—he is literally hundreds and hundreds of feet tall.

9. (p. 176) *three faces on his head... where the Nile falls valley-ward:* By giving Lucifer three faces, Dante uses a physical shape to provide a parody of the Christian Trinity. The phrase, "where the Nile falls valley-ward," refers to Ethiopia, where people are black, and that is

the color of one of Lucifer's faces; the others are red and yellow-white. Some commentators have associated these colors with traits opposed to the Love, Power, and Wisdom associated traditionally with the Trinity.

10. (p. 176) *Sails of the sea . . . three winds proceeded forth there-from:* Lucifer belonged to the highest order of the angels, the Seraphim, creatures who are described in the Bible, Isaiah 6: 2, as having six wings. Dante retains the six wings (two for each head), but he changes them from the resplendent things they were in Heaven into bat-like appendages or sails on a boat, and their motion produces the winds in Hell.

11. (pp. 176–177) *he three of them tormented thus . . . is Cassius:* The three arch-sinners tortured by the arch-monster in the deepest pit of Hell all sinned against the divinely inspired Church and the Roman Republic, which eventually, under the Empire, inherited God's favor and protected the Church. Judas Iscariot betrayed Christ; his back is flayed, as was Christ's on the way to the Crucifixion, and his head is inside of one of Lucifer's mouths. Brutus and Cassius conspired against Rome's first emperor, Julius Caesar; they hang by their legs with their heads down (a somewhat lesser punishment).

12. (p. 177) *night is reascending, and 'tis time:* Virgil continues to tell time in Hell by reference to astronomy. It is now Easter Saturday and approximately twenty-four hours have passed since the journey began, roughly 6:00 P.M.

13. (p. 178) *where he had had his legs:* Some scholars have made a convincing argument that the "he" in this sentence refers not to Virgil but to Lucifer. To understand why this might be the case, it must be remembered that the middle of Lucifer's body would correspond to the absolute center of the earth, of earthly gravity, and of the Ptolemaic universe. Dante is confused when he thinks Virgil is turning around and going back upward the way they came down before. Virgil first sets out climbing down the legs of Lucifer as if on a ladder, and when he reaches Lucifer's shanks (Longfellow employs the more general word "legs"), Virgil and Dante must turn in the other direction as if they were now climbing up a ladder: When reaching the center of the Ptolemaic universe, in other words, "down" suddenly becomes "up." Clutching Virgil's back and with

his arms clasped around his guide's head, Dante is naturally confused and frightened by this apparent shift of direction. In l. 90, the Pilgrim quite understandably sees Lucifer's legs upside down.

14. (p. 178) *What the point is beyond which I had passed:* This is the center of gravity and of the earth.

15. (p. 178) *"the sun to middle-tierce returns":* Mysteriously telling time by the reference to the sun (which is not visible in Hell), Virgil informs the Pilgrim that it is halfway between the canonical hours of Prime (6:00 A.M.) and Terce (9:00 A.M.)—or 7:30 A.M. In l. 68 Dante informed us that it was about 6:00 P.M. (see note 12). The sudden shift in time may be explained by the hint we are given in this line that the time is being calculated by the sun, not the moon. We are now past Earth's center and have moved into the Southern Hemisphere on our way to Purgatory. There the time is twelve hours ahead of the time in the Northern Hemisphere.

16. (p. 178) *"Where is the ice? ... Has the sun made his transit?":* Like the reader of these passages about the final geography of Hell, the confused Pilgrim wants answers to three questions: (1) where is the ice?; (2) how did he come to turn around?; and (3) how did the time jump ahead 12 hours? Virgil responds to his queries in ll. 106–120.

17. (p. 178) *"the fell worm":* Virgil compares Lucifer's position in the center of Earth to that of a worm in the core of a piece of fruit.

18. (p. 179) *Judecca:* The fourth and last section of Cocytus is finally named. The Italian term for this region (la Giudecca) is also the name of a quarter in Venice, inhabited at one time by the Jews of the city.

19. (p. 179) *"Upon this side ... and back recoiled":* Virgil now explains that Lucifer's body fell through the Southern Hemisphere into the earth's core. The land that was once there fell under the surface of the sea ("made of the sea a veil"), causing the land in the Northern Hemisphere to rise higher above the waters. The land where Lucifer made impact rushed upward ("and back recoiled") to form the mountain we shall eventually see in *Purgatory*, the next canticle of *The Divine Comedy*.

20. (p. 179) *Beelzebub:* This is another name for Lucifer.

21. (p. 179) *Of a small rivulet ... into that hidden road now entered:*

This small stream is never identified, but many scholars believe it to be the River Lethe. This stream apparently washed away a space ("Through chasm within the stone, which it has gnawed") below the land that rushed upward to form the Mount of Purgatory, and it is through this opening that the travelers climb from Lucifer's "tomb" to Earth's surface.

22. (p. 179) *to rebehold the stars:* The *Inferno, Purgatory,* and *Paradise* all conclude with the word "stars" (*stelle*), the direction man's journey toward God must take. The sight of these stars has been denied to the Pilgrim during his journey through Hell, and there is a palpable sense of relief when the celestial bodies finally come back into view. Although the *Inferno* represents the most violent, disagreeable, and despicable place in the world of the afterlife, the fact that the Pilgrim encounters the stars once again ends his journey happily. Dante's definition of a comedy, it must always be remembered, stressed a happy ending.

Six Sonnets on Dante's *The Divine Comedy*

BY

HENRY WADSWORTH LONGFELLOW

(1807–1882)

I

Oft have I seen at some cathedral door
A laborer, pausing in the dust and heat,
Lay down his burden, and with reverent feet
Enter, and cross himself, and on the floor
Kneel to repeat his paternoster o'er;
Far off the noises of the world retreat;
The loud vociferations of the street
Become an undistinguishable roar.
So, as I enter here from day to day,
And leave my burden at this minster gate,
Kneeling in prayer, and not ashamed to pray,
The tumult of the time disconsolate
To inarticulate murmurs dies away,
While the eternal ages watch and wait.

II

How strange the sculptures that adorn these towers!
This crowd of statues, in whose folded sleeves
Birds build their nests; while canopied with leaves
Parvis and portal bloom like trellised bowers,
And the vast minster seems a cross of flowers!
But fiends and dragons on the gargoyled eaves

Watch the dead Christ between the living thieves,
And, underneath, the traitor Judas lowers!
Ah! from what agonies of heart and brain,
What exultations trampling on despair,
What tenderness, what tears, what hate of wrong,
What passionate outcry of a soul in pain,
Uprose this poem of the earth and air,
This mediaeval miracle of song!

III

I enter, and I see thee in the gloom
Of the long aisles, O poet saturnine!
And strive to make my steps keep pace with thine.
The air is filled with some unknown perfume;
The congregation of the dead make room
For thee to pass; the votive tapers shine;
Like rooks that haunt Ravenna's groves of pine
The hovering echoes fly from tomb to tomb.
From the confessionals I hear arise
Rehearsals of forgotten tragedies,
And lamentations from the crypts below;
And then a voice celestial that begins
With the pathetic words, "Although your sins
As scarlet be," and ends with "as the snow."

IV

With snow-white veil and garments as of flame,
She stands before thee, who so long ago
Filled thy young heart with passion and the woe
From which thy song in all its splendors came;
And while with stern rebuke she speaks thy name,
The ice about thy heart melts as the snow
On mountain heights, and in swift overflow
Comes gushing from thy lips in sobs of shame.
Thou makest full confession; and a gleam,
As of the dawn on some dark forest cast,

Seems on thy lifted forehead to increase;
Lethe and Eunoe—the remembered dream
And the forgotten sorrow—bring at last
That perfect pardon which is perfect peace.

V

I lift mine eyes, and all the windows blaze
With forms of saints and holy men who died,
Here martyred and hereafter glorified;
And the great Rose upon its leaves displays
Christ's Triumph, and the angelic roundelays,
With splendor upon splendor multiplied;
And Beatrice again at Dante's side
No more rebukes, but smiles her words of praise.
And then the organ sounds, and unseen choirs
Sing the old Latin hymns of peace and love
And benedictions of the Holy Ghost;
And the melodious bells among the spires
O'er all the house-tops and through heaven above
Proclaim the elevation of the Host!

VI

O star of morning and of liberty!
O bringer of the light, whose splendor shines
Above the darkness of the Apennines,
Forerunner of the day that is to be!
The voices of the city and the sea,
The voices of the mountains and the pines,
Repeat thy song, till the familiar lines
Are footpaths for the thought of Italy!
Thy fame is blown abroad from all the heights,
Through all the nations; and a sound is heard,
As of a mighty wind, and men devout,
Strangers of Rome, and the new proselytes,
In their own language hear thy wondrous word,
And many are amazed and many doubt.

Inspired by the *Inferno*

Gustave Doré, whose haunting illustrations of *The Divine Comedy* are included in this volume, and Michelangelo, who portrays Minos and Charon being dragged down to Hell in his famous fresco *The Last Judgment*, are just two of the many artists and illustrators who have used their talents to visualize the extraordinary landscape of Dante's epic.

It is said that Dante once broke the baptismal font in the church of San Giovanni in Florence to save a drowning child. Today the baptistery houses one of the great monuments of the Italian Renaissance, the Mosaic of the Cupola, completed in the thirteenth century by a collective of the day's premier mosaic artists. Closely following Dante's text, the mosaic depicts a many-mouthed Lucifer, perched among human carnage. The devil, five times the size of his victims, is crowned with two great horns, and snakes protrude from his long ears; numerous demons scattered around the huge Lucifer continually load mortals into his gaping maws.

In the 1480s Lorenzo di Pierfrancesco de' Medici commissioned the Italian artist Sandro Botticelli to illustrate Dante's *Divine Comedy*. Botticelli enveloped the onlookers and Dante and Virgil in robes of royal red and blue, and rendered the condemned, who writhe in torment, a pasty white. Botticelli never finished his illustrations, and the sheets, in varying stages of completion, were scattered across Europe. In September 2000 a collection of ninety-two surviving Botticelli drawings illustrating *The Divine Comedy* were assembled as a cycle again for the first time in five centuries and shown in museums around the world.

The celebrated English poet William Blake (1757–1827) was also a gifted painter and illustrator. His works include 102 illustrations based on *The Divine Comedy*. Because most of the drawings are unfinished, large portions, which were meant to be colored, remain blank, lending an almost celestial brightness to Blake's depictions of Hell.

The major work of Italian illustrator Amos Nattini are considered to be the hundred lithographs dedicated to Dante's *Divine Comedy*, completed between 1923 and 1941. Nattini's dreamlike *Inferno* images present writhing seas of sinners, gnarled branches, winged devils, and almost sentimental portraits of the condemned.

To celebrate the 700th anniversary of Dante's birth (1265), Spanish surrealist Salvador Dalí produced a series of wood engravings based on *The Divine Comedy*. (The Italian government withdrew a commission that had started the work, but the artist completed it anyway.) In the colorful images, Dalí employs the elongated limbs, crutches, and melting colors that are typical of his work to create serpentine demons and cannibalizing sinners whose faces drape over surfaces.

For his *Inferno* series (1959 and 1960), Expressionist artist Robert Rauschenberg produced thirty-four drawings, one for each canto. The scratchy quality of Rauschenberg's work, which has buried within it figures and impressions that the viewer must unearth, makes for an apt translation of Dante's *Inferno*, as do his textured browns and blacks, punctuated by the red and orange of hellfire. Rauschenberg's Lucifer—triple-mouthed, lion-headed, and wearing a pair of bloody wings—is one of the most frightening devils ever depicted.

Illustrator Barry Moser achieves a ghostly and ghastly feeling in his stark, black-and-white drawings of Dante's *Inferno*, completed in 1980. He brings a clinical, anatomical approach to images of physical torment—from the spikes of a crucifixion to an eyeless soul spreading open his chest with his fingers to reveal the bones underneath—that resonate with fear and horror.

Painter and printmaker Michael Mazur completed his series of forty-one etchings for Dante's *Inferno* in 2000; thirty-five of the works had appeared alongside poet laureate Robert Pinsky's translation of the *Inferno*, published in 1993. His black-and-white etchings, broodingly dark, feature searing, unforgettable imagery: disembodied heads raining down from the sky; souls with their heads twisted backward; thrashing, winged demons; a hideous, multifaced Lucifer enshrouded in shadow; and a redemptive closing panel of the stars splashed with a brilliant blue.

Comments & Questions

In this section, we aim to provide the reader with an array of perspectives on the text, as well as questions that challenge those perspectives. The commentary has been culled from sources as diverse as reviews contemporaneous with the work, letters written by the author, literary criticism of later generations, and appreciations written throughout history. Following the commentary, a series of questions seeks to filter Dante's Inferno *through a variety of points of view and bring about a richer understanding of this enduring work.*

Comments

REV. HENRY STEBBING

The distinguishing characteristic of Dante's poetry, though far from wanting in occasional passages of exquisite tenderness and beauty, is its sublimity, and hence by general consent the *Inferno* is placed at an almost immeasurable distance above the other two parts of the *Commedia*, which required a milder and more brilliant fancy. In respect to sublimity, Dante has but one superior, our own Milton. The scenes he depicts have the terrible distinctness of places beheld in a vivid dream; the language of his personages makes an equally powerful impression on the mind—it is short, pointed, and abrupt, and such as we might expect to hear from miserable beings dreading the fiery lash of pursuing demons, but retaining their sense of human sympathy.

—from *Lives of the Italian Poets* (1831)

ROBERT BROWNING

Oh, their Dante of the dread Inferno,
Wrote one song—and in my brain I sing it,
Drew one angel—borne, see, on my bosom!

—from *One Word More* (1855)

THEODORE W. KOCH

Although the early American students of Dante were not without their influence in creating a local and limited interest in their author, yet they left but little lasting incitement to the study of him. They did not succeed in bringing Dante before the American reading public, or in giving him the audience he merited. To Longfellow this honor chiefly belongs. No one in America has done so much in the service of this master. The homage paid by the first of our poets to Italy's chiefest singer of rhymes is a significant bond of union.

—from *Dante in America* (1896)

GIOVANNI BOCCACCIO

Many persons, and among them wise ones, ask some such question as this: Inasmuch as Dante was a most distinguished man of learning, why did he choose to compose so lofty a subject as that of his *Commedia,* in the Florentine idiom, and why not rather in Latin verse, as preceding poets had done? To this question I reply that two principal reasons, among many, occur to me. The first is that he did it in order to be of the most general use to his fellow-citizens and to other Italians. For he knew that if he wrote in Latin metre, as previous poets had done, he would have been useful only to the learned, while by writing in the vernacular he would accomplish something that had never been done before, without preventing his being understood by men of letters. While showing the beauty of our idiom and his own excellent art therein, he gave both delight and understanding of himself to the unlearned, who formerly had been neglected by every one.

The second reason that moved him to employ the vernacular was this. When he saw that liberal studies had been forsaken by all, and especially by princes and other great men to whom poetic works are commonly dedicated, and that, as a result, the divine works of Virgil and of other lofty poets not only were come to be held in light regard, but were almost despised by the majority, he actually began, as his lofty subject demanded, in this manner:

Ultima regna canam, fluido contermina mundo,
Spiritibus que lata patent, que premia solvunt
Pro meritis cuicumque suis, etc.

There, however, he let it stand, for he believed that in vain would crusts of bread be put in the mouths of those who were still sucking milk. He therefore began his work anew in a style suited to modern feelings, and continued it in the vulgar tongue.

—from *Life of Dante,* translated by James Robinson Smith (1901)

HENRY WADSWORTH LONGFELLOW

The *Divine Comedy* is not strictly an allegorical poem in the sense in which the *Faerie Queene* is; and yet it is full of allegorical symbols and figurative meanings. In a letter to Can Grande della Scala, Dante writes: "It is to be remarked, that the sense of this work is not simple, but on the contrary one may say manifold. For one sense is that which is derived from the letter, and another is that which is derived from the things signified by the letter. The first is called literal, the second allegorical or moral.... The subject, then, of the whole work, taken literally, is the condition of souls after death, simply considered. For on this and around this the whole action of the work turns. But if the work be taken allegorically, the subject is man, how by actions of merit or demerit, through freedom of the will he justly deserves reward or punishment."

It may not be amiss here to refer to what are sometimes called the sources of the *Divine Comedy*. Foremost among them must be placed the Eleventh Book of the *Odyssey,* and the Sixth of the *Æneid;* and to the latter Dante seems to point significantly in choosing Virgil for his Guide, his Master, his Author, from whom he took "the beautiful style that did him honor."

Next to these may be mentioned Cicero's *Vision of Scipio,* of which Chaucer says:—

> Chapiters seven it had, of Heaven, and Hell,
> And Earthe, and soules that therein do dwell.

Then follow the popular legends which were current in Dante's age; an age when the end of all things was thought to be near at hand, and the wonders of the invisible world had laid fast hold on the imaginations of men. Prominent among these is the "Vision of Frate

Albercio," who calls himself "the humblest servant of the servants of the Lord"; and who

> Saw in dreame at point-devyse
> Heaven, Earthe, Hell, and Paradyse.

This vision was written in Latin in the latter half of the twelfth century, and contains a description of Hell, Purgatory, and Paradise, with its Seven Heavens. It is for the most part a tedious tale, and bears evident marks of having been written by a friar of some monastery, when the afternoon sun was shining into his sleepy eyes. He seems, however, to have looked upon his own work with a not unfavorable opinion; for he concludes the Epistle Introductory with the words of St. John: "If any man shall add unto these things, God shall add unto him the plagues that are written in this book; and if any man shall take away from these things, God shall take away his part from the good things written in this book."

—from his notes to his translation of *The Divine Comedy* (1909)

CARL GUSTAV JUNG

A man who has not passed through the inferno of his passions has never overcome them.

—from *Memories, Dreams, Reflections* (1963)

Questions

1. Can the *Inferno* be read with pleasure by someone who does not believe in God and an afterlife?

2. Are all the punishments meted out to Dante's sinners just? Would you modify or change entirely any one of them?

3. Consider the Farinata episode: Do you see any disparity between the attitudes of Dante the character and even Dante the poet, on

the one hand, and Dante the depicter of divine retribution, on the other? Do you see mixed emotions elsewhere in the *Inferno*?

4. Where would you place certain recent American public figures whom you consider sinners?

5. Professor Bondanella in endnote 3 to canto II says, "One of the most important lessons Dante the Pilgrim needs to learn in Hell is that God's punishments are perfectly just. Human pity for the damned is a sure sign of spiritual weakness." Do you agree? What episodes would you cite to support your position?

For Further Reading

Bio-Criticism

Anderson, William. *Dante the Maker.* London and Boston: Routledge and Kegan Paul, 1980. The most comprehensive biography of Dante, with extensive information about the poet's life and times.

Auerbach, Erich. *Dante, Poet of the Secular World.* 1929. Translated by Ralph Manheim. Reprint: Chicago: University of Chicago Press, 1961. A classic by the greatest literary historian of the twentieth century; still required reading.

Bergin, Thomas G. *Dante.* New York: Orion Press, 1965. An older overview that still rewards examination.

Hollander, Robert. *Dante: A Life in Works.* New Haven: Yale University Press, 2001. Perhaps the best book to approach Dante's life through his writings, with important discussions about the critical problems that have occupied Dante's critics from the early commentators to the present; if you are going to read one book on Dante, make it this one.

Lewis, R. W. B. *Dante: A Penguin Life.* New York: Penguin Putnam, 2001. A brief discussion of Dante by one of America's foremost biographers.

Quinones, Ricardo J. *Dante Alighieri.* Revised edition. New York: Twayne Publishers, 1998. An excellent and very readable examination of Dante's life and works with useful bibliography and information on translations of the works.

Criticism of Dante's Divine Comedy *with Special Reference to the* Inferno

Bloom, Harold, ed. *Dante's "Divine Comedy": Modern Critical Interpretations.* New York: Chelsea House, 1987. This anthology contains essays by different hands, including some of the most influential interpreters of Dante's poem, such as Ernst Robert Curtius, Erich Auerbach, and Charles Singleton.

Caesar, Michael, ed. *Dante: The Critical Heritage, 1314(?)–1870.* London: Routledge, 1989. An exhaustive collection of historically important essays on Dante, with which the reader can trace the changing views on the poet and his masterpiece from the first commentaries of the fourteenth century to the nineteenth century. Critics include important figures from Italy, England, France, Germany, and the United States.

Clements, Robert J., ed. *American Critical Essays on "The Divine Comedy."* New York: New York University Press, 1967. One of the best essay collections on Dante, reprinting classic essays by major Dante scholars working in America.

Freccero, John, ed. *Dante: A Collection of Critical Essays.* Englewood Cliffs. NJ: Prentice-Hall, 1965. Contains historically important essays by such diverse critics as Bruno Nardi, Gianfranco Contini, Luigi Pirandello, and Leo Spitzer.

Gallagher, Joseph. *A Modern Reader's Guide to "The Divine Comedy."* Liguori, MO: Liguori Publications, 1999 (original title: *To Hell and Back with Dante,* 1996). A canto-by-canto discussion of the poem, useful for the student reader.

Giamatti, A. Bartlett, ed. *Dante in America: The First Two Centuries.* Binghamton, NY: Center for Medieval and Early Renaissance Studies, State University of New York at Binghamton, 1983. A fascinating anthology of essays linked to the birth of American interest in Dante generated by the writings of Henry Wadsworth Longfellow, Charles Eliot Norton, and James Russell Lowell, plus such more recent voices as T. S. Eliot, Ezra Pound, and other twentieth-century Dante scholars.

Hawkins, Peter S., and Rachel Jacoff, eds. *The Poets' Dante: Twentieth-Century Responses.* New York: Farrar, Straus and Giroux, 2001. An eloquent tribute to Dante's impact upon working contemporary poets, including essays by Eugenio Montale, Ezra Pound, T. S. Eliot, William Butler Yeats, W. H. Auden, and many others.

Iannucci, Amilcare A., ed. *Dante: Contemporary Perspectives.* Toronto: University of Toronto Press, 1997. A recent collection of fine scholarly essays written expressly for this volume on a variety of Dante topics.

Jacoff, Rachel, ed. *The Cambridge Companion to Dante.* Cambridge: Cambridge University Press, 1993. Useful introduction by a variety of experts to the major problems of Dante criticism, arranged by topic: Dante and the Bible, Dante and the Classical Poets, Dante and Florence, and so forth. The essays were written expressly for this volume and are aimed at the student.

Lansing, Richard, ed. *The Dante Encyclopedia.* New York: Garland Publishing, 2000. Indispensable English-language reference to every imaginable topic, character, and problem in Dante's poem, containing nearly 1,000 entries by 144 contributors from twelve countries.

Lee, Joe. *Dante for Beginners.* New York: Writers and Readers Publishing, 2001. The amusing cartoon drawings and sense of humor in this student-oriented guide do not detract from its excellent canto-by-canto discussions of *The Divine Comedy.*

Mandelbaum, Allen, Anthony Oldcorn, and Charles Ross, eds. *Lectura Dantis: Inferno—A Canto-by-Canto Commentary.* Berkeley: University of California Press, 1998. Thirty-four interpretations of the *Inferno,* one for each canto, by academics from a variety of perspectives, suitable for the more advanced reader.

Mazzotta, Giuseppe, ed. *Critical Essays on Dante.* Boston: G. K. Hall, 1991. A collection of pieces by different authors, particularly useful for its reprinting of a number of the early medieval and Renaissance commentaries on the poem.

Selected Internet Sites for Dante and Dante's Inferno

I. Danteworlds

danteworlds.lamc.utexas.edu

This site is one of the most attractive and useful internet sites available and is devoted entirely to the *Inferno.* Besides an audio component of the most important lines of the poem read in Italian, a video component presents virtually all famous illustrations of the work from medieval manuscripts through Botticelli, William Blake, and Gustave Doré to the present and are arranged by canto. Major themes are outlined, important characters and images are discussed, and study questions for each canto are provided. Additional materials for *Purgatorio* and *Paradiso* are in preparation. The site is supported by the University of Texas and operated by Dante scholar Guy Raffa.

II. Digital Dante

dante.ilt.columbia.edu/new/index.html

This website includes the entire Longfellow translation of Dante's *The Divine Comedy* and permits the visitor to compare it to the original Italian or to a more recent translation. In addition, the site includes other works by Dante, a search engine, a resource for illustrations of Dante's work by famous artists such as Sandro Botticelli, Salvador Dali, among others, along with numerous useful links for the student and scholar.